MORTIS

THE HORUS HERESY®
SIEGE OF TERRA

THE HORUS HERESY®

Other Novels and Novellas

*Many of these titles are also available as abridged and unabridged audiobooks.
Order the full range of Horus Heresy novels and audiobooks from*
blacklibrary.com

THE HORUS HERESY®
SIEGE OF TERRA

MORTIS

John French

BLACK LIBRARY

A BLACK LIBRARY PUBLICATION

First published in 2021.
This edition published in 2022 by
Black Library, Games Workshop Ltd.,
Willow Road, Nottingham, NG7 2WS, UK.

Represented by: Games Workshop Limited – Irish branch,
Unit 3, Lower Liffey Street, Dublin 1,
D01 K199, Ireland.

10 9 8 7 6 5 4 3

Produced by Games Workshop in Nottingham.
Cover illustration by Neil Roberts.

A CIP record for this book is available from the British Library.

ISBN 13: 978-1-80026-246-1

See Black Library on the internet at

blacklibrary.com

Find out more about Games Workshop
and the world of Warhammer 40,000 at

games-workshop.com

Printed and bound by CPI Group (UK) Ltd, Croydon, CR0 4YY

For Carl Tuttle, Ead Brown and Aaron Dembski-Bowden.

—THE HORUS HERESY·—
SIEGE OF TERRA

It is a time of legend.

The galaxy is in flames. The Emperor's glorious vision for humanity is in ruins. His favoured son, Horus, has turned from his father's light and embraced Chaos.

His armies, the mighty and redoubtable Space Marines, are locked in a brutal civil war. Once, these ultimate warriors fought side by side as brothers, protecting the galaxy and bringing mankind back into the Emperor's light. Now they are divided.

Some remain loyal to the Emperor, whilst others have sided with the Warmaster. Pre-eminent amongst them, the leaders of their thousands-strong Legions, are the primarchs. Magnificent, superhuman beings, they are the crowning achievement of the Emperor's genetic science. Thrust into battle against one another, victory is uncertain for either side.

Worlds are burning. At Isstvan V, Horus dealt a vicious blow and three loyal Legions were all but destroyed. War was begun, a conflict that will engulf all mankind in fire. Treachery and betrayal have usurped honour and nobility. Assassins lurk in every shadow. Armies are gathering. All must choose a side or die.

Horus musters his armada, Terra itself the object of his wrath. Seated upon the Golden Throne, the Emperor waits for his wayward son to return. But his true enemy is Chaos, a primordial force that seeks to enslave mankind to its capricious whims.

The screams of the innocent, the pleas of the righteous resound to the cruel laughter of Dark Gods. Suffering and damnation await all should the Emperor fail and the war be lost.

The end is here. The skies darken, colossal armies gather. For the fate of the Throneworld, for the fate of mankind itself... The Siege of Terra has begun.

DRAMATIS PERSONAE

| THE EMPEROR | Master of Mankind, Last and First Lord of the Imperium |
| HORUS | Warmaster, Primarch of the XVI Legion, Ascendant Vessel of Chaos |

The Primarchs

PERTURABO	'The Lord of Iron', Primarch of the IV Legion
JAGHATAI KHAN	'The Warhawk of Chogoris', Primarch of the V Legion
ROGAL DORN	Lord Solar, Praetorian of Terra, Primarch of the VII Legion
SANGUINIUS	'The Great Angel', Primarch of the IX Legion

The I Legion 'Dark Angels'

CORSWAIN	Seneschal
ADOPHEL	Void Commander, Chapter Master
VASSAGO	Librarian
TRAGAN	Captain of the Ninth Order

The IV Legion 'Iron Warriors'

| Kydomor Forrix | 'The Breaker', First Captain, Triarch |

The V Legion 'White Scars'

| SHIBAN KHAN | 'Tachseer' |

The VII Legion 'Imperial Fists'

| ARCHAMUS | Master of the Huscarls |

The IX Legion 'Blood Angels'

BAERON	Line adjutant – Marmax South, Hold Point 78
OCEANO	Commander of Curdir Bastion, Dreadnought

The XVI Legion 'Sons of Horus'

ARGONIS	'The Unscarred', Equerry to the Warmaster

Legio Ignatum 'Fire Wasps'

CYDON	Princeps Maximus, *Imperious Prima*, Principal of First Maniple
BAZZANIUS	Princeps Senioris, *Magnificum Incendius*, Principal of Second Maniple
CLEMENTIA	Princeps Senioris, *Exemplis*, Principal of Fourth Maniple
TETRACAURON	Princeps Senioris, *Reginae Furorem*, Principal of Sixth Maniple
DIVISIA	Moderatus, *Reginae Furorem*
CARTHO	Moderatus, *Reginae Furorem*
XETA-BETA-1	Enginseer, *Reginae Furorem*
ARTHUSA	Princeps, *Helios*, Principal of Seventh Maniple
SENTARIO	Legio Strategic Liaison

Legio Ordo Sinister

AURUM	First Prefect of the Chamber Orientalis
CADAMIA	Prefect, *Orientalis-Echion*

Legio Solaria 'Imperial Hunters'

ESHA ANI MOHANA VI   Grand Master, the Great Mother of the Imperial Hunters, Princeps of *Luxor Invictoria*

ABHANI LUS MOHANA   Princeps, *Bestia Est*

House Vyronii

CARADOC   Scion, pilot of Cerastus Knight-Castigator *Meliae*

ACASTIA   Bondsman, pilot of Knight Armiger *Elatus*

DOLLORAN   Bondsman, pilot of Knight Armiger *Cyllarus*

PLUTON   Bondsman, pilot of Knight Armiger *Thaumas*

The Adeptus Mechanicus

VETHOREL   Ambassador, proxy of the Fabricator General

KAZZIM-ALEPH-1   Magos emissary to Rogal Dorn

GERONTIUS-CHI-LAMBDA   Magos emissary to Legio Ignatum

The Neverborn

VASSUKELLA   The Chorus of the Denied, Song of Endless Rapture, Daemon Prince of the Ruinstorm

Imperial Army

NIORA SU-KASSEN   Solar Command Staff, former Admiral of the Jovian Fleets

NASUBA   General, Inferallti Hussars, Commander of Shard Bastion

SULKOVA	Major General, Shard Bastion Command Cadre
KURRAL	Colonel-Elite, Shard Bastion Command Cadre
COLE	Second Lieutenant, Massian Fifth
KATSUHIRO	Trooper
STEENA	Trooper

Imperial Personae

MALCADOR THE SIGILLITE	Regent of the Imperium
HELLICK MAUER	Boetharch of the Command Prefectus
AHLBORN	Conroi-Captain, Hort Palatine, Command Prefectus
SOLSHA	Lieutenant of the Command Prefectus Militia
KYRIL SINDERMANN	Historian, Head of the Order of Interrogators
ANDRÓMEDA-17	Personified-scion of the Selenar
EUPHRATI KEELER	The Saint, former Remembrancer
VASKALE	Warden, Blackstone

Slaves to Darkness

UGENT SYE	The Orchardist

Others

ACTAE	
BASILIO FO	An inmate of Blackstone
JOHN GRAMMATICUS	Logokine
OLL PERSSON	
LEETU	Legionary

DOGENT KRANK	(Numinus 61st, fmr)
BALE RANE	(Numinus 61st, fmr)
GRAFT	Servitor menial
HEBET ZYBES	
KATT	

'To sleep: perchance to dream: ay, there's the rub;
For in that sleep of death what dreams may come,
When we have shuffled off this mortal coil,
Must give us pause: there's the respect
That makes calamity of so long life.'

– attributed to the dramaturge Shakespire, fl. M2

PART ONE

WAKING

THE WARP

∞

Heat shimmers from earth to sky. There is no sun here, but the light is blinding. The heavens are a dome of brilliant white, clamped over the dry ground. The earth is cracked, skimmed with dust and crusted with salt. The image of the world is flat, an endless plain running to a lost horizon. The air is still, throbbing, an echo of the absent sun's hammer. It is not a true place, for nothing in the Realm Beyond is true, but this place of thirst and heat has always been and always will be.

The tree stands at the centre of the desolation. It is a cedar tree, bare of needles, lightning-struck and blackened. From a distance it would look like an ebon crack running through the sky, an inverted bolt of black lightning. The only shadows in this place lie under the tree. They are thin, tangled in the dust. A trickle of water seeps from the ground at the tree's root, vanishes as soon as it bubbles up. A man sits with His back against the trunk. His limbs are thin, the dark skin drawn taut over bones, cracked around dried lips. The blue shift wound loosely around Him is frayed and

sun-bleached. He is as still as the burnt tree at his back;
His eyes are closed.

Slowly, as though to do more would cost too much, the
man's eyes open a crack to the blazing land. His left hand
moves to a hollow He has scraped in the ground by the roots
of the tree. A little water has gathered there, and He scoops it
up in His palm and brings it to His mouth. Thick with silt,
it is barely a sip.

A breath of air stirs the fold of fabric covering His head.
He looks up, lowering the hand that cupped the water that is
already falling as dust from His fingers.

A whirling column is forming in the air, skidding across
the land, pulling up the dry earth. The light blurs around it,
shimmering, turning the distance into mirages that might be
an army marching over the horizon, or a distant, broken city,
or a lone figure striding from the empty land.

The man beneath the tree waits and watches.

The dust devil dances closer. The wind rises. The dry branches
of the tree rattle. A figure coalesces at the centre of the dust
column: broad, proud face; silver-scaled armour over white
robes; sword sheathed at his waist. A golden crown sits on the
newcomer's brow, burning like flame with reflected sunlight.
The wind unravels. The dust settles. The warrior in silver and
white looks down at the man beneath the tree.

'Father,' says Horus.

The man beneath the tree does not look up.

'There is no refuge, father, nowhere left for you to flee.'
Horus crouches, balancing on the balls of his feet so that his
head is level with that of the man sitting in the shadow of
the tree. Somewhere, out of sight, a crow caws into the shimmering air. A snake hisses and rattles, the sound that of sand
blowing through dry bones. Horus reaches down and picks
up a handful of earth. He is staring into the distance, his eyes

brilliant mirrors to the baking heat. For an instant, his fingers seem claws, long and shining, the ground beneath them a star-strewn night. The earth crumbles between his fingers. 'This was your secret land, father. The warp, the realm that you denied us. Here is the source of all your power, all the paths to your gilded ambition. You are nothing without this place, just a man who stole what was not his and then kept it from others – a beggar-thief with stolen coins.'

There is pity in Horus' eyes.

'Look at you now – withering in a realm of thirst.' Horus stands. 'You must have known this was inevitable. You must have known that your deeds would have consequences. You said that this place, with all its power and possibility, was dangerous – that none should touch it, that none should know its true secrets. Magnus came close to realising you had lied, and you sent wolves to run him down. Lorgar, poor Lorgar, ever searching for a cause, saw the shadow of your ambition and thought it the mark of a god. Burned cities and shame was his reward. And me, father, was I close to knowing too much? For all those years after we found each other, how many times did I nearly realise what you were – a liar and a thief, clad in scraps of false glory? Is that why I was banished from your side? Did you fear this moment, father? If you did, you should have known that it was inevitable – that your deceived son would come for his birthright.'

The wind rises, blowing powdered salt and dust into the air. Silhouettes form in the heat shimmer, at once close and distant. Towering shapes, shapes out of myth and old stories: Cyclops, hunched reaper, flayed angel, serpent Adonis.

'You made us with the fire you took from the realm you forbade us. How could you think we would never realise, would never wonder, would never come home to the place of our birth?'

Horus' gaze moves over the four shapes writhing in the mirage.

'They are here now,' said Horus. 'Your sons, my brothers, returned home. I am their king, not their father, and this realm is mine. The power you denied us is mine. All of it. There is nothing left for you. The night and the day, the dreaming and the waking, all move to my will.'

The man beneath the tree lets out a breath, stretches out His left hand and pulls a finger through the dry earth. The ground shakes. Dust explodes into the air to hang as a layer above the ground before slamming down. The leafless tree grows, stretches, its dead branches reaching shadows in a wide circle. Horus does not flinch, but in the heat-glare, things unseen hiss with the voices of snakes and hounds and dying birds.

The man's hand stops moving. A line marks the dust, a finger's width, but also a canyon, a wall, a mountain range. He withdraws His hand and looks up. His lips and skin are cracked, but His voice is strong as He speaks.

'No,' He says.

Horus steps forwards, but the ground beneath his feet crumbles and cracks, flowing down into the opening abyss beneath. For a moment the man beneath the tree does not look like a man, but a shadow within an inferno. He looks at Horus, and Horus returns the Emperor's gaze. The brightness in the sky reverses to charcoal black, the shadows of the tree become flames.

Horus' eyes are two stars in their sockets.

'You will die, father. See yourself, see yourself diminishing, failing, clutching for shade in a barren land.' He pauses, shakes his head as though in pity. 'You grow only weaker. You shall fade. Your soul shall wither with thirst, and you shall die the slow death that you have too long tried to outrun.' Then Horus turns his back on the tree and the man, and walks away, calling back but not looking over his shoulder. 'I will give you mercy before that end, father. I owe you that, but nothing else.'

Beneath the tree, the man reaches again for water that is already drying to dust as he brings it to His mouth.

ONE

Last light
Script
Overload

The Imperial Palace, Terra

As the sun rose on the twenty-seventh of Quintus, the last of its light broke through the smoke and chem-fog to touch the highest towers of the western edge of the Ultimate Wall. In its shadow the light of sporadic gunfire flared. Shells and energy bursts streaked up to punch the void-shrouded wall and burst on the ethereal canopy of the aegis above the Inner Palace. Across the six hundred-kilometre arc from Western Hemispheric to Indomitor, exhausted soldiers blinked at the golden light from gun embrasures and firing steps. Most had not seen the clean light of the sun since a time that seemed now a dream. A few smiled. A few wept. To many, the fading light felt like a promise. To a few it felt like a farewell. As the sun slid further down the sky, some of the millions watching it muttered prayers to a man who denied He was a god.

The new day's light slid across the bowl of the Inner Palace and its precincts. In past ages, each part would have been large enough to be the greatest city on Terra; now they were just segments of the last circle of defiance against the Warmaster. In the enclaves of the Viridarum Nobiles, the light only touched the highest towers, and few saw that bright moment; the millions that sheltered there shunned the high places. Most had fled to deeper parts of their domains. Some had used every coin and favour they could turn to put themselves as close to the core of the Inner Palace as they could. A few – old or defiant or deluded – walked through shuttered halls and pretended that they could not see the cracks growing on their painted walls as the shells fell.

The light caught the rain that fell inside the shield. Oily rainbows streaked the tower tops. Ugly gun batteries clung to the stone next to the gargoyles and grotesques. If the aegis failed their fire would provide a short-lived resistance to the next stage of catastrophe.

On the top of the innermost precinct, the gilded pyramids and statues gleamed briefly. Beneath them, far below the layers of stone and bedrock, the Emperor sat unmoving, eyes closed, locked into a throne of gold and holding the nightmare back from an ever-shrinking circle.

To the south the stone fist of Bhab Bastion punched up into the light, and for a few moments the rainwater streaming down its walls shimmered silver. Within those walls the mechanisms of command turned without cease. Regiments of command staff slept in blocks of time, the norms of day and night, of sleep and waking broken down into slots, to rotation between the light of pict screens and dreams of wide blue skies and cool water. At the heart of the bastion, Rogal Dorn stood in the Grand Borealis Strategium. The cold light of holo-projections caught the marks of recent battle on his armour. Around him the layers of command radiated outwards, invisible, harnessed to his will. He watched, as he had for the hours since his return from the Saturnine Wall. Then, with the smallest nod, he turned away, and made for the chamber doors and the stairs that would carry him up to the bastion's parapet and a brief sight of the rising sun.

Out through the districts to the walls of Indomitor, Mercury, Saturnine and Europa, the light deepened the shadows in the zigzag highways cut through the buildings. Close to the walls, whole road and street systems had been filled in, blocked by demolished buildings and sealed by rivers of poured ferrocrete. Gun nests and fire points lodged in the flanks of hab-blocks. If – when – the walls were breached, the traitors would enter a kill maze inside them that would make them bleed for every step they took. In their firing nests, troops looked up from their autocannons and rocket mounts and saw a distant ghost of brilliance, high above.

On the eastern arc of the defences, shell bursts sent plumes of dust into the air as though trying to veil the sun's face. This was Anterior, once the gateway from the Outer Palace to the Inner. Hundreds of kilometres of plazas, avenues and buildings cast in marble, glass and polished metal, now a chewed pit of ruins, the lines of the defences stacked on and cut into the bones of the Palace. Here were Marmax, Gorgon Bar and Colossi, hundreds of kilometres of front marked with blast craters, wreckage and corpses, like the tideline on a sea of slaughter. From here, the sun would rise above the wasteland that had been the Outer Palace. The last of the night pooled in the shells of buildings and ran down streets that held only silence.

Over the desolation, fallen walls rose like the broken fingers of dead hands, and then spearing into the sky was the Eternity Wall space port. In its lee, slave crews worked on the parapet of the Daylight Wall, hauling down the guns and munition stores from the positions where they had fired on the port.

The guns were needed elsewhere. Most of the slaves had been soldiers who had defended the walls they stood on. Now their lives were measured in the labour they could do before they expired. Most of them did not look up as the sun poured its new light across the world. They knew that there was no point in looking, no point in hope, or truth in dreams, or salvation in prayers to false gods. There was just the release of brief sleep and the hope that they would not wake to another day.

Marmax South, Anterior Barbican

There was not much left of the lines. Ascending layers of trenches, walls, ditches and breaches had become a chewed maze of blast craters, debris slides and slumped blockhouses. Rain no longer fell here. The layered void shields, which had bred the false storms that had filled the craters and scars, were gone. Now there were just dry clouds that reached down from the bruised sky. Heat was pulling the moisture from the ground, cracking it, and distilling the pools of rainwater to black slime.

All the way from the Gorgon intersection to the remains of the zonal block complex in the north it was the same. As far as the eye could see. And you could see a long way. From up on the parapet of Hold Point 78 you could gaze all the way across to where the black-orange clouds clung to the shadow of the Anterior Wall's eastern circuit. A long way, and all of it a desolation where a city had stood. The broken teeth of great buildings jutted into the air. Heaps of debris smothered roads. Slumped structures formed lines of hills. Flashes of light pinpricked the dawn gloom: lightning, detonations, gunfire. Above it, high in the distance, a dirty orange glow was brightening the jagged horizon.

Katsuhiro paused to watch the light spread.

'Get moving!'

A shove at his back.

He dropped his gaze and started to climb the steps again.

Behind him, the sergeant – Katsuhiro could not remember being told the man's name – was pushing the others up and on. There were twenty of them. Where they had come from, Katsuhiro had no idea. Most of them had the washed-out skin and dead eyes of people who had been on the line since the start. Their kit was a patchwork of colours, patterns and states of repair. Stains marked every inch of them, and since coming onto Marmax all had begun to acquire a layer of grey dust, like a gritty second skin. Behind him, one of the others spat down the inside of the walls.

'Don't do that,' he said, half glancing back.

'Delicate manners, script?' came the whining reply. Steena, of course, her acid drawl rising loud above the sound of trudging feet. 'What the hell else are we supposed to do, swallow the damned dust?'

'Spit and you'll need to drink,' replied Katsuhiro, 'and there hasn't been a water ration since we got on the line. You haven't got spit to spare.'

'Well, isn't that me told and educated? What the hell made you so all-knowing and wise, script?'

'Script', short for conscript, short for anyone who had been scooped up by the mass induction protocols, short for someone who wasn't a real soldier. It had started a while back when the population repurposing had begun, before the enemy had actually come to Terra. It was a way for the real soldiers, the volunteers, the members of some regiment or formation raised before the draft order came, to say that they were on a different level to the millions of men and women who had been diverted from their old lives to become soldiers. The reality of the war had killed the distinction. Old and new soldiers died and were dying by the hundreds of thousands on each front of the battle. Steena, though, had hung on to the term and used it alternately like a slur and an accusation. Katsuhiro didn't care. People held on to what they could. That was another thing the battle had done – planed down the terrain of life to a few basic points: breathing, shooting and, of course, the other thing, the thing that actually mattered.

Katsuhiro kept climbing the steps. Every now and again he caught another glimpse of the land beyond the parapet. Tiers of walls dropped down to the ground-level trenches a kilometre distant. All of it was damaged: chewed rockcrete, split and holed armour panels, demolished blockhouses. In places whole sections had vanished, the walls and buttresses slumping into craters. In places the damage had been repaired, filled with poured cements and fast-welded webs of girders. They looked like scabs over badly healing wounds. There was not time to do better.

Artillery struck in an irregular but consistent rhythm along the line, even when there was no direct assault – long-range rockets fired from hundreds of kilometres distant. Orbital dead-fall munitions dropped without sound or warning. Clouds of cluster munitions scattered from high-altitude bombers. There were snipers, too, out there in the wasteland, watching soldiers come and go and then reaching out with a hotshot blast or hyper-kinetic round to murder a sapper as they worked to repair damage.

Kill units, some of them up to brigade strength, also hit the lines with sporadic ferocity. Slithering forwards under cover of night to breach, kill and lay traps before withdrawing. It was worse when they were Legiones Astartes. A strike by enemy in midnight-blue armour draped in flayed skin had apparently hit the line just below the Cordus Tower the night before last. They got all the way into the third line before pulling back.

What was left were not just conventional casualties; most of them were still alive when the line section was retaken.

The terror assaults, just like the bombs lobbed from distant batteries, were to a purpose. Hours passed between strikes sometimes, and then the world would be thunder and fire and then silence again. It seemed random, but it wasn't. It was a very precise kind of irregular rhythm that took you to the edge of thinking that you could breathe out and then crushed that respite. Genius, cruel genius, the gift of the Lord of Iron and his zone commanders. It was working, too. As much as the large-scale assaults had broken lines and pushed back the defenders to the Ultimate Wall and Anterior lines, the arrhythmic violence ate at the defences and the spirits of those that stood behind them.

Katsuhiro reached the top of the steps. A long walkway ran along the wall's parapet, eight strides wide, open to the inner side, lined by eight-foot-high crenellations. Through the firing slits you could see clear to the next wall down, and then beyond to where the walls met the ground and gave way to trench lines and ditch-works.

An angel waited for them on the parapet. Dust covered it just like everything on the line. Grey ceramite showed through the red armour lacquer in places. It looked battered and worn, but the sight of it was still enough to make Katsuhiro and the rest of the scratch platoon stop in their tracks. Even after all he had seen – especially after all he had seen – there was a presence to a Space Marine, a hammer blow to your awareness that could not be ignored. More and more the Legiones Astartes had been seeded through the mortal forces defending the Palace. To boost morale or to increase discipline, Katsuhiro could not be sure.

The angel turned towards them. A black stripe ran down the faceplate of his helm between glowing green eyes. He passed a dataslate to one of a pair of ragged-looking officers. The gun clamped to the angel's thigh was as big as Katsuhiro's torso.

'I am Baeron,' said the angel, and somehow the voice held a note of music even through the growl of the speaker grille. 'Ninth Legion, line adjutant for this section. You are assigned under my command.' Baeron's glowing gaze moved over them, swift but precise, assessing. Katsuhiro felt pinned in place as the glowing eyes touched him. 'Integrate into the line units of this section. Captain Ulkov and Lieutenant Sabine are unit command under me. Find your firing points. Check weapons. Be ready.' Baeron looked them over again, then turned away, moving down the walkway, eyes now on the world beyond the battlements.

'Alright, you heard the adjutant,' called one of the officers, a squat woman, face half covered by grey bandages. 'Reassigns, pair with someone who has been on the section more than a night. Get on it!'

Katsuhiro blinked, only now looking around and seeing the other human soldiers on the walkway. There were men and women of at least half a dozen units, and some with the marks of more than one mixed into their kit and colours. That was the new normal. Fronts like Marmax, Gorgon Bar, Artiala and the Kanazawa Fold ate soldiers and chewed up the old divisions and order. What was left were those that were still standing, scraped together, and dumped into the next kill-zone. Katsuhiro had been shifted down the Anterior battle zones three times in as many weeks. The lines had changed in that time too, fortresses broken, old hard lines rubbed out and new ones drawn. He wondered if there was something or someone who actually knew where each soldier was, which tank had been abandoned in retreat and which one had been ridden by a different unit as they moved from one zone to another.

In each of the places he had been, there had been a different rhyme and reason to how new troops on the line were handled. On the Dacia turnpike, new arrivals had been divided by block, herded together and then sliced into portions by the shouts and gestures of a major in the tattered greens of the Albia Fifth Rifles. There had been scribes on Marmax North, Line Section Two, twenty of them in fact, going down the crowds of redeploys, pinning numbers on uniforms with plasteel staples, each one marked on pink pulp paper. Here, well, no one had asked or told him anything, just ordered him and a block of others from the cargo haulers up onto the lines. He had acquired a sergeant whose name he didn't know and a new unit in the half hour it had taken to reach the parapet. Some with him, like Steena, he knew from the ride down from Marmax North. Most he did not. That was the new norm, too: to be anonymous, to be unknown to those you stood beside, to become a unit strength increment, a body on the line, a number on tattered pink parchment.

Someone knew, though. Someone knew each and every one of the men and women on the lines and knew what they did. He knew, and He watched them, and where He could He protected them. That truth was all that mattered, all the rest was just the churn of the chaos.

'The Emperor knows,' Katsuhiro had said to himself, in the rattling, cramped dark of the cargo hauler that had shifted him down the line. 'The Emperor protects.'

He must have said it louder than he meant to because someone had echoed the words.

'He protects…'

And then a few more before the phrase had faded.

He said it again, now, in the dawn light on Marmax South, and knew it was true.

He moved towards a section of parapet, checking his lasgun

as he did. A trooper was leaning on the chipped ferrocrete merlon. He looked young, but it was difficult to tell under the grime. Katsuhiro opened his mouth to greet him. The trooper's head jerked up, eyes flicking from horizon to sky.

'You hear that?' he asked.

Grand Borealis Strategium, Bhab Bastion,
Sanctum Imperialis Palatine

'Full assault incoming, my lord, right across Marmax South from the Flavian sub-bar lines to Gorgon Intersection,' called Icaro.

'Strength?' asked Archamus, glancing up from the glow of the main tactical feed.

'Main force,' said Icaro.

'Titans?'

'None sighted,' called Vorst from the console beside Icaro. 'Knights, armour and a full air-support element. Indications of Legion elements, too. Intel is from the craft we still have in the air, visibility to ground is limited.'

'Distance to lines?' asked Archamus.

'Uncertain – three kilometres, maybe,' replied Icaro.

'How in Sol's light did they get that close?' snapped Vorst.

'Signal the line commanders on Marmax South,' said Archamus, his voice level. 'If we've only just seen it, they might not have.'

Archamus, second of that name, master of the Imperial Fists' Huscarls and current watch commander for the greatest battle humanity had seen, allowed himself a moment to find stillness in a slow breath. It was all he could afford. The human command officers like Icaro and Vorst would have to rotate out soon. Exhaustion was already degrading their effectiveness.

Vox-connection indicators flashed on the tactical displays.

The hum and growl of voices in the strategium rose. Holo-displays suspended in the centre of the hemispherical room re-spun to show the lines of Marmax. Uncertain amber runes and data jostled across maps drawn in cold blue light. Even as Archamus watched, half of the tactical data dissolved and rearranged itself. Communications to the front lines were becoming unreliable. Scrap code was seeping into the signal system. Comms discipline was breaking down in the mortal troops. Beyond the wall they were reduced to the eyes of those on the line and the systems built into the defences themselves. On a front like Marmax, which weeks of war had crushed but not broken, those eyes and systems were far from infallible. With every watch that Archamus stood on the strategium's command dais, their ability to see the war they were fighting was shrinking, clarity fading like the world seen through a clouding eye. The Saturnine breach had held yesterday, so had Colossi and Gorgon Bar and Marmax. They had held. The fight had been carried at cost. Where all could have failed, the defenders and defences had proved the equal of their enemies.

That victory was yesterday. The reality of ongoing war was what the Palace woke to.

'Line command on Marmax acknowledged,' said Icaro.

The doors to the chamber opened. Rogal Dorn entered. His amour still bore the stains and marks of battle, his face set in the hard expression that had carved ever deeper into his flesh in the past months. As per his standing command, none of the hundreds of officers in the strategium paused to salute him. His presence was enough to dim the tide of noise. Two Huscarls followed the Praetorian and with him the willow-thin figure of Armina Fel, the primarch's senior astro-path. Rogal Dorn met Archamus' gaze and tilted his head, the gesture as clear and direct an order as a shouted command. Archamus bowed his head in brief assent.

'You have theatre command,' said Archamus to Icaro. 'Apprise me of any change.' The Praetorian moved towards one of the secure antechambers.

What ill has come on us now? wondered Archamus as he followed.

Marmax South, Anterior Barbican

'Can you hear it?' said the trooper beside the wall. Katsuhiro could hear it. A high and distant note, like the call of a dying bird. All along the line, faces were turning to the clouded horizon. Down on the lower lines, he could see red figures moving, huge, their amour skimmed with dust, movements curt and fluid. Legion warriors, sons of Sanguinius, just like Baeron. They were moving to the parapets, guns up.

'Stand ready! Stand ready!' The shouts came down the line. Bodies hurried and shuffled to firing points. Hands grasped guns, clutching, fumbling, holding on.

'What the hell is that?' called Steena. She was next to him, looking up and around.

'Stand ready!'

The high note was rising, splitting, becoming more than one note, shifting direction.

'Attack incoming!'

A battery of aerial defence guns started firing from one of the higher lines, rounds pumping high and far at targets out of sight. Katsuhiro saw Steena flinch. The high note was still clear over the sound of the guns, buffeting now, splitting, growing strands of sound. Was it... was it a voice? A voice singing?

'Rose and rain, and petal on the bough,' his sister sang. *'Oh, where will my heart find true home?'*

He laughs.

She smiles, the notes of the next line of the song fading.

'It's supposed to be a sad song, silly,' she says, giggling, still smiling down at him. She is ten years old. She is so very real. She picks up one of the faded blocks that he has scattered on the floor around them in a game of making as much mess as they can.

'Again!' he calls.

'Again,' she says. 'Really?'

'Again!'

'Alright,' she says, 'again, but just one more time.' He laughs. She is smiling. 'Rose and rain and petal on the bough–'

A column of light burned through the air above him. Katsuhiro ducked, eyes flooded with brilliance. His head hit the barrel of someone behind him. His jaw smashed shut. Blood in his mouth. Ringing in his ears. Shouting and the clatter of gunfire, and more shouts saying to stop firing. The high sound was still there too, still audible, sliding under the roar. Sharp. Oscillating. Aching in his bloody teeth. He wanted to stay down, to go back to whatever moment the memory of song had promised. His eyes were shut, he realised.

'Rise!' the voice boomed along the wall. 'Rise! Weapons ready! Rise!'

He pushed himself up. Eyes open.

The sky above was burning. Energy beams, hard rounds, missiles loosing into the sky in a tattered sheet of flame. The other troopers on the parapet were milling, guns in hand, some looking up at the sky, some down at the wasteland beyond the outer line of trenches. Baeron was pushing his way down the walkway, dragging troopers to their feet, his voice punching from his helm's speaker grille.

'Rise! Weapons ready!'

There were more human troops on the line, grey-dusted, swarming out from whatever places they took as shelter.

The orbital strike hit the edge of the outer defence works five kilometres away. A column of light punched down from the clouds, fifty metres wide, neon white, screaming. Rockcrete and steel vanished into gas and ash. Thunder rolled out. Katsuhiro was already ducking back, half-blinded, weeping. Then the blasts punched down again and again, a drumbeat of wrathful gods shredding the broken world of mortals. The deluge of anti-aircraft fire stuttered.

'Air cover!' someone was shouting. 'We need air cover!'

'Rise! Stand ready!'

'Where's the enemy?' Steena was beside him, shouting. 'There's no enemy. Why are we–'

'There,' said Katsuhiro, his eyes suddenly steady.

Something in his tone must have caught Steena's attention, even over the din. She stared in the same direction as him, shaking her head as though she was about to say that she couldn't see anything. Then she did see and went still.

Gold.

Gold glittering against the hazed light of the new day. Flecks of gold in the far distance, bright against the sky.

Katsuhiro watched. The sound had faded from his ears. It was still there, but now it was just a vibration working its way in from his skin to his bones. It felt good. Like half-waking in warmth with the sweetness of a dream still wrapping you...

Gold. Hundreds of flecks of gold, dancing against the drab sky, spiralling, flitting between explosions and lines of tracer fire. He knew they were aircraft... Part of him knew they were aircraft, hundreds of them, fuselages gilded and polished to shine like the faces of the sun. Aircraft with colours rioting across their wings. Warplanes. Gunships. Strike fighters. He knew what they were but...

Flak was pouring out into the sky...

Golden birds falling...

Broken wings...

Black threads of smoke...

Serenity, tiny slices of perfect time. The colour of the explosion as an aircraft hit the ground two kilometres out from the outermost line: first yellow, the light pure, then orange curdling to black, the cloud drawing colour together as it rose like the head of a burning flower. He could watch it forever, just the sight of this, amid the pulse sound of the world's heart racing to beat its last.

'Watch forever…' said a voice that he realised was his own. Why couldn't he think? What was going on? He felt… He felt like he wanted to stop. Just to stop and watch and listen to the song that was coming out of the distance.

'For the Emperor! For our oaths!' Baeron was bellowing down the parapet line.

Katsuhiro blinked, breathing hard, trying to see, trying to focus. Sound was beating around him, gunfire, shouts, his own breath, all of it. Half of the troopers were standing staring out at the distance, eyes wide, mouths slack.

'Protect me,' he said to himself, and then louder, snarling, 'Please protect me as I protect You.'

He was steady, gun in hand, face forward.

Flocks of golden aircraft were dropping lower and lower, skimming the ground. The scream of their engines boiled dust into the air. Closing fast. Flak and missiles raked the sky as they tried to trace their targets to the edge of their declination. Fire struck one from the sky a kilometre north. Another south. The golden craft were almost on the ground, weaving from side to side. Fire began to flick from the lines. The shriek of the jet engines syncopated, merged, like a screaming voice. Like laughter.

'What is this?' Steena was shouting into his ear. 'What is happening?'

The aircraft were almost on them now. The fire from the walls was a ragged torrent. Las-beams cut wings. Missiles struck.

Red... Great banners of red unfurling behind some of the aircraft. For an impossible instant Katsuhiro thought they were bleeding. Then he realised it was dust, red dust. Plumes of orange and cyan vented from the rest of the aircraft, spilling behind them like a brightly coloured cloak dragged across the ground. They were almost at the outer lines, plunging towards the earthworks. They flicked upwards, spiralling and weaving, engines howling. As they rose, fire followed them from the parapets and tiered lines. The aircraft climbed, near vertical, spearing away. The gunfire chased them for a moment before falling silent.

Above, the blanket of blue, orange and red dust began to drift down.

'Masks!' shouted an officer.

Katsuhiro was already pulling his on as the calls rose. Everything was suddenly quiet, just the sounds of people scrabbling to pull on breath-masks and hoods. His breath was loud as he dragged air through the plug filter. The visor was pitted and scratched. He looked around. Baeron was a statue of red, his helmed head cocked as though listening. Katsuhiro realised that the shrill whine had stopped too. The coloured smog drifted lower, unhurried, gaudy and vivid. It reminded him of chalk dust on a scholam board. He was sweating inside his gas hood and mask. He could feel heat building under the fabric of his uniform. His gloves felt heavy on his fingers. The coloured cloud was just a few metres above them now.

'Full hazard condition,' called Baeron. 'No exposed skin. Weapons ready.'

Troopers along the line fumbled for gloves and uniform fastenings.

Beside him Steena pulled up her hood, gasping, coughing.

'Can't breathe!'

'Trooper, replace your mask!'

The dust was just above head height. Katsuhiro could taste sugar and burning plastek.

Along the line, the coloured dust was draping the troopers. Some froze. A trooper who had not covered his hands with gloves turned and fired, pouring las-bolts into those beside him until a round blew the back of his head out. Explosions flashed out. The smog was a rainbow kaleidoscope of light and colour.

'Enemy in front of the lower lines,' called Baeron. 'Thirty-degree down angle, continual fire.'

Katsuhiro got his gun onto the parapet angled down and sighted along the barrel, and froze.

Dust fogged the view, but he could see the outer trench. A tide of shapes was breaking across the trench lines, things with pale flesh and long limbs, with quills and razor smiles. Beasts or humans or machines, all distinctions failed. Banners of gaudy silk snapped above them. War machines bounded at their sides. They should not have been there. They should not have been able to reach the lines so quickly. It was as though they had congealed from the smog right on top of them. Gunfire chewed at the tide. Flesh blasted to red slime. Metal deformed. But the assault wave was not slowing. It was accelerating. Katsuhiro watched as a thing that must once have been a smaller Knight war machine hit the rise above the outer trench and leapt high. Its armoured shell was ivory white. Troopers in the scoop of earth beneath raised their guns to fire. The Knight landed amongst them, chrome claws and spinning blades extending, and suddenly the length of trench was filled with bloody pulp, and the tide of attackers was spilling over it and up the other side. The ivory Knight arched its back, piston legs pushing it up like a preening bird. Its white carapace split. Inside, something pink and soft and red and slick shivered and whooped a bubbling cry into the air. Katsuhiro could hear it. Somehow from a kilometre distant he could hear it as though it was next to him.

A rocket hit the wall line fifty metres below him and blew out a ten-metre section. Bodies flew up. Debris and smoke scattered. A chunk of rock hit Katsuhiro on the helm. His head snapped back. Pain exploded in his neck, and with it the world was in focus again.

He started to fire. Aiming down, squeezing the trigger, adding his shots to the ragged volleys coming from the layers of walls and parapets. He was one of the few. Most of the human troopers were standing, draped in toxic colours, staring like dumb cattle. A few were lying down as though the ground was a bed. Only the Blood Angels on the lower line responded together, firing and moving with perfect unity, the dust shaking from the red of their armour. They did not pause. Fire speared from the angels. Missiles and bolt fire chewed chunks of the enemy into pools of meat. Lascannon blasts hit in clusters on war machines surging through the tide of flesh and sparked them to burning ruin.

Katsuhiro felt something yank his arm. He looked around, half ready to spin his weapon to fire. Steena was on her knees beside him, bare face painted in pigment dust. She was trembling, eyes wide, lips pulled back from teeth. She looked like she was laughing. Bloody, pink tears were cutting paths through the dust on her cheeks.

'Get up!' shouted Katsuhiro, the words lost to his mask and the cacophony.

Her mouth was moving.

He tried to shake her free. There were other troopers on the parapet, some still firing. Some were staggering. One was cuffing their head as though trying to knock something loose. There was blood on their fist and skull. Katsuhiro blinked. His thoughts were slowing again. He looked down at his hand.

Where was his gun? Where was his glove? Orange dust covered his hand. Steena was laughing and weeping.

Something hit the other side of the parapet. For a ridiculous second, he thought it was a raindrop. He leaned towards the gun loop, his thoughts the soft kind that came just after waking.

The bomblet that had embedded in the outer parapet exploded. Shards of stone pinged off his helmet. The shockwave vibrated through him. His ears burst. He was tumbling on his back as jet wash boiled the clouds of coloured dust. Gunships plunged down, cannons firing, missiles and rockets loosing. Huge figures in power armour stood on the edges of open hatches. Discordant colours and patterns covered their armour: tiger-striped gold, acid green and violet scales, plumes of fire-orange hair. Tubes and pipes festooned them, coiling around bloated guns of chrome and black graphite. A greasy heat haze hung around them as though the air was cooking as it touched them. They had been Space Marines, once; now they looked like a fever dream. Katsuhiro felt the vomit gush from his mouth before he could stop it. His hands came up and ripped the mask and hood off his head. He gasped. Dust poured into his mouth.

The world snapped into focus.

Into perfect focus.

His nerves lit.

Every pain and ache in his body screamed.

The blood and burnt-sugar flavour on his tongue flooded his mind. He could taste the smoke of the gun discharge and the exhaust of the gunship as it banked low above them.

One of the giants in the gunship dropped down onto the parapet thirty metres from Katsuhiro. Stone cracked where it hit. Some of the troopers near it ran. Others turned towards it with docile confusion. It swung the mouth of its weapon down towards the wall. Katsuhiro could see all the way down its throat, could see that inside the chrome muzzle there was a real throat and tiny, perfect white teeth.

The gun fired. Steena yanked him down. The troopers who had been beside him hung in the air, skin and bones and organs shivering to red mist, wave patterns forming in the gore. The giant moved forwards, the neon colours of its armour flowing like oil on water. The sound of its weapon was beyond hearing, a migraine pain pouring into the brain. Katsuhiro could not think.

Baeron came down the walkway from behind them, rock-crete shattering under his strides. Bolt shells exploded across the multihued warrior. Iridescent shreds of armour blew from the impacts. It turned, pulling its weapon around. The shriek of the silver gun rose as the warrior swept it towards the Blood Angel. Sections of the wall burst into dust. Shells exploded in mid-air as they plunged into a wall of sonic energy. The Blood Angel did not slow. He accelerated, drew a knife and leapt. The edge of the shriek-cone caught Baeron's leg as he leapt. Red armour deformed and shredded from knee to foot. Baeron landed, stumbled. The chrome gun came around towards the fallen Space Marine. Baeron sliced his blade across the cables linking the enemy warrior to his gun. Blood sprayed out from the severed tubes. The shriek of the gun was now a gurgle of pain. Baeron struck again and again, under arm, pistoning the short blade up and into the warrior's gut. The abomination was staggering, shedding blood and shards of ceramite, but it was not dead. A pearl-and-silver fist lashed into Baeron's faceplate, once, twice, three times, buckling ceramite, shattering eye-lenses. The angel kept stabbing, shunting the enemy warrior backwards. They hit the parapet. Rockcrete shattered. A section of crenellation broke, and the enemy warrior was falling over the edge, down the face of the wall to the spikes and wire at its base. Baeron straightened on the parapet's broken edge. There was blood on his armour, darker than the dusted lacquer, clotting as it ran through dust.

'Up! Up!' roared Baeron.

There were more figures dropping from gunships up and down the line. Shrieking weapons fired. Armour became shards. Flesh became jelly. Waves formed in powered air, overlapping. Katsuhiro could not move. Everything was colour and sound and vibration and the taste of sugar and bitter lemons and vomit. He could not...

He protects.

A memory of golden light. Heat pouring into him and running down his spine.

He is our shield. He is our light. He is our truth...

And he was screaming, screaming as the kaleidoscope world around him became real, became raw.

He could move. He was standing. Somehow, he was standing and moving to a firing loop, picking up a fallen gun.

'He protects, He protects, He protects...' he gasped, hands reloading, blood running from his ears. He looked down the barrel of his rifle, felt himself weep as he focused on something that shook and wobbled and sliced along the lower lines. There was a roar of more gunships coming in.

He was going to die here. The moment was coming, a promise delivered at last. He would die and no one would remember him, but he would die in defiance, not in fear. 'He protects,' he said, and squeezed the trigger. The shot hit the thing at the end of his gunsight. Blood and scorched fat splashed out. It swayed and slid down, deflating, thrashing. He looked up, searching for the next target, and stopped.

Something was happening. All along the wall and lines that he could see, the enemy was pulling back, bladed bodies and war machines draining away into the multihued pall. Gunships cut in, hovering as giant warriors leapt through hatches, cradling wide-mouthed chrome guns. Gunfire blew craft from the sky. Volley fire, scattered at first and then increasing in cohesion, reached into the fog to rip chunks from the vanishing assault. Katsuhiro fired with the rest, reloading and firing and firing... And then, just as suddenly as the enemy had come, it was gone.

Quiet. Ringing quiet all around. The low crack of las-shots dull behind the pulse of tinnitus in his ears. He stared. Then felt something tug at his arm. Steena had crawled to the wall next to him. Her eyes were bloodshot in her dust-painted face.

'Water...' she gasped. He was taking his canteen from a pouch with shaking hands when a shadow fell over him. He looked up.

Baeron had removed his helm. The face beneath was bloody, the meat and bone of the right cheek mashed and torn, the left eye closed in a clotted mass. The Blood Angel was looking out beyond the parapet.

'What...' asked Katsuhiro, the sound of his voice a surprise to him. 'They... they left... What happened?'

Baeron made no sign of having heard. Then he looked down at Katsuhiro. His open eye was bright green. He stared for a long moment and then back to beyond the parapet.

'I do not know,' he said.

TWO

End to uncertainty
Red waking
Incandescence

Grand Borealis Strategium, Bhab Bastion,
Sanctum Imperialis Palatine

Three figures looked up at Rogal Dorn as he entered the war room. Malcador leant on his staff, the hood of his robe a shadow to the sharp lines of his face. His eyes caught the pale glow of Terra cast in slowly rotating hololight at the centre of the room. He glanced up as Dorn entered followed by Archamus. Beside him stood a tall woman in a red robe and beside her a hunched form in white with a head of bare metal and eyes that were crystal lenses. Both nodded a greeting. Archamus knew them both: Ambassador Vethorel of the newborn Adeptus Mechanicus and Magos-Emissary Kazzim-Aleph-1. Though Vethorel seemed the more human of the two, she only appeared that way. She was adaptable, subtle where she needed to be and brutally direct where she could not be subtle. Archamus liked her. The magos-emissary was a different matter. Focused only on whatever narrow world existed in definitions of his faith, he was ill-suited to the times and to represent the Cult Mechanicus at the war council. He was even less suited to navigating the next stages of coordination between the defenders. That was why Vethorel had come, Archamus was sure, because the next stage of the war would involve the servants of the machine more even than it had so far.

'Connect us,' said Dorn as the door sealed behind him and Archamus.

A single tactical command officer worked the controls of a block of machinery, from which vox-horns rose like the cups of chrome flowers.

'We have connection,' said the officer. The sound of distant explosions and the overlapping rattle of gunfire hissed into the air.

'My brothers,' said Dorn, 'lord Custodian.'

'*We hear you, Rogal,*' came Sanguinius' voice, distorted but as distinct as a bell chime.

'*Lord Praetorian,*' said the voice of Constantin Valdor.

'*Speak,*' said Jaghatai Khan.

'We have held, we endure,' said Dorn, 'but with the ports in his hands, the enemy will now bring the force to bear that he has held back. Encirclement will become total assault.'

'The calculations are not favourable,' cut in Kazzim-Aleph-1. The cogs in the magos-emissary's skull rotated, stopped, and started again. His voice crackled with static, for some reason reminding Archamus of someone chewing their lips. Rogal Dorn's gaze bored into the emissary, but Kazzim-Aleph-1 gave no sign of having noticed or of stopping talking. 'The materiel within the remaining domain depletes at a rate that exceeds that of the enemy. Across all of the projections our effective strength crosses over with the most favourable estimates of enemy strength. It does so within a threshold that does not extend past seventy-six days at the low edge of reliability. The projections with a higher probability rating give a substantially lower value.' At last the magos paused and seemed to reconnect with current reality. He looked up, eyes whirling as they focused. His cranial cogs clicked briefly. 'The calculations are not favourable.'

'I am aware of the position, magos,' said Rogal Dorn. 'To put what you say in summary – it is unlikely that our current defences will hold past a few weeks.'

'That summary lacks nuance but is accurate.'

'Lord Praetorian,' said Vethorel, and her voice was clear and firm. Like her face it read as perfectly human. 'While I would ask you to make allowance for Emissary Kazzim-Aleph-1's mode of expression, it does represent the summation of judgement within the Adeptus Mechanicus. On behalf of the Fabricator General, I must ask – what are you going to do?'

'What am I going to do?'

Archamus saw a flash in his lord's eyes that he could not read. His time in the personal presence of the primarch had been long enough to know that the fire of emotion did sometimes move beneath the cold layers of control. Whether it now sparked in annoyance or amusement or admiration, he could not tell.

'There are other factors,' said Malcador. 'The warp is... changing, aligning.'

'*As it did before,*' said the voice of the Khan, '*at the onset of the assault.*'

'No,' said the Sigillite. 'This is something more total. Broader. Deeper. The forces within the Great Ocean are intensifying. Its influence creeps into reality. Chance, emotion, consequence, all of it begins to bend to an end that is not ours. Reality, I fear, begins to serve our enemy.'

'*How so?*' asked the voice of Constantin Valdor.

'*Ill winds,*' said the Khan. '*We ride not just against the enemy but the elements and against our own natures. Every thought is influenced by the immaterial, every decision and instinct tainted. There are daemons dancing in our desires and dreams. That is what he means.'*

'Morale is corroding,' said Sanguinius. *'Darkness seeps into the thoughts of those that remain.'*

'We still have strength,' said Dorn, and his voice was the clear ring of a hammer striking steel. 'In spirit and sinew.' He turned his gaze to Vethorel. 'And strength in iron, too. Is that not so, ambassador?'

Vethorel gave a single shake of her head.

'There are complications,' she said. 'Besides Legio Gryphonicus and Ignatum, the Titans that walk in our defence are remnants and fragments of broken legions. The same is true of the Knights and bound cohorts that walk at their side. They are not unified, and there is dissent and disconnection within the Mechanicus.'

'A problem that you solved before, ambassador,' said Dorn.

'That was a schism based on data, caused by an unresolved equation of succession. This is not. Some wish to withdraw from the defence. Some wish to use all the strength we have now to push back. Some are caught between unresolved decision calculations. It is discontinuity.' She glanced at Kazzim-Aleph-1. 'It is emotion. It is fear.'

'The weakness of flesh…' said Archamus.

'Daemons dancing in our dreams,' said the voice of Sanguinius, softly.

'It shall be dealt with,' said Vethorel. 'But you must be aware that we are on the edge of a critical intersection of loyalty, will and doubt.'

'A crisis,' said Malcador.

'Yes,' said Vethorel.

'Then resolve it,' said Dorn. 'By whatever means. We enter

the last stage of this war. We shall hold. That is our only purpose. Whatever wall they attack, we shall hold. Whatever challenge is brought to us, we will be its equal. We shall have to use every part of what might and will remains. It shall be enough. I have no doubt, for the tide does not flow only in the enemy's favour.' Dorn's eyes moved around the circle of those directly present. 'They are coming.' Rogal Dorn's words settled into the quiet. 'Guilliman, the Lion, the Thirteenth and the First are coming.'

Archamus felt the words flow through him. Conviction radiated from Dorn as he looked around at them all, firm and true, like stepping onto dry land after an age on a storm-tossed sea.

Malcador looked at Dorn keenly.

'That was always the projected basis of your strategy, but there is more than hope in your words.'

'There is,' said Dorn, but added no more. 'Much will be asked of us in the days to come, more than has been given already. We must hold the circle that remains. Our walls must hold. The enemy's strength must be met. But if we hold true then victory will come.' The room was still, the vox a crackle of static over waiting ears. 'We hold and the enemy will be undone.'

The cogs turned in the magos-emissary's skull.

'Much remains uncertain,' he said.

Rogal Dorn looked at the magos for a long moment, and then smiled.

'Then we will do the one thing that will put an end to all uncertainty – we will win.'

Tulcan Precinct, Sanctum Imperialis Palatine

A fly buzzed through the heat-thickened air of the bedchamber. Bloated, its body the size of a blackened fingertip, it corkscrewed up to the ceiling. It found one of the spatters on the stucco flowers that was still damp and began to eat. Its body was egg-heavy. Once it had taken this last meal, it would begin to plant its seed. Thousands more of its kind had already done just that, but there was time and food and fecund ground for its children to grow in.

Sated at last, it released and dropped, listing as it half flew, half fell through the air. It struck the sleeping man on the cheek. His face twitched but his eyelids remained closed. The fly skittered across the skin, wings beating. The man's face twitched again. He was half-naked. Stained sheets wrapped him and trailed from the chaise to the floor. He was armed even while he dreamed. The knives were scattered across the room, but he had one of the guns tucked under a hand. His eyeballs flicked back and forth under his eyelids, flick-flick, flick-flick. The skin around the sockets puckered. He did not wake.

The fly lofted itself into the air again. The man was of no interest to it. He was alive and that meant he would not provide food to its young once they hatched. It buzzed low over the sodden, red carpet, weaving between the gilded legs of chairs and the discarded glasses. The remains in each would normally be a delight to it, but in such a land of riches it passed them by. The main heap of food was towards the corner by the door. That was where it would lay its clutch of eggs.

The door rattled quietly in its frame. On the chaise longue, the sleeping man flinched. His fingers moved on the grip of the gun. His eyes flicked under their lids.

Flick-flick-flick…

The door rattled again, polished wood and brass hinges flexing in the stone frame.

Flick-flick-flick-flick…

The door blew in. Shards of dark wood spun through the

air. Figures in red body armour came through the blast, guns raised. The man's eyes snapped open as he came off the chaise. The sheets fell from him. He was stripped to the waist, feet bare beneath velvet trews, unscarred skin taut over a lean frame. That gun in his hand came up with him. It was a duelling piece, ancient and expensive, and rarely used. Implosion rounds filled the five chambers of its cylinder. Each bullet was a work of lethal art and worth more than a mid-level menial's yearly labour. It roared. The first figure through the door took the shot full in the chest. Bones split and blood burst out as the implosion generator in the round crushed their torso and sent them cannoning back into the door frame.

The next trooper through the door was already firing.

A blast of shot ripped the upholstery of the chaise where the man had just been. He was already moving though. Neural-lacing, paid for by his parents when he came of age, sent him diving out of the way. The duelling piece roared again. The round hit a portrait on the wall. The implosion compressed canvas, plaster and stone to dust in a flash of blue energy. The trooper with the shotgun ducked back behind the stone frame of the door, but the woken man was moving again, aiming, gun steady, finger squeezing on the trigger.

A woman in black tumbled through the door, rolled, came up and fired twice. The shots caught the half-naked man in the hip and stomach, and blasted him backwards. He hit the chaise and toppled over it.

More figures in red armour followed through the door. Silver visors covered their faces, wide-nosed shotguns braced against shoulders, covering the room.

The woman in black rose to her feet, the pistol in her hands steady on where the target had fallen out of sight behind the chaise. Her face was dark above the high collar of her coat. Cheap, long-dead electoos spidered her bald head with the silver shadows of lions and eagles. Rejuvenat and hard training had kept her features lean, but the narrow braid hanging from the base of her skull was white with time. A compact breath mask clutched her nostrils and plugged her mouth. She was called Hellick Mauer and she had once been a soldier. Now, she was not sure what she was.

The rest of the squad were already at the doors leading to the interior of the manse. The dead trooper from the assault unit would be dealt with later, once the position was secured.

Shotgun blasts shattered locks and hinges. A second later the boom of photon grenades echoed out. Mauer didn't blink at the sound as she walked forwards.

'He's still alive,' called a crimson trooper from the other side of the chaise.

The half-naked man lay in a widening pool of his own blood. The shots from her hand-cannon had ripped him half apart. The first trooper to him had kicked the gun clear of his grasp. Blood was foaming from his lips and running down his chin and cheeks.

Mauer looked down at him.

'Thaddeus Rhihol-Sen,' she said. The man on the floor gurgled, his pupils wide holes in the whites of his eyes. His head twitched as though he was trying to nod, and a fresh froth of blood came from his mouth and nostrils. Mauer reached up and took the breath mask from her face. The reek of the room hit her in a wave as she took a slow breath. She had stood on battlefields after the slaughter, and knew the smell of death too well, yet it still took an act of will to keep the instinct to vomit from showing on her face.

The room was the main reception chamber in the manse. The man she had shot was the first in line to inherit both it and the familial power it represented. Old power, old wealth, going back all the way to before the Emperor welded the

Imperium together, power enough to ensure that they had this residence within the confines of the Inner Palace, wealth enough to have decorated it with art and finery that could have bought a frontier city on distant worlds. Gilded sculptures of cherubs and mythical beasts clung to the ceiling. Cream-white curtains framed portraits and pictures in bright oils: red skies, green fields, blue waters. Islands of upholstered chairs and couches sat on a thick carpet that had been the colour of snow. Soft light shone from drifting glow-globes. There were no windows, just the framed views of ancient idylls painted in oil pigment. Once it might have been possible to sit here and think the world outside nothing but an idea. Even with Horus' forces filling the sky, here there might have been a form of peace, even if that peace was a lie. Once but no more.

Blood spattered the walls, congealing in drops on the faces of the gilded cherubs. Bodies lay in tangles of limbs, some piled at the side of the room, some left where they had expired. Most had been cut. Blood and body fluid had soaked the carpet. Expiring insects and their eggs squirmed in the body heaps and drenched floors, making them seem to flex and twitch. Crystal goblets lay on the floor. The dregs of wine were the same colour as the congealed blood.

Mauer let the nausea fade. She took a step closer to the man she had shot. Her booted foot squelched bubbles from the carpet. It would not be long now; the thread of life in Thaddeus Rhihol-Sen was done down to its last, fraying fibre. Long enough for a last breath, though, long enough to answer a question.

'Why did you do this?' she asked, quietly.

He twitched. A red bubble grew from his lips, burst.

'Waking is despair…' he sputtered. 'They will dream for-ever now.'

Mauer nodded, slowly, then straightened. She aimed the gun and fired.

The crimson-armoured trooper nearby glanced at the dead man.

'No other questions you wanted to ask him?'

'No,' she said, and turned towards the door. Too late again. It was a pattern she had a feeling was going to continue. The sound of shotgun blasts came from deeper in the manse as the assault team cleared the rest of the rooms on this level. It would be just like the rest. 'Get our casualties bagged up and then flame units in once the sweep is done,' she called back as she walked from the room.

'No evidence gathering?' asked the crimson trooper. He was called Solsha, and had been an arbitrator; now he had fallen into being something like her second. It was a duty she knew he had neither wanted nor liked.

'Evidence of what?' she said, turning to look at Solsha. 'He was like the others – unable to cope with the reality he found himself in.'

Solsha looked down at the dead littering the floor. Reflections of corpses flowed across the silver of his mask.

'This is…'

'Not something to think about,' said Mauer. 'Get it cleaned up. Take four hours' rest leave, and then get back on station.'

She did not wait for a reply but stepped through the door. Four hours. There would need to be a report, as nominal and pointless as it was. It seemed not even the possible death of the Imperium could end the need for paperwork. Maybe, though, it was time to report in person. Yes, it probably was – someone had to know it was getting worse. She was sure that they would rather not have something else to worry about, but she had once made a career of doing what was unpleasant but necessary. She would make that report later. First, she would need just a little time for herself. An hour maybe, then, just an hour somewhere away from other people. She really wanted to get some outside air, even if it reeked of void-shield static. Air, and perhaps a drink. Just a small one. No sleep, though. She did not want to sleep.

Cavern 361, sub-shelter level seven,
Sanctum Imperialis Palatine

They called it the incandescence. By convention, within the Collegia Titanica and the Martian Priesthood, the mind-interface between Titan and crew was called the manifold but to the Legio Ignatum it was something more. Bonded by direct neural link it was a space of neither human sensation nor targeting and systems data. It was a union of the two, a world made in the connection, in the overlap of human and machine. Data became sensation, sensation became data. The will of a princeps augmented by their moderati became the actions of a war machine that could destroy armies and level cities. It was a mechanism, a fundamental biomechanical sub-system. That was only part of the truth, though, the truth that could be understood without living the reality. For those that commanded the Titans of the Legio Ignatum the manifold was not a mechanism or interchange of command. It was fire. Divine fire. A world made by the lightning between man and divine machine, life lived in the flash of a thunderbolt.

Incarnated.

Burning.

Incandescence...

Red was the world. Ghosts of green tactical data spun in at the edge of Tetracauron's senses. Spheres of light radiated from him, flickering in orange, yellow and white.

<Engine!> The shout roared within him, and he felt the threat-presence to his right. He turned his head. Pistons lengthening, sensors reaching across the shimmer-images of the fume

stacks and manufactorum blocks. The enemy engine came from behind the forest of chimneys at a run. Ground shaking. Tetracauron lit with fury. Red target mandalas bleached white. Data roared in his synapses. Chain teeth the size of sword blades buzzed on the fists of the enemy engine. It was swift, so swift. Fuel pipes burst under its stride. The ferrocrete slab road exploded into shards.

<Fire!>

<Primary weapon charge building…>

<Impacts on void envelope…>

Bubbles of fire shivering off his cloak of shields. The glitter of fire coming from low buildings to his left.

The enemy engine was closing, accelerating. Its strides the peal of thunder.

And he was striding to meet it, one step then another and another, forward into the kill.

<Fire!>

<Not yet. Not yet!>

<Primary weapon charged.>

His limbs were burning. His heart a sun.

<Charge secondaries!>

<Reactor output at ninety-three per cent and rising. Red tolerance reached.>

<Charging secondary weapons.>

<Reactor output at tolerance.>

<Targets locked.>

<Fire! Fire! Fire!>

And the instinct to let the fury go was equal to his will, pulling ahead.

The enemy machine was there, a stride from him. Black-and-red iron. Its fists lightning, its face a mask of ivory. It crossed the last stride, fist rising with a boom of extending pistons. The target locks in Tetracauron's sight were the red of forge iron.

<Fire!>

<Yes.>

White light. Blinding. Retina-bleaching. Voids collapsing like sheets of glass. Armour becoming vapour. Face of ivory charring black in the inferno…

<Engine kill.>

<Immersion termination protocol initiated.>

The brilliance dimmed.

<No!> His thought stabbed out as the vision broke apart… fragments of grey ash on the wind.

<Princeps Tetracauron, prepare for connection dissonance.>

No…

But neither the word nor his will could hold the world together as it dissolved. Colour and heat and fury drained to grey.

His eyes opened.

Another world filled his sight, metal and dull stone and light seeping from a data screen. He could see. The sensations of his incandescence clung to him for a lengthening second. Ghost echoes of the roar of reactor response and target lock overlaid the grey world. For that moment he was in two worlds, the sense of his limited body stretched over something vast and magnificent. In his eyes the vista of war-data still spun. The breath held in his chest was a roar of star-fire. The spark of his will the ruin of cities… Yet here he was, just a web of sinew and flesh again, dragged back down to the leaden feeling of his muscles and limbs in the throne.

The second sense to return was smell. The air reeked of human sweat, his own no doubt, diluted by the spice of electro-static. He was in a devotional chamber, sat on a throne of hard iron. Cables snaked from the throne to machines that lined the wall. The core of his familious adepts cohort filled ranked banks of consoles, the light and displays glittering in their eyes. A mere forty-five out of those needed to make his Titan truly walk to battle.

'Disconnection complete.' Enginseer Xeta-Beta-1's voice was a harmony of machine notes. 'Confirm sensory reharmonisation.'

He blinked, still adjusting to the feeling of a heart beating in his chest and breath drawing between his teeth.

'Confirm sensory reharmonisation,' she said again.

'Confirmed,' he said.

'Submit secondary audio confirmation, princeps.'

Tetracauron gritted his teeth and forced his tongue to move. A bitter taste lingered as he swallowed.

'Walks in beauty,' he said, chewing the words like pieces of gristle.

'In full and clear please, princeps.'

'She walks in beauty, like the night,' he said, forming the old, familiar confirmation phrase. 'I am fully dis-incarnated, Xeta, no ghost of the flame is puppeting me.' He looked at his hand resting on the throne's arm and pushed away the feeling that it wasn't his. The fingers flexed. He pushed himself up and took a step.

A step… pistons extending. Ground shaking. Gyros spinning as the weight of a divine machine moved on the earth.

His booted foot rang on the grate.

'A little heavy in your first mortal steps today.' Xeta-Beta-1 glided into sight, her dozen brass claw feet raising chimes from the floor plating as she moved. Articulated arms of chrome arched over her shoulders, holding a quartet of dataslates in front of her. She tapped at them, fingers a blur. The digits were still flesh. Tetracauron had once asked her why she had not had them replaced, and she had replied that it was a tragedy but that augmetics could not match the dexterity and feedback of bone, nerve and ligament. Her current hands were not her own, of course; those had been lost in a plasma venting on Sahba-21.

The graft replacements had come from a Martian artisan and been bonded to arms that were machine from the wrist up. For an enginseer trusted with guarding the spirit and systems of a Titan, she was eccentric, her communication spiced with the precise poetry of flesh-bound language, her temperament exacting but given to flights of stray cognition. For the hard-line creed followed by many of the Martian Priesthood, she would seem bordering on errant. She was also exactly suited to the Legio that was her tribe and life's devotion.

'Does the god-machine still echo in your blood?' she asked, looking up from her dataslates. The quad-ocular lenses of her eyes whirred to refocus.

He winced as a ghost sensation of weapon discharge flashed through him. He nodded.

'We must walk,' he said, 'by cog and code we have to walk soon.'

Xeta did not reply; she was already moving away to the other cradles housing Divisia and Cartho. His two moderati had the privilege of exiting the sense immersion after him. His returning first was supposed to be a mark of rank, but Tetra-cauron thought that remaining connected for longer would have been a more fitting recognition of status. Traditions did not change though, least of all in the Legio Ignatum, oldest and most decorated of the first Triad of Titan Legios to walk the surface of Mars.

He scratched the interface plug at the back of his skull. It still itched whenever he was out of connection. It had been refitted and upgraded thirty-five times, but the itch remained. At the last refitting Xeta had wondered out loud if it might not be something to do with him rather than the sacred equipment fitted to him. He had not answered. She was almost certainly right. She normally was. He winced as a ghost echo of reactor data bleached his sight for a second.

The chamber he had woken in was one of the deep caverns beneath the Imperial Palace sanctified and given over to the Collegia Titanica, their crews, support enclaves and god-machines. For now it was, essentially, home.

From across the chamber, he could hear Xeta's intoned commands and the clatter of data conduits and pistons as each of the enclosures around his two moderati's thrones disengaged. They were unsteady as they rose from their seats. Divisia was tall and fleshy, the shock spikes of her hair electric-blue and acid-green. Red geometrics covered her cheeks beneath her eyes. The chrome of her teeth flashed when she winced as she took a step. Cartho was forged as though to form a perfect contrast. Short and willow-thin, the flesh of his face pulled over fine bones, shaven scalp flowing with vivid flame electoos in red, gold and black. No expression showed as he stood, though inside the man would be snarling with discomfort.

'You both look terrible,' Tetracauron said to them.

'The honoured princeps senioris…' began Divisia, and retched. Vomit spattered the metal decking. Tetracauron ignored it. Divisia suffered more than most after dis-incarnation, always had. Her bond with the incandescence was close. One day soon she would walk as princeps of an engine. That was right; she had earned it and proved herself worthy of the honour. He would miss her. In the world where they were both one with *Reginae Furorem* she was a part of him, their wills and instincts overlapping in the well of the god-machine's spirit. To see her go would be to lose a part of himself. She vomited again, gasped, and forced out the rest of what she was saying. 'The honoured princeps does not look much better than dreadful himself.'

'I concur,' said Cartho dryly. The second moderatus was upright but swaying as he tried to find his balance.

'You are both wrong,' Tetracauron said, and smiled. 'I look much, much worse than dreadful.' Xeta emitted a blurt of purring cogs that was probably a proxy for a laugh. Divisia straightened and raised an eyebrow. Her irises shifted to fire orange.

'Is that the best you could do?' she asked.

'Are you telling me you could make a better attempt at levity, moderatus?' he replied.

She tilted her head as though considering.

'Fairly certain, yes,' she said.

He smiled, the sensation of the movement a heartbeat out of synch with his perceptions, and opened his mouth to reply.

A blurt of machine code echoed down the chamber.

Tetracauron, Divisia and Cartho all turned in perfectly synchronised movements. A robed figure was drifting towards them from where a door had irised open at the far end of the chamber. Red robes dragged beneath and behind it. The oily haze of active anti-grav clung to it. A hood with a black-and-white-checked hem half covered a lump of cables and green lenses, which sat in the rough position you would expect a head to be on a typical human. Weapon servitors had activated across the chamber. Targeting beams reached towards the figure as it came on. The tiers of familious adepts turned to stare, machine fingers paused above keys, data markers blinking on unpatched screens.

A brass limb rose from beneath the approaching figure's robes; there was a brief glitter of light and the servitors went still, guns cycling down to inactive.

'Well, this does not bode well,' muttered Divisia.

The floating figure halted six paces from them. Tetracauron could feel the pulse of its grav-field in his teeth. The lump of its head pivoted, and another blurt of machine code sounded through the air. Xeta replied, the enginseer's code a melody to the stranger's growl. It turned its eye-lenses back to Tetracauron. There were twenty-four of them, he noticed, the smallest

no larger than a nail head, the largest wider than a fist. This
was a member of the priesthood, and an exalted one at that.
Another blurt of code. Tetracauron tilted his head and raised
his eyebrows. The silver rings bonded with his jawline clinked.

'The emissary will have to convey his meaning by analogue
methodology,' said Xeta from beside them.

Another blurt.

'Yes, there is no secondary communication option,' said
Xeta.

'This is a temple of the machine,' said the priest. 'The necessity to sully it with the organic is an insult.'

'An insult to what?' asked Divisia.

'To the machines of this place, to the spirits that move in
the holy interfaces, to the god-machines that sleep within the
vaults beneath us.'

Cartho was two strides towards the priest before Tetracauron's arm caught him and shoved him back. The moderatus
raised his arm, head turning, and Tetracauron could feel the
echo of the movement in his own nerves, pistons tightening
to raise the power claw, gas flushing to pressure feeds ready
to ram it forwards. Maximum force strike. Engine kill. Armour
and plasma washing out, and the war-horns shouting righteous victory...

Tetracauron met Cartho's eyes. The moderatus stepped back.

'Who are you?' asked Tetracauron, turning to the priest.

'I am designated Gerontius-Chi-Lambda, emissary from the
Fabricator General.'

Tetracauron nodded.

'Tell me,' he said, carefully, 'does your function as emissary
include access to data on our Legio?'

'It does.'

'And it's impossible that an exalted functionary within the
sacred-cog turnings would not have reviewed that data prior

to entering our Legio's sanctum.' He turned his head, eyes level as they fixed on Gerontius-Chi-Lambda. 'Impossible that it would have escaped such a functionary's notice that the Legio he comes to is the oldest.' He stepped towards the tech-priest. 'That the Legio has been the house of the Omnissiah's avatars of ruin since the birth of our faith's truth…' Another step. Fire rising through his core. 'That it has burned more enemies than any other. That it walks at the will of the Machine-God alone…' Stride, stride, full focus forward. Target's eyes whirring. 'That those who walk with it live for that purpose alone.' Target one-metre range. 'That the link between us and our machines is the only binding we have to the Omnissiah.' Target not withdrawing. Optimum close-range weapon discharge achieved. 'That we do not sully our connection to our god with augmetic, noosphere or code…' His face was a hand-span from the emissary. Weapons primed. Targets ordained. 'That we speak not in its voice but our own, and that to profane such tradition is not insult. It is provocation.' Weapon release on command.

Gerontius-Chi-Lambda shifted back. Tetracauron smiled and felt the echo in his blood of plasma draining into charge coils.

'But no emissary of the Fabricator General would be so foolish,' he said. 'So, I must presume that you have not made a complete review of the data before coming here.'

Gerontius-Chi-Lambda shifted where he floated. Tetracauron forced himself to relax, glancing at Divisia and Cartho. Both were staring at the emissary with gun-barrel focus. They sensed his shift back from aggressive posture and mirrored it, muscles deliberately relaxing in face, jaw, shoulders and limbs like struts and pistons releasing in sequence. He let the heat of anger sink down until it was just an ember in his gut.

He knew Gerontius-Chi-Lambda, or rather he knew his type. Not Martian, but one of those born and trained in one of

the forge worlds or machine holds reclaimed by the Great
Crusade. Hard line to their interpretation of the Omnissiah's
truth, unseasoned by deep tradition, and wanting to bend
the universe to their will. Purity mattered more than truth to
such people, and in the betrayal of Kelbor-Hal and half the
Mechanicum they saw both justification and the opportunity to press their case. They had found an ally in Fabricator
General Kane and enacted his will with direct ruthlessness
while feeding the brutal calculations of his mind. Tetracauron
could not stand them and was certain that the regard was
mutual.

The Legio Ignatum was ancient, one of the Triad Ferrum
Morgulus – the first of the Titan Legions, who had walked to war
since the earliest ages – whose god-machines had souls which
lived in mechanisms crafted by lost forges and fires. They were to
be revered, holy-beyond-holy manifestations of the Omnissiah's
wrath in war. Yet the Legio did not bow and scrape or look like
the priests of this newborn age. They lived for the fire of battle,
and to fulfil the purpose of the machines they guarded. Princeps and moderati alike did not augment themselves beyond
what was needed to link to their charges. They did not sleep
like mortals but dreamed within their neural cradles, linking
their minds to an echo of the slumbering god-machines. They
lived the fire and fury of war and iron. It was a sacred connection, fundamental and all-consuming, the lightning arc between
iron and flesh where the Machine-God spoke in blazing reality.
That fire consumed many, but that was their purpose: to hold
the inferno and become it, and to live in the heart and dreams
of their god while they burned.

'Why are you here?' asked Tetracauron, at last.

'You are summoned,' said the emissary. 'You and all your
Legio. You shall attend the Princeps Maximus Cydon, and all
of those who answer your command shall attend with you.'

'I am commanded by Princeps Maximus Cydon, and he has not commanded me so.'

A buzz came from Gerontius-Chi-Lambda, and he pivoted and began to float towards the door.

'He will command you so. It is a certainty. Three hours, five minutes, six seconds. Princeps, you shall attend to this command.'

Tetracauron watched the tech-priest pass through the door into the chamber and felt his brow crease.

'What is that about?' asked Cartho in a low voice.

'I am not sure,' replied Tetracauron. 'But I have a feeling it's likely to be my least-favourite feature of our exalted and honoured bonds with the eternal and blessed Martian Priesthood.'

'What feature?' asked Divisia.

'Politics,' answered Tetracauron.

THREE

Unmarked-Unknown
Boetharch
Outcast

Unmarked-Unknown

He was not falling. He needed to remember that. Not falling. Not sliding down the incline of darkness. Not plummeting. Not screaming. He needed to remember that here you could not fall.

'Oll…'

Falling.

Stars.

Black.

Cold.

Burning.

But he was falling. Falling all the way down. Down to the underworld. Down to where the krakens dreamed, and the dead were. They were all there: wounds red in white faces, blood on hands, hair waving in water. All of them. Had it been too long? Had they forgotten him? Would they know him, all the dead of a life lived in aeons?

He thought of Medea, beautiful, wronged Medea with the witch-light held just behind her eyes… all that time ago.

He thought of the stone and mud-brick walls rising from the dust and the patchwork green of fields. Home. Home to a boy who ran the irrigation ditches with the calls of his mother behind him, and a laugh on his lips. Home an age ago.

He thought of a friend and hero dragged through the dirt behind a chariot until he was just a bloody rag. When was that? When…

'Oll.'

He thought of Orpheus, poor Orpheus, walking up out of the dark and trying not to look behind.

Don't look behind you. Don't look back at what has gone. Don't look back at what you're going to lose. Don't look…

He was not falling.

'Oll!'

He stopped falling.

His eyes were open. There was noise all around him, noise like breaking glass and ripping silk.

'Oll, you need to get up,' said Katt, voice firm, eyes looking down at the floor. Oll blinked. He almost looked up, then stopped.

'How long?' he asked.

'A couple of seconds,' said Katt.

'It's getting worse,' called Rane.

Oll started to rise. He felt cold, clammy, like something had taken a sip from his veins and not returned it.

'Trooper Persson,' said Graft, and Oll felt the servitor's metal limbs steady him. 'I have you, Trooper Persson.'

He blinked again. His eyes were stinging. He kept wanting to raise his head.

'Who's got the count?' he called, and heard the hardness in his voice.

'Three…' came Krank's voice, starting strong then fading to nothing. 'Three minutes, two… er…'

'Come on!' he snapped. 'The count, now!'

Krank swore.

'Three minutes twelve seconds,' called Katt. Katt, of course Katt. Sometimes Oll wondered if they would have made it even this far without her. She was not just smart and psi-gifted; she was sharp.

There were five of them, five souls taken from the battle on Calth, which was now a long way away in every sense. None of them were the same any more. At least none of them apart from Oll. There was Graft, one-time Militarum loading servitor, still that in most respects, gears and flesh still running but its back hung with kit taken from across the arc of human time. Hebet Zybes, a farmhand, a pay-by-day who had gasped and shook at things he had seen, though not so much any more. Still scared, but calm, hardened, like a piece of wood held in a fire until just before it burns. Bale Rane, a soldier for a war that had never happened, a boy who had become a man while walking in cuts between worlds. Dogent Krank, a soldier who had started this road old in soul and had only got older. Then there was Katt: plain, quiet, very quiet Katt – all dull-eyed and silent on that day when they had come from Calth. Something else now. All of them Oll's problem. All of them the people who had kept him going and alive in all the time since he had cut a slit in the air on Calth and begun this last voyage. All of them not the people they should have been.

'Something is coming!' called Zybes. He was crouched, lasgun up, not looking directly along the sight. Tears were running down his cheeks under the edge of his goggles.

Oll reached for the compass, found it already in his hand. The needle was a blur. Unreadable.

'Three minutes thirty-one!' hissed Rane.

The knife! Where was the knife?

'It's almost here!' called Zybes.

And you could feel it now, the bow wave of its approach like the breath from an open furnace door.

'Trooper Persson...'

'Three minutes thirty-nine!'

Where was the knife?

'Trooper Persson, are you in need of assistance?'

'We need to go!'

The knife... the damned knife had been in his hand already. He hadn't seen it. Hadn't felt it. As though for a second it hadn't been there. Or he hadn't been there.

'Three minutes forty-one seconds!'

He looked at the compass. The needle snapped still. He brought the knife up.

Oll looked up. For this moment, to do this thing, he had to look up.

Up. Everything went up. Light. Shape. Dimension. Colour. Sound. All of it stretched upwards to a vanishing point as Oll raised his gaze. He was smeared, pulled, a string of matter and thought and sensation stretched between nothing and eternity. Pain as well. Pain as a fact that just went on and on, like a looped freeze-frame. That was what you got from cutting so fine on the edge of time and space; you got to walk its fraying edge. A schism-zone was what Katt had started calling it, and that was about right, Oll thought. They were caught on the edge of where they had left and where they needed to be. There were a few rules in this place that they had learnt over gods knew how long they had been in the schism. Don't look up, don't miss the count for when the compass should point true. Don't think about falling. Don't fall. Make the cut.

Make the cut.

He brought the knife up. The point of it was a black splinter at the edge of his sight.

Make the cut, Oll.

Now.

'It's here!' shouted Rane.

Oll heard the sound then, like cartilage popping, like dry skin stretching over bone. He felt breath on the back of his neck, warm and reeking. It was behind him. It was always behind him. There were a lot of things hunting them, but this one was close and no matter how they tried, it kept finding them. Always just out of sight. Always just behind them. They had realised it was there six cuts back, but Oll had a feeling it had always been there, patient rather than swift, closer each time, like something moving in the blink of his eyes.

'It's…' Krank's voice rose, broken, shrill, the tough layer of everything that had made him a veteran solider cracking. 'It's… it's touching… me.' Oll felt it too just then. Fingers on the base of his neck, weak and light, the touch of someone in the last moments of life trying to find comfort. He wanted to scream. He wanted to turn around.

He cut.

The stretched skin of the schism-zone parted. Space peeled open as the knife in Oll's hand slid down.

'Through,' he called. 'Now!'

The others ran past him, and then he was through the cut too, and the sensation of fingers on his back and the breath on his neck vanished.

Falling…

Now he just needed to remember about not falling.

Grand Borealis Strategium, Bhab Bastion,
Sanctum Imperialis Palatine

Mauer watched and listened as she waited. The sound in the Grand Borealis Strategium was the rumble of a tide: snapped

orders, the clatter of cogitators, the hum of muffled voices
caught in vox-sets and the ping of alert buzzers. A fug of
human sweat and burning wires filled the gloom. The pale
glow of hololight and read-out screens lit the faces of men
and women sat at data and signal stations. A projection of the
Imperial Palace filled the central space. Red and amber flickered across it from Anterior Barbican and around the Eternity
Wall enclosing the Inner Palace regions. Each spark was an
active engagement. In places – Marmax, Gorgon Bar, Sanctus
Wall – the shards of light spawned and spread even as Mauer
watched. It might have been beautiful had it not meant what
it did. The enemy was still attacking, in spite of its failure to
breach at Saturnine. The Magnifican extended to the east, a
great, dark expanse, devoid of the light of battles, an abandoned and conquered realm. Two months. Just two months
and a handful of days separated that desolation from the
city it had been. No matter the victories, the battle remained
poised – time bought, nothing more.

'Boetharch.' Mauer turned and looked up at the sound of
Archamus' voice.

The Master of Huscarls did not look tired; Space Marines
did not tire, but she had noticed that fatigue played its own
game with them. There was a glasslike glint to his gaze, and a
tautness around the eyes and jaw, as though he was focusing
on the moment by an act of sheer will.

'Master Huscarl,' she replied.

'Follow,' he said, jerking his head towards a side chamber,
and then stalking towards it without a backward glance. Mauer
watched him for an instant and then followed. She had spent
a long time, a lifetime in fact, around war and watching the
effects of war on people. She knew humans, and how humans
changed when faced with horror, when pushed to their limits.
Space Marines were not people, but there was a heritage that

remained even with all that was done to make them. Transhuman they might be, but that status began with human and
did not leave it entirely behind. If Archamus had been a man,
she would have said that he was operating at the edge of stress,
fatigue and control – functioning, coping, but with parts of
his nature compressing as the weight of the largest and most
complex warzone in history bore down on him. She wondered
what that load was doing to the Praetorian. She knew what it
was doing to the humans of the command echelon: nothing
good, and a lot of bad.

The door to the side chamber sealed after her. A light blinked
green on a security auspex display mounted on the stone table
at the room's centre. There were no chairs, and the lights
remained cold and dim.

'It's getting worse,' she said, without waiting for a prompt.
'Three incidents in the last four days. Fifty casualties from a
munition supply depot – the prefect-senior simply shut down
the air supply. When we found him, he had cut off his own
eyelids. An entire materiel transit hub dormitory that went up
in flames after a loading crew torched it. Half a district dosed
with fatal levels of sedative narcotics by a medicae primus
who got to the water supply. This morning, a senior zone
commander found in his manse with the rest of his extended
family cut up and stacked like timber.'

'Noted. That is information that could have been submitted
by the usual mechanisms of your office, boetharch. Next time
use them.' Archamus began to turn away, stepping towards the
door. Mauer felt her own jaw clench.

'My office?' Mauer heard herself speak. Her voice was cold.
Archamus turned back. A frown was deepening on his forehead, words forming on his lips. She spoke before he could.
'That office barely exists and did not exist at all until sixty days
ago, and if you can tell me what the rank title of boetharch

means, honoured Master Huscarl, you will be doing me a favour.'

'You exist to keep the influence of the war from damaging morale within the body of the command echelon and those areas that influence and bear on its operation.'

'And how do I do that, Master Archamus?' Another frown from him. She raised an eyebrow. 'I am doing my share of shooting, if that is what you are thinking, but the truth is that neither you nor the Praetorian know what is happening inside the heads of the people within these walls. You have grabbed me, and anyone else you can reach, pinned a fresh rank on us, given us authority and sent us out to solve a problem you can't explain and you don't know exactly how to solve.'

A muscle twitched in his cheek. She was not certain if it was a sign of anger or, impossibly, of amusement.

'Are you finished?' he asked.

'Not even getting started.'

It was his turn to raise an eyebrow. She breathed out and unbuckled the collar of her coat. She had worn the full formal attire of her rank, such as it was: black storm coat, the silver rosette of the new Command Prefectus fastened between the red enamelled buttons running in twin lines down the front. Her pistol sat in a patent leather holster at her waist, heavy and awkward compared to hanging in its normal thigh rig. She had even cleaned the gun until the worn metal gleamed. Crimson gloves itched on her fingers. Part of her wondered who had had the time to consider how a newly conjured division of Imperial authority should be dressed. At least there was no hat.

Archamus waited, silent and still, his face unreadable. She pressed on.

'I am here now because it is getting worse. Not just more frequent. Worse, you understand? Morale, crime, atrocity is like a tide – it surges, it ebbs and flows in humans, but it has a rhythm, a cause and effect. A mob is seized by a cause, a regiment weakened by hardship and then poisoned by sedition. A commander who cracks because he has lost everyone around him and has just been ordered back onto the line. Cause and effect. You can trace it back. If there is a pattern, then there is a cause. But what is happening has no pattern, no root in the rational.'

'We are fighting a war for the existence of humanity as we know it,' said Archamus. 'Millions are dying by the tick of the minutes. Is that not cause enough?'

'No,' said Mauer. 'That is not what is happening now. If it was, we might be better off.' Archamus held her gaze. 'The man I executed this morning was a hereditary officer of the Valhara Armoured, family in service going back to the dawn of Unity, even to before. His manse was a gift for the service his sires did the Emperor. Three weeks ago he led a column back from the fall of Lion's Gate space port. Field reports show that his machine was the last in – he was part of the rearguard fighting to cover for the column right until they reached their lines. Three days in a tank with rounds pinging off the side. No relief, no sleep. Air strikes. People burning to death in torched machines. He held it together for all of that, probably saved eighty fighting lives and a couple of dozen tanks. If anyone was still noticing such things he would have been lined up for a citation and decoration. It was enough to earn him a relief furlough, twenty-four hours off the field. He was Palace-born, so he went home. Then he drugged his family and killed them all.'

'Trauma, an acute example of its effect on a mind.'

Mauer shook her head.

'It wasn't.'

'How can you know?'

'Experience, Master Huscarl,' she said, and heard the weariness in her own words. 'The things I have seen. The things I have done.' She rubbed a hand over one of her eyes, blinked. She would need a stimm dose soon to stay awake. 'The man, the dead man from this morning, he said that he did it because waking was despair. He wanted those he had killed to dream forever.' She paused. 'I have heard that before.'

'Where?'

'From every target I reached while they were still alive.'

'That's not in any of your reports.'

'It's what I am here to report now.' She paused. Archamus' face was still unreadable. Intellect moved behind those eyes, though, she knew – the kind of intellect that could hold, dissect and understand an entire warzone battle plan without straining. It was not that he wasn't understanding, but she could not tell what her words were doing behind that unblinking gaze. 'As I said, it's getting worse.'

'And do you think it is...' He stopped, closed his mouth, then started again. 'What do you think it is?'

'I don't know.'

Archamus gave a slow nod.

'Thank you, Boetharch Mauer. Return to your duties.' He moved to the door and released it and made to step back into the main strategium chamber.

'And what are my duties?'

He paused, looked back at her for a second, his gaze hard.

'To protect us,' he said, then stepped out without another word.

Mauer blinked for a second and then shrugged.

'At least it didn't take long,' she said to herself.

Magnifican

The wind woke Shiban Khan from the dream of death. He opened his eyes. Blue sky. A crack of blue sky in dirty clouds scudding across the roof of the world. He blinked. The wind breathed grit across his face. Quiet. Just the sound of the wind. There was pain coming. He could feel it, a storm just beyond the horizon.

'Who are you?' The voice came from above him. He tried to move but whatever was holding the pain from him was also holding him on the ground. A shadow passed over him faster than a blink. He tried to rise again. Failed. He went still. The blue sky had vanished. The sky was a sea of clouds the colour of bile and pus, yellow and frayed green. The wind breathed again, and he heard the click of rock fragments shifting nearby.

'Who are you?' he called before he could think. He could speak at least, even if he could not move. The storm of pain crackled closer. Fire lit at the edges of his nerves. He could remember the blast, and then falling, out and down, down and down, tossed by wind, bleeding. Eternity Wall. He had been at the Eternity Wall space port. He had fallen from the edge of heaven... Down to the land of the dead.

'No,' said another voice from out of sight. 'Not dead. Not yet.'

He knew the voice. He just couldn't remember...

'You are going to have to get up,' said the other voice.

Dead, all dead, all those who had stood at the Eternity Wall. Given to the hungry jaws of this battle, spent like a tyrant's coin, fallen, forgotten, gone to the wind.

'It will be hard,' said the second voice.

An arc of pain shot through him. How much damage could transhuman physiology take? He had kissed death before, and knew its taste. It was here again, grinning, breathing into his mouth as the storm of pain broke through him. The sky above him vanished.

Whiteness. Pure, blank-white pain extending in every direction. A blank world with no edge, a world where you could ride forever, where nothing would ever end.

He breathed, feeling the thread of air into his lungs, forcing the plateau of pain to take a shape. Splintered bones. Fine augmetics yanked out of flesh. Torn cables. Mashed neural machine interfaces. Blood. Oil. Pain arcing through his body like lightning playing over mountain peaks.

'Reassuring in a way,' said one of the voices. 'There is still enough of you left to feel this much.'

Shiban chuckled. The sound was wet and exploded fresh pain through his neck and chest.

'I know who you are,' he said.

'Do you?' said one voice.

'Do you?' echoed the other.

'You were there when they remade me,' said Shiban. 'You spoke to me then, too. You are dead, Torghun. You are a mind ghost, Master Yesugei.'

'If you say so,' said Yesugei's voice.

'You are going to have to stand, brother,' said Torghun.

Shiban moved his fingers first. He found that he could not feel anything of his right arm. The attempt almost sent him into spasm. Bit by bit he found what of his body still remained. More than he had expected, but some part of him could not help wondering if that was fate's joke – he had nearly died once, been remade twice, and now broken again, but not enough to die. He had been left with just enough strength to bear the pain of living.

His living was a marvel, though. He had fallen so far that death should have been a certainty. As it was, the damage was deep and touched every part of him, but had left him alive. He was sure that a great deal of that was thanks to the work of the tech-priests in his second remaking. The subtle and refined augmetics that the Mechanicum had spliced into his flesh and bone were not just crude replacements; they had been enhancements. Cybernetic infusions had bonded shattered bones, ceramite and adamantine plates laminated his skull and joints, bio-plasteks and neural grafts threaded his body. All of it had been integrated with specially crafted armour, so that flesh, augmetics and battleplate worked together seamlessly. Body and machine were a distinction that no longer really applied to him. They had said that he would not just be repaired, but that, with time, he would exceed even the speed and dexterity that he had had before. That promise would now not be fulfilled, but the skill of the tech-priests meant that he had lived through the impossible.

The truth of his situation emerged with every exploratory movement. The damage was subtle and insidious. Nothing torn off, nothing shredded. The most obvious sign of hurt was a split running down his right arm from elbow to wrist. Clogged oil and clotted blood caked the break in the armour. The fingers on the hand moved, but without sensation. The rest of his injuries ran through every part of him – crushed muscle, thousands of cracks running through bone, ceramite and metal. It was as though he had been pulverised by hammers that had somehow left his skin unbroken.

The pain blinded him twice as he pulled himself to standing. Acid and copper burned in his mouth. Once he was upright he slumped to the right, stooped, like an old man under a burden. The thunder of pain rolled through him without end. Above him the dome of poisoned clouds flowed on. The wind brought a wave of dust to rattle off his armour.

He let out a breath and looked around. A wide drift of ash and dust must have caught him as he fell. The metal bones of a building rose from the crest of the nearest dune. Two ragged birds perched on a metal pole jutting from the ground. They were gazing at him with black, pearl eyes. Vulture-crows, the Terrans called them, but they were neither crow nor vulture, but something bred by time, pollution and a diet of food scavenged from the spoil heaps. Filthy black feathers coated their bodies and wings, and iridescent quills cowled their necks and heads. Their beaks were black and sharp, and smooth. They were seekers of carrion and watchers for the dead. In the last months, their murder-flocks had spread across the land as thick as the smoke clouds. For them, this last war of humanity was a time of plenty. Shiban laughed.

'It was your shadows that woke me, then,' he said. 'Am I close enough to death for your tastes?'

The birds did not answer, but shifted, frayed black feathers ruffling. There were more further off, he saw, a flock of them clustered on a tangle of girders projecting from the dust.

'You two are the brave ones, eh?' he said to the pair, but the words turned into a wracking retch that sent a flash of agony through him. The world became a sheet of white for a second. He did not fall. When he opened his eyes the vulture-crows were still there. He swallowed. His throat and mouth were already dry. A bad sign. He took a step, felt the pain crackle through him and snarled. The sound sent some of the birds rising from the tangle of girders. His eyes rose to follow them.

A wasteland of dust and pulverised rubble ran to a horizon where broken buildings clawed at ochre clouds. He turned his head slowly, noting the almost imperceptible shift in light behind the clouds, feeling the wind and reading the patterns of everything he could see. He was in the Magnifican, somewhere in the zones west of the Eternity Wall space port – hundreds of kilometres west, somewhere whose features had been ground down by the tide of war that had flooded the million square kilometres of the Greater Palace, a tide that had now rolled on. The battlegrounds of months and weeks before were now a desolation.

Shiban breathed out. He had a long way to go. He allowed

himself a moment of stillness and then looked up at the remaining pair of vulture-crows perched on the nearby pole.

'I am going to have to take your throne,' he said. 'For this I crave your indulgence.' The birds did not move until he reached out to grasp the pole. They hissed and beat a slow spiral up into the sky. Shiban grasped the pole and yanked. It came free of whatever had rooted it beneath the dust. He hefted it, testing its crude weight. Plasteel, hollow down the core, dented and rusted, a stand for a sign perhaps, or prop for a street lamp.

'In ages of change, things find new purpose,' said Yesugei's voice from behind him.

Shiban spun the pole, then clamped his jaw shut at the wave of nausea and agony that rose within. He gripped the pole, and looked up at the point on the horizon where he judged the Inner Palace would be. Orange-and-white light pulsed on the horizon for an instant. Above him the vulture-crows circled.

'No backward step,' he said, and began to walk.

Command Prefectus chambers, Sanctum Imperialis Palatine

The flicker of blue data feeds snapped and spat through the chamber. Drifts of paper and dataslates lay in stacks on the floor. Bound report files formed teetering towers of paper. Bulbous screens fizzed with static and flashes of pict-cap images. The one functioning glow-globe cast a haze of yellow light over a riveted iron desk. Live hand-cannon shells dotted the surface, brass gleaming. It smelled of static and spaces where people had been breathing too long without ventilation. The heat held heavy in the still air. The door to the side office where Mauer had taken to resting – sleeping when she could not avoid it – was open a crack.

These rooms and the tower they sat in had been an unused

record space, a volume in one of the buildings of the new Administratum, built but never filled. The Command Prefectus had filled the tower in the last month, pouring people, equipment and the detritus of life into the rooms with haphazard thoroughness. Cell levels sat at the top of the tower, under the landing pads. Cables for data-feeds snaked up the stairwells. Rookeries for cyber-avians dotted its flanks. Things piled up because there was not time to put them anywhere else. There were not many in the Prefectus but still the tower felt cramped. As the most senior active member of the unit, Mauer had got the pick of the rooms for herself. She had chosen one that had a window.

She looked around, not seeing the debris. The hammer of fatigue was coming down heavy now. She had been kept young in body by virtue of rank and service that had brought rejuvenat treatment, but she had always thought that age lived in more than blood and sinew. Gene-washing, bone threading and organ reconditioning meant that you could roll through doors and fire guns like you were thirty, but you carried the seventy-five that you had lived in the moments that came after. She had not stopped since the last execution operation – mission debrief of assault team, full written report, dressing to suit the part of her rank, then the journey to the Grand Borealis and back, thinking all the while.

'Should have said no to being young,' she muttered. 'Would have had a viable excuse not to get involved if I had been a crone.'

'I doubt it,' came a voice from the side office. Mauer had her gun out and was ducking aside before the words fully registered.

Female, she thought. *Voice reads young. Confident.*

She came up beside the door. A different person, a person following prudence or advised engagement protocols, would have either emptied half her pistol clip through the door, or got out of the chambers, sealed them and called for a security detail. Mauer kicked the door, and went through, gun up.

The girl in grey sat on the cot in the corner of the room. A chromed mane of hair hung from her head. Her skin was pale. The eyes that looked up from the dataslates spread in front of her were dark.

'If you want an easier life,' said the girl, 'best shoot now.'

Mauer lowered the gun. She knew the girl.

'Archamus sent you,' she said.

'Archamus, Malcador, providence, fate – take your pick,' the girl replied, and looked back down to the data scrolling in glowing green on one of the slates. Mauer holstered her gun and went back into the main chamber. She went to the desk and looked for the box of stimms. She found them under a stack of low-level informer reports. The pills were orange and white, military field grade, good for an extended patrol cycle each. She swallowed two.

'You were a discipline officer,' said the girl's voice from the other room.

'You are correct,' replied Mauer, not bothering to raise her voice, but the girl seemed to have no problem hearing from the next room.

'Isn't this all a bit undisciplined for one of your kind? I was expecting Munitorum standard. Sheets pressed to perfection. Mirror-glossed boots. Everything stowed and in order.'

'You think that is what discipline is?'

'It's what the army thinks it is.'

Mauer clicked her neck, and winced. It would take a while for the dose to kick in. She went to the window. It was an arc sheet of slatted glass that ran from floor to curved ceiling. Dust filmed the glass. Beyond it, the towers and domes of the Inner Palace rose to a dark sky. It was night again. Lightning crackled across the clouds that had formed on the inner skin of the aegis shield. Lights dotted the distance, glowing from other buildings that crowded the hundreds of kilometres between here and the wall.

'You know who I am, don't you?' asked the girl. She had come from the other room almost silently.

Mauer shrugged, but did not turn from the view.

'It's my job to know who you are, Andromeda-17. I know you are a member of the Selenar, maybe the only one on Terra. I know you have the Regent's ear. That you have done work for both the Regent and the Praetorian.'

'You are proud of that, aren't you?' asked the girl. 'Knowing, I mean, being competent.'

Mauer laughed. 'Yes,' she said. 'I am.'

A silence formed. Lightning flashed in the distance.

'You are not going to ask me why I'm here, either,' said Andromeda-17 after a while. 'Are you?'

The girl was looking at Mauer with an unblinking gaze.

'We are going to get there eventually, aren't we?' said Mauer. 'You're hardly going to leave without dealing with whatever brought you here.'

'Fair point.'

Another pause. Mauer could feel the stimms begin to worm into the space behind her eyes. She could taste salt and metal on her teeth. The world sharpened a little.

'Archamus sent you,' she said again.

'Sent is a strong word. The Master of Huscarls talked to me, yes. He was concerned by what you reported.'

'He didn't seem so at the time.'

Now it was Andromeda's turn to laugh.

'It's not in their nature to show what they are thinking. Most of the Astartes breed function along narrow lines of thought and behaviour, and the Seventh Legion most of all.

He heard what you said, and he didn't know how to resolve it, so he came to me.'

'Straight to you?' asked Mauer. 'Not the Sigillite or Praetorian?'

'They would have said to come to me anyway. I am a fluid factor. It's my nature and chosen function to flow outside of the lines. I provide outside context. Your problem is my kind of problem.'

'Proud of that,' Mauer said, and looked around at Andromeda. 'Aren't you?'

Andromeda gave a small shrug and a half-smile.

'Have to be pleased with something, don't we?'

Mauer turned, leant her back against the view of the Palace skyline and crossed her arms. Andromeda sat on the iron desk, legs folded underneath her. Her chrome hair looked gold in the dim light of the glow-globe. The girl was not sweating despite the heat.

'You would have reviewed the written report I put in,' stated Mauer.

'And all of your field reports, and what raw data and intel you gathered – top to bottom, flesh and bones.'

'And?'

'And I agree. There is an upsurge in a certain kind of despair, and a certain kind of idea–'

'The idea of slicing people or blasting them apart to save them from waking, or sending them to sleep so they can enjoy dreaming.'

Andromeda nodded.

'More or less. The violence is the consequence of the idea, but the idea is the heart of it, the nasty bit, the pernicious bit.'

'Cause and effect,' said Mauer.

'If you like,' said Andromeda.

'The question is why.'

'Oh, come on, boetharch,' snorted Andromeda. 'I have read

and absorbed every bit of indicative personality and intelligence data on you. You know the answer, even if the part of you that is still a soldier and rule keeper does not want to say it – the warp, the answer is the warp. The sea of souls, the vast immaterium from which our minds draw the ineffable and all the denied horrors come. You are not supposed to know that much about it, but like you say, you are proud of knowing and very competent so you will have found out what you needed to one way or another.'

Mauer did not change her expression. So far, every word the girl had said was as accurate as it was condescending.

'An infection,' said Mauer, 'unleashed by the enemy and spreading through the immaterial realm, infecting people and sending them into violence.'

'I don't think so,' said Andromeda, tilting her head and biting her lip. 'The warp is not quite like that. It's not just another place like this. Psykers say it's like water in the ocean. It has tides, ebbs and flows – it's plastic, responsive and causal. All its horrors are parasitic to consciousness. Anyone thinks a thought or feels an emotion and the immaterium responds. One frightened soul is a ripple on the surface. It rises and sinks back into nothing. Many souls all in terror make ripples that are stronger. They meet, add together, and now that terror is a wave. It meets another wave and grows, it drags currents behind it. Soon it is big enough and strong enough that it does not dissipate, and it does not matter what other waves it meets, they are just going to be absorbed.'

'This… wave in the warp,' said Mauer, raising an eyebrow. 'That's the idea, yes? It is breaking over the people in the Palace, sweeping up their minds into insanity?'

'Not insanity,' said Andromeda sharply. 'There is nothing insane about despair or the wish for escape. Not normally and certainly not now. That's the thing, the wave is not just breaking over us. We are making it stronger. It's not just sweeping people up, it is finding those that are feeding it most strongly. The noble-soldier-turned-murderer that you put a bullet through this morning – how many times had he wept in his sleep and forced himself into his tank and put on a brave face for his troopers?' Andromeda-17 paused and picked up the box of stimms from the desk, turning it over in her hands. 'How many of these do you take so that you don't sleep?' She looked up, eyebrow arched in question.

Mauer met her gaze and did not blink.

'Not enough,' she said.

'That's the thing, though,' said Andromeda, dropping the box. 'It's not just something being *done* to us – we are part of it, feeding it even as it feeds us. It is accelerating, spun by opposing forces – escape and despair, powerful forces.'

Mauer was silent for a moment, and then shook herself and straightened.

'I see…' She moved from the window towards the door. She would go up to the launch pads. The air reeked of promethium up there, but it would be cooler than in here.

'Is there a way to stop it?' asked Mauer. 'To counter it?'

'We need to find one.'

'We?'

'Outside context, Boetharch Mauer. Different angles on problems, outside of the lines. Did you think it was something that another higher power worries about? Because if so, my proud old mistress of war, the truth is those higher powers are busy. This is the war now. What was it you said to Archamus – "what are my duties?" Well, this is it. You know things. You are frighteningly competent and you want to actually solve the problem, not just shoot it.'

Mauer found she was actually smiling.

'I am being completely played, aren't I? You are a specialist in behaviour, right? How much preparation did it take to map my drives, and compose that little tune you just played with me?'

Andromeda-17 shrugged. 'Honestly, I was mainly improvising – I find it's more effective.'

'This part is going just how you thought it would, isn't it?'

'Pretty much.'

'Including the part where I realise what you are trying to do, yes?'

Andromeda nodded.

'What am I being recruited into?'

'A just and necessary cause.'

Mauer laughed. 'That's how it always starts.'

FOUR

Legio
Drain the heavens
Blind zone

Gathering chamber, sub-shelter level seven,
Sanctum Imperialis Palatine

Sound filled the bowl of the gathering chamber. Tetracauron paused as he entered, looking up at the stone tiers rising from the space at its centre. The commanders of the Legio stood in loose clusters, over four hundred men and women, their hair and faces gaudy blooms of ink and dye above the graphite black of their uniforms. Crests of neon green, chromed skin, geometics and designs in the colours of jewels and chem run-off. Tetracauron's own hair was a crested blaze of red and black stripes. An indigo-blue band ran down his face from brow to neck. Silver rings decorated the line of his chin. Each one was a cog etched with a date that marked a machine kill. The irises of his eyes were topaz yellow, dyed by self-inflicted toxin bleaching. All this gaudy pageantry worn on their faces was another of the Legio's marks, the reflection of the soul of war as they fought it, an echo of the spirits of their engines borne on the skin.

Divisia and Cartho walked at his side as he crossed the chamber floor. The princeps and moderati of his maniple inclined their heads in acknowledgement as his trio approached. Others nodded respectfully. A few shouted greetings that he returned as he made for the crowd on the lower tier.

A squat figure detached from the nearest group as he approached. He smiled.

'Honoured Princeps Arthusa,' he said.

'You look terrible,' said Arthusa. The princeps senioris of Seventh Maniple sported shifting electoos of red cogs, which turned and intermeshed on her skin.

'So people keep saying,' Tetracauron replied and clasped forearms with her. 'But I think you are all just jealous.'

Arthusa gave an 'if that's what you want to think' shrug, and nodded to Divisia and Cartho.

'Princeps,' they replied and bowed their heads briefly.

'Any idea what this is about?' he asked.

She shot him a look, and he could read the 'you know very well' in her eyes.

'The priesthood…' she said carefully.

'Ah…' He looked at her and raised an eyebrow. 'So it is politics. You know, I once thought that a war like this would have swept that all away, for a while at least.'

'You were never that naive,' she snorted. 'War is power. The bigger and more cataclysmic, the more the power involved, and politics is just the feeding frenzy for power. The possibility of annihilation doesn't stop that – in fact, it probably just makes it worse.'

'Were you always quite such a philosopher?'

'Yes,' she said.

He laughed then.

'The priesthood are panicked,' she said, lowering her voice, 'and that's got more intense in the last few days, and not just the lower tiers. The higher up you go, the worse it gets. The machine, blessed above all, is logic, but I think… I think they are afraid.'

'Of what?' he said. 'Of losing?'

'Of losing everything.'

He looked at her again. There was no smile on her face now.

'How do you know this?'

'Because, honoured princeps, I use my time to stay linked to extraneous data when I am not incarnated. I like to know what the battlefield within is like before I walk out to the other one. I can tell you one thing, though, the princeps maximus is not happy – not happy at all. Neither is Bazzanius, or Clementia. The priesthood want something, and we don't want to give it. The cogs are turning and when the wheel stops, who knows…'

'What was it you said about politics and power…?' he said. 'Much more of this and you will be in line to be the next princeps maximus.'

She made a face, and the red electoo cogs on her cheeks reversed their direction of turning.

'Don't be an ass, Tetra. I know it's hard for you, but do try.' Arthusa grinned. 'Talking of ascending,' she said, gesturing at Divisia, 'when will this one walk on her own? Past time if you ask me – no offence, Cartho.'

The older moderatus bowed his head, expression unmoving.

'None taken, princeps. I am grateful that I am graced with being content with my function in the greater turning.'

Tetracauron looked at Divisia, who was trying not to look too pleased.

'When the cogs align,' he said, 'not before.'

Divisia shifted, uncomfortable under the gaze of the two senior princeps.

'If I may ask,' Divisia began, 'is there any more data on why we are here?'

'Politics,' said Arthusa and Tetracauron together.

A bell echoed through the chamber, first once, then twice, then a third time.

The double doors into the room opened. White mist fumed in through the gap. The bell struck again. Throughout the chamber, every one of the hundreds of princeps and moderati straightened. A double file of secutarii hoplites marched from the dark beyond, silver armoured, high shields blazoned with the yellow and black zigzags of Ignatum, red pennants trailing from spear tips. Chromed servo-units flew above them, scattering hololight images of jagged geometric designs in fire orange and vivid blue. Behind them came a man and woman in black uniforms, bareheaded, faces hard beneath crests and shocks of hair. These were the princeps of the Maniple of Maniples that were present on Terra, Bazzanius and Clementia, commanders of two of the Legio's Emperor-class engines, and part of the inner council of Princeps Maximus Cydon. Their moderati followed with them, equally grim-faced. There was a pause, a moment filled with the striking of another bell, and then Cydon entered. To have walked at the head of the oldest Legio for ten centuries and linked with god-engines for as long again might have brought many princeps to the embrace of an amnion-tank or an exo-frame. Not Cydon. He walked. His face was lean, dark skin withered back onto a narrow skull. The crest of his hair was silver, with black pearls bonded to the strands. Golden flames burned across his cheeks in subtle electoos. His left eye was milk-white with blindness, the pupil of his right a shattered star at the heart of an amber iris. His mouth was a thin line above a set jaw. He looked old, and hard, and furious.

Everyone in the room bowed their heads as the procession unwound into a circle that filled the lowest tier. Cydon took his place last, standing with Bazzanius on his right and Clementia on his left. There was a moment of quiet. Tetracauron could feel the tension in the air, taut and stinging like a rising charge in a gun capacitor. Cydon shifted and Tetracauron knew that the princeps maximus had felt the same thing, had thought the same thing. The old man turned to look at the men and women of his Legio filling the higher tiers. He gave a nod.

'Steady, my warriors,' said Cydon. 'Try to keep your tempers. Leave losing it to me.'

A chuckle like low thunder slid around the chamber.

The bell in the ceiling above struck again.

Gerontius-Chi-Lambda entered. He did not come alone. A trio of heavy battle servitors followed and flanked him, their cannons lowered, their red amour gleaming with sacred hexa-decima coding etched in hair-fine gold. Two lesser priests came with them, each bearing a vox-emitter on a long pole. Last, clanking and hissing, came a battle automaton, its carapace the grey-black of graphite. The procession came to a halt at the centre of the room. The automaton and battle servitors locked into place with a perfectly synchronised clang. Binharic boomed from the vox-emitters held by the lesser priests.

None of the princeps or moderati moved. Cydon was unimpressed.

Gerontius-Chi-Lambda turned the lump of his head to look up at the tiers of figures and then back at Cydon.

'The Omnissiah knows all...' his voice boomed from the emitters.

'For knowledge is divine,' said Cydon. His voice was level.

'You are called to heed the will of the machine,' continued Gerontius-Chi-Lambda.

'We are listening,' said Cydon.

'You are coded and commanded–'

'No.' Cydon's words cut through the amplified voice. Tetracauron felt it. Like ice. Like the dead weight of a neutron star. The hairs lifted on his neck. He could feel the princeps maximus' fury, the cold fire held in the breath he had just taken. He felt it, and knew that across the chamber four hundred and fifty-nine of his comrades had just felt the same. Interface synchronisation, they called it. Apparently it occurred in other legions, too, but in Legio Ignatum most of all. It was because of the incandescence. The crew of the Legio did not sleep or rest like others, but dreamed in connection with the battle archives of their engines. Their dreams were the shared echoes of past glory and loss. Within that connection they lived the battles fought by the dead and the living. It brought them closer to true incarnation with their engines, to the oneness that some Titan crews feared but which Ignatum knew was the sacred flame of truth. Thought patterns and instincts bled across that link, imprinting them all. Sometimes, a shared stimulus would bring those patterns viscerally to the fore within the Titan crews, and for a moment they would experience the world in the same way. Synchronised, tuned, like a hundred clocks all set to chime at the same hour.

Gerontius-Chi-Lambda's eyes whirred as they refocused on Cydon.

'As emissary and voice of the will of the Mechanicus, you shall hear me and you shall–'

'No,' said Cydon again. Then he tilted his head forwards. 'Do you wish me to say it again?'

Gerontius-Chi-Lambda did not reply, but the clicking of focusing rings slowed.

'It is the will of the guardians of the Omnissiah that you heed the words of the emissary that stands before you.'

'Better,' said Cydon. 'But the answer will still be the same. The same as I have spoken twice already to you now.' He shook his head once as though in disappointment. 'You should have sent Vethorel, but then I doubt she would have come. She is not a fool.'

The tech-priest pivoted his head, looking up at the ranks of princeps and moderati.

'It is the will of the protectors of the most sacred truth of cog and code that you ready your sacred engines. That you prepare to walk.'

Silence again.

'Is this the petition of the Fabricator General, of Praetorian Dorn, of the Council of Terra?' Cydon's voice rose in volume as he spoke, fire leaking from within.

'It is the will of the machine.'

Tetracauron could tell that this was an exchange that had already happened, and was now being repeated on a wider stage.

'The will of the machine...' said Cydon slowly, controlled carefully. 'Do you claim to speak for the Omnissiah?'

'Knowledge must be preserved,' said Gerontius-Chi-Lambda. 'The sacred must endure. You must obey that imperative. You must walk.' The magos turned his gaze from Cydon, lenses scanning the tiers of Titan crew. 'The machines bound to you must wake, they must walk. You shall heed this imperative. This is the will–'

'Where shall we walk?' asked Tetracauron. Gerontius-Chi-Lambda looked at him. Tetracauron looked at Cydon; the princeps maximus gave a relaxed nod of assent. 'Should we walk to war beyond the walls? That is our desire, so why do you demand it? But you are not talking of walking in the war that is being fought here, are you, magos?' Every eye of the Legio was locked on the tech-priest. 'You are not here at the command of the Fabricator General. You are here to compel us to walk in retreat. You are trying to build support for the Mechanicus withdrawing from this battle, and the way you see that being possible is by the strength of the Titans.'

'What remains must be preserved,' said Gerontius-Chi-Lambda. 'It is the imperative. It is the truth.'

'What of the imperative of hierarchy? What of the command of oaths, of loyalty, of honour?'

'All considerations must bend so that the cog may continue to turn. You must walk. You must aid us in bearing away what we have while there is still opportunity.'

'The battle is in flow, not lost.' Arthusa spoke now, her voice snapping from across the circle from Tetracauron. 'Three great assaults have broken against the Palace in the last days, or are you deleting that data from consideration?'

The magos' lens eyes flicked and focused on Cydon, Bazzanius and Clementia. The princeps maximus and the two commanders of the Maniple of Maniples looked back at him impassively. Tetracauron wondered whether the magos had demanded this gathering, hoping to break the unity of the Legio by appealing to its line commanders. If so, it was a foolish move, and one that spoke to ignorance, an abundance of hubris and fear. The magos did not relent, though. Whatever desperate line of logic had brought him to this point, Gerontius-Chi-Lambda rolled on, like a mechanism that would break itself before deviating.

'The Eternity Wall port has fallen,' said the magos. 'The data projections for conflict escalation are clear. The victories of yesterday only delay the fall. The force ratios have shifted in the enemy's favour, the scope for decisive materiel application have shifted in their favour. The probability of collapse magnifies, and with it the probability of preserving our sacred truth diminishes. The outcomes dictate a simple set of imperatives. Flight and survival.'

'Theory, hypothesis,' said Bazzanius from beside Cydon. 'But most importantly not the will of the Omnissiah nor His Fabricator General. You come here to sell your fears as though they are fact, and your desires commands. They are neither. You want us to join a faction to press a case that has already been denied by all. We shall not do so.'

'You will consign the sacred mysteries and machines we possess to corruption, to entropy.'

'We stand by our purpose,' said Cydon, and for the first time he raised his voice. It rolled through the chamber. 'We are not hounds to be called. We are the first of the Triad. We are those who walk into fire, who bring fire. We do not break. We do not run. We face down what would dare stand against us.' Cydon smiled then, broadly, humourlessly. 'And, most importantly, magos, we win.'

Gerontius-Chi-Lambda was silent for a moment and then half turned away, his head rotating slightly side to side. It was the most human gesture Tetracauron had seen the magos make, and when he spoke it came from him alone, a low voice that sounded weary.

'You cannot win,' he said.

'You speak rank sedition,' said Bazzanius. 'You bring weakness in the hour where strength is needed. It is you who shall suffer censure.'

'That fact and eventuality is irrelevant. The outcome of my life equation is irrelevant. I wish the data were not as it is, but above all I am a servant of the machine's truth – annihilation is coming.'

'You are in error,' said Cydon.

'Am I?' asked the magos, and turned to move away towards the door. The tech-priests, servitors and automata fell into step behind him. He was at the door when he halted and pivoted half back. 'There comes a stage when the equation to be resolved is not how to win, but how to survive.' Then he turned and passed beyond the chamber. The commanders of the Legio watched him go.

'There goes a greater fool than I would have believed could serve the turning of the cog,' said Tetracauron to Arthusa as the gathering's formality dissolved. She frowned; the cogs of her electoos had stopped turning.

'I hope so,' she said and looked towards the door that the tech-priest had passed through. 'I hope so.'

Northern wall circuit, Mercury Wall Zone, sub-horizon belt

The three Knights stood still as the dawn mist rolled off the plain in front of them. Each was of the smaller breed – three times the height of a man, a body of smooth armour balanced on back-slung piston legs. Weathered ivory and emerald lacquer covered their plate. Red-and-silver pennants hung from their weapon arms, heavy and damp in the dawn dew. Two bore blunt-nosed thermal spears and chainblades. Drops of condensed moisture hung from the still chain teeth, and ran from the vents of the guns. The autocannons of the third pointed up at the sky, an echo of the lances borne to war by the knights of another age. Ivory and crimson spiralled the long barrels, the colours bright and clean.

Within the quiet of her cockpit, Acastia watched the mist draw back from the brightening world. *Elatus'* sensors could have painted the view in data, in thermal, electrostatic, motion-corrected or tactical abstracts, but she had chosen to look at it as her eyes would. From here she could see the peaks of the mountains to the north, white-tipped teeth biting up at the sky. Beneath it the ground was still shrouded, grey vapour hiding its scarred skin. This was a flattened land.

The will of the Praetorian had levelled the cities and districts that had stood here. Labour armies and machines had scraped buildings and towers and homes down to earth and dust. Hab-blocks, shanties, manufactories, basilicae, nascent hives – all of them gone, broken and pounded down into a plateau that stretched from the feet of the distant mountain back to the walls that circled the Inner Palace. It was intended as a killing ground and it extended for one hundred and twenty kilometres from the wall. Acastia and her banner comrades stood on what the gunners on the walls called the horizon line – the point where line of sight from the highest wall sections hit the curve of the earth. From here, if she looked back towards the Palace, she could just see the battlements atop the Mercury Wall. Thunder clouds crowned that view, billowing up from where the aegis void shields interfaced with the atmosphere. Flashes of lightning strobed within the clouds. Between where the trio of Knights stood and the wall lay the Mercury-Exultant kill-zone: one hundred and forty kilometres of undulating ground spidered by shifting rivers of water, debris hills and crevasses. The labour armies had flattened the settlements beyond the wall, but what remained was a testament to the fact that you could never make anything truly flat, not on this scale, not with the time and tools that had been used. Out there were settlement-sized tangles of machines, the root masses of hives that had defied the efforts to break them. The Praetorian's will had been done, but what had been achieved was a desolation under the eyes and guns of the wall. Thousands of kilometres squared, it was a battlefield waiting for a battle.

It was beautiful in a way, thought Acastia; seen from here, at this time, there was a slow-moving serenity to it, a peace and freedom that denied the wider context.

Distant flash of lightning...

White gauze of mist melting...

Thin light catching clouds...

'We should proceed.' Dolloran's voice sounded in Acastia's ear.

'Soon,' she replied. She did not want to move. Not yet. Dolloran was impatient to begin, she knew; she could feel his impatience over the sympathetic link between the machines. He wanted to move, wanted to stride, and so did his mount.

Cyllarus was a Warglaive, a direct kin to *Elatus*, born in the same forge, a twin sharing the iron of their creation. They were both machines of fire and fury, impatient as they were swift. Acastia could feel the instinct of her own mount growling across the neural links in her helm. There was a joy though in denying the call, in feeling the power of her mount held in place by her will. It was a song in her nerves, a rising beat in her heart. Soon that would be gone, drowned in the clench and extension of pistons. A few hundred metres more and they would be past the sight line of the guns on the wall and into the blind zone beyond, hunting for the enemy. They would run free, and *Elatus'* instincts would rule as much as hers. In the land beyond the sight of the wall, they were the eyes and claws of the defences. And there, for a while, she could imagine that she was free.

'All systems and sensors are calibrated,' said Dolloran, 'there is no need to wait any longer.'

'Soon,' she said again. She felt the buzz of a one-to-one vox-connection opening.

'I think you may have indulged yourself enough, Acastia.' Pluton's voice was level, the patience in the old vessel's voice as clear as the note of chiding.

'At the setting out, in the quiet stillness, there is beauty, who should leave such a gift squandered.'

'True and well formed,' said Pluton, 'but we have a duty and it will not wait for beauty and poetry.'

For a moment she wanted to snap at him, but she bit the instinct back, holding her irritation in place with the same will that held *Elatus* still.

'Very well,' she said, breaking the link, and released some of the tension in *Elatus'* drive. Its pistons extended. Metal feet pawed the ground. Weapon arms flexed. She felt its snarl of joy echo through her temples. Her lips peeled back from her teeth involuntarily. Beside her, the other two Armiger Knights shivered to readiness.

'Now,' she said, and the three Knights began to stride into the land beyond the horizon.

The Imperial Palace

They drained the heavens. As dawn came on the twenty-seventh of Quintus, the sunlight reached across the curve of the world and touched the spines of ships as they sank through the upper atmosphere of Terra. Ark ships and warships slid into contact with the upper spires of the Lion's Gate and Eternity Wall space ports. Docking umbilicals locked into place. Blast doors hissed open in the bellies of ships. More ships dropped past them to latch on to the lower flanks of the port spires. Gunships and macro lifters settled on landing pads. Cargo began to vent onto conveyors. As soon as ships were unloaded they broke dock, and the next moved into place, stacked across low orbit and up into the void, moving towards the ports like the teeth of turning cogs.

Within the ports the adepts of the New Mechanicum and the labour cadres of the IV Legion worked the transit mechanisms without cease. In times of peace, the great space ports of Terra had moved billions of tons of cargo and millions of people from orbit to surface and back every hour. Now they were turned to a single purpose: to move every scrap of remaining men and materiel from the Warmaster's fleet to the surface of Terra. The cycle of ships and landing craft turned tirelessly, each one locked into a schedule and pattern that ran to the minute. Iron Warriors helmsmen and tugs guided the ships of those forces that were too far gone to meet the Lord of Iron's requirement and precision.

Thunder shivered up and down the orbital spires as ships

came in or broke dock. Rust and caked corrosion flaked free from tower sections the size of mountains. Vibration compensators sang as they worked to stop the mountains of metal shaking apart from competing forces. In the docking limbs and landing pads everything was movement and the clangour of machines and labour. Crews of servitors and whipped slaves dragged containers of shells, cylinders of plasma, boxes of rounds. Tanks rolled directly from the guts of ships into macro hoists. War machines stalked, skittered and dragged themselves into transit chambers and began the drop down to the lower levels. Regiments of troops, herds of things that had bred in the shadows of the warp, and a tide of the lost and the damned flowed down to the surface of Terra. On and on it went, like water gushing from an opened sluice, like blood pumping from a beating heart.

Forrix, First Captain and warsmith of the Iron Warriors, watched the operation unfold from the Tower of Logisticators on the Lion's Gate space port. Here the high clans of transit and the merchant factions had made their seat, and watched as the hunger of Terra bloated their wealth. They were gone now, fled into the Inner Palace or slaughtered. A few had bent the knee to the true cause and now helped turn their place of greed into a conduit for the armies that would remake the Imperium. The tower pinnacle was two hundred metres wide and enclosed by a crystal dome that gave a view across the curve of the earth. Forrix could look down to see the glimmering flashes of battle in the Palace Anterior kilometres below, half hidden by the cloud layer. Above, the light of the stars was vanishing behind the blue dome of day. In the chamber behind him, banks of cogitators pulsed with a drone that ached in his teeth. All of the staff in the chamber had lost the ability to move from their posts bit by bit as the techno virus unleashed by Volk into the port's machines spread and multiplied. With every command and input, they were becoming the machines they worked. It had not seemed to reduce efficiency or accuracy; if anything it had increased it. Now there were no vocal comms, just the flow of signals and command through the human shapes slowly becoming one with the data of destruction. Through here the summation of the entire deployment phase was channelled, pooled and flowed on.

They had prepared for this ever since the Lion's Gate fell, but the reality of it still woke a spark of awe in Forrix's mind. Billions of points of data, timing, estimation and coordination all interacting and adjusted so that the flow from sky to ground never halted. By looking up he could see those operations move the world. As he watched, a ten-kilometre-long war barque detached from the spire dock and came about, engines flaring to push it up into the sky. Behind it, an armoured macro hauler in the colours of the Legio Fureans was already taking its place – jets of flame firing from fifty-metre-wide altitude adjusters as it lined up with the docking limbs.

It was like the ticking of a clock, he thought, each minute a unit of force added to the pressure of the assault on the surface, each second a decrement to the remaining life of the Imperium.

They had held back so much strength. Even with all of the millions poured into the battle sphere, even with the bulk of six Space Marine Legions deployed and active, even with numbers and strength enough to take and retake star empires, still they had held back their full might. It was, as it always was, a matter of numbers. Forrix had reviewed and arranged the secondary orders for the movement into this phase of the battle.

The Saturnine gambit had failed, but that did not matter. Dorn had saved himself from a swift end, but the outcome was still inevitable. The Outer Palace was gone, a thousand-kilometre-wide ruin no longer contested. They held both the Palace space ports now, and the outer ports like Damocles to the north. They had applied pressure to the Inner Palace walls. They had taken the defences to the point of breaking on two fronts. Now they would simply make the whole circuit of the Ultimate Wall a front, all thirteen hundred kilometres of it. In a matter of days, every last unit of the Warmaster's armies would be on the surface of the Throneworld. Total pressure. Crushing force from every angle until the circle shattered. The defenders did not have the bodies, or the bullets, or the will enough to prevent it. This was war as a progression of multiplying equations, victory as a cold inevitability.

A low chime brought Forrix back from his moment of contemplation. He looked down at the communication controls mounted on his wrist, reading the indicator runes on the display. He frowned, keyed a control, and a projection from the collar of his armour filled his eye. He blinked at the brief spiral of data, then shut it off. His lips had pulled back from his teeth. Then he let out a breath and turned towards the centre of the chamber.

Perturabo, the Lord of Iron and Siege Master to Horus, sat in a data-cradle at the room's centre. Screens and holo-projectors moved around him on rails and articulated limbs. Direct interface cables plugged into his armour, snaking between weapon pods and over slab-plates. Only the primarch's eyes moved, flicking from screen to screen as they flowed past his field of vision. He was absorbing the data from the battle sphere raw: from the ammunition levels in the Anterior forward reserves, to the kill screeds from Legio Vulpa Titans, all of it, from micro to macro. This was as deep in the battle flow as Forrix had ever seen his primarch. The Lord of Iron was at one with the obliteration he was creating, his being focused down to

a point, like the aim of a gun barrel or the edge of a knife.
There was a beat to it, too, an almost organic rhythm to the
cradle's movements and the murmur of its machines. Like
breathing. Like a pulse. Forrix could feel it every time he had
to approach his primarch.

'Lord,' he said, coming to a halt beside the data-cradle. A
screen buzzed past on a rail, the information on it a blink-fast
flow of battle data. Perturabo did not respond. Forrix waited
twenty seconds and then spoke again. 'Lord.'

The movement of the screens and projectors slowed. Perturabo's
eyes continued to follow the flick and trace of the information.

'What is it?' said the Lord of Iron.

'The Warmaster's equerry is coming,' said Forrix. 'His gunship
touched down three minutes ago. He is two minutes from
the chamber.'

Perturabo was silent. Forrix waited. While the Lord of Iron's
focus and awareness of the battle sphere was near total, it was
also directed. One very particular subset of data was omitted.
Anything to do with the Warmaster himself came through
other channels, word of mouth, messengers. Forrix did not
wonder why; he knew why. Winning this battle required focus.
Focus of a kind that a being like Horus could break in an
instant. It was a conflict waged on behalf of the Warmaster,
but not with him. 'There is no further data as to why,' Forrix
added after a long moment. No data, but he could guess –
the losses at Saturnine: the Mournival, the finest of the Sons
of Horus, trapped and slaughtered in a failed gambit.

Perturabo's eyes stayed fixed on the shifting battle data.

'Admit him,' he said.

Forrix bowed his head and stepped back.

Admit him... as though there was another choice. Argonis
might be many things, and very few of them Forrix liked, but
he was the equerry of the Warmaster, and when he came as

emissary it was with Horus' will and authority. You did not bar the path of the Warmaster's will. It was not wise. Forrix knew that. He hoped that his primarch still did, too.

The doors into the chamber pistoned open, and Argonis entered, helmed and cloaked. A squad of Sons of Horus legionaries in red-crested helms followed him. In the fading light coming through the dome, their armour was the black of a sea at sunset.

'He is in the cradle?' Argonis said to Forrix as he stalked past with barely a glance at the First Captain. Forrix's arm shot out to bar Argonis' path. The guns of the Sons of Horus legionaries rose with a clatter. Iron Circle automata stamped from the edge of the chamber. Argonis looked down at where Forrix's armoured gauntlet rested on his chest.

Unwise, said a voice in Forrix's head, *very unwise.* He found himself surprised at what he was doing, but he didn't move. *Perhaps there is still an edge of old iron in my blood,* he thought, and almost smiled.

Argonis reached up and removed his helm, looking directly at Forrix. The equerry looked tired, like a man who was living out a life that made less sense by the day. There was something else in his eyes, too, something that Forrix would never have expected to see there. Pity.

'Let me past, First Captain,' said Argonis, his voice low.

'What is this?' said Forrix.

'Let me speak to him, Forrix,' said Argonis.

'Not without knowing what is happening.'

Argonis was silent for a long moment.

'Nothing that can be prevented,' he said at last.

'Why are you here?' the voice of the Lord of Iron growled across the air. Perturabo rose from the data-cradle, interface cables snapping free as he straightened. Weapon pods cycled on his arms and shoulders, like dogs shaking off slumber.

'I am here in the name of the Warmaster, beloved and obeyed by all,' said Argonis. 'He demands your presence.'

'Where?' said Perturabo.

'On the flagship. On the *Vengeful Spirit.*'

Northern wall circuit, Mercury Wall blind zone

Acastia and her fellow Knights passed the outposts at noon. Here in the blind zone, the northern wall circuit was a memory left out of sight. Battles had spilled across this area and shell bursts and munitions from both sides had left it a pock-marked, broken place of bare ground and debris. Here and there the metallic remains of dead skitarii lay in jumbled drifts, the flesh hanging from their augmetics in wet, half-rotted webs.

The fighting along the northern circuit had been in the early weeks of the siege. Prosecuted by the forces of the Dark Mechanicum on the part of the traitors, and by the houses of Knights and the armoured and motorised elements amongst the defenders. The traitors had encircled the defences and pushed close into the shadow of the Mercury and Indomitor walls, but the guns and scale of the defences had held them back. The Northern Circuit had become a rolling tussle fought between platoon and company-scale forces in the kill-zone in sight of the wall guns and the blind zone beyond the horizon. The traitors tried to establish footholds in the forward areas: forward operating bases, artillery enclaves, observation posts. When they succeeded they spread, digging in and funnelling more supplies, engines and troops forwards. They were trying to push themselves far enough forwards that they could lob medium-range artillery directly onto the wall. With that they would be able to directly assault, and apply the kind of pressure that had breached the Helios Gate. So far they had not

108   JOHN FRENCH

succeeded in securing a stable forward base within the sight
of the wall. They just did not have the numbers, in Acastia's
opinion. There was a reason the east held the hot zones of
fighting: the ports would let the traitors bring more strength
from orbit faster, and the lines in the Anterior before Lion's
Gate were formidable but nothing compared to the scale or
resilience of Mercury, Indomitor or Exultant. Why throw forces
against the strongest fortifications, when you could grind down
the weak point and then breach the Lion's Gate? No, the war in
the Northern Circuit was about each side denying the other respite or the chance to redeploy forces to other areas. A smaller,
necessary, grubby battle fought so that the day could be won
elsewhere.

It was a near-perfect echo of her birth and life, reflected
Acastia.

'You will never be raised high,' had been her mother's words
since she could remember. Bastard born, bound by blood to
service and obedience, but always to the side, placed a little
above the serfs and oathmen of the house but only a little.
Permitted to steer a mount but only one of the lesser kind,
never an Errant, never a long-shanked Cerastus or powerful
Castellan. War and glory and beauty ever in sight but never
touched, never fulfilled.

'*Identify.*' The voice came over the vox-link, heavy and mono-
tone. They were at the outpost line. A drum-shaped blockhouse
rising from the desolation, it looked like a giant shell casing
dropped in a battle between gods. Four storeys of poured rockcrete braced by metal plating, gun ports shuttered. Acastia
heard the chimes of signal and target lock as they approached.
Blockhouses like these ran in a chain through the wall guns'
blind zone. Some had been lost but most were intact. Tunnels
reached down from each of them to supply and ammunition
reserves, and linked each to the next outpost in the line. Like

Acastia's trio of Knights, their main purpose was to give wall command alert of enemy movement. That, and to challenge a force moving into the plateau before the wall. The outpost's guns and defences would not last long against a main-strength formation, but had Acastia and her trio been hostile, they would have lasted minutes at best.

'Greetings from the house and riders of Vyronii,' replied Acastia. *Elatus'* systems purred as it transmitted identification engrams. The three Knights slowed their stride. Acastia felt the needle-point sensation in her skull as gun sensors painted her mount. One flick of a hand on a trigger or a misfunctioning target protocol and she would be chewed apart by bolt shells.

The cockpit instruments pinged, and the sensation of needles vanished.

'Pass,' said the voice over the vox. *'Good hunting, Vyronii.'*

'Acknowledged,' she said, then impulsed the vox over to the rest of the lance. 'Let's push. I want to be a hundred kilometres deep in the zone before we revert. Pluton, push your auspex left flank, maximum gain. Dolloran, mirror right. I have the lead.' She kicked the pace cycle pedal before the others responded. *Elatus'* stride lengthened. Plasma flowed through conduits. Beside it, *Cyllarus* and *Thaumas* matched pace, spreading wide to either side. Outside the land spread, stacks of building debris rising in artificial mesas. Crags of rock from where the mountain feet had been imperfectly ground flat loomed around them. Fog was rolling across the land. Wind tugged past the Knights, pulling their gun pennants out behind them.

'It's quiet,' said Pluton, as the distance count rose. 'Nothing on auspex. Not even weapon discharge remnants.'

'Disappointing,' said Acastia.

'Concerning, surely,' said Pluton, and she could almost hear him frown. 'There should be something, even if it's low level.'

'He's right,' said Dolloran. 'This sector has been crawling with false Mechanicum units. Why is there nothing?'

'Because they knew we were riding out,' she snapped. 'What more reason does any dog need to run back to its hole?'

'It's an ill indication,' said Pluton.

'So we should wheel and withdraw?' she replied.

'We should be on our guard, and ready.'

'A worthy reminder to yourself to wake up, Pluton.'

The vox lapsed into silence.

The empty land passed. The auspex chimed low and soft as it reached beyond sight and found nothing. Acastia felt the annoyance roll and disperse as the rhythm of *Elatus'* stride rocked her. She knew Pluton was right. This empty quiet did not feel like peace. It felt as though the sea had pulled back from the shore, and they were running along the exposed seabed before the waves crashed back. She would not turn back, though. To go back would be to give up freedom before she needed to. And she wanted a kill. She would force Caradoc to mark *Elatus'* hide with an honour mark. The thought of her liege's face, jaw set, eyes cold, setting the mark, and knowing that it meant that on the field she was his equal... that would be a reward sweet enough to stride this uncertain land for days.

'Onwards,' she said, and the three Knights paced on.

The Imperial Palace

The armies of the Warmaster marched across the ruin of the Palace. They marched from the great space ports of the Lion's Gate and Eternity Wall, and from Damocles and the landing fields on the southern plains. The labour armies went before them. In the Outer Palace Magnifican there were no highways for them to follow, so they made their own. Battalions of slaves and levelling engines ground and blasted and bulldozed through the carcasses of city-sized districts. There was no subtlety in what they did. The forces already on the ground and those in orbit needed to flow as fast as possible to the walls of the Inner Palace. The speed and volume at which they could do that was the dominant factor. The ocean of annihilation needed to flow to the walls of the Inner Palace.

Lines were drawn across the thousands of kilometres of the Outer Palace, and they became mass highways, hundreds of metres wide, leading from the space ports westwards. Structures were detonated. Rock and iron were beaten to shards and pounded flat. The hands of thousands of slaves sifted the ground for unexploded munitions before the war engines and troop transports advanced in their wake. In some cases, the advancing forces overtook the slaves, and ground the carpet of panicking souls into the beaten rock and dust. Supply auxilia scrambled to build fuelling and resupply camps ahead of the tide, vast reservoirs of crates, generators, fuel and water bowsers. Most had been taken from within the Palace itself, secured from the defenders by strike teams commanded by the IV and XVI Legions. Now, the stores that would have kept the defenders fighting would feed their enemies. To plan for such necessities, even as the Outer Palace fell, took a particularly cruel form of pragmatism. Such was the truth of iron that flowed in the veins of Perturabo and his sons. While others went with the rage and the fury, theirs was the purity of obliteration: considered, eternal, remorseless.

Much of the strength of the Iron Warriors was here, on the roads being ploughed through the Outer Palace. Overseers watched over the mass columns of tanks, war engines and troops. When delays or conflicts broke out they were ended with gunfire and slaughter. The corpses of those who impeded the advance were pinned to pylons sunk beside the roads. Flies swarmed the corpses. Blood formed slick, sticky patterns on the dust. Some of those passing wailed from fear or piety at the sight. Onwards the rivers of iron and flesh flowed, the roads carrying them laid down hours before they were trod. Relentless, eating towards the Inner Palace through the turning of day and night.

At the space ports the mass formations of war engines began to arrive. The remaining Titans of half a dozen legions, Knights bearing the heraldry of great houses, tank divisions numbering in the hundreds. With them came things bred from the alliance Horus had made with the powers of the warp. Beasts the size of buildings, dragging cold iron chains, things that had been machines but now loped, and howled and gurgled. Above them soared flights of aircraft, pure atmospheric craft that had made the spires of the space ports their roosts. They wheeled above the columns like bats.

On the easternmost lines and walls of the Inner Palace, the defenders felt the surge advance as a shiver in the air. On the crumbling parapet of the Colossi works, Jaghatai Khan felt the tremble and looked up at the gloom of the eastern horizon. Behind him his warriors and Stormseers stood. Their white armour was pink with blood. Some of it their own. There was weariness in the Khan's eyes as he looked into the distance, and only the humour of the graveside spiced the smile that split his face.

'A storm that shakes the earth,' he said, dryly. 'I sense that this may be an ill omen that even I can read.'

'Shall we ride to meet it, my Khan?' asked Naranbaatar. 'Pluck out the black lightning before it can fall on the land.'

'And what if we fall as we ride?'

'Then we die having ridden beyond the horizon, my Khan.'

Jaghatai Khan did not answer, but stood looking into the distance, unblinking.

* * *

To the south, Sanguinius felt an echo of his brother's silence as a breath of air across the fever heat of his thoughts. Fire and ruin turned in his skull as he felt the ground tremble. The day before he had found hope in the darkness, but now… what? Not darkness but something else: a question? A question that he could not yet hear, waiting in the inferno that was the future, a question to which the only answer was blood and murder.

In his gunship, flying east between aegis shield dome and building tops, Rogal Dorn saw the surge as a rising trickle of reports from forward units at the eastern walls. In the dark, alone, he was silent. He thought of the words he had spoken to his brothers and commanders: that they only needed to hold, that help was coming. He knew they were true. He hoped that he believed them.

FIVE

From the dark cometh angels
Labyrinth
Bearers of light

The Wrath's Descent, *Saturn close orbit*

The beast in his dream is dying. There is blood on the snow, pink slush, entrails steaming in the cold air. The boy is shaking as he comes closer, pistol raised, barrel steady, white breath sawing between his teeth. The beast tries to move as it sees him, tries to claw towards him. Its movements slosh in the blood-melt. The boy can see the creature's black eyes looking at him as he comes to stand over it. There is an intelligence in those black depths: intelligence and recognition. The boy lowers his pistol. The beast gives a huff of breath. Pink liquid bubbles between its teeth. The boy slides the sword from its scabbard. It is as tall as him, a blade that he should not be able to lift, much less turn and wield. He holsters the pistol, lifts the blade. The dark trees shiver around him. The wind lifts the edge of his hood. The beast's eyes go wide as it looks up at him. The boy lifts the sword high above his head.

'Forgive me,' he says. The beast snarls. The boy strikes down.

In the dark of his cell, Corswain woke. The white and red

of the dream faded to black. For a moment he was still. The stiffness of old wounds poorly healed clung to his muscles.

'Your grace,' said the voice from the vox-link bonded to his skull beside his ear.

'Yes,' he replied, standing in the dark and walking to the cell door. Locks clattered open at his approach. Candles lit the chamber beyond. Black-robed serfs and servitors were already lifting the sections of battleplate and weapons from their racks. The air smelled of gun oil and tallow.

'It is time,' came the voice from the vox-link.

'Understood, shipmaster,' he replied.

He stopped in the centre of the chamber, arms outstretched. The serfs surrounded him. Layers of armour weave sheathed his muscles. The first pieces of plate snapped tight over connection ports. At the side of the room, a tech-priest muttered code as it brought the armour to life a piece at a time. Until this ritual was complete, the dead weight of layers of ceramite hung on him like sins waiting for forgiveness.

It was strange to sleep while in sight of the site of the largest battle in human history. But sleep he had. It was necessity as much as prudence. He had not slept while they had raced through the warp. For every watch he had stood on the bridge, his mind split between waking and the half-comatose state that was a gift of his geneforging. Around him the *Wrath's Descent* had creaked as it cut through the aether tides, and the beast had stalked at the edge of his denied dreams. In the quiet of those watches, he had heard the voices of his fears in his half-dreams:

'Too late, too late...' said the ghost voice of Alajos.

'The Imperium is already dead,' rasped Konrad Curze. 'The Emperor is a corpse on a throne.'

'I am placing my trust in you,' said Lion El'Jonson. 'Do not fail me.'

On and on, slowly circling as the Dark Angels warships passed through the Sea of Souls towards the flickering light of Terra.

And now they were here, and here alone, and so now fear had new whispers: where was the Lion? Where was the Legion? They should have been there. The storms had cleared, and the primarch would have heard the call of Terra just as Corswain had – wouldn't he? Unless he couldn't. Unless the Legion was no more. Unless those warriors that Corswain had brought to the Solar System were the last of his brotherhood...

Ten thousand men and two dozen warships – the core of Corswain's command renewed by reinforcements from Caliban that had been waiting for him at Zaramund. A great host... Nothing. Against the forces that swarmed on Terra and swam the Solar voids, nothing. He had seen it on the face of the Admiral Su-Kassen when her ships had found them.

'You bring so little and too late...'

If there was a note of disappointment in her voice, Corswain knew it was an echo of his own. He had been certain that the Lion and the rest of the Legion would already be on Terra. They should have been there. That was what Su-Kassen had been waiting for, too; that was what her fleet was for, to meet the reinforcements, join with them and drive a path through the enemy to Terra. They had been waiting for months, preserving their strength, striking only where needed, gathering intelligence and planning for the moment when reinforcements arrived. They had thought Corswain's fleet a herald fleet, riding ahead of a main force.

The survivors of the Solar War lay in the shadow of Saturn's rings, folded in the planet's radiation and magnetic fields. It was an armada, hundreds of warships pieced together from those that had stood against the onslaught on the Solar System: ships of the V, VII and IX Legions, of the Jovian Fleet, of the

Saturnine Flotilla, and with them warships that dwarfed all the rest: the *Monarch of Fire*, the *Red Tear* and the *Phalanx*. Huge and silent, legends of war sleeping in darkness, active systems powered down to silent running. They had asked Corswain to join them, to become part of the armada waiting to secure the gates to the Solar System when the forces of Jonson, Guilliman and Russ arrived. He had thought about it, as the eternal night lapped at the hulls of his ships. Then the light of the Astronomican had vanished from the sight of their Navigators. No one knew why, or what calamity had occurred on the Throneworld to steal its beacon light, but all knew that it meant the chances of more ships coming from the night to relieve Terra had gone with it. It had, though, settled something in Corswain's mind.

The doors to the arming chamber opened. The wash of air stirred the candles. Three warriors in black plate strode in. All but the last were bareheaded. Tragan was first, the captain of the Ninth Order, his power fist and left pauldron bone-white, the new armour still gleaming with fresh lacquer; then Adophel, the Chapter Master cloaked in the silver-threaded cloak of void commander, his face an axe blade of scar tissue; last came Vassago, the Librarian alone wearing his helm, the psychic conduits and arrays hooding his armoured head. Silver keys hung from his waist, and a mace was clamped to his back. He alone bowed his head as he entered. Corswain returned the gesture. Vassago and the Calibanite reinforcements they had met off Zaramund were still adapting to their places in this new, active command. They were good warriors all, but this was a long way from Caliban and the decades of having few concerns beyond the raising of fresh recruits for the Legion.

'The gunship is prepared,' said Adophel. 'Are you sure you do not wish to take more warriors?'

'More?' said Corswain. At his back, the spinal connections with his power pack sparked as they linked.

'Yes,' said the void commander. 'Do you trust them?'

'If they wished me dead then they could have fired on the gunship before we even reached the *Phalanx*.'

'There are other things they might try.'

Corswain gave Adophel a sharp look, then nodded and closed his eyes for a second. The dream still clung to the inside of his eyes.

'That is why you and Vassago come with me,' he said, 'to make sure that a witchling thing does not come back wearing my face. Though I doubt any would want to – as ugly as this war has made it.'

None of them smiled. They had all seen too much of what the enemy could do to laugh at the jest.

The last plates locked into place. Mag fields snapped true. Power fizzed through fibre-bundles and neural links. The weight of the armour vanished. Corswain held out his hand for his sword as a serf fastened the white pelt across his shoulders. 'Stand the ships ready to break silent running and fight free if we do not return within the time.'

'Do you think they will agree to help?' asked Adophel.

Corswain did not answer, but walked from the room, sheathing the sword.

The journey from the *Wrath's Descent* to the *Phalanx* was by gunship. Squadrons of First Legion craft flanked them until the whole formation was bracketed by vessels in the yellow and black of the Imperial Fists, until the lone Stormbird carrying Corswain and his honour guard slid into the *Phalanx*'s launch bay. A full company of VII Legion warriors met them as they disembarked, weapons ready. It was not a warm welcome. They were cautious, and suspicious.

Corswain noticed the marks of battle damage as he stepped from the gunship.

Halbract, Su-Kassen and a White Scar that Corswain did not know waited for him, flanked by a pair of Dreadnoughts. A warrior in the yellow of the Imperial Fists and bearing a staff and psi-hooded helm the echo of Vassago's watched from the rear of the group. The First Legion were not alone in breaking the Edict of Nikea, he noted. The Imperial Fists Librarian leaned in close to Halbract and Su-Kassen as Corswain's entourage approached.

'You bring a psyker with you,' said Halbract. Corswain looked at the Imperial Fists commander. He knew of him, one of Rogal Dorn's finest, a stone man, as unyielding as a cliff face. This was the first time they had met, though. Terminator plate bulked his frame, yellow with crimson bands across the shoulder guards. There were battle marks on the plate, unrepaired even though the armour was clean, like scars worn as medals.

Corswain reached up and removed his own helm, and met the cold blue of Halbract's gaze with his own, emerald stare. He turned his head to look at Vassago, then back to the Imperial Fists Librarian beside Halbract.

'We have learnt to be cautious,' said Corswain. 'In these times it is hard to tell friend from foe at sight.'

Halbract's face did not change.

'Your brother will make no use of his abilities,' said Halbract. 'If he does, we will know, and you will be treated as hostile.'

Corswain held the Imperial Fist's gaze for a full second, and then turned and nodded to Vassago.

'It is done,' said Corswain, looking back to Halbract and the admiral. 'You have also learnt caution, I see.'

Halbract did not answer.

Su-Kassen took a step forward. She was void-born thin, her bones fine, her eyes dark. The starburst and orbiting rings of the Solar Naval Command gleamed on her uniform. Like Halbract, Corswain had heard of her: an old warrior born and made in a different time.

'Welcome, Lord Seneschal,' she said. She did not bow her head. She was mortal, but here, on this ship, and in her fleet, she was the mistress of all. By her word, weapons made to kill empires spoke. If the weight of that power was a burden, none of it showed in her gaze.

'You have considered my request to join your forces to our fleet?' she asked.

'I have,' he replied.

'But you have not come to agree,' she stated.

'No,' he said. 'I have come to ask your aid.'

Unmarked-Unknown

Oll woke with stone under his face. Cold stone, smoothed by footsteps. He pushed himself up, hands clutching for the knife and compass.

Nothing. Nothing in his hands but cool, empty air. He looked around.

Stone walls, finished and fitted close, forming a corridor just wide enough for him to have stretched out his arms to the sides. He looked in both directions. Blackness ahead and blackness behind. An oil lamp sat on the floor just beside where he had been. He recognised its style, the finish of its bronze and the patterning on the handle. It was from a kingdom that had become rubble a long time ago. He looked at the walls and floor again. It was familiar, like the face of an old friend, or an older enemy.

He was getting a feeling that he did not like; it was a feeling that he knew where he was and when he was. They must have been thrown out of the schism zone after they made the last cut. They had landed back in the tangle of true time. That had to be it… but why? He had spent a long time going between times and places in the last seven years, walking a path back to the old world, to Terra, to do something that he was not even certain he wanted to do. Early on he had been following the path set for him by John Grammaticus as the psyker nudged him from place to place on a winding, hidden road. He had not heard from John directly in a long while. He had tried not to think about that more than he needed to. Looking into the dark beyond the lamplight, he was starting to wish he had heard from John. He was starting to wish he knew more about what was waiting for them if they made the next cut.

Cut…

His hands closed reflexively. He looked around.

The knife was gone.

The others were gone.

'Katt?' he called. 'Rane?'

No reply came from the dark, not even the echo of his own voice.

He opened his mouth to call again, and stopped.

Footsteps… the sound of far-off footsteps on stone, in the distance behind him.

Shuffle-tap… shuffle-tap… Rhythmic and slow.

He turned.

Silence again.

Carefully he bent down and picked up the lamp, wondering who had lit it and why it had been left beside him as he woke. Whose was it? Who had put it there?

'Some choices to be made soon,' said a voice behind him.

He whirled, fist clenching to strike. The man sat at the bottom of the wall. There was blood on his tunic, under the hands that rested on his stomach, red seeping through the fingers. The man looked up at Oll, smiled. His teeth were pink. 'I should have listened to you. I should have raised the white sails.'

Oll felt cold. He knew the face. It was the face that had smiled with the joy of leaping bulls, that had gone down into

Minos' Labyrinth without hesitation, the face of the man who Oll had told to raise white sails but had not.

Oll knew where he was.

'You were always good at choices, old friend,' said Theseus, 'but these ones ahead are going to be the worst of all, no clear path, no thread back this time.'

Oll brought the lamp closer. The light showed more blood, a lot more, more than a man could live without.

'What choice are you talking about?' said Oll. 'How do you know?'

A bellow came from the dark, echoing off the stone. It sounded like something in pain, like something that was hungry.

'It told me,' said the dying Theseus, his eyes looking into the dark as the sound faded. 'After it... after it did this, it told me all the things that it knows. It told me that you would come. It told me where you are going. It told me that it is waiting for you, here, and that you cannot get out – even if you think you are free, you aren't. This place, it's not just a riddle in stone, old friend... Should have known... How could a puzzle of stone hold the bastard-child of a god? I should have known. I should have listened to you. Daedalus did his work well.' Theseus' back arched. His eyes and mouth clenched shut against the pain.

'You got out,' said Oll. 'This is not what happened. You slew the beast. You got out.'

'No,' he said with a bloody grin. 'I'm still down here, and I always will be. Made...' He gasped, and the blood was bright on his lips now, pink froth, spilling down his chin. 'Made the wrong choices. No thread, no way back. A fool... You were right then, but now you are here again, just like it said you would be.' Eyelids began to flutter. His head lolled onto his chest.

'How did I end up back in here?' said Oll, suddenly urgent,

his hand going to Theseus' shoulder. 'Is this you, John? Is this you trying to tell me something? How do I get out? How do I go on?'

Theseus' eyes flickered open for a second, but the pupils were small, unfocused.

'Who... who is John?' he asked. His eyes closed, and went still. Oll froze, then took his hand away; it was wet and red.

His head twitched. Somewhere in the distance there were footsteps, coming closer.

Shuffle-tap... shuffle-tap, shuffle-tap... Faster, picking up speed as though hurrying.

He turned towards the sound.

Something came from the dark behind him.

A breath of air blew across his cheek. The lamp flame guttered and went out.

Blackness.

'Two minutes one second!'

The voices were above him, around him, loud, urgent, afraid: Katt, Rane, Zybes.

'Oll? Oll? Can you hear me?' Katt, definitely Katt.

'It's going to be here soon. We're going to get caught!'

'Oll? His eyes are opening.'

'What's wrong with him?'

'I don't know.' Katt again.

'He looks like he's going into shock.' Krank. Yes, that was Krank.

Oll saw light, smeared light. Nausea rising in his mouth.

'Two minutes forty-one seconds!' Rane.

Oll tried to move, but he was numb, floating, cold.

'Knife...' He forced the word out, tried to rise again. He could feel the knife in his hand, still there, as certain and true as it hadn't been there in the... in the Labyrinth. The thought jammed like a knot in a spoiling rope.

'Three minutes!' Zybes, loud now with fear.

Oll tried to move, felt his limbs flop like cut lengths of cord.

'He can't do it!' Rane again, almost pure panic. 'We're done! We're–'

'I've got it,' said Katt's voice, low and close, calm, controlled. Oll felt the knife tugging out of his grip, closed his hand tighter. The world was spinning. He was falling. 'Let go. I've got it. Just let go, okay, Oll.'

The knife, the knife he had brought all the way from Calth, that had sliced them to safety and now to here. The knife that he had a feeling was not just a knife. Their only way out, their only way on, their only way to stay alive.

'You were always good at choices,' said Theseus' voice in a quiet corridor of memory. Oll thought of Ariadne making a web of thread between her fingers as she smiled at Theseus.

Oll relaxed his fingers. The knife slipped free.

'What are you doing?' Rane, sharp with terror. 'Katt, what are you doing? You don't know... You can't–'

'Be quiet,' said Katt, voice clear. Oll's eyes opened. He saw Katt standing above him. She had the compass in her hand, the black, stone knife raised, very still. Clever Katt, watching, listening, learning, growing for seven years.

'Three minutes thirty seconds!' shouted Zybes.

Metal arms lifted Oll. The smell of machine oil and sweat filled his nose.

'I have you, Trooper Persson,' droned Graft.

Oll felt the cold blast at his back, heard the skeletal song of a death rattle. Katt flinched. The knife wobbled. There was a heat haze in the air, a shadow at the edge of sight, just behind Katt, just behind Graft, behind them all, standing with them.

'Three minutes forty-one seconds!'

The knife in Katt's hand sliced down.

* * *

The Phalanx, Saturn close orbit

Su-Kassen and Halbract did not speak for a long moment once Corswain had finished.

Battle and fire marked the audience chamber they led him to. The doors were heat-buckled. Gouges ran across the stone floor. Burn marks crawled over every surface like trapped shadows. There was a smell, too, sharp and bitter, like pyre fumes and copper.

Vassago was watching him, he could tell. Halbract, too. The four of them alone stood in the echoing quiet of the chamber.

'Is it your hope to die in battle?' asked the admiral at last.

Her gaze was level, he noticed, perceptive – the gaze of a predator-hawk.

'The hope remains the same, does it not? That aid will come from the Ultramarines and my liege and Legion brothers. Without the beacon of the Astronomican to guide them, they will never come.' He closed his eyes for a second. Twitched as a snake of old pain reared through his rebuilt spine. 'We came here to have purpose,' Corswain said, and opened his eyes. 'We shall go to Terra and if the beacon light has fallen, we shall relight it.' The admiral and Imperial Fist were staring at him. He met each of their gazes, unblinking. 'You have your orders and your duty, and I know well enough of Lord Dorn's sons to know that they would never break with such an oath – and such a quest is the work of warriors, not the guns of starships. I had hoped to stand here at the Lion's side, but I will not wait in the dark for him when without a light to lead him, he will never come. Dark Angels… so are we called, but we will be bearers of light. The beacon shall be relit.'

'Or die in the trying…' said Su-Kassen.

'We are ten thousand knights of the Lion, we shall see it done.'

He saw a smile twitch at the edge of Su-Kassen's mouth.

'Something tells me that all objections and talk of hopeless odds of survival will not even make you blink,' she said, and smiled more broadly. 'And, to be honest, I would be disappointed if they did.'

Corswain bowed his head.

'You will not pass unnoticed,' said Halbract. Corswain met the Imperial Fist's eye. He understood what the other warrior meant. He had listened for an hour while Admiral Su-Kassen had summarised the battle state of the Solar System. Every part of the dark held some of the traitor's taint. Kill craft and reaver squadrons haunted the voids. Things from the warp churned on the gulfs of reality left ragged by the sorcery that had brought the bulk of the Warmaster's fleet to the inner system. The traitor fleet had not paused to conquer every planet or rock, but none of them were untouched or would offer safe harbour.

The masterless killers and corsairs that followed in Horus' wake were still fighting their own battles of spite and atrocity in the orbits of Saturn, Mercury, Neptune and Venus. Mars belonged to Kelbor-Hal's Dark Mechanicum. The Iron Warriors had refortified the orbits of Pluto and Uranus, and left garrison forces and battle groups that could hold any force trying to penetrate into the system by either of its two main warp gates. Close to Terra, the void swarmed with thousands of traitor vessels, many of them the greatest and most terrible of their breed: the *Terminus Est*, *Conqueror* and *Vengeful Spirit*, blood-soaked empresses of void-slaughter. Closer still, in the high and close orbital spheres, the density of warships was enough that their engines dimmed the lights of the heavens when seen from the surface.

'What else remains to us if we leave our swords sheathed, and deeds undone for the lack of hope?'

Halbract nodded slowly.

'Would that we had more time,' said the Imperial Fist. 'I think I would have liked to have known you better.'

'There is a way it might be done,' Su-Kassen said, and shot a look at Halbract. 'With the right weapon, no wall or gate shall bar our path, isn't that the truth your Legion hold to?'

Halbract's still face narrowed as he frowned. Then he shook his head.

'No, it cannot be used so. It is–'

'It is a weapon without purpose,' she cut across him. 'I am charged with holding the might of our fleet intact until it is called or until allies come.' She nodded at Corswain. 'They have.'

'The fleet must remain intact and ready.'

'One ship,' said Su-Kassen. 'One ship for a cause. To bring the Angels of Caliban to the soil of Terra, to the beacon of Terra.'

Halbract shook his head again, but in thought rather than disagreement.

'They do not answer to you. They may not agree.'

'They will,' she said.

Corswain watched and waited.

'What makes you so sure?' asked Halbract.

'It will appeal to them.'

'You think you know their minds?'

Su-Kassen gave a small nod. 'Enough to know they will agree.'

She turned to Corswain. 'We have a way to help you reach the Throneworld.'

He bowed his head in brief thanks, then asked the question that had been held behind his teeth.

'My thanks, but what ship do you speak of?'

Su-Kassen smiled then, and her dark eyes seemed to light. 'A ship that once carried the light of the Imperium,' she said.

SIX

Totality
When it was called Earth
Sighted

The Vengeful Spirit, *Terran orbit*

It was not a ship any more. Once it had been one of the greatest and grandest daughters of war and iron to light the void with fire. Forrix had known it in those old times, had seen it in battle, jewelled by weapon impacts and radiant with its own fury. He had seen it burn alien fleets to cinders, and looked up from fields of triumph to see it hanging like a banner in the sky. Now it was a shadow of that past, a shape created by its lost light. Things watched from the shadows at the edge of passages they walked through. The eagles carved into the walls wept silver tears. Banners of sable, of skin, of smoke-thin silk hung in place of the triumphs of old. Forrix thought he heard the voices of the past speaking words just below hearing. *Vengeful Spirit…* If it had been in his nature to feel humour, Forrix might have found laughter in the name.

Perturabo walked flanked by a quartet of Iron Circle automata, preceded by Forrix and three Terminators of the First

Grand Company. Argonis walked at Forrix's side, helm under one arm, staff of office in the other. Perturabo's dark eyes did not move from the path ahead, but one of his weapon mounts clattered and reloaded as the whispers followed them. Argonis, too, was silent, face set. The Warmaster's equerry had been that way since they had ascended from Lion's Gate Port. There was something in that silence that worked on Forrix more than the whispers and shadows that haunted the ship. Argonis was a Cthonian through and through, but there was a killer's swagger to that nature, a knife-cut sneer at the world. At the moment something else had taken the place of that confidence. Had Argonis been mortal, Forrix might have thought it was fear. Or regret.

The doorway to the throne room loomed before them, so sudden in its presence that Forrix halted with surprise. He had a clear memory of the ship, had been this way before, but had recognised none of the features or passages leading to the command chamber. *Throne chamber,* he reminded himself: not a place of command or greeting, but a place of power. A skull-aching buzz rose in his head when he looked at the doors. They had been plasteel, layered with red iron and adamantium. Now they looked like obsidian, polished smooth, reflections moving beneath the surface like smoke.

He was suddenly aware of the figures in black Terminator armour standing to either side of the doors. How had he not seen them? The Iron Circle pivoted, weapons arming, shields rising. Perturabo twitched his head, and the automata froze. Forrix's trio of Terminators shifted into a triangle, guns outwards.

'Stand down,' Perturabo said. 'We are in my brother's house. What harm could befall us here?' His gaze shifted to Argonis. The equerry did not reply but stepped forward and raised his staff. The doors split open and hinged back. Air hissed from within, cold white, like the breath of winter.

Argonis turned.

'Enter,' he said. Perturabo did not move for a second, his eyes black pearls. Then he stepped forward, the plates of his armour catching the light like the edges of knives. The Iron Circle and Terminators remained where they were. Forrix followed.

For a moment there was darkness, complete and total. He had the sensation that he had stepped off the edge of a cliff. Then his foot touched the deck. Light poured into Forrix's eyes, so bright that his vision bleached for a second to compensate. Sunlight poured in through the circular viewport set in the far wall. Golden light gleamed on gilded pillars and the mirror-sheen floor. No shadows lived here. They couldn't. Only light, pure, brilliant, dazzling.

Horus sat before the viewport. His armour was black but also radiant, as though he were a prism that caught the light and then cast it back out, as though he were the source of all illumination. A halo of crystal and gold framed his throne. The burnished skull of Ferrus Manus rested under the blade claws of his left hand. His face was open, serene, welcoming.

'My brother,' said Horus, standing as Perturabo advanced. Forrix held a step behind his lord. Argonis had moved to stand beside the throne. The equerry seemed out of place beside the dazzling presence of the Warmaster of Mankind.

Perturabo bowed his head briefly.

'My Warmaster,' he said.

Horus walked down the steps of the throne dais. At the corner of his eye, Forrix thought he saw something shift in the glare, like a smudge of oily smoke above a burning horizon, like a mirage.

'You have done it,' said Horus, stopping before Perturabo and placing a hand on the Lord of Iron's shoulder. 'No place beyond our father's last wall is not ours. Our forces shake the ground. A crumbling circle of failure is all that remains to Rogal. Totality. As I asked and as only you could create.'

Forrix felt his heart rise, felt the fatigue, of which he had not even been aware, lift. He felt exalted, fulfilled, as though everything that had come before was a dream and everything that would come after was a promise of bliss.

Perturabo gazed at his brother for a long moment, eyes seeming to not reflect the golden light of the room.

'It is not complete,' he said. 'It shall be. The walls will shatter. When that is done, and our brother's pride lies in the ruins of what he made… Then we shall call it totality.'

Horus' smile broadened. He held his hand on Perturabo's shoulder. Warmth, understanding and complete control radiated from him.

'As ever, your craft is matched only by your diligence.' Horus let his hand drop and half turned away, his fingers gesturing glowing displays into being. The images hung in the air, pin-sharp accurate, the markers of unit strength and tactical data drawn in multicoloured halos. Details crawled over the images, tiny movements that echoed some vast shift on the surface far below. It was beyond real, as though it was not data or projection. As though it was the vision seen by a great, all-seeing eye.

'The space ports are mine, as you said they would be,' said Horus. 'My might moves in full across the arc of the Earth.'

'Almost your full force. Only the last Legion and Titan Legio elements remain. Once they are committed then the last phase begins.'

Horus was tracing the claws of his left hand through the visions of the Palace. Forrix thought he saw the glitter of explosions where the blade tips touched the image. The Warmaster was not looking at Perturabo.

'The rest of my sons and the machines of Mortis…' His voice was low, casual, the threat of a predator's purr.

'The Third flees the battle space,' said Perturabo. 'Their numbers and strength must be replaced.'

'Strength...' said Horus, the word hanging in the air. His claws were poised in the images of the battle sphere. Unit values and threat markers gleamed on the razor edges. 'Will you spend my sons as you did at Saturnine when I commit them in full?'

The tone of his voice was still the smooth warmth of before, but Forrix felt the cold crawl down his spine. This was the reason why the Warmaster had summoned the Lord of Iron: three companies of the XVI Legion and the Mournival lost in the fissures and spaces beneath Saturnine Wall, a ruse imagined to bring swift victory turned into a bloody defeat and slaughter. They had been read by Dorn and he had been waiting. Abaddon had survived from the strike force, the rest buried or cut down. It was a bitter loss, made worse by the fact that the Sons of Horus' elite had not acted with the direct sanction of the Warmaster. It had been kept from him, hidden by omission. Had it worked, victory would have ensured forgiveness. Now Perturabo would have to face the consequence.

'Loss is a factor in all victory,' said Perturabo, his voice cold, his black gaze unblinking.

'Do you seek to tutor me, brother?' Horus let his claws drop from the projection. He smiled at Perturabo. 'It is no matter – an action worth the risk and the loss. Were it otherwise I would not have permitted it to proceed.' Forrix felt himself blink with surprise and then the cold crawling down his spine sharpen. The Warmaster was still smiling. 'Did you truly believe that I did not know? All is revealed to me. I am illumination.' He stepped closer to Perturabo. The air felt suddenly heavy, storm-charged and thick. Forrix felt a pressure in his skull. The taste of sugar, of blood, of ash was in his mouth. There was something moving at the edge of his sight, something in the golden light – something that was just behind him, just out of sight. Black veins spidered Perturabo's face, bulging as muscles tightened to cords. Forrix saw heat glow red on his armour. Then, for an instant, the Warmaster seemed not a man but a shadow at the heart of an inferno...

Then he was just as he had been, radiant and smiling, hand reaching to pat Perturabo's shoulder. The pressure vanished. The light resettled. 'My good brother,' said Horus. 'Iron within, iron without, iron for eternity. You have done all you have promised. What more could I have asked?'

'It shall be complete. True totality. Then I will call it done.'

'You will call it done?' said Horus, and now there was a soft edge of humour in his voice, like a distant thunder growl. 'And what of your Warmaster – what of what he commands done?'

'I am giving you what you want.'

'Are you?'

'It is the only way.'

'A slow grinding of equations. Walls pulled down by the clicking of ratios in cogitators. The only way? Where there is no way, I shall make one.' Horus turned slowly. He raised his hand. The displays dissolved, all but one. It grew, until a section of the Inner Palace and its wall filled the space between the primarchs. Horus reached a silver claw into the sphere of light. Its razor tip held on a section of wall sketched in red light. 'Here,' he said.

Perturabo was silent, his face set as he looked at where the finger blade rested. For a moment Forrix thought that his eyes and mind were playing him false. Mercury Wall, two hundred kilometres of defences that stood almost intact. Almost twelve hundred metres high from parapet to base, it was a tiered mountain range of rockcrete, metal and shaped stone. Two bastions that were fortresses in their own right, all watching over a kill-zone that extended one hundred and twenty kilometres from the wall to the horizon. Together with Exultant, which lay to its east, it was amongst the most substantial sections of the Ultimate Wall that ringed the Inner Palace.

'An assault there will not succeed,' said Perturabo.

'It shall be done,' said Horus. His gaze was fixed on the image. 'You shall ring the walls, brother, just as my might shall encircle our father. There shall be no respite from where the sun rises to where it sets. And Mortis shall walk as one. They shall open our way within.'

Legio Mortis, the Death's Heads, largest of the Titan Legios, first to bow to Horus and the new age – a legion whose name was a promise to those who would face them in battle. Until now they had not walked on Terra, but slept in coffin ships in the dark of the void above the world. Slept, and waited.

'They will not reach the wall,' said Perturabo. 'The projections are clear. Wait until the encirclement assault takes its toll and every wall shall fall.'

Horus' clawed finger lowered, slicing through the light of the display before it vanished. He turned his back on Perturabo and Forrix, and walked back to his throne.

'If Mortis walk against Mercury now, they shall fail,' called Perturabo, and Forrix felt the anger and will that edged his voice.

'They shall reach the wall, and it shall fall,' said Horus. He turned and sat, and when he looked down at them, Forrix had to avert his eyes.

'How can that be?'

'Because I will it so,' said Horus.

Starspear, Lion's Gate space port

The ark ships of Legio Mortis came to the spire of the Lion's Gate space port. The other ships that had been dumping their cargoes into the docks withdrew back into higher orbits like courtiers making way for a high executioner. The ark ships came in slowly, holding perfect formation. Each of them was vast to the point of obscenity. Black hulled, air frost forming on their flanks as they sank into the upper layers of atmosphere. On the docking platforms, the servants of the New Mechanicum waited. Some wept corrupted binary. Some watched the arks descend with the utter stillness of supplicants seeing a prayer made real. All of the servitors and slaves in the upper docks had been assessed and purged, so that those who remained were worthy to look upon the most holy of the walking god-machines.

The first of the arks descended. Its bulk swallowed the dome of stars and the glare of the sun above the clouds. Thrusters fired along the kilometres of its hull. The thin air churned. On the dock platforms, machine acolytes and serfs were blown into the sky. Minutes passed as it sank the last hundred metres. Mooring gantries swung out of the spire top. Clamp cradles opened hundred-metre-long fingers. Docking tugs, little more than blocks of thruster engines, began to nudge the ship into place. The first moorings touched and gripped the hull and began to pull it in. The ship began to shudder. Its thrusters flared brighter. Tornadoes spun into being on the platforms. The tugs pushed more as the gantries reached and gripped the hull. Inch by inch it drew in to the spire top. Docking limbs mag-clamped to its cargo doors like sucker fish to a leviathan. The waiting priests looked up at the hundred-metre-high door in the hull metal. Micro debris impacts had pitted its surface, and condensing atmosphere ran from it in silver tracks, pattering on the priests as false rain. The vibration of the thrusters keeping the ship in the air now trembled through the top of the tower. As more of these vast siblings docked, compensator engines in the structure would have to work to stop them shaking the spire apart.

Clangs echoed out as locks released. Then, slowly, the doors began to grind open. Darkness, mottled by red light. The air inside became a fog as it met the atmosphere. Some of the machine priests were falling to their knees. Some trembled. Others fixed their gazes on the darkness within. Prayers of binary and scrap code clattered from speaker grilles. A cluster of spider-limbed servitors expired in a scatter of sparks as their machine components overloaded. A pulsing drone of silent code echoed through the data connections: numbers cycling down into pits of null calculation, wave forms collapsing, time decrementing with the sound of blown sand.

Within the hold, a shape moved. The clang of struck iron. The thump of pistons driving forward thousands of tons of metal. An aching buzz of chained power. A shadow of a vast figure. The drone of numbers was deafening now, bleeding from data into thought, scratching like flies on corroded tin. The shadow filled the door opening.

The priests could not think, could not calculate, could not move. All that existed in their minds was the promise of perfect annihilation. Zero. Heat death. Ultimate entropy. Data abyss. Null.

The machine stepped through the door. Even the most defiant priests bowed then, folding themselves to the ringing deck as the first Titan of Legio Mortis walked into the light.

Old Terra – Unknown

The voices came first after the fall. For a second, Oll was not certain if they were from the now, or from another time. The fall after the cut had been bad, a drop all the way down. It had gone on, then stopped. Then the voices.

'Are we here?' Rane asked. 'I mean… this is somewhere, right? Is it…'

'I don't know,' replied Katt.

'What did you do, girl?' snapped Zybes, voice hard, threaded with fear.

'I made the cut,' she said.

'How did you know how?' Zybes was scared, Oll could hear it: really scared and angry. That was something that had taken a while to come out of the big labourer. Zybes had hardened over the years, become a survivor or at least someone who could continue. One of the ways he had done that was by letting his fear become anger, and with it he had let a seed of unkindness take root in his heart.

My fault, thought Oll. Another thing to add to the ledger of sins, another price for having started this voyage with them.

'How did you know how to cut through?' Zybes growled. There was the clink of a gun coming up.

'Easy, Heb,' said Krank to Zybes, 'easy, alright.'

'No!' snarled Zybes. 'How did she know how to make the cut? Oll said it's not the sort of thing normal people know. So how did she? Something has got into her mind.'

'Heb, look, just…'

'Where did you bring us?' Zybes said to Katt. 'Why?'

Where… They were not making the count, Oll realised. He could smell something, too. Something so familiar but something that he could not put his finger on.

'Lower the gun, Heb,' said Krank. Firm voice now, the old soldier still there. 'We'll sort it out, but things are okay.'

'What you going to do, kill me? I tell you, there's something wrong here, and with her. Something got to her, in the schism space – something could have latched on, brought us to a dead end again. We know she's a–'

'A witch,' said Katt. A quiet descended. The word was not one that had much use in the time they had come from. But they had picked it up, along with all the other trinkets and lessons of their voyage. They had never used it about Katt, though. Psyker, that was what she was. Exactly how strong, Oll did not know. She was growing into it, though.

Oll felt his eyelids move, and then the sensation of flesh and bone return. Something was wrong but it was not with Katt. It was with him. He was not an easy man to frighten, but waking in the black with just the voices did frighten him, most of all because he didn't know why.

'It's not her fault,' he said. He could see sky when he opened his eyes. Sunset bruising a sliver of blue at the edges. He pushed himself up. His limbs felt numb for a moment and then became his own. They were in a long cave that looked to have been cut and widened into a broad tunnel. The stone of the walls and floor was smooth, as though worked by the flow of a river. The walls tapered to a narrow opening high over-head. It all felt crushingly familiar, but not quite recognisable.

The others were all looking at him. Zybes still had his gun raised, but his mouth was open. Krank had his hands up, placating. Rane stood five paces back from both of them. Graft was stationary by Katt. She met his eyes and nodded.

'It's not her fault,' repeated Oll. He looked around at all of them. 'We should all be thanking our lucky stars and her that she pays attention.'

He held out his hand to her. She handed back the knife and compass. He noticed that the needle was not spinning behind the crystal.

'Where are we then?' asked Zybes.

'Not sure,' said Oll, turning to look at Zybes as though discussing where to mortar in a fence post. The pay-by-day still had the barrel of his gun up, still looked jittery. Oll had seen that look before. Some journeys broke people before you reached home shores. Too much time below the horizon, too much time riding the storm waves and wondering where you were going. He just hoped he could get them somewhere before it became a problem. Zybes met his eyes, nodded and lowered his gun.

'Thanks, Heb,' said Oll, his tone level, almost casual. 'I know you always have our backs.'

Zybes nodded again.

'Are you…' he began, 'are you alright, Oll?'

'Fine,' said Oll, 'just fine. Shouldn't have looked up at the wrong time. My own fault. Getting old, you know.'

That got a nervous laugh from them all. Zybes blinked, then nodded.

'Okay,' he said.

'Thanks,' Oll said, and picked up his own gun and kit. The rest had spread out and dropped down to watch the tunnel to either side of them, and the opening above, guns ready, fingers on triggers – the habits that had kept them alive.

Oll checked his gun and looked around. The tunnel sloped up to one end, the view fading out in the twilight. Following the downward slope, it turned around a bend. A breeze slid along the tunnel, carrying the smell of cool rock, and an edge of salt. Oll blinked, and then almost smiled. He knew where he was.

'Looks like an old watercourse,' said Krank.

'It was,' said Oll. 'Made to carry a river's worth of water. Took the reign of two emperors to make it.'

'Two emperors?' said Rane.

'Long time ago,' said Oll. 'An emperor was a smaller idea then. Water flowed right down here in a torrent. If we had stood here when I last saw it, we would have been swept away.'

'Where is it though?' asked Krank.

'Terra,' answered Katt. Oll turned to look at her, so did the rest. All but Zybes, still looking away down the tunnel. 'Terra from the past, I mean,' she continued, looking at Oll. 'When it was called Earth.'

'Yeah, that's right,' said Oll. 'About thirty thousand years in the past from when we left Calth, give or take.'

'Thirty thousand…' said Krank. 'So we are off course. We were supposed to be getting closer, narrower times, and now…'

'No,' said Oll. 'I'm not sure why we are here exactly, but if the compass held true…' He glanced at Katt, who nodded. 'Then something brought us on this turn.' For a second he thought of Theseus, looking up at him in the dark of the Labyrinth, blood on his lips.

'Couldn't this just be another place from your past, like the others that we went through?' asked Rane.

Oll shrugged.

'All the other places on Old Earth that we went through were places I had been at the time I was there, but I was never here at this time. That's why I didn't recognise it – never saw it from down here, never saw it without water.'

'Why here then?' asked Krank.

'It's close,' said Katt. Oll frowned. The breeze slid down the tunnel again. The sliver of sky above was darkening.

'Close to what?' Rane again.

'Where the path ends,' said Katt. 'Different time, same place.' She looked at Oll for confirmation.

'No…' he said, turning to look around him, then striding off down the slope of the tunnel. 'No, that can't be right.'

He heard them following as he turned the bend and saw the tunnel mouth open to a view beyond. He stopped at its threshold. The ground ran down from the tunnel, the dry course of the stream that flowed in place of the torrent a pale scar cut into the ground. Waves broke on a long beach in the distance. The breeze rose. He smelled salt spray, the smell of the old sea of monsters and islands, the scent of a sea that he had crossed and recrossed many times in ages past. He blinked as he looked at it, thinking of the story of the sneering bastard from Ithaca – blown off course in sight of journey's end.

'What's wrong, Oll?' asked Katt as she came up beside him.

'You're right,' said Oll. 'If we are here it must be because this is close, and if not in time then in place. But then we shouldn't be here, the last cut should be to the meeting point… If we cut from here, and the next cut is the last, then we are going to be a long way from where we need to be. That's how these tools work – they respond to what we want. And we didn't want to be here. So we either made a mistake, or…'

Oll pulled the compass out then, opened the lid, held it up to the thinning light. The silver needle was a spinning blur behind the circle of glass.

The wind whipped around them, suddenly cold at his back.

'What was that?' asked Katt.

A tapping, dragging step, echoing on stone.

Shuffle-tap… shuffle-tap…

'The count…' Zybes was half moaning, half growling. 'We lost the count! We should have gone already. It's got us!'

Rane was panting, eyes wide. The dark was thickening. The sound of the sea distant.

'It's coming,' panted Rane. 'It's here.'

And it was. The thing that had been trailing them. Suddenly right there, just a step behind.

Oll could feel it on his neck: the hot pressure wave, the fever prickle on his skin. He turned to look into the dark of the tunnel.

The steps were speeding up, closing down the tunnel they had come from.

Shuffle-tap, shuffle-tap, shuffle-tap–

He looked down at the compass. The needle was jerking between two directions.

'Oll…' moaned Rane. 'Oll, I can feel it… It's behind me. It's right behind me.'

The needle snapping from north to east.

Shuffle-tap, shuffle-tap, shuffle-tap–

The sounds of quickening steps were almost with him.

Shuffle-tap, shuffle-tap, shuffle-tap–

'Oll!' shouted Katt. 'There is something in the tunnel!'

His head came up. The tunnel was in front of him, a wide and dark mouth. The steps were almost on top of them. At his back he felt the warm blast of wet breath. Behind him.

Shuffle-tap, shuffle-tap.

The sound of the steps were in front of him. In front. A shadow, in front of him, someone dragging themselves into the edge of sight.

'It's got us!' called Krank.

The touch on his back. The slow hunter now with him. Dead end. Dead here and now.

A figure stumbling just inside the tunnel mouth, falling.

Oll stepped forwards.

A face looked up, bloody and gasping, screaming in silence.

+Oll!+ screamed John Grammaticus' voice in his head. +Oll, where are you?+

Then the face was gone. Bloody handprints black on the stone just in front of him. He looked at the compass. The needle was still, dead on the direction where he had seen John's face. Straight into the mouth of the tunnel. Behind him he could feel the dead fingers on his back and the sound of a dying breath rattling behind a smile. He still had the knife in his hand.

'With me!'

He cut.

Northern wall circuit, Mercury Wall blind zone

'Contact seventy degrees from north,' called Dolloran. He slowed the stride of *Cyllarus*. Acastia and Pluton matched the pace change. *Elatus*' sensor gaze swung to follow Acastia's attention. The return fizzed at the edge of the auspex screen.

'Metallics and heat,' she said. 'Could be a lone unit or multiple.'

'Or a dead machine with heat bleeding from a plasma unit.'

Acastia looked at the screen for a second, blinked. It had been quiet for hours now.

'Let's see,' she said, and kicked the motive spur at her foot. *Elatus* jinked onto a new line, stride lengthening. 'Hawk and archer,' she called, but the other two had already guessed the troop formation and were sliding into position – *Cyllarus* matching *Elatus'* pace and arcing wide, *Thaumas* holding to the slower stride, guns lowering, scanners and targets to maximum as it paced behind. They kept their thermal cannons and ion shields cold. If it was just a tank or low-grade automaton, even if it saw them, it would not be able to read exactly what they were until they had a kill position.

'Hard sensor read,' called Dolloran. 'It's stationary. Threat status amber.'

The stride shook through *Elatus*. Acastia felt it and grinned. Freedom. This was it, finger held on the gun trigger before firing.

'It's moving!' called Dolloran.

'Not a dead wreck,' replied Acastia. The sensor return was moving. Energy readings spiralled. Red, multiplying.

'Energy spike! Honour of the ancestors – that's an active void shield.'

'It's seen us,' said Acastia. 'Raise ion shields. Weapons to the trigger.' *Elatus* shivered as its shield canopy lit, dorsal heavy stubber armed, power flushed to its lance. And then suddenly there it was, on her left flank, closing under its own power. An ovoid of armour plates set above a heavy track unit. Red sensor lenses shone from its central mass. The light shimmered around it, sliding into oily rainbows. It was hostile. It reeked of hostile. Range and target locks pinged. Weapon runes shone green.

'Engaging!' called Acastia, and spurred forwards. The thing's torso rose and pivoted. 'Look at me…' she muttered. Weapon pods uncoiled on metallic tentacles. 'That's it.' She fired the heavy stubber. Rounds chugged at the machine. Beams lashed across the distance, but Acastia was already prancing sideways, holding the stubber fire true. Rounds splashed into its shield. Black lightning cracked the air around it. The machine's beams burned across the air and struck the ground where *Elatus* had been. Dust and grit flashed to glass. Static boiled across the auspex as the beams passed. Viewscreens flashed to black. Pain stabbed into her head as feedback leapt across her helm's nerve connections. For a second she felt *Elatus'* balance tilt, the fire from the stubber faltering.

'Shit! Shit!' The machine was accelerating, its shield and envelope distorting the air around it. 'It's an abomination-engine.'

'Coming in,' said Dolloran over the vox. 'Keep it on you.'

She swore again, not bothering to cut the vox, and spurred into full stride. *Elatus'* upper torso rotated, its legs a blur, one metal hoof barely in contact with the ground. Another beam lashed towards them. Her ion shield aligned just in time to take the hit. White light flashed out. Inside her cockpit, Acastia bit down as feedback shrilled through her skull.

Abomination-engine. Silica-anima. Heretek construct. Woe-machine. That was what this quarry was. Once unspoken dreams made by the schismatic tech-priests of Mars, now multiplied and sent out from the Dark Mechanicum's camps ringing the Palace. Driven by forbidden, false intelligence and armed with weapons that fused the material with the immaterial and defied the reality that had borne them. They were amongst the worst of the weapons unleashed by the enemy. Their forms were diverse and ever-changing, but they were never less than lethal. A lone Armiger Knight was no match. Even Acastia would admit that she should not have engaged such a machine alone. But she was not alone.

Cyllarus came in fast, crab-dancing across the compacted scree. Stubber fire exploded across the abomination-engine's void shell. It half-pivoted, its weapon pods rearing like snakes. Dolloran did not wait for it to fire; he was close enough. *Cyllarus'* heat lance shrieked. A line of blue heat scored the air. The enemy engine's shield flared. Black lightning crackled. In her cockpit, a third of a kilometre away, Acastia felt something scream in her head.

'Shield down,' shouted Dolloran.

The targeting rune was green in Acastia's sight. She keyed her trigger. The enemy engine reared, its form flickering and blurring like a smear of paint in rain. The beam of *Elatus'* heat lance stabbed out, boring through air where there should have been metal.

'Shit!' swore Acastia. The target display was a fog of red shards.

'Where is it?' came Dolloran's voice. 'Where the hell is it?'

Acastia was about to reply. The bulk of the engine loomed out of the pixel fog, closing, accelerating, weapon pods glowing. She slammed *Elatus'* ion shield around. The enemy engine fired. Light exploded around *Elatus*. Its ion shield collapsed with a concussive bang. Red light flooded its cockpit. Acastia tasted blood. Her mount's stride wavered, pitched. Cockpit screens clouds of static. Alarms sounding. Acastia felt her head reel as if she had just taken a punch. Red and static and the blare of oncoming death. This was it. Over now. She found that she was not sorry.

The sound of cannon fire juddered through her ears.

Heavy impacts close by, one after another, overlapping. *Elatus* caught its balance, and Acastia kicked it into a circle, still alive, ears and head still ringing. The abomination was shaking, armour plates deforming as munitions struck it.

'Kill it now,' said Pluton's voice over the vox as *Thaumas* paced forwards, cannon arms chugging out rounds into the enemy engine. It was still moving, fluid venting from holes, heat building in its weapons. Acastia kicked *Elatus* forwards. The chainblade on its left arm spun to a blur an instant before she buried it in the enemy engine's central mass. Acastia shivered in her seat as her mount juddered. Teeth bit. The engine twisted, as she forced the spinning teeth into its core.

'Get clear!' shouted Dolloran. Acastia ripped the blade out of the top of the engine and bounded *Elatus* back. And not a second too soon. The plasma core at the engine's heart split. Sun-fire heat snapped out. Metal blew to liquid, to gas, to ash.

Acastia was breathing hard, her head pounding.

'My kill,' she breathed through her gritted teeth.

'Yours,' came Pluton's cold voice. 'And it nearly cost you your life and *Elatus*.' *Thaumas* was stalking forwards, guns still locked steady on the wreckage of the engine. 'You should have held back, waited for us all to have it under our guns.'

'You will hold your tongue,' she snarled, and felt *Elatus* gun its chainblade in sympathy.

'I speak as I see.'

'Why was it alone?' Dolloran's voice cut through the vox. *Cyllarus* was already in stride, pacing out north in an arc, head and gun scanning the distance. Light was failing fast now, pushing shadow across the land in a thick veil.

'What?' Acastia's head was still fogged from the neuro-feedback. For a moment, for a beautiful moment, she had thought it would all stop.

'An engine like that does not move on its own, too easily outclassed. Too easily killed to be worthwhile sending out alone.'

Acastia twitched, suddenly cold. She was bringing *Elatus* around, its sensors at maximum gain as she looked out across the darkening land. Pluton was doing the same, bringing *Thaumas* into line with its lance kin.

'I see nothing,' said Pluton.

Acastia was about to echo his words when she saw it – red and bright on the auspex screen.

'Enemy,' she called. 'Eleven hundred metres, sixty-degree angle, and narrowing.'

'I have it,' replied Dolloran. 'I'm reading active weapons, metal hull, heat output. It's big. An armoured unit?'

'We take it,' said Acastia, and she began to push *Elatus* forwards.

'Hold,' said Pluton.

'Command is at my word,' Acastia growled. 'We make the kill.'

'Look,' said Pluton, his voice edged by control. 'Look with your eyes, as you do at the dawn.'

Something in the old man's voice held the words in her throat. She blinked, holding *Elatus* still, and flicked the screens to an unfiltered external view.

The darkening land was still, the ground-down grit of buildings rolling in low hills towards a vanishing point. There was nothing. Nothing. Just the last of the light fleeing the world and leaving the air bruised black. Then she saw it. A light. Yellow, shrunk to a pinprick by distance. Then another, glimmering into being. Then a scattering along the line of the black-mauve sky, rising up like sparks from a burning forest. The auspex began to ping. A snow of red runes began to blur across sensor screens.

It wasn't a column. It was a tide flowing across the land, east to west. Armoured units, transporters, automata walkers, Titans, air cover a firefly cloud above, all moving in a mass beyond the sight line from the Palace walls. On and on, the vibration now shaking the ground and the frame of the cockpit around Acastia. She swallowed with a dry mouth.

Enemy distance to wall: 150 kilometres, estimated.

PART TWO

KILL-ZONE

THE WARP

∞

Night falls in the desert, but it brings no comfort to the man beneath the tree. Above Him the glare of the white sky fades to indigo then to deep blue, and then to black. Stars appear, flickering in the dark. They are not real, any more than the dust and the smell of distant fires are real. They come from Him. Stars, scent, image – even the concept of night as a metaphor to clothe this brief respite in the battle He is fighting – all are the way they are because this is the clothing His mind has made for what He endures. Here in the realm beyond sight, there is nothing that is not brought by those that come here. Once, long ago, but also only a moment past and in a moment to come, this realm was void, without even the idea of dimensions or duration so that it could be called empty. Long ago… Long, long ago… Now it is a place filled with the refuse of its travellers: the husks of grand ambitions and dreams, the shadows of atrocity, and the secrets of the countless dead and the yet to be born. It is both a lie and the truest thing to ever be.

The man beneath the tree watches the pinholes in the sheet

of night for an age that is shorter than a heartbeat. They are all
there, clustered in patterns that had been forgotten by most:
Perseus, Aphrodite, Ursa... Memories, all of them, just like
the dryness and the heat and the thirst... A memory... He
lets His gaze drop.

A figure stands nearby, barely visible in the starlight. He
wears a robe of tattered white, holed and trailing threads.
He has a stick in his hand. Nothing so grand that it could
be called a staff, just a branch from a thorn bush, stripped
of barbs and bark, surface smooth with the wear of hands,
and made hard by time and sun. His face is young, but his
eyes are still.

'Peace and greetings,' says the young man. The man beneath
the tree slowly raises a hand in acknowledgement and opens
His cracked lips, but a reply either will not or cannot come.
'May I draw near?' asks the young man. 'I have water.'

The man beneath the tree nods. Then lets His head roll
back so that it is resting against the trunk of the tree. The
young man comes close. Above them, the bare branches of
the tree stir. The wind that moves them smells only of dryness and thirst.

'Here,' says the young man, kneeling down and holding up
an unstoppered waterskin. The man beneath the tree raises a
hand to grasp it, tries to grip the skin's neck. The skin slips
and the young man catches it. Droplets of water fall from the
spout. For a moment they rest on the ground, small domes
of crystal catching the starlight. Then they seep into the dust.

The young man holds the waterskin up again, but this time
to the man's mouth. A trickle flows at first, then a little more.
The man beneath the tree drinks and drinks, slowly at first and
then insistently, glugging and gurgling the water down. The
young man takes the skin away when there is just a mouthful
swashing in the bottom. The man beneath the tree looks up

at him, and His eyes are dark holes and there is nothing kind in the grasp that grips the young man's arm.

'I must keep something,' says Malcador, re-stoppering the skin and hanging it over his shoulder. 'For the journey back.'

The man beneath the tree, who here is far from an Emperor and too close to a god, nods, then slowly releases His grip.

'My thanks,' He says, but His voice is thin and dry, the sound of dust rattling over half-buried stones.

Malcador nods in reply.

'How…' asks the man. 'How long?'

'Not long,' says Malcador, then shakes his head. 'A little longer.' The man nods. Malcador watches Him. In this place his own emotion becomes a breath of wind and the shadows stirring across his face. 'I do not know if I can return again. The wheel is turning. Things are falling apart. Flesh, will and spirit, all of it. He and those with him are stronger than I dared think.'

The man rests His head on the bare tree again; His eyes are closed. 'A little longer…' He says.

'Do you see something?' asks Malcador. 'I have looked but the cards and signs speak of nothing but the call of crows.'

The man shakes His head.

'Do you see nothing?'

'I see…'

'There was one card out of place in the spread,' said Malcador. 'Just in the last reading. The Wanderer, his face turned away, his aspect turned to the Lightning Tower.'

'I see…'

'There was something in his hand, something held close that I could not see.'

The man's head comes up, and His eyes open. There is fire where His eyes should be.

'You must go,' says the Emperor.

Malcador looks up then.

There are eyes in the dark, round and silver, like grave coins. Shadows of hunched backs and fur and wide laughing jaws shift silently. They do not blink but shift. They are silent. Waiting. When the sun rises in the sky that is not a real sky they will become mirages, pillars of shadow and false promise in the blinding heat. For now they do not move or leap, but just watch. They have time. Here in the desert that is the world for the man beneath the dead tree, they have all the time that can be.

Malcador moves slowly, straightening. He looks at the water-skin and then drains the last gulp of water from it. It vanishes as he lowers it, the idea of its shape falling as dust. He grips his stick, eyes on the circle of waiting shapes.

'Thank you,' says the man beneath the tree.

Malcador nods.

'I will return with more,' he says.

'No,' replies the man beneath the tree. 'Not again. There will be no way here.'

'How will you endure?'

The man beneath the tree does not reply. Then He closes His eyes.

'You will have to be swift,' He says. 'Go. Now.'

And then, in a single moment, there is a roar and there is light. Not the hammer blow of the heat in the sky. The light of falling lightning. The light of a sunbeam on the crest of a wave. It flashes out, and the watching shadows flee, mewling and growling.

Malcador is already running, bare feet pounding the parched ground, running and running into the distance, back the way he came and the way he cannot walk again.

The light blazing from the man beneath the tree stutters, fades.

The man is alone again.

He closes His eyes.

The coolness of night drains away. The sky is a hammer blow of white heat again. In the distance the calls of crows and jackals rise with the wind and dust. The dead tree stirs, twigs rattling as they move. Beneath its meagre shade, the man sits and waits and endures.

SEVEN

Annihilation strength
Family
Solaria

Mercury Wall kill-zone

The wall rose before them. Storm clouds crowned its highest
parapet. Cliff faces of rockcrete cut down from sky to ground,
so vast and sheer that it felt that the eye shrank them to fit a
sense of mortal scale. Macro cannon barrels became hair-fine
spines. Hundred-storey towers shrank to the proportions of
candles mounted on lamp holders. Half a kilometre wide at
its narrowest point. Touching thirteen hundred metres high
from where it rose from the ground. It was not a wall, not
truly. That was too small a word for a creation of this kind. Its
kin were not the rings of stone thrown up by the fearful kings
of old; its kin were the mountains who it had supplanted.

Shard Bastion jutted from its face like an axe blade left in
the shield of a foe. Running from the base of Mercury to its
uppermost parapet, it had been the core of a mountain. Rogal
Dorn's warmasons had peeled the rock from around it, cored
it out and lashed the wall to it as it grew upwards. When the

rare sunlight caught its edge, it shone as though it were a piece of freshly knapped flint.

Acastia felt herself shivering in *Elatus'* cockpit. She had been riding now for three days without sleep. The last hundred kilometres had been a winding sprint, the wall ever in the distance, the promise of the enemy's vanguard ever at her heels.

'Signal again,' she called.

'Vox distortion has not abated,' came Pluton's voice in reply. 'There is no point–'

'Just do it!' She cut the link and keyed her own broadcast control. 'Come on… come on…' she muttered. Around her, *Elatus'* stride jolted her across the broken ground, and the wall grew before her. Static broke through her ears, rolling like the surge of a tide.

They had passed an outpost bunker and found it burning. Kill automata lurked in the smoke that boiled from it. Soot had covered their limbs and pistons. They had made swift kills of the machines, not slowing, the pride of the action not breaching the thoughts that filled her head, rising up in the blackness of eye-blinks.

Machines… a moving mountain range of machines… ground shaking… something buzzing in her ears… her heartbeat. Static. The pulse of a vox tuned to a dead frequency…

The enemy harbinger units were already in the kill-zone moving to the horizon line. The wall command would know that something had happened, but not what; they would not know what was coming. The vox, and even buried cable links to the outposts, had been failing since the fall of the Lion's Gate space port. That was why they sent units like hers into the blind zone.

'Respond…' she muttered, keying the long-range vox again. 'Respond!'

Signal clarity had been getting worse for months. Damage

to key systems, loss of personnel, lack of time to repair. But out in the kill-zone, Acastia had often felt that it was like a cloud falling over everything, muffling, corroding, breaking the defenders into small pieces not by force but by the soft hiss of static. Now it felt like not just a fog but a presence, as though the cloud of isolation and signal failure were chasing them as they ran.

A pop and screech burst from her helm speakers. She swore, ears ringing.

'Nothing,' said Dolloran.

'Distance to wall ten point two kilometres,' said Pluton.

'There is something behind us,' said Dolloran.

'I cannot see anything,' said Pluton. 'Negative contacts on auspex. Negative on visual.'

'I can…' the inter-Knight vox-connection slurred. 'I can feel it. Can't you?'

'Quiet,' snapped Acastia. 'Keep the stride.'

She knew what Dolloran meant though – her back prickled with sweat. She wanted to look back. She blinked…

Huge shapes moving… a tremble… a buzz of static and grinding metal… like the tread of a god… like a pulse… like a dying voice counting its last seconds…

An alert chimed. Acastia's eyes flicked to the power plasma output gauges. *Elatus* was running at the edge of power output, and into the red warning zone of fuel depletion.

'Come on,' she said to *Elatus*. 'Come on… do not fail us now. Run this last course for me.'

She could see the outer lines now, the folded earth beneath the wall where trenches and mazes of kill traps and mines tangled the ground in the shadow of the wall.

Half without hope, she keyed the long-range vox again.

'Mercury command – this is Vyronii Lance Hymettus, acknowledge.'

A buzz and shriek of static.

'Vyronii Lance Hymettus, this is Mercury command.'

For a second she was silent, the jolt of *Elatus'* stride seeming distant. *What will happen after this?* she wondered. *What will happen after I speak?*

'Intelligence from blind zone – total priority – assault force sighted and inbound to Mercury. Repeat, assault force inbound to Mercury Wall section. Estimated distance to wall one hundred and fifty kilometres.'

Silence for a moment, the buzz drone of vox distortion.

'Received and understood, Vyronii Lance Hymettus,' said the voice over the vox. *'Confirm force strength estimate.'*

Acastia paused, attempting to find a word that encompassed what they had seen walking up towards the edge of the world.

'Annihilation,' she said at last. 'Annihilation strength.'

Grand Borealis Strategium, Bhab Bastion,
Sanctum Imperialis Palatine

'Is that your full report, bondsman?' General Nasuba's voice crackled over the top of the holo-projection of a Knight pilot. The woman nodded. Even over the distorted transmission, Archamus could see that the House Vyronii bondsman was on the edge of collapse. To be expected. A long-range mission and return, then four hours of intense debrief would do that – that and the word that she had brought and what she had seen.

'That is everything,' said the Knight pilot. *'By the honour of Vyronii.'*

The holo-image froze.

'Do we have any secondary corroboration?' asked Kazzim-Aleph-1. The magos-emissary twitched as he spoke. The exposed cogs looping out of his skull stuttered in their turning.

Fear, thought Archamus, *fear*.

'*There is no active air cover in that zone,*' said the voice of Wall Master Efried.

'*Our reconnaissance units have not been able to penetrate deep behind the enemy's lines,*' came the voice of the Khan, the whooping of the vox trying to cut up the power of his voice. '*I believe this rider of House Vyronii, though. She speaks truth – you can hear it.*'

'*The other pilots in her formation also gave the same report,*' said Nasuba.

For a second a wave of buzzing static filled the war room as the overlapping vox-feeds clashed. Archamus could smell burning plastek in the air. They had barely been able to reach the Khan, and the connection to Lord Sanguinius in the Anterior had failed completely. The scratched voices of Efried, Nasuba, Raldoron and Field General Vetrive on the Adamant Wall formed a clicking chorus of static. Only Rogal Dorn, Archamus, Malcador and the two representatives of the Mechanicus were physically present in the room.

'Ground vibration sensors on the northern walls are consistent with a mass formation of armour, infantry and god-engines moving towards the Mercury Exultant sections,' said Ambassador Vethorel, shooting a look at her fellow tech-priest.

'There are a number of ways of interpreting the data,' said Kazzim-Aleph-1.

'It is real,' said Dorn. Archamus looked at his lord. The Praetorian shifted his gaze to Kazzim-Aleph-1. It was like the realigning of a gun barrel.

'*It is a strange move,*' said the voice of Vetrive. '*To march against where we are strongest.*'

'*Is it?*' asked the voice of the Khan. '*Breach Mercury and they pierce us to the heart. Just as with the attack at Saturnine, so at Mercury. What they could not do by guile they do by raw strength.*'

'What strength could they bring to breach the wall?' asked Archamus.

'Mortis,' said Vethorel. 'The Legio Mortis.' Kazzim-Aleph-1 twitched again. 'The Death's Heads have been absent from the battle sphere but we know they came with the enemy. A full Titan Legion and all that can come with it.'

'Just so,' said Dorn.

The buzz and crackle diluted the moment of silence.

We cannot pull forces from the rest of the walls and lines, said Raldoron. *The pressure of assaults is increasing. If we do, then they will force a breach elsewhere.*

'This moment was always going to come,' said Dorn. 'We have strength to meet it. Mortis walks to our walls. They must be denied. Strength for strength.'

Dorn looked at Vethorel. Kazzim-Aleph-1's head rotated around in surprise to look at his fellow priest. Vethorel held her gaze on Rogal Dorn.

Vethorel keyed a control on the projection table.

A fresh cone of light replaced the image of the Vyronii bondsman. Pixellated snow boiled in the cold light. A face formed in the deluge, flickering even as it hardened.

Kazzim-Aleph-1's cogs whirred and his eyes buzzed as they focused.

My greetings, said Princeps Maximus Cydon. *The Legio Igna-tum, by the command of the Fabricator General and the will of the Praetorian of Terra, prepares to walk.*

Arteria 29, Interior Kill-zone Arcon,
Sanctum Imperialis Palatine

The Titans of Ignatum walked the empty streets of the Palace. They walked in single file, zigzagging through the arterial roads that led from their underground hangars to the northern walls.

Over fifty engines in a four-kilometre column from the grand Warlord at its head to the missile-heavy Reavers in the snake's tail. Every few kilometres the lead Titan sounded its war-horn, and the call would roll down the column from engine to engine. Rainwater poured from their backs. The buildings they passed shook and shook with the rhythm of their tread. People huddled in their homes and shelters heard and felt the god-machines pass. A few wondered if it was a sign of the end; some went to windows and high places to try to catch a glimpse of the machines. Soldiers stationed close to the route looked up, mouths open as the red, yellow and black figures walked on.

The interior kill-zones ran forty kilometres back from the walls. No one lived there any more, and the empty shells of buildings had been fused together with rubble and rockcrete mix to create blocks tens of kilometres wide. Fortress-builders had blocked roads and streets to create winding routes that anything going to or coming from the walls would have to pass through. Gun nests covered every turn. Most were likely unmanned – the soldiers pulled away to the walls until the breach came. Buildings filled with explosives stood ready to detonate and block the path of attackers. Tanks of volatile chem-refuse sat in ranks ready to be lit and poured into the streets. Layers of mines dotted the sides of the deserted buildings. If... *when* the walls fell, the enemy would die here for every step they took. Until then, it waited, the barrels of the guns and the empty eye sockets of the buildings watching the vanguard of Legio Ignatum march to the Mercury Wall.

After they had gone, the columns of bulk haulers would follow. Blocks of red steel, blazoned with black and yellow and bearing the marks of Legio Ignatum, they would take hours to pass. Within were the machines and crews that kept the Legio walking: vox-sensora-fanes; munition caches the size of small hab-blocks; forge-fires; racks of armour plates, each a metre

thick; plasma-charge fonts. The soldiers of the skitarii went
with them, their red coats slick with rain, red light burning
from eye slits in chrome visors. Heat rose from them, cooking
raindrops to puffs of steam. When they reached their desti-
nation these units would unfurl into the caverns and hangars
at the wall base and make ready to welcome the full strength
of the Legio Ignatum, which walked a day behind them. Three
hundred personnel for each Titan, from lowest servitor to
highest magister of flux or binder of signal-aetherics. On and
on they walked to the Mercury Wall, and above them the false
thunder rolled and the ground shook to the tread of iron.

House Vyronii enclave, Shard Bastion, Mercury Wall

Caradoc found Acastia in the ablutions chamber. It was small,
a box of rockcrete holding the foetid air and the smell of sweat,
leather and metal polish. Faded house colours hung on the
walls. Grey recycled water ran tepid from faucets into metal
bowls and troughs. In the time they had been there, rust had
started to creep over the fittings, and mould had begun to gather
like solidified shadows at the edge of the walls and tiles. It was
hot, the summer heat greater than the sluggish air circulation
could cope with. Dolloran was sloshing water over his hair and
attempting to smooth it back above the glossy skin of his face.
The fires that had remade him had left him with pain that he
hid, and a layer of scar tissue over face, shoulders and hands.
Sweat and water gathered on his nose as he closed his eyes for a
second. He looked as exhausted as Acastia felt. Here, separated
from the machine-nerve link of the Helm Mechanicum and her
steed, the fire had drained from her, leaving a grey numbness.

'Tried to sleep,' said Dolloran.

She looked over at him. His eyes opened. Red veins threaded
the whites.

'Think I got to the edge of it…' He gave a smile that rear-ranged the scars of his face. 'Then everything just slammed back, you know?'

She had thought of sleep; her position meant that she could rest as needed. But the few dreams she had when she had closed her eyes in the last few days had been unpleasant: thick, like hardening amber, flecked with things she wanted to forget trapped inside.

'Better to be awake,' she replied. 'Better yet to ride.'

'Indeed,' he said. 'For house, for honour.'

'For house?' she said, looking down into the bowl of water in front of her and stirring it with her fingers. 'Why not just because we choose to?'

She could feel him frown.

'I am not talking of this, Acastia,' he said.

'No,' she said and could not keep the sneer from her tone. 'You never do or will – it is comforting to be a loyal dog at the hearth, isn't it?' She did not look at him, but down into the bubble-flecked water in the bowl, but she could almost see him give a small shake of his head.

She had just brought a hand of tepid water to her face from the bowl when the metal door released and slammed wide. She began to turn, but he was already across the water-spattered floor, and into the space behind her. She turned the last part of the circle so that she was looking at him full in the eye.

Caradoc, scion of House Vyronii, the Emerald Lance, and sixth in descent from the high chair, returned her gaze. His face twitched, lips curling over pearl-enamelled teeth. Sweat was pouring from the dark hair pulled back along his scalp in a ponytail, and running down his face. His cheeks were flushed, and there was the tang and flavour of spice liquor on his breath. He was in full armour, she noticed, caparisoned in chain mail, boiled leather and white and green chequered pressure plates. Beads of sweat had gathered on the tips of his moustache. He was very, very angry, she could tell. Her brother had always had poor control of his bile.

'My lord,' she said, and bowed her head. 'How may I serve?'

Caradoc's jaw clamped tight. His eyes were hard points of night.

'Kneel,' he said, the word a hiss from behind his teeth.

Acastia went to one knee, slowly, aware that Dolloran had already knelt. The water was still sloshing into the bowl on the stand behind her.

'How may you serve?' he said, the words low, but rising in tone like a stone gathering an avalanche as it rolled down the mountain. 'How may you serve? You serve by duty, by humility, by keeping to the place you were born to.'

'If I have given offence, sir, it was not my intention,' she said.

'Intention?' he snarled, face flushing red above the collar of his armour. 'Who gives a shit what you intended? You ride beyond these walls for us, for Vyronii!'

She knew why he was angry, had known why since he slammed open the door, and had suspected that something like this would happen as soon as she gave her report of what they had seen in the blind zone not to him as her liege, but to the command staff officers in Shard Bastion, and soon after to General Nasuba and Wall Master Efried. To them it was a simple matter of strategic intelligence. To Caradoc, being the bearer of such information to high commanders was an honour, one he should have shared in. His prize and the gilding of such contact had been taken from him. The rest of existence might be falling, but to her half-brother and honoured lord, the world still fell into a pattern of pride and cruelty that was called chivalry. This was not a moment of desperation or simple, military expediency; it was a chance to shine. He was right too, in one respect – she had stolen that moment from him and known that she was doing it.

'I am sorry, lord,' she said, neutrally, 'but I do not understand.'

He stepped back, looking at her, the smile on his lips an ugly gash across his face.

'Do you not, Acastia?' He reached down and began to pull the gauntlet off his hand. It was heavy, hardened leather, lined with chain mail and metal plates. The flesh of the hand beneath was damp with sweat. 'The blood that ties us is a privilege. Bastard born though you are. It binds us. It harnesses you to my will, and though you do not appreciate the fact, it binds my hands.' He was very close now, the gauntlet held between pink fingers, light and soft, as though it were a sleeping dove. 'You are protected from so much...' His voice was low, almost a whisper. 'And that protection exists by the honour you scorn.'

He turned to Dolloran, looking down at the kneeling man.

'This one is not like you. Low-born, no trace of misplaced nobility in his veins. Just a will to serve his lord. He knows his place. Knows that he is ours. Knows that he honours and obeys us with his every deed.' Caradoc rested the empty gauntlet on Dolloran's shoulder. 'You know that, don't you, serf?'

'Yes, my lord,' replied Dolloran.

Caradoc looked up at Acastia.

'You see?' he said. 'Loyal, obedient... like a hound.' He looked down at Dolloran. 'Lift your head up.'

Acastia began to shake her head. Dolloran swallowed, and raised his head.

'No—' began Acastia.

Caradoc was fast, muscle surging under armour and mail. Dolloran did not have a chance to rise. The gauntlet lashed across his face. Blood and teeth spewed across the floor. He pitched sideways. Caradoc struck again as Dolloran's head came back up.

'Do you see?' he snarled, striking. The impact a wet smack of mashed flesh and cracking bone. 'You are protected!' Another blow. Blood splattering the tiles. The water brimming the bowl on the stand overflowing. 'You ungrateful…' A low crunch. '…cur!'

Caradoc straightened, breathing hard. Dolloran was still. Water was pouring across the floor, diluting the blood to grey-pink foam.

Acastia felt herself flinch forwards, then stopped herself.

'You serve our house. First and last and forever.'

On the floor, Dolloran gave a moan that formed bubbles in the spreading pool. Caradoc turned, stepped over him and walked out of the door. Acastia lunged forwards, pulling up Dolloran, blood-warm water on her hands.

'Dolloran? Dolloran!'

A sound that might have been a word or a rasp came from the red meat of his lips.

Something moved outside the still-open door. Acastia looked up. Pluton stood just beyond the threshold. He met her eyes. His old face was a mask. His gaze hard. Their gazes held for a long second, and then he turned and followed Caradoc out of sight.

Legio Ignatum Vanguard Strategium,
Shard Bastion, Mercury Wall

Legio Liaison Sentario swept into the sub-command space. The Inferallti Hussars guarding the doors came to attention. Targeter eyes gleamed. Sentario kept moving forwards. Orbiting servo-units peeled away from her and buzzed into the cavernous gloom. An army followed her: enginseers, calculus tacticae adepts, servitors, signal augurs and skitarii marched in, fanning out, carrying and wheeling floats of machinery. Shouts and blurts of binary flooded the silence with echoes.

Sentario locked on to the cluster of figures waiting opposite the main doors. Her augmetic eyes tagged, logged and identified them all in the space of a blink: Wall Lieutenant Angiol of the VII Legion; Colonel Vastri of the Inferallti Hussars, bastion command cadre; Magos Intanil-7-Delta-Chi-Gimmel and Magos Fer-Ultio-4, governors of ordnance and sacred-signal traffic on the walls respectively. Behind them an arc of officers and adepts.

She gave them a bow of her head as she swept towards them.

'Liaison Sentario,' said Angiol. 'Welcome to Shard Bastion.'

'My greetings,' said Sentario without breaking stride. Signals flicked across her noospheric link, blurs of code and blessed cipher-packages. There were smudges of distortion, too. Scratched tangles of code interference bleeding in from the bastion's outer shells of data transfer. She thought-flicked to direct transmission and sent a signal to the Legio units pouring into the space. <High degree of localised transmission fidelity failing. Command: site our noospheric and transmission cleansing units. Institute full counter protocols before we conjoin the spirits of our systems to the outer data links.>

She felt the command link ping with acknowledgements, as she opened her mouth to speak.

'I tender honour and respect from Princeps Maximus Cydon and the Legio Ignatum. Is this the complete liaison cadre?' she asked, still moving forwards, eyes sweeping the space, noting blocks of machinery touching down on the rockcrete floor, calculating the efficiency of movement. Time was decrementing in a cascade of minutes and seconds at the edge of her awareness. A Legio strategium emplacement was not a simple thing to install. Hundreds of personnel and systems needed to be sited, locked, tested and brought online, and this was just the first of five that would be installed in the Mercury Wall before the Legio walked as one.

'It is,' said Angiol, and Sentario noted that the Space Marine seemed to be smiling.

'This is the summary of current tactical position and readiness across the wall section and kill-zone,' said Vastri, holding out a cylinder of ribbon-bound parchment.

Sentario took it and held it out to two of her servo-units. The floating devices seized the cylinder and unfurled it with manipulator claws. Scanning beams swept over the sheets. Information began to unfurl across the noosphere.

'There are scout forces in the kill-zone,' she said.

'Legio Solaria units,' said Vastri, 'and lance formations from House Vyronii, Konor and Cadmus, with fast armoured squadrons from the Vordate Armour Brigades backed up by Seventh Legion elements.'

'A thin net,' said Sentario. Behind her, slab containers were rolling through the doors. Each was a signal and data pod to be trunked in and powered up.

'A fine enough mesh to catch an assault of this size,' said Angiol. 'It is of main assault strength.'

'Let's hope so,' she said.

'Strategic integration stands ready,' said Intanil-7-Delta-Chi-Gimmel. 'What is your estimate of readiness?'

'The first engines are already here and ready,' said Sentario. 'Last enemy distance to wall was one hundred and fifty kilometres estimated. The vanguard force must walk in five hours. This enclave will be installed and functional within two hundred and seventy-four minutes. We will be ready.'

Adeptus Mechanicus enclave, Sanctum Imperialis Palatine

Abhani Lus Mohana looked up from where she had been crouched beside the head of her Warhound. A sound was moving through the forge chamber. Noise was a constant here: the rattle of chains, the pulse and thrum of charge coils and the whoosh of steam, but all those sounds had a rhythm.

It was the layered heartbeat of the machine. This noise was different. It was rising unsynchronised with the beat of the forge chamber.

She glanced to where her two moderati sisters crouched on the other side of the data console.

Abhani nodded. 'Let's take a look…'

The forge cavern was part of the Adeptus Mechanicus enclave. Buried under the Inner Palace, not so deep as the great dungeons, but a city under a greater city. Here was the exiled heart of the true servants of the Omnissiah: all the secrets and devices saved from lost Mars and the great forge worlds, all the exiles and scraps of strength and knowledge, held beneath the earth like the hoard of a mythical worm, circling, eternal… until and unless the defences failed. Until all was lost.

Abhani moved out of the shadow of *Bestia Est*. The Warhound Titan had not seen action since a raid beyond the Western Hemispheric Wall into the False Mechanicum forces massing there. That had been five weeks ago, a limited action sanctioned by the priesthood and the Collegia Titanica. Only one Legio, great Gryphonicus, was continually and completely engaged. Its engines were spread across battlefronts like nails trying to hold the tattered map of the Palace in place. Ignatum, old and at near full strength, had been held back, she had heard. A decisive reserve of strength waiting for the hour of need to arrive.

The rest of the Titans were a menagerie of many Legios, most the survivors of the Titan Death at Beta-Garmon. Some had lost so much that their legion lived in only a single engine. Others, like Abhani's own Legio Solaria, were a fraction of their former strength. Battered, broken, reduced to relics of glory. She thought that was why they were permitted to walk so sparingly: the fear of losing more after so much had already been lost.

She reached the end of the passage. A crowd flowed down

the central arteria. She could see priests in the cloth of dozens of denominations, electro-priests, magister-coders, enginseers-majoris. A cacophonic drone of machine code and voices surrounded them, growing in volume and agitation. At the head of the wave walked the slim figure of Ambassador Vethorel, and a cluster of priests and skitarii guards in gilded plate. Abhani could see the crowd was churning in Vethorel's wake, calling to her, trying to overtake her and being pushed back by her guards.

'What is happening?' asked one of Abhani's moderati from behind her. 'Does the ambassador bring word from the Fabricator General?'

'I don't know,' said Abhani. 'We should follow.' She stepped onto the arteria and joined a flow of Titan crew coming from the side passages and niches where the god-machines rested. After a few strides Abhani had a feeling she knew where they were going. They did not have to follow far for the feeling to be proved right. Vethorel halted in front of a towering recess. A Warlord Titan stood within it, wrapped in scaffold, its head separated and suspended by a web of cables and chains. Red covered its metal skull, and mottled green its skin of metal. It was called *Luxor Invictoria* and it was the principal Titan of Legio Solaria.

'Is the Great Mother awake?' asked Vethorel. Seamless noospheric connections sent her voice to vox-grilles in the cavern walls and ceiling. The ambassador's voice echoed out, though her tone was even. The hubbub of machine and flesh voices faded.

'I am,' came an answer. It crackled from the head of *Luxor Invictoria*, the voice of a war god aping that of a human. The voice of the Great Mother, Grand Master of the remains of Legio Solaria. Her mother's voice.

'Great Mother,' said Vethorel, and the tone was lighter, softer – intimate even, though still loud enough to carry through the caverns. 'I come to you to ask for your aid.'

'When has the proxy of the Fabricator General ever asked for aid? The machines turn at the word of Zagreus Kane and so by your word, too. You command.' A pause and crackle from the god-machine's speaker horns that made Abhani remember her mother's dry chuckle. 'I appreciate the gesture, though. What do you ask?'

'The enemy has unleashed the last of its forces. Mortis walks, Great Mother, here, on Terra.'

There was true quiet then. The stunned silence of calculations paused and equations suspended. For a second, Abhani imagined that she heard the rumble of the cavern's turning mechanisms halt. Legio Mortis, first of the traitors to turn against the Omnissiah, largest of the Legios, born on Mars itself in the age that saw the truth of the Machine rise to create the Priesthood. Ancient. Mighty. Remorseless. She had seen their work on Beta-Garmon. Many of the surviving Titans and crew in the caverns owed the near annihilation of their Legios to the Death's Heads.

'All of it?' said the Great Mother in a croak of electrostatic and turning cogs.

'Yes.'

'You are certain?'

'The projections based on the data and probability place it in that threshold.'

'They walk as one?'

'That is likely.'

'So you come to ask us to walk against them?'

Vethorel gave a deep nod that was almost a bow.

'Ignatum walk,' she said. A clatter of gears and buzz of code from vox-grilles. 'In entire, as one. They go to meet the enemy beyond the wall and hold them.'

Another crackling chuckle.

'If the Fire Wasps have not changed their stripes, then holding will not be their aim – they will seek to destroy the enemy utterly.'

'Perhaps so,' said Vethorel. 'But they cannot walk alone. Even with all their might, the enemy has greater numbers, and the attacks on the rest of the Palace only intensify.'

Now Vethorel turned, looking out at the crowd of priests and Titan crews around her. Abhani saw it then, the play of this moment, the tactics at work. Here, Vethorel was the hunter seeking to bring down a quarry. This was not just an appeal to the Great Mother of Solaria; it was an entreaty to all of those others listening. Abhani knew that the wounds of the Schism, the founding of the Mechanicus and the losses at Beta-Garmon had run together like cracks spidering through a steel beam. The siege had only forced those cracks wider.

'You ask us to walk into annihilation?' came a voice from the crowd, unaugmented but loud. The throng parted as a man in the purple and green of Legio Amaranth, the Night Spiders, came forward. 'The engines of our legion lie in rust on the fields of Beta-Garmon from the last time we answered such a call.'

Abhani heard a murmur of assent and echoed code buzz from amongst the crowd.

'We have walked beyond the walls twelve times since this battle began. Three more engines gone... Ignatum can walk, but Amaranth will not. Not now. Not for certain loss.'

That was it, thought Abhani, laid bare. We are wounded and afraid, and that has made the masters of the weapons of gods cowards.

The buzz was a rising tide now. Others in the crowd called out, some in blurts of binharic, others with cries of shame and dishonour. But there was a current rolling behind the calls, a growl of agreement with the Amaranth princeps. He looked at Vethorel and shook his head.

'How much more?' he asked. 'How much more when we have lost almost everything?'

'Then we give everything.' The voice of Esha Ani Mohana Vi rolled across the crowd. The crowd of priests and Titan crew were looking up at the head and frame of *Luxor Invictoria*. 'There is nothing beyond this.' A pause and the murmur of cogs in the quiet. 'Solaria shall walk. Even if it is into the night. We shall walk.'

There were nods then, some cries of agreement.

The Legio Amaranth princeps gave a single shake of his head, and turned away. Others followed in his wake as he left the crowd. Abhani noticed that apart from her own sisters of Solaria, those remaining were few. A trio of crew from the Legio Defensor, the lone crew of the only Legio Atarus engine to reach Terra. Vethorel looked around at them.

'My thanks,' she said, 'and the thanks of the Fabricator General and Praetorian.'

'Ambassador,' said the voice of the Great Mother, now coming from a small speaker grille and sounding almost as though it was formed by a mouth. 'I would speak with you.'

Vethorel gave a bow of thanks to the remaining crowd and moved closer into the shadow of *Luxor Invictoria*.

'You as well, my daughter,' called the Great Mother. Abhani glanced at her legion sisters and then followed the ambassador. The head of *Luxor Invictoria* lowered on its chains as they approached, until its chin was level with their heads.

'Abhani Lus Mohana,' said the voice of her mother. 'You will go first to this hunt. I have reviewed the data supplied by the Praetorian's command. They will need hunters to find the enemy before the main forces can engage. Ignatum have strength but your maniple can be in the field first. This is your honour and my will.'

Abhani blinked, then tilted her head.

'You knew,' she said. 'Great Mother, you knew the ambassador was coming. You knew what would happen and what you would say.'

'Only a fool walks into a battleground without knowing the terrain, and the ambassador is no fool,' replied her mother. Then she paused. 'You play a dangerous game again, Vethorel,' she said. 'You always have.'

'There is no game here,' said Vethorel softly, and Abhani thought she felt a tinge of something very human and very tired in those words. 'I hoped you would consent. I hoped you would agree to walk.'

'What have we come to when the voice of the leader of a broken army carries more than the entreaties of the Fabricator General?'

'The edge, Great Mother,' said Vethorel. 'It means we have come to the edge.'

Enemy distance to wall: 140 kilometres, estimated.

EIGHT

On the shore of a lost sea
The past came here to die
Faith

Issus Escarpment, East Phoenicium Wastes

There was no sea. The water had long drained and burned away to salt-saturated pools at the bottom of valleys that had once been lightless places far beneath the waves. The shoreline existed still, though, but now it was the shoulder of a hill that slid down into the shimmering distance.

Oll rubbed his eyes. They were streaming. The sky above them was a blue-tinged white, the sunlight hazed by pollution. Heat hammered the exposed skin of his face and arms as he raised a hand to shield his sight.

'Where are we?' asked Rane.

Oll licked his lips and found them dry. A gust of wind slid over him. It was hot, the breath of a furnace that pulled more sweat from his skin. Far off he could see the baked ground roll into hills and dust bowls before sliding into the distance behind the heat shimmer. Empty. Drained. He had looked at the compass, but the needle just turned slowly in place, same with the pendulum. He didn't need them to answer Rane's question, though.

'Where–'

'We are where we were before,' said Oll. He lowered his hand and knelt down. The bone-white sand was dry in his palm. He dabbed it to his tongue, tasted the salt. He thought of the waves breaking on the shore and the smell of the sea – an aeon ago, minutes ago, a cut of a knife ago away. 'This is the same spot we left, or as near as makes no odds.'

'The tunnel, the sea…' said Rane.

'Gone,' said Oll. 'The sea went and the tunnel will have been ground down or buried.' He stood, wiping the dust from his hands, and turned to look at his crew.

His crew… The word had come to his mind without consideration. Was it because of where he stood – on the edge of the sea that had been his home for much of the first age of his life? Was it because in some way that was what they had always been to him, and he had only just felt the truth of it? They had no ship, but were they so different from those who had sailed the *Argo*, or leapt the waves under the black sails of the ship of Theseus? Perhaps that was why he had brought them so far with him – not just to keep them alive, but because that had always been the way of the great journeys of the past.

They did not look like much: a bunch of vagabonds in mixed military and civilian kit. Zybes was looking around, his gun held half-ready, finger beside the trigger guard. He was squinting at the distance, head wrapped in a faded blue kerchief against the sun. Krank was drinking water from a canteen. Oll noticed that the old soldier's hands were shaking slightly as they held the canteen. He was sweating hard. Rane was standing close to Krank, checking the pouches of his kit compulsively. Graft was motionless, machine components still, shoulders slumped. The skin of its flesh was reddening in the sun. Katt was frowning under the brim of a slouch hat she had taken from a pack. Her eyes were set on the distance.

'This is it?' asked Zybes. 'This is where we were supposed to be?'

Oll didn't answer. He thought of John's face looking up at him in the dark of the tunnel, blood on his cheeks, mouth wide as though trying to scream.

'Where we are supposed to be…' he said, half to himself. In truth he was a long way now from where he thought he needed to be. That place was a couple of thousand kilometres off across the wasteland that had once been a sea. They had been supposed to meet there, he and John, and… and Her.

'This is Terra, then?' said Rane.

'It is,' said Oll, shaking himself, wiping the sweat that was gathering on his forehead. 'This is the Issus Escarpment, and the sea we saw in the other time covered all of that land beyond. Goes on for hundreds of leagues now, just dust and drift camps, and the ruins of old cities.'

'But it's the right time?' asked Krank, corking his canteen. 'We are at… it?'

'I reckon so,' said Oll. He pointed up at the sky just above the horizon. The glare was blinding and the haze thick, but there were shadows in the heavens. Big serrated shadows, like notched axe blades wielded by myth. 'You see them?'

'Ships,' said Krank. 'Void-ships in close orbit.'

Oll dropped his hand, nodded.

'Those are big ships…' breathed Rane.

'That won't even be the half of it,' said Oll. 'They will have brought every tug that can haul a shell to this. I would. Above the centre of things, they will be stacked all the way up to the stars, and slinging down thunderbolts.'

'And that's where we are going?' asked Rane. 'To where that's happening?'

Oll let out a breath.

'I reckon, but not first.'

'Your friend,' said Zybes. 'John, that one – he led us here, right? Back there in the tunnel it was witch-sight or something, and that led us here? Because he is not here. Feels a lot like being lost again.'

The thread… play it out behind you or you will be lost…

Oll was about to reply, when Katt spoke.

'That way,' she said, and pointed east. They all looked at her. 'There is something…' She paused, shivered and tilted her head as though trying to shake something free. 'I can hear something, and it's coming from that way.'

Oll looked at her for a long moment. She wasn't even asking if the rest of them could hear it. She knew only she could. A witch thing. A psyker thing.

'What kind of thing?' Oll asked.

She shook her head.

'Not sure. It's pulling at us. Like a voice that is a thread pulling.'

Oll blinked at Katt and then at the way she had pointed.

'What's that way?' Zybes asked Oll.

Oll was still looking east. The haze was thickest there and the crest off the escarpment hid the distance.

'There should be a macro conurbation,' he said. 'Hatay-Antakya Hive. If it's still there.'

'Any chance that your friend John could be there?' Zybes again, pressing, almost angry, afraid and wanting to move on, to be gone. That was another thing that happened on a voyage like this, thought Oll. People got so used to moving to stay alive that they never wanted to stop. Oll had been like that once. Deep down he guessed he still was.

'Could be,' said Oll carefully. It was possible, but part of him could not help thinking about that bloody-faced apparition of

John Grammaticus screaming in the dark. Part of him thought that they should turn and find a way across the empty sea to the place they had been supposed to be going.

'Okay,' Zybes said, and looked around at the rest of them before starting up the slope towards the ridge crest. 'Okay, let's get moving.'

Rane and Krank did not move. Katt glanced at Oll. He met her eyes. He frowned, then shrugged, and nodded.

'Okay,' he said and made off after Zybes. Behind him the others followed.

Plaza of Remembrancers (former), Sanctum Imperialis Palatine

The groundcar stopped twenty paces from the building. Rain streamed off the blue-green copper roof and bubbled up from where drainpipes vanished beneath the paving slabs of the plaza. Mauer waited for a minute, keeping the engine of the vehicle running and the auto-targeting top gun active. Nothing moved except the raindrops dancing on the wide pools of grey water.

'A little paranoid?' asked Andromeda from the passenger cradle.

Mauer did not reply, but just watched the plaza and the front of the building, then flicked her gaze back to the auspex screen in the control console.

'No movement,' said Mauer.

'Who else do you worry will come looking?'

'We have just entered into a conspiracy,' said Mauer. 'At this point everyone is a concern.'

'Do you know much about the Lectitio Divinitatus?' *Andromeda had asked as they crossed the Palace. Most of the mass transit system had been closed down, so they had used a Prefectus groundcar. Through the armoured glass slits, they had seen*

*rain-glossed streets dotted with tank traps, and the sides of build-
ings hung with gun nests.*

'The cult of Imperial divinity,' Mauer had said. 'I know of it.'

'You've read the texts, I'm sure,' said Andromeda.

*Mauer nodded, waited. She had not known where they were
going. That was one amongst a growing list of reasons she was
almost regretting agreeing to Andromeda's proposition. Almost.*

*'Not a convert then?' Mauer felt her face harden. Andromeda
smiled. 'I wouldn't care, but given your nature it was improb-
able. That, and the number of them you've killed. Still, I thought
I would check.'*

'They can be a threat,' said Mauer carefully.

*'Oh yes, they can,' said Andromeda. 'They really can, but right
now they also might be useful.'*

'How?'

*Andromeda had grinned widely, but Mauer felt the coldness in
the expression.*

'In a way that makes no sense.'

Mauer watched the rain fall for a little longer. This part of
the Sanctum was deserted, the refugee populations housed
elsewhere. It was too close to the heart of things to be open
to wide numbers of people – a straight up security risk. It
had been zoned and grown to house the various non-military
functions of the Great Crusade, from the Conservatory, to the
Officio Universalo. The buildings were still all there, but the
only people walking the streets were soldiers in sweep patrol.
The building she watched was the Symposium, the nominal
place that the remembrancers had left from to go and immor-
talise the Great Crusade. The plaza was named after them,
too. Mauer wondered if any of them had ever seen their supposed home.

Still nothing moved in sight or on screen. She keyed the
vehicle's vox-control.

'Scryer-zero-six, this is Noon-zero-one, code check – one-alpha-seven-two.'

A crackle and then a clipped voice with the accents of the Med-basin cities.

'*This is Scryer-zero-six, code confirm – six-seven-niner-one.*'

Mauer nodded.

'Target still in place?'

'*Still in place.*'

'Good. We are coming to you, out.'

She cut the vox, released the door and stepped out into the rain. Andromeda followed, swearing as she wrapped a plastek rain cloak over her grey robes. Mauer moved down the street and across the plaza towards a side door set in the Symposium's wall. Her gun was in her hand, ready but held loose at her side. The door opened when they were five paces away. She saw an increasingly familiar face.

'In,' she said to Andromeda, and paused, scanning the street one more time before following. The hall inside smelled of damp stone and disuse.

'You were clear to the door,' said Ahlborn, fastening the locks. 'No one out there – at least if there is, they are better than me.'

'Chances are low then,' said Mauer, shaking the rain free of her coat. 'Keep it locked down until we are done.'

Ahlborn nodded. He was another one of the new recruits – were there any other kind? – to the Command Prefectus. Sharp, efficient: Mauer rated him highly and trusted him, as did Master of Huscarls Archamus.

'Where is he?' she asked.

'One floor up, third door after you come off the landing.'

'How many do you have on that level?' she asked.

'Two of my best, very carefully out of sight. Another two on the next floor and two on the roof.'

'Nice and tight, eh, conroi-captain?'

'Absolutely, boetharch,' he replied.

Mauer started down the corridor.

'He knows something is happening,' said Ahlborn, from behind them. 'Can't say how or why, but don't be surprised if he is not surprised.' Ahlborn paused and gave the smallest shake of his head. 'He's clever and sharp. Doesn't look like much but… he's dangerous in his own way.'

'I hope so,' said Mauer, and moved on.

They climbed the stairs, found the door and pushed it open. The room beyond must have been a library, but its high shelves and crystal-fronted cabinets were almost bare. A few volumes sat at the edge of cases, some on their side, a few open, mildew spotting the pages. A man stood beside a wide table of polished wood. He was old, and the creases of his face and the depths of his eyes held a life that had seen the universe turned upside down as he watched. He held a pair of books in his hands, one open, a finger jammed in the pages of the other. A battered dataslate sat on the tabletop by him.

'You are Kyril Sindermann, so called Chief Interrogator and former Iterator Prime.'

'Yes,' he said. 'And who are you?'

'I am Boetharch Mauer of the Command Prefectus, and this is Andromeda-17 from…'

'A non-explicit line of authority.'

'I see,' said Sindermann, putting the books down on the table. He looked totally unsurprised and totally unfazed. 'Please, take a seat. Let's talk.'

Lion's Gate space port

The emissary of Horus came to the Lord of Iron where he sat in the dark tower. Forrix met him as he emerged from the macro hoist. Argonis, as before, strode towards the doors of the command chamber. He came alone, his staff of office in one hand, his helm held in the other. Forrix did not try to stop him, but moved to the equerry's side.

'I have an order, for your primarch,' said Argonis without breaking stride.

'From the Warmaster,' said Forrix.

Argonis did not answer, but Forrix thought he caught something move across the legionary's expression, a shadow of an emotion that should not have been there. Forrix recognised it. He had seen it before on the *Vengeful Spirit* as they had entered Horus' presence. In the stillness of the emissary's face there had been sorrow.

They stopped as they reached the data-cradle. The Iron Circle automata closed ranks as they approached but did not try to stop them.

'Lord Perturabo, I bring word and command from the Warmaster of Mankind.'

Perturabo did not respond or move. The data-cradle hummed and spun about the primarch. Flows of code blinked across screens, machines buzzed. But the eyes of the Lord of Iron did not move in his face. He had barely moved for the last twelve hours. Three hours into that time, the Lord of Iron had stopped calling up fresh data-sifts and report streams; he had just let the data wash over him in whatever format it came. In the last four, he had stopped issuing new commands. In the last thirty minutes, Forrix was not even sure if his lord was assimilating the data at all. But still he did not move from the cradle. It was as though a finality was creeping into Perturabo, a dreadful passivity in the face of whatever he was seeing. It was terrifying.

Argonis took a breath to speak again.

'Mass errors with the strategic data flow,' said Perturabo. 'So many errors and points of corruption that I can barely see the war.' He looked around at Argonis. His eyes were dark mirrors. 'I am becoming blind.'

'Lord,' said Argonis. 'The Warmaster commands you–'

'It does not matter,' said Perturabo. The Lord of Iron stood from the cradle. Cables snapped. Sparks fizzled across his armour. Screens flickered and filled with static. 'I know what you are here to say, emissary. Before my sight dimmed, I saw. It was there in the troop movements. In the sensor flow. Too great a change to not be ordained.' Perturabo's gaze held on Argonis. The primarch's armour purred. 'But speak your words, equerry. Let it be done.'

'You are ordered to move your location. You shall disperse your Legion warriors amongst the assault forces. You shall take command of the assault on the Sanctus wall section.'

Forrix felt the breath become cold in his lungs.

'The surge of forces is near completion,' said Forrix. 'Without strategic oversight, how will we guide the–'

'I will not,' said the Lord of Iron. Forrix just watched his primarch. Perturabo turned and looked at the terminals and jungle of cables filling the chamber. They all already had a wet, muscle-like sheen. 'Mortarion and the Death Guard are moving, they are coming here,' said Perturabo. 'Is that not so, emissary?'

Argonis nodded.

'That is the Warmaster's will.'

'We are to be displaced?' Forrix could hear the disbelief crack the hard control of his voice. 'We can see victory and you would take its architects away before it is complete. Who will order the battle?'

'Order…' The word seemed to echo though Perturabo had not raised his voice. 'There is no order here now. This is not a war any more. This is a storm. And you see it, don't you, emissary, equerry to the Warmaster who was once my brother?

You see it. I am blind but now I can see as you see. The Legion war is dead. The cause we raised arms for is a corpse. There is nothing that happens from here that can be called victory.'

'What are you saying, lord?' said Forrix, his mind and voice moving out of sync with what his primarch had just said – with the impossible thing his primarch had just voiced.

Perturabo walked to one of the chamber windows and keyed a control. Blast shutters pulled up, grinding and squealing. Layers of fog and cloud hid the ground below. In the distance, the tops of towers rose from the folds of vapour. The orange light of a fading day folded over both. As Forrix looked, an explosion lit in the distance, large enough to shine through the murk. He had a feeling that he should walk away, that this was a moment that did not include him and should not be observed. He did not move.

'How long to stand here,' said Perturabo, his voice low. 'A lifetime, many lifetimes as most mortals live them.' He raised a hand, servos whining, exo-bracing and armour plates shifting. His hand opened, metal-clad digits reaching delicately for the distant towers of the unconquered Palace. 'I never wanted to be put to any of the uses you put me to, father. All you have ever valued is destruction. All you have ever praised is weakness and pride. All that I wanted has been taken.' Perturabo's gaze was distant, as though he were focusing beyond what he could see to some infinite distance. 'He is just like you, father. Horus, your bright son. You both made us want to serve you, and you then made us kill our dreams with our own hands.'

Perturabo looked out for a moment more and then his fist closed, and he turned away from the view.

'Know this, equerry,' said Perturabo. 'I pity you. You see, and you know, and you fear for your Legion and wonder what the oaths you swore mean now. Yet you do not have the strength and the power to do the only thing that is left to do.' Argonis looked as though he might reply, but the Lord of Iron had turned to Forrix. 'Send a signal to all of our forces, full withdrawal. Bring our fleet into dock and begin to embark. We will move to the system edge and translate. This is immediate.'

Forrix did not move. The words he had just heard rang like bullets hitting iron.

'Lord...'

'It is over,' said Perturabo. 'Horus has given this battle to sorcerers and beasts. The war of Legions is over. Mortarion comes here to take this place. He and what he has become is what this war is now. He comes at the will of Horus to be the agent of what will happen.'

'But he did not order our withdrawal.'

'I order it,' growled Perturabo. 'It is my will. There is no victory here, just creatures and parasites pulling down a dying beast. It is gone. The Legion war is dead. The chance is gone. The cause is gone...' Perturabo paused, and then shook his head. 'We will not bleed for this. We will not break the circle of our iron for this.'

Forrix nodded then.

'As you will it, my lord.' He began to turn away, and then stopped.

'All the blood of your Legion, all of the red iron spilled, was it worth it to come this far and go no further?' asked Argonis.

Perturabo was silent for a long moment. Pistons and weapons clicked. Shells exchanged between guns and ammunition feeds.

'It was worth it to learn the truth – this universe does not care. We could bleed our last and it would not matter. Pour the blood of my warriors into the earth and all that grows is the hunger for more.' He began to move towards the doors.

'If you go,' called Argonis, 'if you defy the will of Horus, then your ships shall be burned from the stars.'

'They shall not,' said Perturabo. 'Just as you shall not draw
your gun and shoot me now, though you should. Horus has
bartered your strength for doubt and false promises. But our
strength is still ours and our iron is still true.'

'You shall be outcast,' called Argonis at Perturabo. 'He will
hunt you. Once the Warmaster has taken the throne, he will
hunt you.'

Perturabo paused.

For a moment Forrix thought he saw something shift in the
shadow of his master, as though it was not cast by the thin
light of holo-screens but by the light of fires falling through
the heaped blades and guns of broken enemies. In the back
of his mind he heard the chuckle of bullets rattling into boxes
and the hiss of sharpening swords. The echo of pride faded
from his thoughts.

We are damned, he heard his own thoughts say. *Damned
no matter what choice is made here or how far we run from this
folly. Damned in a universe with only false gods and no salvation.*

'So be it,' said the Lord of Iron.

Perturabo turned his back and walked from the room. At
his side walked the Iron Circle. Forrix walked, and within his
hearts he heard a drum roll of iron.

Magnifican

The night slid across the land, and Shiban kept moving. The
heat clung to the air, thinning but never fleeing as the light
bruised to purple, to muddy red, to black. There were no
stars, and the lights of the ships in orbit did not pierce the
cloud. The flash of distant explosions faded from the horizon
as though following the sunlight down, and out of sight. The
world became black. Shiban's eyes were such that he could see
on a starless night as though it were day, but there was nothing

here to give that comfort. He could not see the ground under his feet. Soon the staff was his only guide, its tapping telling him of shifting rubble and water-filled sinkholes. The darkness was not wholly natural, he was certain of that. He was no Stormseer, but he knew that what lived between Heaven and Earth did not follow the lines of thought that humans wanted to call truth. He was walking not just through a night caused by the turning of planets. The darkness was alive. Breathing with the pulse of all the breaths drawn for the last time on this ground. Sounds shivered in the dark. Hootings. Moans that sounded like voices calling for help. But the land was empty of life, except for him.

He had followed one of the moaning cries the first time he heard it, followed it into the shell of a road tunnel where the bones of macro haulers lay silent in pools of oil and fuel. There was a light, too. A little warm glow hanging at head height, like the glow of a small fire or lumen pack. He had followed the sound of tears and the light until he saw what was crying. Something with a body of loose, rotting skin hung from the apex of the tunnel, hidden in the gloom. Only Shiban's rare eyes let him see it; without them it would have just been a bulge in the shadows. Fleshy tubes flexed in place of its mouth, piping the sound of fear and pleading into the air. The light hung from it on a rope of soft white sinew. Bones littered the ground beneath it. Strings of flesh held some together enough that he could recognise a hand, a foot and a jaw in a skull without a crown. The creature shifted as he drew near but did not move. The moans had got smaller: a child lost in the dark, an old man stumbling towards hope.

He had turned and left, pausing only to strike a spark from the metal pole on a rock. The tunnel mouth had filled with flame as the spilled fuel and oil burned. The thing on the roof had cried out as it died, squealing in a hundred stolen voices.

Shiban had gone back into the night and walked until the fire was a dot, then a mote, then gone. He had heard the cries again, several times, each from different directions. Things were making this new Earth their home, and he wondered if the nights that fell in the future would all be like this: blind and filled with the cries of things that hungered.

'It is not done, until you say it is,' Yesugei had said to him from over his shoulder as the night went on. 'While there is will to resist, to ride on, then there is still a way.'

'A way to win?' he had replied, aware of the flat echo of his voice in the dark.

'I did not say that. A way to continue.'

'Is that comfort?'

'It is truth.'

'What do you think, Torghun? Each step carries us to what end?'

If Torghun's ghost had an answer it kept it to itself.

Eternity Wall… The memories and faces came to him in the dark, again and again. Dorn had known… He had known and had marked its fate as annihilation. It was that land they rode through now, a land of desperation where the sacrifice of one's own strength and blood was a price not just paid, but offered. Thousands killed by the blades of the enemy, but at the will of their commander – that was war, he knew it; he wished it was not the war they were fighting. How much more would have to be given? What would remain of their souls even if they won?

In the distance, a column of lightning shot from the earth to the heavens. It boiled up from the line of the ground, defining it as it climbed through the sky: ghost light, yellow and bile green, red the colour of drying blood. It flowed across the bellies of clouds, so that they looked like coals glowing under a bed of ash. A shape sat at the core of the column,

hidden by the shifting glow. Shiban blinked, staring, his mind
scrabbling to process what he was seeing for a second. Then
he realised. It was the Lion's Gate space port, sheathed and
lit by coils of light that were flowing up its walls. Its tower
formed a black void within the arcs, an absence darker than
the banished night. He had not realised he was so close to
it. Or perhaps it was no closer, but only felt closer. Closing.
Imminent. Like a threat.

As he watched, the clouds rippled and flowed, shunted aside
like sea froth before a leviathan. He could see the stars, and
between them and him the shapes of vast ships moving through
the boundary atmosphere, their thrusters and grav-distortion
shimmering like water. Behind them, the spire of the space
port they had left glowed then faded to cold black again. The
distances flexed and contracted as the ships rose, and for a
moment he felt he stood just beneath them, staring up at the
pitted iron of their hulls. The *Iron Blood* and her sisters come to
take their lord back into the abyss above. They rose, and then
the distances snapped true again and they were just dots of light
fading as the cloud layer rolled back. The lightning around the
Lion's Gate space port faded. Night returned. Silence wrapped
around Shiban again.

'Where am I?' he asked.

'A different world,' said Torghun.

'Still on Terra?'

'The land changes,' said Yesugei's voice. 'The place is the
same but it is not the land you walked before. The fulcrum
tips. The past came here to die, and this is just one death
amongst many.'

'The death of what?' he asked.

'The death of the wars we fought and the lies we told ourselves as we fought them.'

Shiban did not reply to the voices. Standing still in the

silence of the night, he listened to see if more words would come.

None did, but high above he thought he heard the call of carrion eaters as they circled in the dark.

He took another step and kept moving. There was no choice in that. Day or night, darkness or light, he would keep moving.

Plaza of Remembrancers (former), Sanctum Imperialis Palatine

'I hear that you have lost your faith,' said Andromeda as she sat on the tabletop and crossed her legs beneath her. Sindermann paused as he pulled out a chair then lowered himself into it.

'You hear the strangest things,' he said carefully.

'Frequently,' said Andromeda. 'But is it true? You were an iterator of the Imperial Truth, secular to the core. Then you became a convert to the *Lectitio Divinitatus*, a disciple of the so-called saint, a fanatic to a new cause. You claim to have seen the evidence of the Emperor's divinity. But you spend a long time looking at drops that might kill you for a man with the certain belief in a god.'

Sindermann held Andromeda with a long, careful gaze.

'You really do hear a lot, don't you?'

Andromeda shrugged.

'You renounced your faith,' said Mauer, 'as a condition of your freedom and the formation of your band of recorders of history.'

'Interrogators,' said Sindermann. 'They are called interrogators.'

'A strange name for non-combatants with quills and pict-capturers,' said Mauer.

'The interrogation of the present before it becomes history, or do you think that the only interrogation happens in cells?'

He paused and looked between Mauer and Andromeda. 'Or across tables?'

'Your faith…' said Andromeda softly. 'You very carefully did not mention your faith.'

'I did not renounce my faith. I promised to keep it to myself. No preaching. No spreading the word. I have kept my promise, too.'

'But you still believe that the Emperor is divine?' asked Mauer.

'Believe? No, I don't believe it, boetharch – I know it. You can't believe in a fact. It just is.'

'You sound as though you resent it,' said Mauer.

'I might as well resent the rain…' He shook his head. 'Questions… It all comes down to questions. Old questions, as old as thought and the idea of gods.'

'If the Emperor is divine, how can He permit the suffering and disaster that is occurring?' said Andromeda.

Sindermann nodded, his eyes on the books he had placed on the table, his gaze distant.

'And He *is* divine – I have seen the truth. Philosophers of a different age would use the same question to undermine the concept of a higher power – there is suffering and darkness and so gods must be false. But gods are real, and there is suffering, so that must be because they permit it… I have not lost my faith. I have found that I believe in a God-Emperor who is less than the divinity I wanted, but the only thing that is true.' He was quiet then, staring into whatever infinity he saw before him. Mauer did not break the silence. Sindermann blinked and looked up at them. 'Is this really what you came to ask?'

Mauer shook her head.

'We came to ask you to help us.'

'Help you how? As you say, I am a master of nothing but people with quills and picters. A propagandist with a lost truth and a flawed faith. You two are in a very different business to me.'

'The same business,' said Mauer. 'We have the same business. The preservation of humanity in the face of annihilation, and the survival of the Emperor.'

'All your interrogators,' said Andromeda, 'what are they doing if not trying to save the present for the future?'

Sindermann was still for a moment, and then gave a single, slow shake of his head.

'I think you may have rather overestimated both my power and your own.'

'No,' said Andromeda. 'I don't think so. You interrogate history and events, so tell me – how many times have the turning points of events come down to just a few people with the insight and will to act?'

'Not as often as many would like to think.'

'But sometimes,' said Andromeda. 'Sometimes history tilts on an edge that's just that narrow. You know that – you believe that.'

Sindermann did not reply for a second.

'How do you think I can help?' he said at last.

'Very soon, everything will fail,' said Andromeda. 'Our defences, our will to fight, our strength to resist – all of it will crumble, and it will crumble from within without the enemy needing to raise a sword or fire a bullet.'

Mauer pulled a dataslate from her coat pocket and slid it across the table to Sindermann. He picked it up and began to scroll through, eyes flicking and focusing.

'I see,' he said. 'I see.'

'Yes. I think you do,' said Mauer.

'Tell me,' he said, his gaze distant again but focused as though he were seeing facts and ideas forming into a pattern in front of his eyes, 'how has it been spreading and manifesting?'

'The dreams,' said Mauer. 'The dreams and the despair that comes in waking.'

She closed her eyes and pinched the bridge of her nose for a moment, then let her hand drop from her face. She felt her thoughts twitch towards the cylinder of stimms in her coat pocket.

'Despair, anger, total loss of perceptual balance. The conviction that there is a better world that is beyond, in dreams, a paradise that can be reached somehow.'

'Violence?' asked Sindermann.

'Yes,' replied Mauer. 'Conforming to a pattern but not a common cause. Like a slow, secret hysteria.'

'Instances both more acute, and more widespread?' he asked.

Mauer nodded.

'And this is not sedition or the whispers of propagandists – take it from me. It used to be my trade. No... even without the details, just looking at your faces, I know I have hit the mark. These atrocities, this rising tide – they are like miracles, but not, like the shadow of miracles. Almost ineffable, but not quite. Something from beyond, something from the realm of new truth we find ourselves in, false gods and cruel gods, daemons and saints.' He looked down for a moment, at the hands that sat on top of his knees. Mauer thought she recognised the look that ghosted across his face. It was the same expression she had seen on the faces of soldiers who joined a war for ideals but ended up living the truth. 'But you knew that already,' he said, looking up at Mauer.

'It is the warp,' said Andromeda. 'The place where faith and ideas rule. That's why we came. We aren't looking for answers. We are looking for a solution.'

Sindermann bit his lip, then nodded.

'I think I see the solution you imagine. You think... you think you want to spread the faith in the Emperor's divinity and that will, like white cells in the blood, force out the dreams and the despair and the whispers of daemons.'

'And?' asked Mauer.

He laughed, the sound dry and humourless.

'You know, even six months ago I might have not just agreed but rejoiced, but things change, do they not, boetharch?'

'Can it be done?' asked Andromeda.

'Maybe,' said Sindermann. 'But it will be dangerous, even with the authority that you are wrapping this in – it is forbidden, and the Praetorian is not one to bend or forgive.'

'Noted,' said Andromeda. 'Will you do it?'

Sindermann shook his head.

'I can't,' he said.

'You can't?' snapped Andromeda. 'You were the Iterator Prime. Half the ideas of the Great Crusade were propagated using methods you developed, by pupils you taught.'

'That was our biggest mistake,' said Sindermann. 'To think that you could spread ideas like seeds to take the place of the human need to believe in something more than the rational, something beyond.' He sighed. 'That is why I cannot do what you ask. This is not a thought puzzle, Andromeda-17 of the Selenar – it is not a bio-conditioning factor to be picked apart.'

Andromeda exchanged a look with Mauer.

'You do not think it will work?'

'I think that it may. I think that you do not really know what you are asking, or what you are playing with. I think that it might be the worst and best hope I have heard anyone speak in a long time.'

'But you won't help?' asked Andromeda.

'That's not what I said,' he growled, 'and do not goad me! You are very clever and very subtle, but I have seen, seen with my own eyes the truth of faith and divinity, and it holds as much terror as it does comfort. The survival of humanity – that was the phrase you used. Who could walk away from that when they had the means to try to prevent it?'

'But you refuse to spread the faith as we need,' said Mauer.

'No, that was a simple statement of fact. This is not about ideas or speeches now. It is about belief. It is about miracles. An old iterator who has seen the face of divinity is not enough. Words alone are not enough. What is needed to begin this is something higher, something touched by the beyond.'

'And you can help us get that?' asked Andromeda.

Sindermann looked at them both, a tired smile on his face.

'Of course I can,' he said, and then he looked from Andromeda to Mauer. He nodded at the gene-witch. 'That is why she came here. Not for me but for who I can reach. She thinks of means to ends, and once she has an end in sight, everything and everyone is just a means. I would not trust her too much if I were you, boetharch...' He paused, and gave a sad smile. 'In fact, trust no one might be a wiser maxim.'

Then he turned and pulled on a rain cloak, picked up a battered dataslate, and made for the door.

NINE

Hunt
Ready to walk
Ignite

Sortie Cavern 78, Mercury Wall

'Get that ammunition feed locked!'

Acastia could hear the shout of Caradoc even over the sounds of the bolt-drivers and the clatter of loading hoists.

'Faster, lock it now!'

She was moving to her own Knight, pulling on gauntlets. A lesser servant of the house followed her, his arms full with the pipes and cables that trailed from her suit, another with her helm. Dolloran and Pluton were just behind her. Dolloran's face was a mass of dark bruises and split skin sealed by surgical staples. He did not meet her eye as she looked around.

She rounded the side of a container of vulcan shells, rattling as they were spooled out onto belts.

She saw them then. Three god-engines in light mottled green, hound heads splashed with crimson, standing in pools of light. Flocks of servitors and tech-priests moved over and around them. For a moment she almost stopped in her tracks.

It was not that she had never seen their like before; she had. On five battlefields she had ridden at the side of machines from three different Titan legions. Her awe of them had never dimmed, and now seeing them without the shell of her own steed she felt as though she was close to something truly dangerous. Violence radiated off the Titans like smoke off embers.

Beside them, the stalk-legged shape of Caradoc's Cerastus and the three Armigers of their lance seemed lesser, as though they were imperfect, incomplete shadows of true majesty.

Caradoc turned from where he stood beside the hoist that would carry him up into the cockpit and throne of his steed. It was called *Meliae*. Its form was cast in the Castigator mode of the Cerastus pattern: long-legged, its weapon arms ending with a powerblade and the rotary barrels of a mega-bolter.

'Make ready to mount,' he called, taking his own helm from a servant nearby. 'The Hunters are inbound.'

'They are here, my liege,' said Pluton. They all turned. Nine women strode down the centre of the room. The one in the lead had a lean face, hard eyes. There was a fluidity and precision in her movement, Acastia noticed. Focused. The control of a predator. Attendants in the colours of the Legio Solaria followed.

Caradoc moved to step forward, his helm clasped under his arm, the features of his face rearranged into something welcoming and serene. She could tell he was preparing to make the one-third bow of greeting to a warrior of higher honour.

'Noble princeps…' he began as the Solaria crews closed.

'I am Abhani Lus Mohana,' snapped the lead princeps. 'You are the Vyronii who ride with us?'

'I am Caradoc, sixth in succession–'

'I know who you are,' said Abhani, continuing towards the Titans. 'We walk in fourteen minutes. The count has begun. Be ready.'

'Yes…' said Caradoc, and for a second his mask of welcoming serenity slipped, and an uglier truth slid across his features.

'All field decisions are bound to my word, if I fall, to that of my sisters,' said Abhani Lus Mohana without slowing or looking at Caradoc.

'As you will it,' he said.

The princeps did not reply. Caradoc turned, and flicked his fingers. Acastia began to climb the grips up to *Elatus'* cockpit. She did not look back at Caradoc. She knew the rage would be there, waiting for a target to lock on to. She could already imagine the sharp goad of his anger biting across the thrall control he wielded over her and the other two.

She dropped into the throne inside the cockpit. Servants began to buckle her in. Controls flashed from amber to green. She heard fuelling cables snapping free. Her hands and eyes were moving over *Elatus'* controls as she took the reins of its waking spirit. A servant raised his hand to confirm she was ready for enclosure. Acastia looked up from the controls, and saw the Solaria Titans begin to stand. Fumes billowed as coolant test-vented. Pistons elongated. Their gun-laden shoulders rolled, and each machine shivered. They turned. Acastia felt her teeth shake in her jaw. She hesitated and then put the helm over her head. The cockpit hatch hinged down above her. Neural links between helm and skull lit with pain. Instruments flashed red, amber, green. She punched buttons. *Elatus* woke, head twisting, gun arm twitching. It wanted to gallop free, and she had to bite down as the goad of Caradoc's neural harness held them in place.

The doors at the end of the cavern drew up into the ceiling. Ion mist was flowing from Knights and Titans as shield generators charged. Caradoc's Castigator flexed its weapon arms and dry-cycled its guns. Acastia could feel Caradoc's anger at having to follow the will of another, Titan princeps or no.

The cavern doors were fully open. Acastia could see the ramp rising to the next door beyond, which was already in motion. Far, far off, she fancied she could see a slice of daylight at the outermost door. By the time they reached it, it would be open to the world beyond and once they had passed through it would close without a second's delay.

The three Solaria Warhounds stalked to the door, paused and hunched down, pistons contracting like muscles in a predator before it pounced.

'My sisters,' said the voice of Princeps Abhani Lus Mohana. 'Knights of Vyronii, now is the hour, now is the need – hunt.'

The Warhounds bounded forwards and ran towards the widening bar of daylight. A second later, Acastia felt the neural harness release, and she was running, too, out into the land beyond.

Command bunker, Shard Bastion, Mercury Wall

'Open it up.' General Nasuba turned from the circle of her command staff and jerked her head at the armour-covered viewslit. 'Let's have a look before we ruin the view.'

A low set of chuckles came from the officers. Nasuba made herself smile.

'Blast shutters releasing,' called a junior. Adamantine plates began to draw down into the lower frame of the foot-high slit that ran across the front wall of the command bunker. Nasuba watched the exposed chain links run through the slow-turning cog teeth. Light flowed in through the slit in a widening band. It was not clean – nothing was any more – but the muddy, bruised murk of twilight. Nasuba stepped forward, holding out her hand for magnoculars. Two of her seniors stepped forward with her. Kurral, pulling his own brass-cased glasses from the pouch hanging from a patent leather belt circling his willow-thin frame, and Sulkova, who just closed her right eye and let the augmetic in her left socket do the work.

Nasuba brought the magnoculars up to her face and snuggled the rubber seals into her eyes. The view shifted as the device tried to autocorrect.

'You would have thought that a few years in the field would have taught me how to use these things,' she said. Another low ripple of chuckles. They enjoyed when she played down what she was and where they were. It was not much, but right now Nasuba would take every fleeting rise in morale she could conjure. Half the war was out there, beyond the drop of the wall, and the rest was in the heads of the men and women on the wall. Right now she was not sure they had a firm hold on either of them.

She flicked the magnification and enhancement dials, and the view blurred as it zoomed out into the distance.

The command bunker sat at the top of Shard Bastion, just below the primary laser and plasma batteries, nearly a thousand metres above the base of the wall. From up here you could see a long way. Even with the naked eye, on the rare clear days you could make out the maximum direct fire line that ran along the arc of the horizon over a hundred and twenty kilometres distant. The peaks of the mountains that surrounded the Palace and its artificial plateau sometimes emerged from cloud and smog to bite at the sky.

The view in the magnoculars swam for a second and then settled. Visibility was poor. Discharge fog had rolled down off the aegis above the Inner Palace and mixed with the mist that rose from the baked land as the day cooled. Distance and range data scrolled at the edge of her sight as she found and focused on the metal spines of Karalia's Grave, rising above the folded ground seventy kilometres out. A press of a control tagged the focal point and a fresh set of relative distances began to unwind as she panned across the ground towards the darkly gleaming water of Lake Voss. The water had pulled back from the shore as the heat had built over the last weeks. Crusts of green-and-pink salts marked its margins.

'What was the last location of the hunters?' she asked.

'Just tracking down the drain rivers past Sinkhole One,' said Sulkova. 'They are making good pace.'

'Direct feeds?'

'Data and visual,' replied Kurral, 'but it's patchy.'

'Isn't everything?' replied Nasuba.

Legio Solaria had put three Warhounds in the field. A lance-tip of Vyronii Knights had gone with them, including the riders that had made the sighting in the blind zone. There were nine other hunter groups out in the kill-zone, all seeking the leading edge of the enemy advance. But all of what Nasuba knew said that if this assault force was coming then it would come down the southern edge of Lake Voss towards the ruins of Karalia's Grave. Get forwards, get a foothold, dig in, maybe throw up a void envelope and site a dispersal node, spread to cover the flanks then wedge forwards. It was what she would do. It was predictable, but sometimes the predictable was that way because it was the best option.

Wall Master Efried's plan of response was equally direct: find the enemy, move main force out to engage and pin an advance at a point that allowed the wall guns to do their work. It was the strategy of the Solar War and siege to date: hold and punish. The enemy might be able to close the distance to the wall, but it would cost them in time and strength. If they made it across the one hundred and twenty kilometre kill-zone, they would not have the strength to do more than shout their fury at the wall. In the months that would take, the chance for victory would have passed. That was the plan. Nasuba knew it would work – for all its simplicity it was a creation of Rogal Dorn. It was just what the reality of that would look like on the ground.

General Nasuba felt the semi-powered carapace of her armour creak as she shifted her weight. This was going to be the start of the real shitstorm. She could feel it. Never mind the strategic data and reports that her clearance as commander of Shard Bastion gave her, she just knew it.

'General,' came the voice of a junior from behind her. 'Communication from the sally-vaults – the lead elements of the Legio Ignatum have arrived.'

'Reply that I will be with them shortly,' she said, lowering the magnoculars and handing them to an aide.

'They have been here for some time already, general,' said the junior. 'The communication chain from the lower wall must have failed.'

Nasuba frowned at that; communication fidelity and discipline had been getting worse and worse in the last week.

'Find out what went wrong with the comms and close the loop. Sulkova, you have zone command. I want to know as soon as the hunters have contact with the enemy.'

Sulkova snapped a crisp salute.

'My general,' she said.

'Try not to cause trouble.'

Another chuckle in the uneasy air of the bunker.

'The Fire Wasps...' said Kurral. 'Do you want some extra troops for your honour guard? The Collegia Titanica are keen on that kind of show, I hear. Particularly if they have been kept waiting.'

Nasuba smiled as she moved towards the door, even as she felt the lead cool and harden in her gut.

'I'm sure they will cope with any disappointment,' she said, and heard the chuckle in her own words.

A real shitstorm... said a voice in her head. *Let's hope we can smile at the end of it.*

* * *

Sally-vault 14, Shard Bastion, Mercury Wall

Tetracauron could feel the headache building in his temples as he walked down the centre of the vault. He blinked a few times, took a sip of a cup of water that tasted decidedly like piss, and tried to focus on what was going on around him. Twelve hours unlinked and he was fairly certain that much more than another day and he wouldn't be able to move for the migraine that was spooling up in his skull. Divisia and Cartho paced in his wake, each dealing with the disconnection in their own way: Cartho with silence, Divisia by uttering a creatively wrought litany of swear words under her breath. The rest of the crews of the vanguard Titans would arrive with their engines in a few hours. They would arrive already connected to their engines and incarnated. Time was already running swift and the rest of his command would walk from here directly out onto the Mercury-Exultant kill-zone. Tetracauron would dearly have liked to have been with them, but this duty superseded his comfort. He took another sip of the piss-flavoured water and looked around.

'Does the work not lift your heart?' asked Xeta-Beta-1, falling in beside him.

'Of course,' he replied, 'and the wait raises my stomach to equal heights.'

'Do you require a dose of suppressants to soothe the disconnection symptoms?'

'About as much as I require a blow to the genitals.'

'Now you are being needlessly profane.'

He did not reply.

The vault was one of a series set in the ground beneath Shard Bastion. Wide enough to swallow multiple hab-blocks, it was linked to both sides of the Mercury Wall by tunnel roads sized to allow the Titans to walk in single file. Rockcrete slab doors sealed the openings at the base of the wall, and multiple blast doors could close the tunnels in seconds. In extremis, explosives could collapse them and flood them with fire. From here, vast forces could deploy to the kill-zones.

The advance cohorts of the legion's support caste and tactile cohorts had arrived with them in the brief cool of the night before. They filled the vault. Arming and repair cradles for forty Titans already towered over the central space. Sparks flew from welding arcs in the webs of girders. Hoists lifted tank-sized boxes of ammunition onto platforms. Binharic shouted through the air in time with the grind of bolt-drivers and the clang of metal. The air reeked of acetylene, ozone and oil – sacred and rich. In each of the other vaults, the same preparations were underway. A full thirty thousand tech-priests, adepts and servitors had poured into the vaults in the hours after the Grand Master had given the order. Another two hours and Tetracauron's vanguard battle group would arrive, and they would walk beyond the wall an hour after that. The rest of the Legio would stand in these buried places.

'How long until we have strategium data feeds?' he asked, glancing at Xeta-Beta-1. As enginseer for the battle group's command Titan she had assumed dominant rank amongst the priests that supported the Legio. She seemed to be coping with the escalation of responsibility with a combination of exasperation and glee.

'Projected at one hundred and two minutes,' she replied. 'The cogitator sifts are still being located and installed, and there is a high degree of discomfort and corruption in the spirits of the bastion's communication systems. Added to which there are fragments of Vyronii and Solaria command systems to account for and integrate.'

'It will be ready,' he said.

'Of course, but it's not a pleasing or seamless integration between our machines and theirs.'

'Let's hope that the human element proves easier,' muttered Divisia.

'Talking of which, command unit incoming left, forty degrees,' said Cartho.

Tetracauron paused in his stride and turned to see a woman in red-and-white carapace armour striding across the vault floor. A guard of four troopers in similar gloss armour bracketed her. All of them bore plasma fusils and volkite energy guns. Servo-bracing extended over their shoulders and arms to assist with the weight of their weapons. Helms of matt-black ceramite covered their heads and faces. Vertical sensor bands ran down the front of the faceplates. The woman wore no helmet, but the back of her shaved skull glinted with interface plugs. She moved like an engine killer, smooth and gunsight-focused. Even without the command briefing he had absorbed, he would have known who she was at a glance – General Nasuba of the Inferallti Hussars, commander of the Shard Bastion.

Behind him, Cartho and Divisia straightened as the general came to a stop three paces from them. She waited, pale green eyes steady on Tetracauron's gaze.

'General Nasuba,' he said, and dipped his head as far as pride and protocol would allow. 'An honour.'

'I'm sure it is,' she said. 'What is your status, princeps?'

Not even a twitch of deference or uncertainty, he thought. *I like this one.*

'As of now I have a growing headache, my mouth tastes of… well, let's not be specific, and I am waiting for the finer details of what we might be going to be killing, but I am coping well enough, general.'

Nasuba smiled and began to stride past them, looking up at the gantries and supply hoists.

Tetracauron caught the amused look in Cartho's eye and fell in beside the general.

'You will be ready to walk?' she said to him.

'We are always ready.'

'Good,' she said, and kept walking.

Mercury Wall kill-zone

The Knights and Titans ran across the land, the green of the Solaria Titans a mottled echo of the emerald of the Vyronii Knights. They ran in two groups: the three Warhounds behind in a loose triangle, the long-legged Cerastus Knight and its three Armigers spread in an arc ahead. They were moving swiftly, power flowing to motive drives and auspex.

Mist rose from the ground as the heat of the day increased. Lichens and fungi and weeds had spread over the plateau of ground and crushed rubble as the cold of winter had become spring, then summer. Ancient seeds and spoors unearthed from the ground by the creation of the kill-zone had blossomed in the heat and water. Dark green and purple leaves floated in pools of run-off. Grey puffballs the size of human heads swelled on crests of rockcrete shards, clouds of dust stirred into the air by hot winds. Tangles of bright green leaves and heavy-headed mauve flowers had grown in thick carpets in places, their trumpets open to the daylight that reached them from the layer of cloud and smoke above. On the wall they said that when the wind turned it sometimes brought the scent of blossom from the wasteland, thick and heavy, cloying, like a call to the sleep of suffocation.

Acastia saw the land pass on the screens inside *Elatus'* cockpit. There was no sign of anything hostile, not machine or man. It was quiet, a land of heat shimmers, fog and the coloured smears of vegetation across the grey blanket of rubble.

'Give me threat and observation status,' came Caradoc's

demand across the vox. He had loosened the leash of neural
control, but yanked it taut again whenever he spoke to them.

'Nothing on visual or sensors, my liege,' said Dolloran.

'Nothing, lord,' said Pluton.

'Likewise,' said Acastia. She could feel the spike of anger
across the helm link. She knew why. Pride, and the possibility that her words had brought him out here on a false quest
that would bring shame rather than glory.

'All units.' The voice of the Solaria princeps rose over the
vox. 'Track south-west on transmitted bearing. Hold formation
and keep your eyes sharp. We are going to skirt the Cradle
and come down to Lake Voss' northern shore.'

'Is there an intelligence update, honoured princeps?' asked
Caradoc, tone smooth.

'No,' said the Solaria princeps, 'but if I were them, that's where
I would start a spear-tip push. Looking at the topography – the
lake and channels give them access into the kill-zone core, and
there is dead ground out of sight from all but the top guns on
the wall.'

'Princeps,' said Acastia. She felt a cold surge across the neural
link to Caradoc. 'Recommend bearing south-south-west to
come in on the southern shore of the lake. If they use it as
an axis of advance, they will be aiming for the dead ground
and wreckage-maze at Karalia's Grave.'

There was a pause, an inhalation of breath in her own mouth.

'Understood and confirmed,' said the voice of the Solaria
princeps. 'My thanks for your insight, bondsman. All units
track south-south-west. Bondsman, set and lock our bearing.'

'As you command,' said Acastia, keying the directional and
waypoint data into broad transmission. Caradoc's anger was
a growing headache at the back of her skull.

The sun had begun to set over the silent land of the kill-
zone. Still they had seen nothing, not even the signs of recent

enemy passing that way. Acastia found it increasingly unnerving. It was as though the presence of their foe had been inhaled back, out of sight. Lake Voss was a mirror to the sky above. She looked at it as they strode on. Heat misted its surface. Insects hovered above it, circling in buzzing murmurations. Acastia paused, then turned the gaze of *Elatus'* head towards the water and pushed the magnification to maximum. The water was rippling. Across the still lake tiny shivers lapped the shoreline. Her eyes went back to the haze of humidity hanging above the water. There was no wind.

'All units,' she said, opening the broad vox. 'Enemy engines are close, repeat, enemy engines are close.'

The vox spat and clicked with distortion.

'What are you doing?' snapped Caradoc across a direct vox-link. 'There is nothing on visuals or sensors.'

'Look at the water,' replied Acastia but on the broad vox.

'You shall–'

'Look at the water,' she repeated.

'Vibration patterns,' came the voice of one of the Solaria Titans.

'Sensors show nothing, honoured princeps,' said Caradoc.

'I can see that,' snapped the voice of Solaria. 'All units, slow and pace, full battle readiness. Enemy in proximity.'

The vox snapped again. An alarm buzzer began to sound in *Elatus'* cockpit. The auspex erupted with red threat runes that spun and exploded into clouds of red static. Sparks danced across the screen as it flickered into a distorted wash of green. She could smell burning plastek and hot metal. She swore, and curbed *Elatus'* forward pace, yanking its head and lens-eyes around.

And there they were.

Figures on the shoreline. Vast figures, legs hidden in the humidity. Shimmering as though they were stepping out of the heat haze. Shadow grey in the failing light. A ragged crowd extending away out of sight. Walking towards them.

She kicked her steed around and began to lengthen her stride as the vox popped with fragments of orders.

Acastia found that sweat was running over her skin inside her armour as she punched a data stamp into the sighting log and hit transmit. Off in the distance, systems and eyes would hear and process a great threat rendered down to a few lines of cold fact:

Enemy sighted southern edge of Lake Voss.
Mercury-Exultant kill-zone.
Grid two-three-one by four-five-two.

Shard Bastion, Mercury Wall

The sally-ports opened beneath Shard Bastion as the dawn broke. Heat was already pulling fumes from the ground and laying them above it as a grey pall. Rain ran down the three tiers of the Mercury Wall. The cap of clouds above the aegis shield flashed with lightning. Sunlight was a diffuse pus-yellow glare rising beyond a frail veil of vapour. *Reginae Furorem* was the first to step into the light. Yellow and black banded its left shoulder plates, deep blue covered its right and the tilting plate that bore the glyphs of its forging and the honours of its name. Red plates clad its limbs. Pennants hung from its weapons, lank in the damp, hot air. Behind the red crystal of its eye slit, Tetracauron saw the world beyond the wall through the eyes of his engine.

Terrain scanners webbed the ground in orange. Behind them, the void generators and guns of the wall buzzed with a sound like distant beehives. He paused, feeling the fire within rise as he and the engine stopped.

<Weapons check,> he sent.

<Powering carapace cannons to firing threshold,> replied Divisia, even as he felt the tingle of the laser blasters' building power.

<Weapon active,> sent Tetracauron.

<Powering volcano cannon to firing threshold,> said Cartho.

<Weapon active.>

A feeling in his hand like a hot coal burning his skin…

<Activating power fist field,> said Cartho.

Lightning whipped up Tetracauron's left arm, spiking into the base of his brain. He gasped, his hand flexing, haptic sensors echoing the movement in the unfurling of *Reginae Furorem*'s slab-thick digits.

Tetracauron felt the fire and lightning roll through his flesh: pain and beauty and true life.

'Vanguard command, this is Shard Bastion command,' said a distorted human voice at his back. *'You have halted. Is there a problem?'*

'No issue,' replied Tetracauron, hearing his machine echo his will across the vox. 'We walk,' he said, and the last word boomed from *Reginae Furorem*'s war-horns in a rolling roar. Behind it, the other Titans in the sally tunnel took up the call. Sound echoed across the land. Through the root of Shard Bastion the war calls of fifty Battle Titans shook the wall's bones.

At the bastion's pinnacle, General Nasuba felt their call as a tremor beneath her feet as she raised her field glasses to her eyes to look at the land beyond.

In the insulated vault of the primary Ignatum strategium, Sentario heard its echo as a cascade of binharic across the noosphere. She signalled a reply, and within a nanosecond it was taken up by all of the adepts and priests and facto- tums: an answering call in simple code, ancient before the

Martian priests preached its truth; an old and primary imperative spoken at the beginning of all that was sacred, the prayer incanted by the smiths of iron over their forges, the breath of code in the turning of the first wheels, the command given by spark to fuel and fire.

<Ignite,> they said.

In *Reginae Furorem*'s cockpit, Tetracauron heard, and smiled.

<Walk,> he willed, and he and his engine strode from the door into the daylight.

Enemy distance to wall: 130 kilometres, estimated.

TEN

Pilgrims
Cries
Conclave

The Blackstone, Sanctum Imperialis Palatine

'It is the authority of the Praetorian,' said Andromeda, tapping the dais beside the docket. The warden behind the desk did not move or respond. 'It means that you will admit us.'

Still no movement. Mauer moved her eyes over the chamber. It was small, one door in, one door out. The outer door was a metre of hardened adamantium with bolts that had taken eleven seconds to disengage to let them in. The inner doorway was just wide and tall enough that two people could pass through at the same time and not scrape the walls. The door was black, its surface a mirror. She could see no sign of lock or keyhole. The worst part was what it reflected. Each part of the room was there: the walls, the outer door, all perfect. Except that there was no reflection of anything else: no Mauer looking back at her, no Andromeda rolling her eyes, no Sindermann tapping his old fingers on the case of his dataslate. They had decided to use the authority Sindermann already had established to enter Blackstone; it was less attention-drawing, and less easily noticed. They were all part of the Order of Interrogation, now. Mauer had removed her insignia and rank marks and fixed a flimsy ribbon of parchment to her coat with the mark and writ that said she was a person authorised to ask and record questions.

'I remember you,' said the warden. He had the uniform and gear of the Solar Auxilia and bore his weight on crutches that spoke of combat injury. He looked sour, too, thought Mauer.

'And I you, Warden Vaskale,' said Sindermann. 'I take it everything is in order and we may enter?'

'Different to last time,' said Vaskale, eyes flicking over Mauer and Andromeda. 'You have new friends. Look a bit more serious.'

'Things change,' said Sindermann.

'What happened to the last one?' asked Vaskale. 'The lad? What was he called? Karri? Tary?'

'Hari Harr,' said Sindermann. 'His name was Hari Harr.'

'Didn't want to come along this time?'

'He went to Eternity Wall,' said Sindermann softly.

Vaskale was silent for a long moment, then licked his lips and looked down at the security wafer.

'All in order. You may go ahead,' he said. 'Once you have entered you will need to be escorted. I will lead you. You will have to follow my instructions.'

'We require no escort,' said Andromeda. 'Our writ as interrogators does not require us to be watched over.'

'You shall follow my instructions,' repeated the warden to Andromeda, then glanced at Sindermann. 'Like you say, things change.'

Andromeda looked like she was going to argue. Then she shrugged.

'Fine,' she said.

The warden did not move, but continued to stare at them.

'We will follow your instructions,' said Mauer.

'Good,' said Vaskale. 'Because it's for your good as much as anyone's.'

'How so?' asked Sindermann.

'Trouble,' Vaskale replied, and stepped back. In front of them the mirror-smooth door cracked. Hairline fractures became triangles, which folded back and in until the door was no longer there. Mauer waited for the warden to demand the gun that hung on her hip, but he said nothing of it.

'You're not worried by someone taking a gun in there?' said Andromeda.

'No,' said Vaskale as he followed them through the opening, but added nothing more.

The door closed behind them, unfolding back into being as they stepped into the passage beyond.

The air was cool and dry, as though the humidity and heat smothering the rest of the Palace was a separate world. The light in the passage was blue-white and stark. None of the walls reflected the light. All were the same glassy black substance as the door. Their steps lifted chime-like notes from the metal floor.

Mauer had heard of the Blackstone. It was one of the things she knew she was not supposed to know about. Before the war its use had been bound up with functions that she was frankly pleased to be ignorant of. Since Horus' coming to Terra it had performed a simpler function – a gaol for those too dangerous to let loose, but that the Imperium for reasons of its own did not want to kill. Mauer did not understand that compassion in such times. If someone was a threat then they were running out of reasons to live, if any existed in the first place. She was far from convinced that this was a place to find answers to the kind of problems they were looking at.

'Have you come to see the same one as before?' asked Vaskale.

'Yes,' said Sindermann.

'Just her?'

Sindermann nodded.

'She's out of her cell most of the time, will take some tracking down,' said Vaskale, pausing at a console mounted into the passage wall and punching in commands. 'Talking to the other prisoners. What's the purpose of that now?'

No one answered. The warden frowned at the console screen.

'Him again…' he muttered and shook his head. 'Follow,' he said, and began to move down the passage.

Mauer glanced at Andromeda, but the gene-witch was already following the limping man, her bare feet padding on the bare metal.

The warden led them down corridors and through echoing chambers. They passed locked cell doors and open shafts that led up and down to darkness. There were a lot of people in the Blackstone, Mauer had been reviewing the figures, but they saw none of them. Silence was their companion.

'Cheerful, wouldn't you say?' remarked Andromeda after a while.

'Better this way. You want to be out when it's night,' said Vaskale.

'What happens at night?' asked Sindermann.

'The stones sing dreams,' said Vaskale, but then would offer no more.

Mauer watched Andromeda idly run her hand along the wall as they walked.

'Almost reminds me of home.' Mauer shot her a glance that Andromeda caught and answered with a facial shrug. 'The fanes of my kind are a bit like this, all smooth, dark rock and layered symbolism. We prefer curves to all these straight lines but if I squint and don't pay attention to the details I could be back up there.'

'You miss it?' said Mauer.

'No,' said Andromeda. 'The Imperium came two centuries ago and killed the Selenar cult. We made a deal to live a little longer, and sold our sacred truth to mass-produce monsters for the Emperor. For that we got to die slow rather than quick. There were hardly any of us left when I made another deal and came to help the Imperium. Now... maybe I am the last of my kind...' Andromeda's voice trailed off. She seemed suddenly not young but very, very old. 'No, I don't miss it. I mourn for it.'

Another shrug. Mauer was wondering how to reply, when the warden leading them slowed and stopped beside a door set in the passage wall.

'Ah,' said Andromeda, her voice quick and light again. 'This must be it.'

The warden fitted a key into the door's lock, then paused.

'The one she is talking to in here...' he began, then bit his lip again. 'I don't know why she talks to him so much. All the rest she has never come back to, but this one... her and the Custodian. They keep coming back.'

'Whose cell is it?' asked Mauer.

'Doesn't matter, does it?' said Vaskale, shaking his head as though trying to dislodge an unpleasant thought, and triggered the lock. 'After all, it's not him you came to see, is it?'

The cell door opened.

Sindermann gave a curious look at Vaskale and then went in, Mauer and Andromeda behind him.

A woman in prison overalls sat cross-legged on the floor. Her hair was an unkempt dirty blonde, and her eyes sharp as she looked up at them. Across from her, a small old man sat on a cot, his back straight, his eyes two black pearls in a broad face. He smiled at them.

'Ah,' said Basilio Fo. 'Are these your friends, Mamzel Keeler? I wonder what they want to talk about?'

* * *

East Phoenicium Wastes

The hive was still there. It rose before Oll and his crew as they crossed the white land, glittering in the distance. The dust beneath their feet was fine. Time had ground down the shells of a lost sea and the glass of dead civilisations to make it, and the winds of Terra had spread it out across hills and valleys to smooth them down. It was blinding. Sunlight reflected, bouncing shimmering ghosts into the air. Oll had had to wind a scarf around his head and reduce the world to a slit to avoid blindness as they crossed the land. They had been walking for most of the day, and the sun had not dimmed. In fact, it had not seemed to move at all, as though its disc were stuck to the dome of the sky. That was just one thing that was not right amongst a pile of wrong things that Oll had been gathering as they trudged on. The hive on the horizon was another.

He had seen Hatay-Antakya Hive before, a short-long time ago, when he had decided to come back to the old places during the early days of the war that had become the Great Crusade. It had been called the new Babylon then, by conservators and ideologues who had no idea what the first Babylon was or why they knew the term. Oll, who had seen the first, second and many other versions of Babylon and Rome and Xanadu rise in name and spirit numerous times, thought that the idea fitted only loosely. The old Babylon and its gardens had been a wonder in its time, made more so by the fact that those were times when to raise a palace or a city took generations and the blood of millions. The price was still the same, and the time too, but the results were on a new scale. Hatay-Antakya was a hydroponic hive. In the desolation of Terra, it produced crops, fruit, propagated plants lost to the rest of the world. Vast hydrological systems pulled billions of gallons through the pipes, pools, tanks and aqueducts that made up most of the hive structure. Crystal domes and enviro-blisters dotted its outer surfaces. Elevated canals swept in arcs between the sub-spires and spurs. On the upper surfaces the craft of the propagation houses were displayed in layered gardens and false lakes cupped in vast bowls of copper.

The rulers of the green-jewel of a hive swam in plunge pools a kilometre across, floating amongst the pads and blossoms of water flora. In the lower levels, huge loops of tunnels were filled with stark light, with plants moving between pressure and temperature-controlled areas as they passed through the cycles of germination, growth, flowering, fruiting and decay. In the depths, huge pits absorbed every scrap of waste matter and composted them in caverns the size of city districts. The heat from the decomposition flowed up in ducts to warm the growth of new crops.

It was remarkable, proof that the drive that had led humans to cut water channels and make the land green could endure even in the desolation that remained where earth had been. Babylon, Eden, Avalon… just like all the rest and yet not, hope and hubris given seed and grown. Oll had seen Hatay-Antakya and wondered how long it would last, and if it would end like all the others.

Looking at the hive's shadow on the horizon, he was not sure he now wanted to know the answer. Sometimes it rose as it should, a low, ragged mountain, but sometimes when he looked up there was something else there, the shadows of domes and towers that had not stood there for a long time, places that Oll knew and had seen burn or fall or drown.

'What's that?' It was Rane. The lad was up ahead, walking just ahead of Zybes. 'Just there at the bottom of the slope – you see it?' Oll looked the way the boy was pointing. There was a line, dark against the white ground, like a wide ribbon of shadow. Oll squinted. The line was moving, like water moving in a river.

'That's people,' said Zybes.

He was right – as Oll focused he could see that it was a long, loose line of people, their clothes and shadows grey against the daylight.

'Look like they are going the same way as us,' said Krank. 'Towards the hive.'

'Refugees,' said Rane.

'Maybe…' said Oll. In the back of his mind a series of things were stacking up into a shape that was neither clear, nor welcoming. 'Except we haven't seen any signs of battle near here, have we?'

'The ships,' said Rane, jerking his head in the direction that they had seen the shadows of the warships in the distant sky.

'But not here,' said Oll. 'No smoke on the horizon, no planes in the sky… It's quiet.'

Quiet, that was it, that was what had been growing as an itch in his thoughts; it was quiet. No cries, barely even the sound of the wind.

'That's why they are here,' said Krank. 'When war comes, those that can get out do and they find the quietest, safest places they can.'

'The nearest major population centre is over two hundred leagues away,' said Oll, reaching up under his scarf to rub the sweat gathering in his frown. He did not like this; most of all he didn't like the feeling that there was something that he wasn't seeing, just around a corner, coming closer. 'If there is no war here, then those people must have walked a long way to get here.'

'People will come a long way to get away from war,' said Rane, then half turned away. Oll knew that Rane was thinking of Calth, of Neve – the wife who was still waiting for him on a dock in a city that no longer existed.

'True,' said Oll. 'True.'

'Oll…' It was Katt. 'Oll, look back that way.'

He turned and looked, squinting as the glare of the sun shifted in his eyes. There was nothing, just the flooded bone white of the wasteland. Katt raised a hand to point as though sensing his puzzlement. He followed the direction of her finger, and saw what she had seen.

Careful, clever, looking behind when everyone else was looking forwards, that was Katt.

There was a shadow in the distance. Small and smeared by the heat haze, just a smudge of grey amongst the white that might have been a leafless tree or stump of rock… But could also have been a figure walking, or running closer. Coming after them.

Shuffle-tap… Shuffle-tap…

Cold in the dark of the Labyrinth.

'How long has it been there?' he asked.

'I don't know,' said Katt. 'I watched it for a minute. It doesn't seem to be getting any closer, but I am sure it *is* closer.'

'The unknown waiting ahead and following behind…' he said, half under his breath.

He was thinking. From here it should have been them all making the decisions, choosing the path: him, John and Her.

He was still thinking when a clank of machinery turned his head. Graft, the old Munitorum servitor that had been with him before Calth and had followed them since, was clanking forwards on its tracks towards the distant column of people.

'Where's it going?' asked Rane.

'Finally blown its last fuse,' said Zybes, snorting.

'Graft,' called Oll, and he moved after the servitor as it trundled down the slope. 'Wait up. Where are you going?'

'This way, Trooper Persson,' said Graft, its voice the same modulated drone as ever. 'This is the way.'

Oll felt a cold thump in his guts.

'The way? The way to what?'

The servitor was moving faster, and Oll was having to run to keep up. The others were following, running down the slope after him. In front of them, the faces of the column of people walking at the base of the slope had turned towards them. He heard shouts, calls and cries. Some sounded alarmed; some sounded excited, joyful. There were colours amongst the grey throng he noticed now, scraps of brightness, smudges of colour.

Graft was still ahead of him, the servitor's units clanking as it closed the ground. There was a buzzing coming from its speaker grille.

Oll stumbled. His eyes were swimming. The hive in the distance was suddenly much larger, much closer, glittering and shining under the sun. How had he thought it was so far away? It was right there, just a short walk away, just another step…

Behind him he heard one of the others shout. Katt? Zybes?

'*No*,' said a voice in his head. '*Do not take this turn…*'

John?

'It's a dream, but it can be real…'

You! You, old friend, but this is not then.

+Oll! Help us! Oll!+

And then the hammer of pain exploded in his skull and he was falling…

But not hitting the ground. Caught in mid-air or between the fall and having fallen. The slope and the sun-bleached sky swirled into white and ochre.

Like sand, Oll thought, like sand churned up by a breaker on a bright shore.

+Oll…+

John? He formed the thought in reply, trying to make it clear.

+I can't do this for long, Oll. It's… this place.+ John's voice was coming from above and around him, moving out of sight.

John, where are you?

+I tried to reach you but got it wrong, overshot, landed where we predicted you arrived, but you were not here. I... we thought you might have been taken to paradise so went looking, got caught. Now...+ There was a stutter in John Grammaticus' voice, a blink in the world.

+Yes, that's right.+ John's voice was suddenly clipped, businesslike, controlled, as though tone and words had been cut from another time and place and glued in place here. +It will be difficult to achieve but not impossible – destabilisation is always more difficult than simple mayhem, but rest assured it can be done.+

John?

Another blink, and now there were clouds of colour fizzing in a black void like a riot of fireworks.

+Haven't you heard that song?+ John's voice was a chuckling slur now, rolling with drink and mischief. +Well I guess I can sing it if you aren't going to shoot me for crudity...+

Something grabbed hold of Oll and spun him up and over. He could feel something wrapping around him, toothed suckers biting through cloth, thorns in his skin. An echo of pain that did not belong to him.

John, can you hear me? We–

+There was a good wife of Europa...+

John, let me go! We are coming for you, but you need to let me go.

The pain broke. The sparking fire of the world snapped off. Oll felt like he was floating, rolled and turned by the surge of the tide.

+Hurry...+ said the distant voice of John Grammaticus. +They know you are here.+

Oll was looking up at the sky. He had not opened his eyes; they were already open. He was sitting on the ground at the bottom of the slope he had run down. The others were nearby,

Zybes and Krank had their guns up. Graft was twitching in place, a low burble coming from its speaker grille. Katt was approaching warily, pistol held out of sight at her side.

The river of people they had seen was still moving. He saw them clearly now: men and women, some old, some in the prime of life. The sun had bleached their clothes and the dust cloaked them in a pale powder. Wire-strung shards of multicoloured glass and plasters hung around their necks like garlands. He could see the bones showing through the skin of some, the flesh sucked from their frames by starvation. Others rolled with fat, sweat pouring from them. All of them were gazing in the direction they walked, towards the distant shadow of the hive. Some were grinning, others drooling, the muscles of their faces slack. Whoops of laughter and a babble of frantic words rose from some and then faded. Most of them did not look at Oll and his companions, but just shuffled onwards. There was blood on the ground, he noticed, red mush and pink sand under the dust-covered feet.

'Do you hear it?' Oll looked around. Two figures had stepped from the crowd, and were standing three paces away. They were very still, Oll noted. One was a bloated, towering thing wrapped and wound in tattered multicoloured fabric that billowed and rippled in the wind. He could see nothing of its face. The other was very tall, thin. A patchwork cloak of velvet and silk tatters hung from her. A veil of frayed red hid the upper half of her face above the mouth. He could see that her skin was cracked by heat and dusted with a powder whiter than the desert sand. Barbed hooks pierced her lower lip and chin, and finger bones hung from them on loops of plastek cord. They rattled as she spoke.

'You hear it, don't you?' she asked, her voice high and melodious.

'Get back!' snapped Zybes; his gun was pointed at the pair.

Behind and beside him, Rane and Krank had their guns out too. Katt was edging wide, poised, eyes focused on them. The fabric-swathed figure turned the lump that must have been its head. The river of people behind them flowed on, unseeing or uncaring.

'Pilgrims,' said the woman, holding up her hands. Oll noticed that they were scarred, the tips of the digits curved by glass blades. 'What do you seek?'

Oll stood, fully straightening, dusting off his hands.

'We thought you might have been taken to paradise,' John had said.

'Yes,' Oll said, and stepped forwards towards the veiled woman. 'We seek paradise. Will you show us the way?'

The Blackstone, Sanctum Imperialis Palatine

There was a moment of quiet as the little man on the cot smiled up at them. Then Andromeda was lunging forwards, snarling, reaching for Mauer's gun. Sindermann was turning in surprise, Keeler's mouth was opening to say something.

'Kill him!' screamed Andromeda.

Mauer moved faster. She hit Andromeda in the gut just below the ribs, open-handed. The gene-witch cannoned backwards, hit the wall and slid down. Mauer had her gun in her hand; she had drawn it as she had hit Andromeda. She held it ready, eyes moving across the faces staring at her. She looked at where Andromeda-17 was gasping, trying and failing to get to her feet.

'Don't do that again,' she said, calmly. 'Ever.'

The little man on the cot was still smiling.

'He…' hissed Andromeda, fighting to draw breath. 'He must die.'

'A little extreme given that we have not even been properly introduced,' said the man. 'You are one of the Selenar, aren't you? My, my, and I thought all of your kind had slunk away to expire.'

'Be quiet,' said Mauer. The man raised his hand as though in apology. 'No one moves. No one twitches towards anyone. Understood.'

Nods all round. Sindermann was looking at the man on the cot, his face unreadable.

'Who is this?' he asked softly.

'His name is Basilio Fo,' said Euphrati Keeler.

Sindermann's mouth opened slightly and then shut.

'You know who he is?' asked Mauer.

Fo tilted his head. Mauer was certain the man was yet to blink.

'He is a monster,' said Andromeda, still breathing hard.

'From your kind that might be considered a compliment,' said Fo.

'I said be quiet,' snapped Mauer. She looked at Sindermann.

'He was a criminal who escaped the Unification War.'

'Oh come,' said Fo. 'I was more than that. You are Sindermann, aren't you? The iterator? We've never met but I've admired your work from afar – cultural mutilation carried out with such precision… my compliments.'

Mauer aimed her gun at him. Fo raised his hands again as though in apology.

'The accounts of the purge of his enclaves during Unification… well, there are phrases used that speak enough – flesh husks, bio-resculpture, gene-phage torture, things that wanted to scream but could not. The others who opposed the Emperor all died – Cardinal Tang, Narthan Dume, the Crimson Walkers all gone, but not him. He got away, somehow. He was hunted for most of the Crusade, under the broadest remit and urgency – complete and total destruction of his works and those who he had contact with. Complete and validated confirmation of termination or capture.' Sindermann looked back at Fo. 'He is the last of the Lords of Old Night.'

Mauer looked at Andromeda.

'If you want to get up without me putting you back down you are going to have to explain what just happened.'

Andromeda was staring at Fo, her eyes bright, but did not answer.

'It might be kinder if you let me explain,' said Fo. 'She has reasons for what she did.' Fo looked at Mauer, face placid, an eyebrow raised. He looked as dangerous as a breath of air. 'Shall I tell you why?'

Mauer hesitated, then nodded. Fo tilted his thanks.

'We have history, myself and the Selenar gene-cults. Old history.' He looked at Andromeda and nodded. 'I remember your clone-kin when your reincarnation counts had barely started to rise through single digits. A lot of failure to their work back in those times. They had this idea of finding spiritual truth through iterations of genetic incarnation. Lovely idea, just a shame it's just another story. They had found some beauty, though, secrets buried down in the cells. Small things, wonderful things. You called me a lord but unlike your Emperor I have humility – I know when someone has reached beyond my own achievements. The Selenar had done so well... but I had to take measures to secure what I wanted from them, and those measures were severe.'

'You are a thief and a defiler,' snarled Andromeda.

Fo's lips twitched.

'I am sure this is out of character for her,' he said. 'Don't judge her too harshly – the hate, it's coded into her. This one has never actually seen me before, but the Matriarchs locked me into their hindbrain threat evolution. Specific pheromone recognition linked to primary levels of kill-to-defend instinct – all baked into her from skin to bone. It's taking her a lot of willpower not to try to reach me. Gene-daemon, is that what you still call me?'

'Sounds like a perfect reason to kill you right now,' Mauer replied, and raised her gun.

'No,' said Keeler, jumping up and raising a hand. 'Wait.'

Mauer did not fire. But she didn't lower the gun either.

'You are Keeler,' said Mauer.

Keeler nodded.

'We came for you,' said Mauer. 'And he is not part of the conversation.' Mauer moved her eye to the right.

'You can't kill him,' said Keeler, and there was something… something in the calmness of her voice that stopped Mauer pulling the trigger.

Fo grinned at her from the other end of the barrel.

'I am being helpful, you see,' he said. 'Maybe I can help you, too. That's why you are here, isn't it? For help?'

'No,' said Andromeda.

Sindermann looked carefully from Keeler to Fo.

'What help could a monster like this be to our cause, Euphrati?' he asked.

'Not to your cause, Kyril Sindermann,' came a voice from by the door.

Mauer whirled, hearing the door sealed with a clink of metal and a whir of cogs. This was a trap; she had no idea why, but she had walked right into a trap with her eyes wide shut. She saw something like a heat-haze shimmer, a glimpse of gold, and then her pistol was tumbling out of her grasp before her trigger finger could squeeze more than air.

A golden giant stood beside the door, pulling the remains of the falsehood from his form.

'Be still and at peace,' said the Custodian. 'This is an important moment and one best approached with delicacy.'

From his cot, Basilio Fo gave a dry chuckle.

Magnifican

The night had turned through the sky four times before Shiban stopped walking. A broken arch curved above him. The sky was dark overhead, stained at the edges by reds and oranges and yellows that bled into the black, flickering sometimes, fading or growing. He had not seen the stars since the cloud of smoke had swallowed the blue sky that had greeted him when he woke. No sun, no stars. A grey-ochre pall dragged across the land he passed through in day, and when the light faded it was to black and the ghosts of distant war. The heat remained though. The impact had damaged the temperature control systems in his armour, so that sweat bled from his body. In the day it was a fist squeezing him. At night it seemed that the dark itself was a black shroud, winding tighter and tighter around him. He would need water soon. Even one of his kind had limits. That lesson had been taught to him again and again. His body was damaged to the core, his will pushing him forward. But he had seen no water, not even polluted run-off or liquid caught in a broken pipe. The land was dry and suffocating. A land to die in.

'Forwards,' he growled to himself, but knew that the word was a dry hiss from his lips. He took a step, pushed into the ground with his makeshift staff, and took another step. The broken arch became a shadow behind him and then vanished out of sight. Another cluster of ruins emerged from the gloom ahead. He was keeping to what cover there was, hugging the folds of the land. There had been no sign of the enemy, beyond the distant glare of fires, but that did not mean they were not there. He knew where he was. Each step and light in the sky slid into the sense that held him true and guided him towards the ever-distant promise of the anterior of the Inner Palace walls. Would they still be held by his brothers? Would the Palace still stand? 'It will stand,' he hissed to himself, and felt a bolt of pain as his step lit fire in his legs. 'No backward step. It will stand.'

'Not everything lasts.' Yesugei's voice from just out of sight.

Shiban did not turn to look. The voices had been silent for the last two days and nights.

'What matters lasts,' he growled back. *Another step… Another step forwards.* He could feel the blades of fractured bone grating against each other as his foot touched the ground.

'And what is it that matters?'

'Was I a poor enough student that you had to pursue my correction beyond death?'

A chuckle that touched his skin with the hot breeze of the night.

'What is it that matters?'

The plains stretching out in front of him. Dawn a line of fire beneath a curve of blue where the light of stars glimmered their farewell. The wind rose across his cheek as he smiled and opened his mouth for the cry as he spurred forwards.

'Nothing that can be held in by anything but the wind,' Shiban replied to the ghost in the dark.

'Just so,' said Yesugei's voice.

Shiban shifted his weight to take another step–

He froze, body and mind suddenly alert.

A cry… He had heard a cry. Close but quiet, as though muffled. High and sharp. Small lungs.

He waited, forcing the pain that roared through him down into silence.

Nothing. Just the beat of his own hearts and the click-purr of his armour.

He shifted, muscles and bones screaming anew as he prepared to take another step.

There it was again. Fainter, close by, somewhere amongst the ruins that waited ahead. He reached up and removed his helm. The air breathed across his face, hot and cloying. He listened. His armour enhanced his hearing, but it had taken as much damage as him, more perhaps. Besides, there was a trust that came only from using one's true senses. He forced the pain down until it felt like it was someone else's burden that he was only carrying for a while, stilled his own breath and heart rates until silence stretched within him.

The warm air was a murmur. Somewhere, a long way away, there was shelling, a dull rumble carried through the ground as much as the air.

The hum of a power cable vibrating in the breeze.

Rattles of glass dust shifting on a sheet of broken iron.

He accepted it, let all the sounds into his awareness.

That was the key to so much, to seeing, to hearing, to fighting, to living – accepting the heavens and earth and letting them tell you what was the truth.

The heartbeats came to him, small drum rolls of blood, next to bone and muscle, one louder and stronger, the other small. A human adult, and an infant, crouched out there, one trying to calm the other without making any noise. There was their breath, the air sliding between lips and through teeth.

He listened for a long moment. He had a long way to go and the end was far from certain. He was injured and half the man he was in strength, and what strength he did have he would need for what lay ahead. He should move, pass by like the wind.

His eyes caught light in the distance, a glimmer in the shroud of the night off to the east. From the direction he had come. From the Eternity Wall. He thought of the last hours of that defence, bloody, desperate, defiant. Of the shouts across the vox, and the fires. Futile. Abandoned by higher necessities, by the will of Rogal Dorn, left to die and not even knowing that they were martyrs left beside the path of history.

The beginning of a cry, seeming loud in his mind now, and now the desperate murmuring hush of another human trying to give comfort and calm.

'If you are going to turn me aside,' he murmured to the ghosts of Torghun and Yesugei, 'then you should speak now.'

The wind was his only answer.

He nodded and moved, quickly now, as though his decision had numbed the pain that flared in him. His armour growled and spat. Another cry, loud, unruffled, and a human rising to standing, running, feet scrambling over shards of rock, breathing hard, heart racing.

Shiban reached a heap of torn masonry and girders, climbed it in a bound. The pain blinded him. He landed, pushed off, and half staggered, half ran past the dead eyes of broken windows. Glass and pieces of stone shattered under his tread. He saw the figure, running away, boots slipping on broken tiles, a heavy coat flapping behind it. He pushed forwards.

'Stop,' he called. It was not a shout, but it hit the fleeing figure like a thrown knife. They stumbled, began to fall, arms clutched close. A sharp cry.

Shiban's hand closed on the figure's shoulder, holding them above the fall. The pain inside him was a sun. He had passed through ten strides in a blink. He could taste copper on his teeth and tongue. The figure writhed, gasping. Shiban pulled them back and turned them to face him. Wide, wild eyes in a gaunt face. Matted hair. A ragged beard. Shiban could smell the sweat and dust and ash and fear. He took in the military-issue coat in a glance, the torn epaulettes, the uniform of the Massian Fifth Infantry, the crude binding over a wound in the ribs. And clutched between the human's arms a bundle, a small face squirming, mouth opening to cry out again. The man saw Shiban's eyes move to the child and jerked back, one hand reaching for a gun holstered at his waist. Shiban locked his gaze to the man's and raised a finger. The man stopped, frozen in place like an animal caught in the glare of a stablight.

'Do not attempt it,' said Shiban. 'It will do neither of us any good, and the sound of a las-blast might bring enemies.'

The man nodded slowly. Shiban realised that the human

could barely see in the half-dark. He stepped closer. The distant orange glow caught the lightning bolt on his armour, white still clinging to the scars.

'I am called Shiban, of the Fifth Legiones Astartes.'

'Co…' stammered the man. 'Cole, second lieutenant, Massian Fifth.'

Shiban gave a single nod. There was nothing further about the man that he needed to know. Not now.

'And this?' asked Shiban, looking down at the infant in Cole's arms. It had gone quiet, but its eyes were wide open looking up at Shiban in the dark. Its face wrinkled as it met Shiban's gaze.

'I… I found him in the ruins two days ago. He was crying. Alone… I do not know who… He was… I took him with me. I have tried…'

The man's voice trailed off.

Shiban looked down at the infant for a second more and then back the way he had come. Back along the steps he had taken. Back towards the Eternity Wall space port. Yesugei's smiling face at the edge of sight and memory vanishing.

'You have food?' he asked without looking around. The man did not answer. Shiban could hear confusion beating out a fresh tattoo within the man's heartbeat. 'For you and the child, you have food and clean water?'

He looked at Cole. The man nodded.

'A little. I have been dissolving ration blocks into water for him. He doesn't like it but he takes a little.'

Shiban nodded and turned to face the direction of the Inner Palace, the direction of the path forwards.

'Good,' said Shiban. 'It will be a long path.'

'A long path? What do you–'

'You are coming with me, Lieutenant Cole. It seems that the wind does not wish me to walk alone or with fewer burdens than it can grant me.'

'I…' Cole began to stammer again, teeth clattering. The infant gave a yawn and closed his eyes. Cole nodded. 'With you. Thank you, lord.'

'Not lord,' said Shiban. 'Not out here. Not now. And there is no thanks to give.'

He took a step. The bolt of agony blazed through him. He shifted weight to the metal staff, and took a second step.

'Lord… Shiban, where are we going?' said Cole, following.

'The only way that's left.'

'What's that?'

'Forwards,' said Shiban.

The Blackstone, Sanctum Imperialis Palatine

Mauer looked at the Custodian. Nothing in the cell moved. Then the Custodian leant his spear against the wall, reached up, and removed his helmet. The face beneath was wide, the skin very dark. The eyes were green, Mauer realised, the vivid green of forest leaves in sunlight. He locked his helm to his waist and took his spear again. Every movement, Mauer noticed, was precise and smooth, inhumanly perfect in range and balance, down to the curling of his fingers on the spear haft.

'I have completed the latest set of notes,' said Fo, and he held up a dataslate. 'Or would you rather we did not talk about that in present company?'

The Custodian showed no sign of emotion, but took a step into the room. For something so large, it was impossible that he moved with such pure and perfect grace.

Andromeda got to her feet; her eyes narrowed as she stared at the Custodian as though seeing him for the first time.

'What is your name?' she asked.

'His name is Amon Tauromachian,' said Sindermann.

Amon closed the dataslate and clamped it to his belt. The

gauntlet extended back over his fingers. Apart from his first words it was as though the rest of them were not there, Mauer thought – something to be resolved after the primary concern.

'How much more?' asked Amon.

Fo shrugged.

'Some – it is not something you just jot down, as I said to you before. And anyway, as I am reasonably certain that you will kill me once I am done, you cannot blame me for taking my time, and I am enjoying my conversations with Euphrati that you so graciously agreed to as a condition for my help. I have missed company.'

He looked around at them all.

'What are you helping him with?' asked Andromeda, and Mauer could tell the gene-witch was exerting a lot of control to keep her tone even.

'Oh, a weapon to end the war,' said Fo. 'And what are you here for, my child of moon and stars?'

Andromeda shook her head slowly.

'You should not be here,' said Amon, looking around at them.

'Shouldn't we?' snapped Andromeda, and pulled a holo-projection disc from inside her robes. A cone of cold blue light snapped into being. Inside, the image of the 'I' of the Imperial Regent and the wreathed skull of the Praetorian turned slowly. 'You know our authority.'

'Yes,' said Amon, 'and you know mine, Andromeda-17.'

They stared at each other for a long moment.

'We came to talk to Euphrati Keeler,' said Mauer. 'And her alone.'

'You will need to tell Amon,' said Sindermann, quietly. 'There is no way around that now. He is here. He knows we are here, and depending on how we proceed we will need his help.'

Andromeda opened her mouth, but Sindermann shook his head.

'You know I am right.' Sindermann looked at Amon. 'Besides, I think he might be more open to the possibility than we might assume.'

'What under the light of the sun makes you think that?' asked Andromeda.

'Because we are alive,' said Sindermann.

Amon turned and looked at them all then. His gaze was neutral but completely threatening, thought Mauer, like that of a feline apex predator.

'What you would say to Euphrati Keeler you will say in my presence,' he said.

'And if you don't like it, you will kill us?' said Andromeda.

'Perhaps,' he said, neutrally. 'But if you do not speak that will be a certainty.'

'That sounds like the summation of no choice,' Andromeda said, and bit her lip. 'Fine.' She looked at Mauer and Sindermann. 'Yes?'

Mauer gave a curt nod and moved to the door.

'You have access to another place we can talk?' she asked.

The others were already moving, Keeler half turning to say something to Sindermann. Andromeda shook herself and took a step.

'No need to leave on my account,' said Fo. 'In fact, stay. I prefer art to conspiracy, but it's more interesting than anything else I've run into in a long while. We have quite the conclave assembled here and it would be a shame if you broke it up.' Amon and the rest kept moving, and did not look back at the little man. 'That was not a request.'

The steel in Fo's voice made Mauer's gun hand twitch up. They all turned to look at him. His expression had not changed but there was a cold depth in his eyes – an invitation to the abyss unblinking above the smile.

'You want me to complete the work, Amon Tauromachian,

and this is a new condition of my cooperation. I remain, and
so do you.'

Amon took a step towards Fo. The gesture was pure, fluid
threat, but the man did not move or flinch.

'Kill me,' said Fo, not smiling now. 'Kill me and you will
never get your weapon. Do not give me what I want now and
you never get your weapon. The end of the war, Custodian,
an in-extremis option to save the Emperor from His monstrous spawn. No more Horus. No more primarchs. No more
Astartes. All gone. Problem solved. So close, all you need to do
is let things carry on.' His lips twitched. 'Like the gene-witch
said – the summation of no choice.'

Amon did not move for a second. Then very slowly he
stepped back, turned and gestured to Sindermann, Andromeda and Mauer.

'Speak,' he said.

Mauer nodded.

Keeler looked to Sindermann, turning her back on Fo.

'Kyril,' she said. 'What are you doing?'

'The right thing.'

'A difficult thing to find,' she said.

'I am doing my best.'

She smiled, put out a hand to his shoulder. Mauer could
see the sympathy and sadness on her face.

'It's alright,' she said. 'But I'm not going to like what you've
come to say, am I?'

'I don't know,' he said. 'You once said that your truth might
be the only thing that could win this war... and the time is
coming when there won't be a war left to win.'

Keeler looked at him for a long moment. Mauer found that
she was holding her breath.

'Go on,' she said. 'Tell me.'

So he did.

Mauer listened as Sindermann laid it out, point by point, fact by fact. It was like watching a master watchmaker reassemble cogwork. She knew what the facts were, what the plan was, but as Sindermann finished, she felt as though the idea of it had settled into her – simple and true. No wonder he had been the man to turn victory into true compliance.

Silence slipped into the moment after he finished.

'It would be a lie,' said Keeler, after a moment. 'I would renounce the right to speak the truth of the Emperor's divinity, to be free, and that renunciation would be a lie.'

'A necessary one,' said Sindermann. 'A lie to serve a greater truth.'

Keeler gave the smallest shake of her head.

'And once I was free, what then? A fugitive in a fortress under siege.'

'Then you do what only you can,' said Sindermann. 'Show that the truth is real.'

'The ground is ready,' said Mauer. 'As much as my office has done to try to control it, the rumours of miracles and the hope of the Emperor's protection are spreading. The only thing that is spreading faster is the despair and the hunger for escape. Those who despair want hope, want something to believe in. It would not take much, but it would have to be…'

'Be what, boetharch? What would that not much have to be?'

'Real,' said Mauer.

Keeler held her gaze. 'You don't believe, do you?'

'I believe that there are forces acting that I can't solve with questions and a gun.'

'If it is relevant,' said Fo, and they all turned to where he sat. 'I think that it might work. I am not an expert in aetheric resonances, although the divide between that and the outer edge of bio-alchemy is thinner than you might imagine – but the theory is similar to the use of viral manipulation to destroy other forms of disease, or parasites to stimulate the bio-resistance to other pathogens. Given the position, Mamzel Keeler, I would do what they suggest.' He gave a shrug. 'Though it will mean that I miss our conversations.'

They all looked as though they had just been punched.

'I am an artist, and a pragmatist. I also like being alive in a universe that is not bound and slaved to the will of extra-dimensional thought-parasites who want to use existence as a playground. I am not an idealist, never have been. That was always the problem with your Emperor, He could never accept anything but the ideal – the one path, His path. And that's the same for the rest of you who follow that path – you all think that if someone does not agree with you they would be happy to see everything burn as long as the Imperium, and its beloved Emperor, burns too. Well, I would rather that He becomes a false god than everything becomes slaved to real gods.' He shrugged again. 'From a purely pragmatic view, you understand.'

'You…' began Andromeda, but Keeler started to speak, her voice distant.

'I can't,' said Keeler. Mauer looked at her and saw that the woman's gaze was distant, her face grave. There were shadows in her eyes, and across her face.

'You must,' said Amon. Mauer's head jerked up. The Custodian was utterly still and looking at Keeler. 'You must do what they suggest.'

'You would permit it?' said Mauer.

'I would permit nothing. I only serve the purpose that made me.'

'But you will be complicit in…' began Keeler.

'I will be complicit in nothing,' said Amon. 'I will leave. You will talk. Mistress Keeler will decide. She may not leave until she has made an avowal of solemn intent not to preach the creed that she believes in. If she does that, I will not stand in her way.'

He turned and went to the door. No one moved or spoke. It unlocked with a chorus of turrning gears and sliding bolts. He began to step through, then turned and looked back at them all, his green eyes moving between Sindermann, Andromeda and then Mauer.

'I would be careful,' he said. 'If Mistress Keeler passes beyond these walls she will become a target. The enemy will sense a shift, they will feel the intent in her words and deeds, they will try to stop her. There are also those of our own who will not stand by to let you violate the decrees of the Imperial Truth. You will be hunted, and I cannot intervene.'

'But you are now,' said Keeler.

'An omission is not an action, according to some – I have done nothing other than give you my opinion and say that you cannot leave without an oath that you will not spread the faith you hold to others.' Mauer thought she saw a smile form and fade on Amon's face. 'Besides, as Andromeda-17 will tell you, the Custodians cannot act from their own feelings, only in service of their purpose.'

'And that is?' asked Mauer.

'The preservation of the Emperor,' said Amon, 'in the face of any threat and by any means.'

He looked away and went through the door, leaving them to look after him, and listen to the locks re-engage.

Sindermann broke the quiet, turning back to Keeler.

'I am sorry, my friend, but I feel time is running fast. Will you do it? Will you take the oath and leave here?'

Keeler was still for a long moment, and then she looked up, eyes fixed on the ceiling, or perhaps on something beyond. Her mouth moved, speaking silent words. Then her head dropped, and she shook herself. She looked up again. There was sorrow in her eyes. For a second Mauer felt as though she was falling, and with her went the voices of all the things she had left behind and never looked back at – her father, dying alone forty years in the past; the friends who had never come back; the man who had been brave before he had become a murderer, looking up at her as she aimed the gun.

'Yes,' said Keeler. 'I will take the oath. I will tell the lie. It shall be done.'

ELEVEN

We are the bearers of fire
Shadows in the pyre
Screaming with our own voices

Lake Voss shore, Mercury-Exultant kill-zone

Lake Voss had been a pool caught in a fold on the ground seven months in the past. Five years before that it had not existed. Three years before that, the nascent Karalia had risen three kilometres into the air from the spot where the lake now sat. Rogal Dorn had ordered the land beyond the Ultimate Wall cleared, and the labour armies and Mechanicum levelling engines had obeyed. Karalia had been pulled apart, its metal going to the war forges to clad fortifications, its fabric ground into dust and gravel. Karalia Hive remained only as a nub of metal and broken machines.

The rains of Terra had come. Channels had snaked across the bare earth, cutting their own mark, making topography in the new land. Small folds in the ground and low hills of spoil became water sheds. Creases in dust and debris became channels, became rills, became erratic rivers filled by spoil water and the melted snow of winter. The pool that would be

Lake Voss began to fill. A macro extractor had left a cut in the ground, perhaps the first of many that did not follow. Perhaps, it was simply forgotten before it began or the machines were re-tasked before they began. Later, water gathered there and found it could not drain down into the soil of Terra. A sheet of compacted and heat-fused metal lay under the surface, the bones of some city raised and reduced to slag in a war no longer remembered. The water could not pass down so it deepened on the surface. Before the Warmaster's ships darkened the skies, it was already eight kilometres long at its longest point. Water channels snaked across the desolation to find and feed it. The water was clear, all life kept from clouding its depths by the chemicals leeched from the ground. The pilots of the patrol craft that went overhead said that they could see down to the deepest point below its surface, and that the shapes of the abandoned excavators lay under the water growing bright flowers of multicoloured rust.

The ordnance masters picked landmarks as they ranged the guns and drew up the fire plans of the wall armaments. Some were given names, granted with little thought or consideration besides the need to bring a form of order to the newly flattened land beyond the Palace. The growing lake took the name 'Voss' for reasons that were never considered and not remembered. It shared the land with ordnance codes, and names granted with equally little care: Karalia's Grave, Drain Reach 45-56, Night Water, and on.

When the Warmaster came and the great aegis shields lit above the Palace, Lake Voss drank deeply and grew. The interaction of the shield layer bred storms inside and above the aegis. Rain fell in deluges on the edge of the wall where shield and air met. The precipitation from inside the Inner Palace drained from its buildings and streets. Torrents gushed down pipe and tunnel networks, some refined to slake the thirst of

those within, but most poured into the land beyond the wall.
New rivers cut their way through the plateau. Some found the
channels already made by the rains and turned them from
irregular streams into tangles of broad rivers. New lakes were
formed and swelled. Lake Voss spread and deepened day by day
until it was a long blade of flat water, twenty-five kilometres
wide and sixty long, cutting through the Mercury-Exultant
kill-zone into the blind zone beyond.

Incursion forces had used it as an axis of advance since the
first troops had touched Terran soil. The undulations in the terrain around it and on its shoreline created dead ground where
even war engines were out of sight of the wall guns over a hundred kilometres away. There had been battles on its margins
before and the corpses and wrecks of those engagements lay
in the mud or on the slopes of rubble. That the enemy would
use it now as the incision point for a new advance was predictable, but they had never come in such force or with such
strength before.

Tetracauron had wanted to see the ground of battle himself, with his own eyes, and so had floated his consciousness
between the machine and his body. The sky beyond *Reginae Furorem*'s eye-ports was darkening, bruising through the
layer of cloud and smoke. They were just coming over a low
rise of grey stone, fifty engines arrayed in staggered lines, the
red, blue, yellow and black a garish shout of defiance against
the draining light. Runs of rubble ran down the slope before
them. With his human ears he could hear the rumble of metal
and the hiss of pistons, a song of thunder voiced through
machines. Behind them the cohorts of the secutarii troops
followed, embarked in transports so that they could keep pace.
Five thousand bonded troops and with them forty Knight
Questoris of the thrall houses of Ignatum. These were not
oathed Knights but warrior machines wholly thralled to the

Legio, their livery red and jagged with yellow and black to mark them as a diminutive of the greater machines they fought beside. In battle, these Knights and the secutarii protected the god-machines' flanks and rear, and countered the threat of infantry and armour units. Though the weapons of mortals were pinpricks to a Titan, en masse a thousand pinpricks could bleed a walking god of strength.

<Closing on enemy,> came Divisia's sending. She was the primary connection to the auspex and signal systems. <The hunter group has them in sight. Thirty kilometres. Projections put the engagement site right on the southern shore of the lake.>

<Signal the hunter group to track them until we engage,> he sent.

<I hear the Solaria princeps in command of them is a killer,> impulsed Cartho. <I'm not sure she will want to hang back while we do the work. They will want to taste blood.>

<This is our moment of fire,> impulsed Divisia. <The torch of battle was given to us to carry.>

<They have cause, Divisia,> sent Tetracauron levelly. <They are a shadow left by the fire of Beta-Garmon. Vengeance matters more when it is all you have left. Signal them that they can join battle once we have fired the first shot.>

<Yes, my princeps.>

<The enemy seem to be advancing without ground unit support,> sent Cartho. <Engines only, en masse.>

Tetracauron closed his eyes to the deepening twilight and let his mind fold back into the brightness of the incandescence. The world shrank back in the whirl of bright data and the breath of reactor heat. He was walking. His stride carrying him forwards. The weight of his weapons a warmth on his hands. The presence of his kin a scattering of flames. The enemy was still out of direct sight, hidden by the deceptive folds in this

MORTIS   249

flattened land and the heat haze still smearing the darkening
horizon. They were there, though, he could feel it. The old
enemy. Mortis, the legion of the cull, the reapers and the coun-
ters of the dead. There had been a time when they had been
allies, bound together as part of the Triad Ferrum Morgulus.
They had defended the earliest truth of the Machine-God on
Mars and stood as the first of the Titan Legios, primogenitors
in tradition and renown before all those that would follow.
Now they walked to war against each other, and Tetracauron
could not help but feel that this was an inevitable moment
long delayed. Here they both were, kin of the forge, the iron
and steel of each poured from the same crucibles, walking to
war for what had to be the last time.

<They will burn...> sent Divisia softly, as though speaking
to his thoughts. <All of them.>

The reactor in his chest growled.

<Hear me,> he willed, and felt the spirits of the engines
answer. <All engines, weapons and shields to full readiness.
We are the bearers of fire...> A moment, a lengthened break
of sensation as he felt the reactor's fury draw breath.

<Merge auspex and targeting data,> willed Cartho.

<They are coming in broad and in depth,> came Divisia's
pulse of thought. <All the turning cogs of Mars, there's a lot
of them!>

<Maintain stride speed,> sent Tetracauron. <They will be
pushed south by the lake unless they want to wade, and Divisia... try to keep it respectful.>

<Yes, my princeps.>

<Not for me, but the machine listens to your soul, remember –
best not to anger it before we have a target. Once we have them
in gunsight then swear all you want.>

<Yes, my princeps.>

<Good. Do the wall guns have range on them?>

<Forty per cent of top guns sighted and zeroed,> replied Cartho, <holding for your command.>

<Just forty per cent?>

<Lines of sight are not clear for direct fire in this area.>

<Forty is good enough. Let's hope that they are as accurate as General Nasuba says. For the rest we will just have to rely on ourselves. All machines, light and charge your weapons. Fire is truth.>

<Princeps, I have the hounds from the Legio Solaria and a lance of Knights closing and requesting data and signal mesh. Code identifiers verify.>

<Granted and link,> he willed. His sight flicked with tendrils of green as the data-link with the other legion's machine-spirits bled across the incandescence. <Solaria, this is Princeps Senioris Tetracauron. I have field command for the engagement – assimilating your auspex and visual log data and realigning battle protocols. We aim to burn them all, but if you are here for blood and fire then lock into step and ready your guns.>

<Our honour and pleasure, Ignatum,> came the voice of Abhani Lus Mohana. Tetracauron felt the snarl of aggression in the Solaria connection. He felt his flesh smile. He liked this one.

<Solaria, you are closest to the enemy,> he sent. <Your formation has target and range control for the wall guns. Guide our wrath true.>

<Compliance,> replied Abhani, and the link faded from Tetra-cauron's sight and senses.

<All Ignatum engines, synchronise weapon firing cycles.> He saw the enemy closing, shadows and red smears in the whirl of flame-orange data. The links to his crew and the engines of his maniple and demi-Legio were so close that they felt like his own thoughts.

<Signal lag compensators and data purge activating.> Cartho.

<Stride at sixty-four and accelerating.> Divisia.

<Target lock held.> Cartho.

<Fire,> he whispered to the soul of the gods he walked with.

Ignatum obeyed. Missiles, plasma shells, beams of heat and light and pulses of exotic energy sheeted through the gloom.

The combined fire hit the advancing Mortis Titans in a staggered attack that marched through their ranks from front to back. Missiles hit, streaking high and falling in a rolling wave of explosions. Blast spheres shrieked out. Fire smeared down collapsing void shields, which burned in glittering cloaks as they fell. A deluge of shells struck at the same moment. Munitions chugged from gatling barrels and streamed from mega-bolters. The void shields on the lead Titans shredded. The shield projectors on a Reaver Titan stuttered and misfired as they tried to come back online, then detonated in a howling explosion. The engine behind walked on into the deluge, its own cannons firing as its forward armour deformed. The energy weapons fired a perfectly timed instant later. Streams of plasma and lances of las-fire reached into the boiling front of flame and stabbed into raw metal. The first true engine kill was a Warlord struck by the volcano and turbo-laser beams from the Reaver twins *Torchbearer* and *Fulgurite*. Their shots struck its central mass and bored into its heart in a flash of vaporising metal, then snapped off. For a second the Warlord swayed, its foot still rising to take the next step. Then its back split apart from inside. Plasma vented out, not in a sphere but in a cloud that howled into the twilight sky, twisting with oily light. The engine fell, thrashing, scrabbling in the sludge of the lake shore. Two more went, blown apart, cored, heads and limbs blown open or into gas. Giants stumbling, falling, crashing down in sprays of mud steam.

The fire wave rolled back through the advancing enemy.

The view through *Reginae Furorem*'s eyes was of a land aflame, rippling, roaring beneath the fog-veiled sunset.

<My princeps, I have vox fire command to Shard Bastion. They are locked and ready to fire on your command.>

He felt fresh waves of power flow into weapons, heat and plasma inhaling into reservoirs.

<Shard Bastion to range and then saturate for effect,> he sent. <The Solaria hunters have target correction.>

In his heart he felt the fire beat against its iron walls. The incandescence pulled his attention back into its blazing heart. He held on for a second to give the command that would loose the guns of the Mercury Wall.

<Be free,> he sent, and let the roar of the fire within and without take him.

The slope down to the lake shore vanished in light. *Elatus* was at full stride when the first ranging shots from the Mercury Wall hit. The aim was good and the shell exploded across the unshielded canopy of a Reaver Titan that was lumbering towards the edge of Legio Ignatum's fire wave. The shell burst, scattering green flare fire into the air and emitting a signal pulse.

Elatus was close enough to see the struck engine flinch as though stung.

'Shard, shot true,' shouted Acastia into the fire control vox-link. 'Repeat, shot true. Fire for effect.'

'This is Shard, confirmed and fir–'

Acastia did not hear what came next. Pressure clamped her skull. Pain bored down through her. *Elatus* lurched in its stride. Behind and to either side of it *Thaumas* and *Cyllarus* stumbled too.

'The call of the hunt is mine!' snarled Caradoc's voice over the vox as his will and anger lashed through Acastia's Helm Mechanicum. She could feel his rage and spite as he yanked her nerves and thoughts like a leash. 'You shall not dishonour me so!'

'I...' she tried to reply. The enemy Titans were so close that she could see the skin of their bodies clearly for the first time as the explosions lit them.

Pocked lacquer peeling from corroded metal...

Ash falling from joints...

And...

And there was something wrong with what she was seeing, something that tried to form into a thought as her head flooded with her half-brother's fury. 'Please,' she said. 'Please, my liege, there is something wrong–'

'You will obey! You will do me honour!'

Elatus was still running forwards. The Titans were looming in her sight, outlines in the fire and las shattering on and around them. And in a flash of explosive light she saw the Reaver Titan that had been hit by the ranging shot, saw it clear as the snap of flame poured across its body. Holes in armour plates, patched in places, open in others. Broken cables dangling from gouged wounds. Pale light within, flickering like a candle burning inside a ruined castle long deserted.

She wanted to shout, to call out, but the pain from Caradoc's command was swallowing everything.

Then the first shot of the full barrage from the Mercury Wall struck. It was a plasma blast, shot from a bombard on the distant parapet. It hit the nearest Titan's back plates and blasted a layer of them to slag. The glowing ball of energy flattened, melting through the metres of armour, feeding on what it burned, sinking into the engine's back like a hot coal on ice. The Titan staggered forwards, shrugging, head twisting. Streams of molten metal were running down its back. More shots landed, shells and blasts of energy, that blanketed the ground and burned away the night.

Acastia felt Caradoc's hold slacken, and jinked *Elatus* aside as a shell hit the ground fifty strides ahead of her and punched a fist of debris and fire into the air. Her ion shield sang with shrapnel impacts. Her head was a shattered sun of pain. Rainbow colours spun in her sight. The ground shook. Fire hid the ground ahead all the way down to the water. The enemy engines were shadows within the inferno. The Ignatum Titans were still coming forwards in an arc along the lake shore, their fire tearing at the shadows within, the rhythm of their guns synchronised.

Acastia caught her breath. She saw the Reaver Titan that had taken the plasma bombard hit stumble from the inferno. It bent over, the wound on its back a glowing crater. Patches of flame clung to its power fist and gun arm. It tried to straighten, legs pushing forwards. Its head came up, and for an instant it was looking directly down at Acastia. Then it fell. Its balance unravelled with a shriek of metal. It pitched forwards, snout ploughing through the bank. Mud fountained up. Water became steam on the hot metal. Acastia thought she felt its fall shake through the frame of her mount.

The strobing tide of detonations filled Tetracauron's sight. Target halos formed and locked, as *Reginae Furorem*'s sensors found the signatures of enemy engines amongst the explosions. In the incandescence, the fire was ragged black. The ground grey. His legion kin were figures of burning gold striding forwards in staggered lines. Knights and skitarii flowed about them, moving in synchronisation with each step. Shadows moved in the flame, trying to walk against the deluge of fire. There were dozens of them. A forest of walking metal and iron. They fell, burning, cut and blasted, limbs and armour melted. The tick of minutes since the battle began a rising count of engine kills.

Target lock.

Weapon icons spun green. He felt the fire loose from his engine a blink before it crossed his vision. A stitched blur from his back. A nanosecond later, a matched blast from his maniple kin, each one firing as the others' reactors drew breath so that the flow of destruction never ceased. Perfect. Delivered as one, striking metal as one, as *Reginae Furorem* and its kin strode into the killing ground, passing the dead, flames glittering off their void shields. An army of god-machines six hundred metres wide, curving as it pressed the enemy down the lake shore.

Target lock.

Firing.

Target lock.

Firing.

Striking metal.

The few void shields on the enemy fizzling and misfiring. Like they were already damaged, or not working.

<All units,> he sent, <confirm the presence of any shield envelopes on enemy engines.>

<Negative,> came the first reply, then the rest, the data flow a chorus in his head.

<Negative.>

<Negative.>

<Negative.>

<Negative.>

<Negative.>

<Negative.>

<Negative.>

<Negative.>

<Negative.>

Three kills, four, five, ten, enemy casualties mounting and return fire only a scatter of wild shots.

<This is not right,> breathed Divisia across the link. <We

should be taking fire. Our damage yield is off the scale. It's as though their shields are not functioning, or as if they had already taken damage.>

<Central command records no engagements with these units,> replied Cartho.

Tetracauron's mind was racing, thoughts spinning through the memories of engagements, of tactical scenarios and patterns, searching in the space of an eye-blink for a model to fit what he was seeing.

<All units,> he sent, <immediate halt!>

The dead Titan lay in front of Acastia, the air burning behind it where the bombardment was still rolling through its kin.

For a moment Acastia stared at it. *Elatus'* stride had slowed. The fallen Titan filled her eyes, its shadow lit by guttering flame, the shroud of steam billowing across it. She was half aware of the tactical data scrolling across the edge of her sight. Ignatum were adding their fire to that of the wall guns, their engines spreading out in an arc to cover any enemy that broke from the bombardment.

'Acastia.' It was Dolloran, coming close, curbing his steed to match her faltering pace.

There… there had… The engine had looked at her before it fell.

'Acastia, what is wrong? Are you injured?'

It had looked at her… Head dipping like a dog with a broken back. She had looked back, and seen…

'Acastia!' *Cyllarus* was abreast of her now, close enough that their guns were almost touching. She was still going forwards towards the downed Titan.

Fire running from its shoulders. And…

One of the Solaria Warhounds went past her, its stride loping, mud splashing up from foot impacts. Its gun and head not looking at the dead Titan lying at the edge of the lake…

Head coming down. The cracked crystal of its eye-ports, lit from within, but not by fire.

Everything seeming slow in her mind, sand scattered by a blast of wind.

'All…' she began to say, her hand finding the broad vox transmission stud. She felt *Elatus*' stride falter. The dead Titan was directly ahead of her. It had looked at her as it fell…

Head coming down, fire inside its metal skull. Cold, pale fire…

'All engine kills still hostile, repeat, engine kills still active.'

'Acastia…' began Dolloran, but she did not hear what he was going to say, nor the other voices coming from her vox.

The dead Reaver Titan dragged itself from the ground. Fire drained into blackened armour. Shattered joints splintered as they moved. Mud and black water fell from it. Its head came up last. Pale light filled the space inside its eye-ports.

'Move!' shouted Dolloran, his voice stabbing across the vox as *Cyllarus* swerved. Acastia was already kicking *Elatus* forward, jinking the Armiger aside as the shadow of the Titan grew against the sheet of fire at its back. Gun barrels rotated. 'Get–'

The risen Titan fired.

<Target active!> Divisia's sending echoed into Tetracauron from the incandescence. <It's right on top of us!>

And it was. A Warlord, its body soot black. Dark liquid draining to the ground. Frost forming on its limbs. Right next to them. Close enough that there was nowhere to go.

<Shields–> But he did not finish the sending. Shells struck *Reginae Furorem*'s shields. Explosions blotted out Tetracauron's awareness. *Reginae Furorem*'s shields blew out in a drum roll of detonations. Feedback lashed through the incandescence. Tetracauron felt his jaw clamp shut with sympathetic pain. He was falling, falling from the rope that tied him to his engine.

He gasped. Blood sprayed from his lips. His eyes were a blur of images from inside his Titan's head. Fire and lightning flashing beyond its eyes. Red lights shrieking across machine surfaces. Beyond it a shadow, the shape of the Titan they had killed stepping forwards, rust scattering from its fingers as its fist rose and reached. He could hear it. Somehow, he could hear it speaking to him, its voice a rattle of broken gears.

The incandescence snapped him back. Power shivered through him. Cold fire flooding him from his core. The enemy Titan a shape of night bracketed by green target locks. Weapon charge. Target ordained.

<Strike.> The command left his mind. He felt it pass to Divisia, felt it become her will and an echo of his command in a time that for flesh would not have even allowed for a breath to be drawn.

Reginae Furorem's power fist came up, lightning arcing along its open fingers. It met the enemy Titan's blow.

White light shattered from the impact.

Tetracauron felt force judder through his engine. His will snapped the fingers of his Titan's hand shut. The fingers dug into rusted metal. Power fields tore through gears and joints.

<Tear,> shouted Divisia, her command to the weapon system boiling out into the incandescence. The reactor spiked. Tetracauron felt fire pour down his own arm. Mandalas of weapon data spun as piston rams fired. *Reginae Furorem*'s fist yanked back. The enemy Titan's fist tore from its arm. A sphere of energy formed and burst around the torn joint and shattered. Shoulder plates and torso mass rippled like cloth as the shock wave passed through it. It was reeling, plasma and ectoplasm pouring from its wound. Its shriek of pain was a blade of static and corrupted code stabbing into his nerves. *Reginae Furorem* cast the hand of its enemy aside. Tetracauron could feel its spirit blazing with rage. It was almost acting without

command, the echoes of its past battles driving it, flowing out from its molten heart. The enemy Titan tried to bring its gun up.

<Weapon primed. Target locked.> Divisia's weapon command blinked through him.

He felt the iron fist of the Machine-God that he served rise. The enemy Titan was before it, trying to straighten, the world behind it ragged with fire.

<Shields!> sent Tetracauron. <Shields now!>

And he felt the shell of void energies begin to reform around him, layer by layer, each an eye-blink, each a slow ripple of time for him.

<Strike!>

Reginae Furorem punched its open fist into the enemy Titan's neck, up into the join between head and torso, up into the mass of cables and power conduits. It closed its hand with a clap of lightning, and ripped its arm back. The enemy Titan's head and half of its upper torso came away. Bile-coloured fire blasted out. Blood poured into the wound, bubbling from the spaces inside. Its legs shuddered, half lifting from the mud, as though an echo of will within it still drove it. *Reginae Furorem* did not wait for the enemy to fall. It struck into the wound of its first blow, the head of the enemy still in its grasp. The enemy Titan exploded in a ragged blaze. Malfunctioning plasma conduits ruptured. The energy still pooled in the stopped heart of its long-dead reactor burst outwards. A blizzard of sharpness and plasma broke *Reginae Furorem*'s void shields an instant after they formed. Tetracauron felt the layers of protection shatter, but the sensation flicked past as his Titan and crew roared with anger and victory.

Tetracauron yanked his mind out of the spiral of burning and flung it wide, through sensors and noospheric links, across his battle force. Every engine was engaged, most at extreme close quarters with dead Titans that had pulled themselves from the ground. There were more closing, a ragged herd of engines coming on, weapons chugging fizzing shells and blisters of plasma. The noosphere link to the other engines rolled with errors and ghost images. Flickers of fire and the sound of alarms and the engines falling under skies that were not Terra's blinked across his vision.

<Impact, upper carapace quadrant,> sent Divisia.

<Xeta?>

<Reactors are fluctuating. Scrap code into peripheral systems. Hostile and corrupt data incarnations across multiple communication bands.>

<Shut them out!>

<I am attending to that task, princeps, but they are not using enemy code ciphers. They are transmitting a dirge. Disharmonious. Broad spectrum. Maximum gain. The blessed subsystems of our engines allowed them in before we could shut them out.>

<How?>

<They are not enemy Legio code cant structures. They are ours. They are screaming with our own voices.>

Enemy distance to wall: 113 kilometres.

TWELVE

Paradise
Sons of Caliban
Ugent Sye

East Phoenicium Wastes

'What are we doing?' Krank had been asking the same question for the last hour. Oll had given the best reply he was comfortable with each time, but he was not sure that it was going in.

'We are trying to find John,' Oll said again. 'Without him I don't know where we are going next. Added to which he was in trouble.'

'Bad trouble?' asked Rane.

Oll nodded. He was keeping his eyes down on his feet or on the back of the crowd in front of him. It was getting harder not to look up at the hive as they got closer. Every time he let his thoughts off the narrow passage he was holding them to, he found himself staring at it. It was brighter than it should have been, a spiralling set of needle towers and bridges, the sun exploding into rainbows and sun patterns from the polished metal and crystal domes.

The rest of the crowd were not trying to look away. All of

them were gazing upwards. Some of them were crying. Some of their tears were pink with blood. There was a smell of sweat and burning sugar and meat to the crowd. Some of them talked all the time, as though they were walking somewhere else other than the baking wastelands. There were blasts of laughter, sometimes of song, sometimes screams. There had been some who had collapsed: a man who had stumbled and slipped, and had his ankle broken by the tread of those coming after him, screaming in pain that he had to reach paradise, sobbing as he pulled himself over the ground; another who must have died days ago, their body dragged by the clothes that had snagged unnoticed on others.

They might have once been refugees, but the crowd were something else now. Pilgrims, Oll thought, pilgrims who thought they were walking to paradise, and who might just be right.

Bad trouble… Oll was certain they were already in that and that it was only going to get worse. That was what was going to happen, down into Hades, into the Labyrinth with the beast… There was no dodging it, and only one way to go: forwards, into it, and hope that you came out the other side.

It had been hard to keep moving, hard to keep the others moving, too – harder to keep them from turning to try to help, or shout, or shoot the tide of people. Rane was the worst, Rane and perhaps Graft. Rane was struggling not to look at the hive. Oll had heard him mumble Neve's name once, a name that Rane had not spoken in years. There was something up with Graft, too. The loading servitor had started twitching, suddenly swinging around as though to a command. The woman with the veil and the bones hanging from her mouth, with her big companion, had stuck with them, too. Keeping close, glancing at them every now and again. The throng kept back from the pair, as though from instinct. That had been useful, and worrying.

'This is a witch path,' Katt said to Oll under her breath as they walked on. 'You know that, right? I mean... I can feel it. I can hear it, and it's... it's like a song, Oll, like before when we left Calth, like the sirens.'

'Yes,' he said. 'That's just what it's like.'

'Once we are in,' asked Katt, 'how are we going to find your friend? Presuming he is in this place?'

'John called us,' said Oll. 'He will have left a sign, or a message.'

'You are sure?'

'No,' he said, and looked at Katt. There was no point lying to her – she would know if he did, he was sure.

'Okay,' she said in reply.

'Look...' The woman in the veil was just in front of them, turning to look at them, pointing up as they rounded a spur of dry earth and rock.

Oll looked before he could stop himself. The hive was there, rising from the dust, glittering, dazzling, rippling in the heat like a gas flame. He felt the sensation drain from his skin, felt the breath hiss from his lungs...

Everything was going to be okay.

They didn't... He didn't need to go any further. This was the place he needed to be. The only place he ever needed to be.

'Just what you wanted,' said a voice beside him, deep, resonant, the voice of an old friend. *'You only ever wanted to stop, to let the world be, and hope that it would let you be for a while.'*

'The... the sea...' he felt himself stammer. 'The ship and the open seas.'

'All of that wandering and adventuring came later,' said the voice, *'once you figured out that the world would not let you rest. Even then you were always trying to get home, really. And now... now you are, and you can rest now, Ollanius.'*

Something hit him from behind. He staggered, and the voice was gone and so was the sight of the hive.

People were rushing past him. The long ribbon crowd that they had walked with was breaking into a mad rush as they saw the hive above them. People were running, scrambling and ripping past each other. He heard gunshots, cries. Oll tried to move, was hit again. His head was aching, his eyes streaming. A high ringing – like a glass struck by a fingernail – filled his ears.

A strong hand caught him and lifted him up. He looked up, expecting to see Graft or Zybes.

The towering figure swathed in coloured fabric stood beside him, a rock that the tide of people flowed around. The veiled woman stood next to him. She was not looking at the hive but at him.

'Here,' she said, 'just a little further, traveller, but you have to move. The threshold is no place to linger.'

He stared at her, his sight blurred, the shape of her a multi-coloured flicker. The river of people were passing in a rush, but they were an island.

'You?' he said, mouth and throat dry. 'Who are you?'

She was smiling, the bones on their threads rattling softly beneath her chin.

'I am a pilgrim,' she said.

'Oll!' Katt's shout ripped his head around. She was coming at him out of the crowd. Zybes and Graft beside her. Krank and Rane following. They all had their eyes held low, down-cast from the sight of the hive. There were tears of blood under Katt's eyes, and red on her chin. She was pale. Shaking. The others too. He saw them begin to run. 'Get away! Run!'

A booming cry filled the air, pulsing and rising, cutting clear over the shouts and whoops of the running crowd. Oll felt the noise rather than heard it, felt it vibrate out from bone to skin.

'Uhhh…' he felt himself gasp, tasted vomit on his tongue. He saw the figure out of the corner of his eye. Big, bigger than could be ignored, standing on a crag of sandstone, coated in armour, glowing with colours and reflections: acid green, deep crimson, fire orange and teal, chrome and bronze. It had limbs and form… god, but it was real, more real than anything should be, a shriek given form. It was looking down at the running tide of humanity, bellowing welcome or glee, or threat. The crowd was running, some towards the figure, others away, or flattening themselves against the ground. There was blood. Blood running from ears and eyes and mouths, and the wounds raked by fingers in flesh. The veiled woman and her giant companion were nowhere to be seen, vanished like smoke before a gale.

A hand grabbed him.

'Oll, stop!' Katt's voice, distant, shouting. 'Not that way, get away from it!'

He looked down; his feet were moving, taking him forwards, towards the figure. A neon burn-image of the armoured figure clung to Oll's sight.

Oh god, he had been going towards it… He still was.

He wrenched himself around, closing his eyes, dragging muscle with will – and began to run. The bellowing cry unfolded in the air above him. At least some of the others were beside him. He was running towards the hive and all he could hear was screaming and all he could taste was vomit and sugar.

The next stride of his run unfolded in front of him. His foot touched down on…

Polished stone. He stopped, halted, blinking, breathing, the red in his mouth fading. There was no crowd. There was no dust. He was standing on a path of green stone run through with pale bands, polished to a sheen. It wound into the distance in a curve that drew the eye on and up. The hive was there, still shining in the sun, but there was a warmth to it now, a perfection to the arcs of its aqueducts and clustered domes. Stairs wound up from the ground into the air, cork-screwing up through hundreds of metres to join delicate bridges. The leaves of plants waved from the balustrades. Flow-ers, heavy with pollen and scent, hung their heads over the sides of stacked balconies. The leaves of trees shivered in the warm breeze that blew from behind Oll's back. Flocks of birds, or perhaps butterflies or moths, with multicoloured wings took flight and resettled on patches of blossom. Grey and yellow pollen puffed into the air, coiling and swirling in drifts.

He took a breath. The air was sweet, edged with smells of salt and lemon blossom and the warmth of earth under the sun.

There was no one else in sight. No crowd, no abomination in armour. Quiet, broken by the distant splash of water and the laughter of bird wings in the air.

He had his gun in his hands, he realised, finger beside the trigger, safety off. He thought about safetying it and slinging it – no need for it here. No need for anything here...

He kept the gun in his hands. A familiar old sensation was creeping over him, like a voice he had not heard for a very long time speaking a half-forgotten name.

'Oll?' He turned. Katt was standing beside Graft. She had her pistol in her hand. Aimed. No waver in the barrel. Behind the sight he could see her eyes.

'It's me, Katt,' he said, very carefully. 'Something tells me that you might need more than that to be certain – but it's okay.'

She lowered the gun after the sound of the last word. Okay – not a word of this time, a word that had come to mean a lot of things to the crew that had crossed the last years with him.

'You went away,' she said. 'It's been hours, but... not for you, right?'

'Right,' he said, looking around again. 'The others went, too?'

She nodded. 'There and then not.' Oll looked at Graft. The

servitor was still, head sunk between piston shoulders. Oll put out his hand to the old half-machine. It raised its head. Looked at him. There was a film of fluid running down its neck from its speaker grille.

'Trooper…' it buzzed. 'Trooper Persson.'

'I looked for them,' said Katt, 'but I didn't want to go far, or call out. There are things here, Oll.'

Oll looked at Graft and let his hand drop. Here he was, just like before, just like always happened when you were trying to get somewhere that the gods didn't want you to reach. People got lost.

'Have to find them,' he said, half to himself, then shook his head. No use… If he was right about what had got John, about where they had run aground, then the others were as good as gone.

'I think I can find them,' said Katt. He looked at her sharply. She nodded in reply, and held up the pendant and the compass. The shard of black crystal on the end of the pendant swayed. He saw that she had his chart too, folded in her fingers. She must have taken them from him when he fell again, in case he did not come back. Clever Katt… 'I can feel them, like they are out there, very distant, but in my head, too, like a voice, or a clear memory…'

'Like a thread,' said Oll.

She nodded.

'And this.' She raised the pendulum, compass and chart. 'It gives you a way to somewhere, or someone.'

Oll smiled. He wondered if it was all the places they had been that had taught her this, all that tumbling through time and looking into the whirlpool of the universe. The terror had burned away, had become the will to look on things that would break others and let her still act. Her psyker talent, well… he still hadn't got a sense of what shape that was taking, only that right now he was very glad they had brought the near-catatonic girl with them from the ruin of Calth.

'Not lost at all, are you?' he said. 'Not even here.'

She smiled too.

'I've no idea where this is – I thought we were back in the schism space somehow, but it's not that. It feels different, worse. Like…'

'Like it's trying to strangle you with softness,' completed Oll. 'Yes, I'm afraid I have brought us to a bad place. A very bad place, in fact.'

'What is it?'

He looked around at the leaves and flowers and falling water, and the pollen hazing the light falling through, and thought of all the names and ways that the idea had changed over time, pernicious, tempting, the truth of it only leaking out in places where stories frayed.

'Paradise,' he said.

Magnifican

'We have to stop, at least for a while.'

Shiban looked around at Cole. The man was sweating, swaying slightly. The infant in his arms was asleep, a small hand clear above the fold of the hessian sheet that had become its sling. It smelled of shit. The man, too. That was good, in Shiban's estimation. If it was defecating that meant that its digestive system and kidneys were functioning and had not rejected the non-standard diet it was being fed.

'There,' said Shiban, pointing with a finger at a curve of girders and pitted metal projecting from the ash layer. 'That will provide shelter, and there are pipes running to it under the surface.'

'Water?' said Cole.

'We will see.'

He moved forwards, eyes passing over the little of the land that there was to see. A dense, humid fog filled the air around them, turning the daylight into a haze, and objects in the distance became phantoms that vanished, never to return. To breathe it was to be suffocated, to move through it like wading across the seabed of an ocean. Taste, smell, vibration and sound had taken the place of sight as key senses. Sometimes there was gunfire, or a swell in the distant rumble of civilisation-ending weaponry. Twice now, Shiban had heard things moving close by, within twenty strides, things that moved with the care and slowness of hunters. He had become still, and held Cole still with a gesture. The infant was always quiet at such moments, as though it understood that silence was survival. Both times, the sounds out in the fog had moved away after a while and they had pressed on. Cole had taken to talking, asking questions mainly. Shiban was tempted to tell the man to be quiet, but that would have served no end – words were this human's connection to a world he could understand.

'Poetry begins with the talking,' Yesugei had said. *'And talking is the shadow of the spirit within.'*

So, he let the man talk and walked on. It was the questions that tried his patience most.

'You have seen him, the Praetorian?' asked Cole.

'Yes,' Shiban said, and kept moving.

'You have been in his presence?'

'Several times.'

'He has talked to you?'

'Yes.'

'Truly?'

'Yes. I have talked to Lord Dorn, and Sanguinius, and my Khan, and Lord Guilliman, and…' He had been about to say the names of Magnus the Red, Fulgrim and Horus Lupercal.

'Yes? And... who?'

'Others,' said Shiban.

'Ah...'

They walked on for a few more steps in silence. Shiban could not help but think of Yesugei smiling with amusement.

'I think I preferred the vultures...' he muttered. The pain had ebbed to a constant dull ache in every part of his body.

'Sorry?' asked Cole.

'Vultures, journey companions to the wanderer. On Chogoris we say that when any spirit is alone, companions will always come with them. Sometimes a rider may become separated from their fellows, or choose to go riding alone, beyond the horizon. No matter why, or how far they have gone, companions will join them, travel with them until they either find their way back or ride beyond the plain of the world. They speak wisdom and truth and keep the wanderer true to themselves.' Shiban glanced at Cole. 'They usually look like birds.'

Cole frowned.

'You are saying that I... that we are like the carrion birds that follow lost people who are going to die?'

Shiban raised his eyebrows, a facial shrug that sent hot needles into his skull.

'I am saying that you talk a lot.'

Cole opened his mouth, still frowning. Shiban waited for another question, but the man raised his head, looking up and away, alert.

'The wind is changing direction,' said Cole.

Shiban felt it then. A thread of cold air was coiling across the skin of his face. How had he missed it and the man had noticed?

He paused, turning to look in the direction Cole was looking. As he moved, the gust strengthened. Cole's coat snapped and billowed. Dust skittered across the ground, rattling. He

shivered, unease rolling through him in place of the relief
that a cool breeze should have brought. He caught a breath
of the air, tasted damp stagnation on it, the smell of a sep-
ulchre kept sealed.

The fog swirled, shrinking, drawing back like inhaled smoke.
The distant sky emerged, hazed, sunlight stained the colour
of old rags. And thrusting up through it was a tower that
reached up and up, its silhouette ragged like the blade of a
notched knife. Shiban felt his eyes lock to it. For a moment
it seemed to lose dimension and detail, so that it seemed like
a black wound in the sky. Light fled it, and he knew that the
wind that had parted the fog had come from it. The Lion's
Gate space port, that was what he was seeing, but in the back
of his skull all he could think of was the sound of the wings
of dying birds, and down in his core, besides the pain of his
wounds, he felt ice form and climb up his spine with slow
fingers. The wind gusted, whispering, breathing, laughing…

'No…' moaned Cole. 'Please, no…'

Shiban looked around. The man was on the ground crouched
in a ball around the bundle of the infant, rocking. Shiban moved
to his side, put a hand on his shoulder.

Cole looked up. Tears were rolling down the man's face
and falling onto the bundle of fabric holding the child. Who
was… asleep, eyes closed, chest moving with the slow rhythm
of whatever were a human's first dreams.

'Cole,' said Shiban. 'Why do you weep? The infant lives.'

'One day he won't,' said Cole, softly. 'One day I will fail. One
day he will be alone out here, screaming for someone to help.'

'That is not certain.'

'It is, though. Look around, Space Marine,' said Cole, and
with that the words were pouring from him, flowing out as
he shook. 'Everything ends in tears and suffering. Everything.
I just… I just wanted to help him. I just wanted to help… I

just wanted for something to be true and whole and to last. One thing… just one thing. Why can't that be true? Why is the rule of the universe cruelty? Everything is gone. Everything… I can see them… This was not supposed to happen. None of this was supposed to happen. But it won't stop, don't you see? This goes on forever, until there is nothing left. Nothing.'

Shiban let his hand drop from the man's shoulder. He could feel the shadow of the Lion's Gate behind him, the breath of the dank wind stirring his hair. He could hear that distant tower calling him to the same despair that Cole had fallen into – like a voice reaching for them across the land.

'Perhaps,' he said.

Cole looked at him then, and bitterness gleamed in his eyes. 'Perhaps? Is that all you can say?'

'Hope is not certainty. It is the light in the distance. Ride towards it, and you may reach it. You may die in the saddle before you see it, but stop and it will always be distant.'

Cole laughed, shrill with bitterness. 'Is that the best of Chogorian comfort?'

'It is truth,' Shiban said, and stood, 'and that is all we have.'

Cole looked down at the sleeping infant. The child's face twitched but his eyes stayed closed.

He shook his head. Shiban watched him. The wind was dropping, the fog folding over the corridor it had opened to the vision of the Lion's Gate space port. At last Cole shook his head and looked up at Shiban. 'One more step,' he said.

Shiban nodded, and reached out a hand. Cole took it and pulled himself up.

'It is not far,' said Shiban, 'but I fear that from here it will not get easier.'

Cole shook his head, he was already walking.

'You really need to work on your motivation.'

Shiban was about to reply, as he glanced back behind them

in the direction of the now obscured space port. He stopped.
The fog was thickening, but for a moment he thought he saw
something. A shadow in the blurred light and haze, bloated,
spiked, standing on a rise of rubble. Unmoving. Looking back
at him across the distance.

The Wrath's Descent, *inner system gulf*

Corswain opened his eyes. The dying beast was still there,
bleeding out, looking at him from the borderland of remembered sleep. The pearl of Terra looked back at him from the
viewport. The bridge of the *Wrath's Descent* was quiet, the
crews at their stations speaking in murmurs or in the click of
keys and controls. Vassago and Adophel stood further back
from the viewport, exchanging a few words that Corswain
did not try to catch.

'We are reaching the initiation point,' said Adophel. Corswain
nodded but did not reply. His gaze shifted to the bulk of the
ship hanging in the void above him. The light of the distant sun
rolled across its golden flanks and snagged on the impact craters
that dotted its surface. This close, it felt as though he were
looking up at the surface of a gilded moon. Its hull and flanks
tapered down to a spear-blade tip. The clusters of its engines
glowed a cold blue, sliding it forwards and down towards the
distant light of Terra. It was smaller than the *Phalanx*, a sister
in raw mass and volume to the great Gloriana-class ships that
led the fleets of traitors and loyalists alike. It dwarfed the Dark
Angels battle-barge and three grand cruisers that moved in its
shadow. There was more to it than its size, though. It carried
a presence that Corswain fancied he could feel across the gulf
between the ships. In the ages when it had gone to war, its
guns had been crewed by devices and half-machines created
not on Mars, but in the Fortresses of Unity on Terra. Palaces

lived within its hull, and its weapons were marvels taken and
made from the dead glory of the past. It was called the *Imperator
Somnium*, the Imperial Dream, golden and bright. It was one
of the three ships that bore the Emperor through the stars on
the Great Crusade. Now it would go home for one final time.

'Are we ready?' Corswain asked, still without turning.

'Aye, lord,' said Vassago.

Corswain gave a nod but nothing more. Ten thousand of
his brothers packed the four Legion warships that moved in
the *Imperator Somnium*'s shadow. Ammunition and crew had
been stripped out, and gunships, landers and assault craft
loaded into every hangar and launch bay. Some bore the
colours of the Blood Angels, Imperial Fists and White Scars,
the vessels gifts to Corswain's cause from his Legion cousins.
Racks of drop pods waited in launch tubes. Kharybdis and
Dreadclaw assault pods clung to the ships' bellies and backs,
all fully loaded with warriors.

'The cause…' breathed Corswain to himself. A cause or a
vainglorious piece of foolishness, a knight riding into the
spears of the enemy, a cry on his lips, sword raised, and his
death and the deaths of those that rode with him a certainty.

'My lord?' said Vassago.

'You do not agree with what we are doing, brother, I know.'

'Lord?'

'You are silent in counsel, Librarian, and that silence speaks.'

'The role of my circle is not to lead, lord, it is to aid those
who do.'

'Then aid me now, by sharing your doubt.'

A pause, a shift.

Corswain knew that the Librarian was looking at Adophel.

'Adophel has heard and seen enough to know that difference
in opinion does not mean dissent or division,' said Corswain,
still keeping his eyes on Terra. 'Speak.'

'As you will it,' said Vassago, carefully. 'Lord, the battle is done. The forces of the Warmaster are greater. They will prevail. There is no salvation coming. We are all there is. Death awaits us on Terra.'

'Better that we let it play out?' said Corswain.

'Better that we preserve what we can,' said Vassago. 'This war shall not end. The stars will burn hereafter. We have some strength, maybe with our allies more. Strength enough to defend what we have, strength enough to begin again.'

'Without the Imperium, without the Emperor.'

'With what remains.'

Corswain's jaw clamped shut.

'Your words could be an avowal of betrayal.'

'You asked me to speak,' said Vassago. 'I would not have done so otherwise.'

'And when I do not take that course?' asked Corswain. 'Will you still be silent?'

'I will stand by your side, sire.'

Corswain nodded, and then glanced at Adophel.

'Give the order,' he said.

The fleet master nodded, and moved out of sight. Ten seconds later, Corswain felt the vibration of the deck change, deepening as the engines and reactors lit. The stars began to slide past faster and faster. The great golden bulk of the *Imperator Somnium* kept pace. There were hardly any living crew on board, just the servitors needed for the reactors and some of the guns, and a trio of Custodians, who stood on the bridge.

'Get to the launch bay,' Corswain said to Vassago, and turned from the view. His helmet clamped over his sight. The world became a red glow of threat markers. In the blink of his eyelids he saw the beast's blood leak onto the snow and its eyes close. In the viewport behind them, growing brighter and larger by the second, Terra glowed, haloed by the jewels of ships and the fires of war.

The ships flew, it would be hours before the fleets around
Terra saw them. Then would come a time of thunder and
fire. Until then they shivered to the growl of their engines
and plunged on.

Down in the near-silent decks of the *Wrath's Descent* Vassago
paused as he moved into his arming chamber. Threads of
thought moved at the edge of his awareness, coils of cold
intent wrapped in shadows of deception. There were three
waiting for him. He knew them all just by the taste of their
minds. He did not need to look at them to see their black
armour and the glow of their eyes in their helms beneath their
cowls. The air of Caliban stirred in his senses as he touched
their minds.

'You should not be here,' he said aloud without turning as
he moved to the gun racks. 'There is nothing to say.'

'We must kill him now,' said one.

'Do that and we will be slaughtered,' said Vassago, 'and those
who we do not kill shall realise our intent and the intent of
the Order on Caliban.'

'This assault will see us all dead to vainglory and fallen ideals.'

Vassago picked up his plasma pistol, slotted the plasma-
charge cylinder into its port and set it to arm. Charge coils
glowed, and a high-pitched whine rose from the gun.

'We are here to save the Order, to eliminate the threat to the
future of Caliban and to bring any who see the truth amongst
our brothers to our cause.'

'Corswain...'

'Is a noble knight,' said Vassago, 'and there is hope for him.
If we act now we lose the chance to gain all that we came for.
There is opportunity in what is about to happen, great opportunity to guide the path of the Order. All we need to do is be
ready to seize what fate and chance cast in our path.'

'So we ride into a battle where we likely will die before we raise a blade?'

'Corswain is a great lord and his plan is as brilliant as it is dangerous. It might work.'

'You admire him…'

'And you do not? He is a peerless warrior, dedicated, ruthless and subtle. He is also honourable. What is there in that for a son of Caliban not to admire?' No answers came. Vassago holstered his weapon, and shook his head. 'Gird and arm yourselves. The time has not yet come,' he said.

When he turned a moment later he was alone in the half-dark.

Hatay-Antakya Hive, East Phoenicium Wastes

Oll and Katt found Krank first. The old soldier was lying on a stone path on the edge of a garden dome. Whatever had happened to the hive had left this small corner untouched. Trees stretched to spread a green canopy beneath a dome of brass and crystal. Water still flowed in the irrigation channels that wound between roots and open patches of ground. It was warm, and smelled of earth and green foliage. Krank lay on his front, face down, his gun just beside him, his hand resting on top of it as if he was asleep.

They paused when they first saw him, ducked back and waited. Watching the trees and the edge of the dome. They had climbed to the dome up one of the spiralling walkways that led them from the point they had entered. They had seen no one in that time, nor any signs of violence either. That had put both Katt and Oll on edge.

'That thing back there before? At the entrance to this place,' asked Katt in a half-whisper. 'That was an Astartes…'

It was the first time either of them had mentioned the giant that had sent the column of refugees into a stampede.

'It looked like one,' replied Oll, and even as he said it the image flashed across his mind. Even in memory it was enough to send spots of mid-range light spinning across his eyes. 'Or like it was once one of them.'

'But that means the war is here,' said Katt, 'but then there should be signs of it.'

'Maybe this is the sign,' replied Oll, 'the silence, I mean.'

He waited a heartbeat more, then stood up and moved out to beside Krank.

No shouts. No shots. No steering pain and the fast fall to the earth.

He reached the old soldier, checked with eyes and then fingers that there was no grenade lodged under him. He kept his eyes on the trees.

A bird, mauve-and-orange-feathered, lofted into the air. He twitched, relaxed. There was no blood on Krank, and when he rolled him over he found a low breath coming from the old soldier's lips. His eyes were closed.

'Why did he fall?' asked Katt, coming up behind him.

'Exhaustion.'

Oll's eyes and gun whipped up. A man in tattered rags was crouching beside the trunk of the nearest tree. The man raised a hand placatingly and then scuttled out beside Oll. He barely gave Oll a glance before looking down at Krank.

Katt had flinched back, her pistol up, but the man scarcely gave her a look either. A tattered pack hung from a strap over one shoulder. He looked worn, his face framed by an unkempt beard, and dirt had caught in the lines of his face and the pores of his skin. The skin beneath his eyes hung in tired folds. It was a kind face though, and the glances he gave to the trees were an echo of Oll's own worry.

'Your friend needs water,' said the man in rags. His fingers were moving over Krank's face. 'He is older than he looks.' He frowned, stood up and put his hands under the old soldier's arms. 'Help me get him up.'

Oll did not move for a second.

'What are you?'

'What kind of damned stupid question is that?' snapped the man. 'I am… used to be a medicae, for all the good that has done me, and I am telling you to lift your friend's feet up and get him moving to under the tree, so I can see if I can make him a little better than he is now.'

The man held his gaze on Oll, who paused for a second and then moved forward. Graft moved to help, but Oll held up a hand.

'As… as you wish, Trooper Persson,' buzzed Graft and held still.

Oll slung his rifle, bent down and lifted Krank by his legs. They moved him under a tree and propped him with his head resting against the trunk. The man said nothing but his fingers began to dance over Krank, pressing flesh, parting lips and lowering his ear to listen. Oll watched. He had seen a lot of medics and doctors work in his time, and could tell that the man knew his business. Katt was still holding back, looking at the pendant as it spiralled over the chart. Every now and again she would wince, eyes closing, grimacing. There was a bead of blood at the corner of her left eye, Oll noticed.

'She's not in the best way either,' said the man, glancing up and then back to Krank. 'I would start at a lack of water and food and sleep deprivation, but something tells me it's a lot more than that.' The man took out a tin flask, unscrewed its lid and tipped a finger-depth of water into the lid. It was clear and clean. 'Mental and physical fatigue, shock and a bunch of other words that just mean you've been through what no one should.' He paused, put the flask down. 'Probably more than that, would be my guess.' He reached out a hand and gently pulled down the bottom of Krank's mouth, and brought the lid of water to his lips, pouring a little in.

'Is all well, Trooper Persson?' buzzed Graft, suddenly raising its head, and pivoting. 'What was your command, Trooper Persson?'

'Nothing,' said Oll. 'Thanks, Graft.'

He watched the servitor for a second, frowning. It was becoming more erratic. He wondered what all the steps of their journey had done to what remained of its human brain.

'Persson,' said the man. 'That's your name then, and trooper – you're a soldier then.'

Oll shrugged. 'Was,' he said.

'There are a lot of people who were soldiers on this world,' said the man. 'Most of them dead. I guess you are of the other type.'

'The other type?' asked Oll.

'The ones smart enough to run away.'

A moment of quiet fell.

'What's your name?' asked Oll.

It was the man's turn to shrug. He had his hand on Krank's chest, fingers spread and loose, eyes half closed as though listening.

'Ugent.'

'Where did you come from?' asked Oll.

'Come from? I didn't come from anywhere. This is where I am from, where I was born.' The man flicked his eyes up from Krank for a second, a small smile on his lips. 'You really thought I was one of the ones that have come here? Most of them have lost their minds. Desperate last scraps of hope in failing bodies, that's what they are. Everything they knew ground to dust, everything they thought they valued gone. War does that, but you know that, don't you? I can tell.'

Oll nodded.

'How long have they been coming?'

The man flicked Oll a sharp look; he was pouring another measure of water for Krank.

'You mean how long since this place changed?' The man grimaced. 'I don't know. Sometimes it seems like a long time, sometimes a few weeks. But once it did, the people started coming, and they just don't stop. All the same – broken down, desperate, hoping that the dream they have had of paradise is real… Then they find the truth.' He sighed, pursed his lips and looked at Krank. 'He needs food,' he said, and stood, looking about.

'The enemy came here,' said Katt, pausing in her work with the pendant and chart.

'Enemy?' said Ugent, still looking around. 'I'm not even sure what that means, you know. There is a war, for sure, going on somewhere, burning and crushing everything it touches. You can see the lights sometimes if you are higher up.'

'The Astartes, Ugent,' said Katt. 'We saw one when we reached here.'

Ugent went still for a second, shivered, then nodded.

'You saw one, did you?' he said, and shivered again. 'Yes, they are here.'

'There are no signs of battle,' said Katt.

Ugent looked at her; there was a frown on his face. 'No one thought enough of this hive to think it worth defending,' he said. 'How much of a battle do you think it was to take?'

'The refugees, though,' said Oll.

'They are following the call,' said Ugent. 'You will have heard it, even if just when you sleep, but its strongest to those that have lost most – those whose world has become grey despair. They hear it and they want nothing more than to be here. They follow dreams and they find themselves here.'

'What happens to them?' asked Katt.

'What do you imagine?' he replied.

'How have you kept alive?' asked Oll.

The man called Ugent turned, took a step towards one of the trees heavy with fruit, and reached up to pick one.

'Alive?' said Ugent. 'I just helped all the people I could, Trooper Persson.' The fruit came loose in his fingers. For a moment, Oll thought he heard something, something high and sharp just out of his ear's reach. He looked at Krank, still lying under the tree. The man's eyes were open. They were open and staring at Oll, filled with terror, screaming in silence. His face was slack, mouth still open from the last drink of water. 'And the more I helped,' said Ugent Sye, turning, holding up the fruit, 'the more I was alive.'

Ugent Sye smiled, and raised the fruit to his lips, and took a bite.

And the forest of trees screamed.

Oll jerked back, eyes clamping shut, hands over ears, as a bright pain lit in his skull. He felt the bile and vomit fountain from his lips. He was choking, gasping.

'It's okay,' said Ugent Sye, voice rolling over the shrieking. Oll forced himself up, gun up, stock to shoulder, finger to trigger. Sye was moving back towards Krank, unhurried. There was red liquid on his lips and chin. The bitten fruit was in his hand. Its outer golden flesh was oozing juice, its core red and wet and twitching. Ugent Sye's teeth were pink in his smile, his eyes bright. The rags shimmering in the light falling between the leaves. He seemed bright, a light source moving the shadows around him as he stepped forwards.

Oll shot. It was an action drilled into him by life upon life as a soldier. The weapons had changed and changed again in that time, string and sling to gunpowder, plasma and las charge, but the action remained the same: sight, angle to target judged in a heartbeat, the flick of will that drove throwing arm, or released string, or squeezed trigger. He was not a peerless marksman, not a dead-eye shot like Locksley had been, or as gifted as poor, foolish Paris, or as lightning fast as Doc, but at this range, and with a clear target, Oll did not miss.

The las-bolt burned through the air past Sye, and punched into the trunk of a tree. Bark fountained, blood and bone showered out from within. The screaming of the trees rose.

Oll fired again, going forward, gun level, switching to full-auto without a blink, and raking a line of shots across Ugent Sye. Puffs of blood and flesh burst into the air as the bolts burst through trees and leaves. Blood spurted from the branches. Not a single shot landed. Sye kept coming, closing on Krank, kneeling, bringing the fruit with its kernel of flesh at its heart to the man's lips. The sight of Oll's gun was on the man's serene face. Clear. Kill shot. Unavoidable… Except he was certain it would go wide.

'It's not real!' shouted Katt. 'Oll, it's not real!'

But Oll was already grabbing for the knife at his waist. The splinter of black stone that had cut their way from Calth came free from its sheath. The light broke as it touched the blade. Colour and distance and space peeled open like a flap of skin as it bit. And they saw what was around them.

Katt was wrong, noted a small voice at the back of his head as the truth poured into his eyes. It was real. It was very real. Too real to bear.

There were still trees, still light falling between leaves, still the shadow of the hive's higher spires beyond the crystal dome above. But this was no garden of plenty. The ground was black mulch, loam-wet and sticky, churned with scraps of skin, fingernails, hanks of hair. The roots of each tree were the limbs of tangled bodies, the trunks stretched flesh spiralled together, every knot a mouth or eye. Arms and legs reached and spread into branches, fingers and toes stretched into twigs. Wounds opened as flower petals. The leaves were not leaves but the detritus of lives still clutched in fists and hung from fingertips that had carried them here in hope: tatters of picts, rings and jewellery, scraps of cloth, a chrono, a ribbon, a quill, pieces of parchment that must have meant everything in a world that was burning. The fruit hung from the branches were droplets of soft fat and skin, borne by pulsing stems. Further off he could see bodies lying nestled in soil, heaped, their bones and flesh already sprouting upwards. And he could see that their eyes were all open. Alive.

'I want to help,' said Sye, and Oll saw him then. He was tall, much taller than he had seemed, his limbs long, his head hairless, youthful, and the robes that hung from him were not rags but silver-white, like a shimmer of sunlight on the sea. 'I want to help you, Ollanius, you and all you care about.' He was rising from beside Krank, coming forward, slowly, remorselessly. 'You are tired, so tired…'

Oll blinked, pulled the muzzle of the gun up one-handed, the weapon braced against its strap, and fired. The las-bolts struck true. White fabric, blood and flesh blasted from Sye, puffing into the air, burning. He kept on coming. Blood ran down his limbs and body like the juice from the bitten fruit in his hand. The trees were shrieking. The air was thick with pollen and the reek of raw meat.

'So tired,' he continued, 'all you want to do is rest, and you deserve that. Come to us. Lay down your burden. It is over, Ollanius, and Katerina – you need to do no more.'

Oll fired again. The bolts took Sye in the face and blew through his skull. He kept walking towards him.

'This is the garden of plenty,' said Sye, his voice now rising from the mouths in the trees. 'This is where there is no more hunger, no more fear, just rest. All of these came here looking for peace, hoping for it, and now they have it and will have it for eternity…' Oll was going backwards as Sye advanced on him, the remains of jaw and tongue still moving in the blown ruin of his head. 'They have found what they wanted most, and so will you.'

Oll fired again. He was not looking at Katt or Graft. He was hoping that they would have done what he would have.

Sye's remaining body was almost in touching distance, arm rising, the bleeding fruit held out to Oll like a gift.

Oll let himself glance away, to where Katt and Graft were lifting Krank from the ground.

He looked at the red and white of Sye. He had the knife in his hand, and he brought it up in a single cut. There was a scream, a high, breaking note like glass shattering. Sye fell backwards, chest parting, black smoke billowing out, organs unfolding into embers from within the sheath of skin.

He turned, looking for Katt and Graft and found them already next to him.

'That way!' shouted Katt, pointing, and they were running down the path that no longer was smooth stone but a channel filling with dark, reeking liquid. Around them, the image of the dome was coming apart like a torn canvas. The trees of flesh and bone were collapsing, the soil was boiling. Insects and birds were dropping from the air, hitting them, splashing into the filth clogging the irrigation channels. Ahead of them an iris door stood open. Rust and corrosion was already crawling over it.

'They know you, Ollanius,' said a fading voice from amongst the collapsing branches. 'They know what you want. They want to give it to you. And they will wait for you…'

THIRTEEN

The dead of Beta-Garmon
Merge
Death's Heads

Lake Voss shore, Mercury-Exultant kill-zone

Fire swallowed *Cyllarus*. The Armiger's ion shield absorbed a fraction of the first shell's explosion. It was long enough for Dolloran to see the flames enclose him. Long enough for him to see the spinning shards of shrapnel glow as they hit the collapsing shield. Long enough for a part of his brain and soul to think it beautiful. Then the heartbeat moment collapsed, and *Cyllarus* vanished.

Acastia felt it die across the machine connection. She let out a shout of pain.

Then the blast hit her.

The pressure wave picked up *Flatus* and threw it down the lake shore. Acastia's head slammed into the back of the throne. The world spun over and over. *Elatus'* legs kicked in the air for the seconds before it hit the water with a plume of white spray. Force snapped through her. The screens in front of her fuzzed. Her mount was half-submerged in black water. She

287

could see the Titan though, could hear its dragging stride in
the boom of waves breaking over her mount. *Elatus'* legs kicked
out, lashing the water. The Titan was almost above her, wading
into the lake shallows, gun chugging shells into the distance,
mud slime and cable fluid drooling from its wounds. The water
was freezing as it struck the armour of its shin plates. Voices of
static and screams buzzed in Acastia's ears. Broken symbols spiralled across her auspex screens. *Elatus'* alarms were a blended
shriek of panic. She could feel fear overwhelming her, pouring across her helm links to her thrashing mount as the dead
Titan closed. It was blank, raw, the bruising total loss of control. It had seen her.

'Pluton!' she shouted. 'Pluton, you shit, where are you?'

She could not feel Caradoc's presence either. For once the
feeling of his will burrowing into her head would have meant
something other than misery.

The Reaver was almost on her. Ice-heavy water frothing
around its stride. There was a sound in the static on the vox,
rhythmic, a drone of numbers like the rattle of lungs half-filled
with fluid. It was the sound of her mother on the cot they
had given her to die on. Last moments measured in seconds
marked by quickened breaths and the clenching of weak fingers
around Acastia's small hand. She had to get out, she had to get
out. Acastia felt herself slam her fist against the cockpit hatch,
felt the bones in her hand break. The dead Titan stopped, and
dipped its head on its broken neck. The light in its eyes fizzed
on the target screen.

Rounds struck its head and chewed into its cracked skin. It
reared up, joints grinding, cannon arm lifting, as a deluge of
explosions boiled across its head and shoulders. A Warhound
in the mottled green of Legio Solaria came from the wall of
smoke and flame, its guns spearing fire into the Reaver as it
staggered.

'Hold on it!' shouted Abhani Lus Mohana. *Bestia Est*'s vulcan mega-bolter fired. Brass cases showered onto the shore mud. Twenty metres of muzzle flame breathed from the rotating barrels.

The enemy Reaver was turning. Its own cannon was rising even as the shells chewed into the engine's mass.

'Brace for incoming fire!' shouted her moderatus. Abhani bared her teeth. Across her link she felt her Titan's reactor snarl.

'Dance for me now,' she hissed.

The Reaver fired, but *Bestia Est* was already running on an angle, firing as it did, accelerating even as explosions danced in its wake. The Reaver tacked its fire after the Warhound, the barrel of its cannon jerking like a half-broken arm. *Bestia Est* was running just ahead of an arc of explosions. Abhani could feel the presences of her maniple at the edge of her sight and touch, close, almost where they needed to be.

'Look at me!' snarled Abhani; her eyes were the eyes of her engine locked on the enemy, painted with target data. 'Look at me, you bastard child of iron.'

'Weapon heat at threshold!' shouted her gun moderatus.

Flash signals pinged green and clear at the edge of awareness.

'No matter,' said Abhani. 'Now, my sisters. Take it now!'

Beams of light struck the Reaver from beside and behind it, spearing into its skin. The other two Solaria Warhounds circled, jinking their runs as they fired. Ghost light and black fluid boiled from the Reaver as it twisted. Turbo-laser fire bored into it. Armour plates melted to slag in seconds. It did not fall.

From her throne, Abhani Lus Mohana watched as glistening black clouds billowed from the wounds, coiling and spreading through the air. It took her a second to realise it was not smoke but insects, black bodies glinting in the flame light, swallowing the las-blasts and exploding to ash.

The Solaria Warhound's steps shook Acastia in her cockpit. Multicoloured shards filled her sight. Her senses were blurred, soft and sharp at once. There was blood on her face and in her mouth. She could feel her mount feebly trying to respond to her half-conscious mind. Another jolt, and the world snapped sharp. She gasped. Waves were breaking over her. The auspex was alight. Her hands and feet were moving over controls. Pain sliced into her. Broken bones grated. Bile filled her mouth.

'Up, up, up! Now!'

Elatus scrabbled for an instant, and then stilled. Its feet kicked once and then bunched tight. Its weapon limbs braced.

'That's it, my beautiful beast!' snarled Acastia, and the Armiger Knight began to rise.

'Bring it down,' called Abhani.

The wider noosphere was alive with flashes of threat indicators and weapon discharge. The ragged light of battle lit the shore of the lake and the plain beyond for five kilometres. There were engines burning, firing, striding, falling. All of it felt distant, the sound of wind or rain. All that mattered was the prey before her.

The three hunters were circling the Reaver. Fire from them sustained without cease. This was one of the hunt patterns of the Legio Solaria. Normally performed by four Warhounds, it was called a gyre kill. One of the Titans drew the enemy to it while the others positioned themselves at each point of the compass around it. Then they fired and moved, spiralling, synchronised in movement, so that a target that turned on one of its tormentors would leave itself open to the others. All the while, each of them would cycle reactor power and ammunition stores between its guns so that while one fired the other reloaded, cooled or recharged. Done correctly it was a hunt pattern that could bring down the largest war engines. With three Warhounds it was just as deadly. But their prey would not die.

Abhani growled as *Bestia Est*'s turbo-lasers fired up into the enemy. The blasts hit it as it turned, and slammed into the damaged wreck of its left weapon arm. For an eye-blink of time they were linked by a glowing rope of light. The remains of the left arm dissolved into slag. A stream of plasma from the warhound *Artemisia* burned through the cloud of metallic insects and struck the enemy Titan's right thigh. Abhani saw the reactor indicator for *Artemisia* flash red.

'Reactor venting, weapon's out,' came *Artemisia*'s voice. She had dumped half of the reactor output into a single plasma blast. The Reaver staggered, slumping to its side. Then, somehow, impossibly, it rose, metal flowing like flesh. Abhani had a moment to notice the Armiger Knight in its shadow, which she had thought dead, rise.

Acastia looked up at the Reaver. From this distance she could see the patterns of un-repaired battle wounds in its armour plates, and the broken cables dangling from its chest. *Elatus*' thermal lance rose. The Reaver's head was distorted and fire-scarred; the ghost light within its cockpit hurt Acastia's eyes. She could still taste her own blood in her mouth. She grinned.

'Burn,' she said.

Elatus fired. A beam of white-blue heat stabbed up from the Knight's arm, up under the Reaver's chin, and melted through the back of its skull and into the mass of its torso. The Reaver's shoulders and chest distorted. Explosions burst within. For a second it seemed to be frozen. Then it arched, straightening, pulling the beam of *Elatus*' lance down its chest. Rusted armour parted. Clogged oil gushed out, burning as it fell. It twisted, reaching up, screaming in silence.

The beam from the thermal lance cut off. 'Back! Back!

Back!' shouted Acastia as she reined *Elatus* into reverse stride.
Mud ground in joints. The Reaver went still. Its pierced torso
lit from within by fire. It lowered its head, almost slowly.
The ghost light was a fading gleam. For a second Acastia
thought she heard a voice, not over the vox but in her ear.
A lone, pleading voice. Red and blue fire blew the Reaver's
back open from inside. Armour plates flew up, spinning. A
second later more explosions lit inside its guts, and blew
through its head and shoulders. The rolling blast wave reached
towards *Elatus* as it withdrew. Acastia felt triumph and relief
rush through her.

Then she felt the ground rock. Once, twice, up through her
mount and into her bones.

'Enemy engine!' called Abhani. Explosions struck *Bestia Est*'s
void shields and burst them like bubbles of foam on water.

From the burning horizon an engine walked, towering,
colours almost scoured black by flame, wrapped in coils of
unlight. Its head was a ruin of cables surrounding a shattered
skull. It bellowed through the air, vox and noosphere, and its
voice was the shriek of breaking machines and overload. Its
presence sent pixels spinning across screens and sensors. She
could hear the buzzing of insects and frayed cables. Could
smell burning oil.

Beams of stuttering las-fire reached from its shoulders and
exploded across the shields of her sister Warhounds. They
were already moving, scattering as this new foe took another
step and shook the ground.

Abhani looked up at the new enemy.

Cold flooded her.

Even broken and scorched, the last of its heraldry still clung
to its shoulders and the lines of its form still spoke from
beneath its skin of ruin. She recognised it. For a second she

felt as though she was floating… Then the scorched Warlord bellowed again, and fired.

Command bunker, Shard Bastion, Mercury Wall

In the command bunker at the top of Shard Bastion, Nasuba winced and lowered the field glasses. The flare compensators had been disabled to help night vision. She had just seen an Ignatum Titan go up in a full reactor detonation. The neon light clung to her sight. She could see the two enemy engines that had made the kill, two ragged outlines in the fire, broken limbed but still moving, dragging the Titan down as it fought. There was a taste in her mouth, too, bitter and metallic, like spoilt milk and blood.

'Summarise immediate,' she called.

'Engagement along the Lake Voss southern shore is intensifying,' said an officer bent over a set of green-lit screens. 'Full battle group is engaged. Enemy engines advancing. Eliminated hostile units activating amongst Ignatum engine formations. Distance to wall – one hundred and seven kilometres.'

'Where is our link to the Ignatum command-and-control enclaves?'

'Errors and intermittent failures on internal comms systems, general.'

'Then send a unit and get one of them up here, now.'

She turned back to the viewslit and raised the field glasses. Even as she did, something big went up in the distance. Blue-white fire punched up into the night sky to light the underbelly of the clouds. Sweat was running down her skin inside her collar and that was only in part down to the heat.

'Target and range units on the upper gun batteries say that they cannot distinguish targets for effective fire,' said Sulkova.

'Ammunition depletion?'

'We have drained a lot of solid ordnance, but the wall plasma reactors and charge coils are functioning. Output at seventy-three per cent effective.'

'Not that effective if we can't pick targets to shoot at.'

'General,' came another shout, 'signal from Curdir Bastion.'

'Link,' she replied, her eyes still on the magnified view of the battle. She could pick out almost nothing. Foe and friend identifier runes spun as unresolved amber.

'*General*,' growled a voice from the vox-speakers. It was heavy, laden by machine modulation and chopped by static. It was Oceano, designated commander for Curdir Bastion, sixty kilometres to the south, the second of the Mercury Wall's sub-fortifications and command points. He was Astartes, or had been, a son of the primarch Sanguinius laid low in battle and returned to serve in the shell of a Dreadnought.

'Commander,' she replied.

A squall of distortion whooped from the speakers.

'*Gener-rallllllll…*' Oceano's voice stretched into the fizz.

'Clear it!' Nasuba called.

'*General*,' came Oceano's voice again. '*We have reports from forward units in the blind zone. Mass formation approaching along Mid Elevation ridge, and spreading north towards current engagement zone.*'

'What position and strength?'

'*Multiple engines, full ground escort, Legion contingents – it is a full Titan legion advance. Close visual confirms. It is the Legio Mortis.*'

Beyond the viewslit another blink of sun brightness, a strobing ripple of explosions.

'Then who are we already fighting?'

Lake Voss shore, Mercury-Exultant kill-zone

Abhani Lus Mohana gazed up at death as it strode to meet her.

Carnifector Noctis had been a proud engine. A beautiful

thing of iron and war, the Warlord had walked on battlefields across the galaxy as the Great Crusade had made the
stars the new Imperium. It had died on Beta-Garmon, fallen
down on the plains of ruin, and its sacred iron had been
left in its grave as the Legio Solaris had fled the Titan Death.
It was mourned. It and all of its lost siblings and cousins.
The oil tears of enginseers had fallen in crucibles of molten
silver. The song of electro-priests had spun the dirges through
capacitor and circuit. It was gone, a sacred fragment of the
Machine-God left on the battlefield.

Noble hunter of Solaria, war engine to a dozen of the sisters
and daughters of Solaria, kin to *Bestia Est*... Dead. Gone. A
memory to be honoured.

Now it walked towards Abhani Lus Mohana.

Its skin of iron hung on its bones. Rust covered its armour.
The kill-wounds of lost battles holed its frame. The fires of
the bombardment drained into it as it walked, inhaled by
the thing that had taken its corpse as a shell. The gaze of its
shattered head was the light of burning oil wells. She felt a
voice reach into her skull, arching across the gap between the
two engines. A wail, a high shout of rage and pain and defiance as souls and spirit vanished into oblivion. It was the voice
of the moment *Carnifector Noctis* had died the first time, the
voices of its systems and the women who had guided it to
war, a cry circling the moment they fell into darkness. Abhani
felt the fire of the dead Titan reach into her, felt its promise,
understood its meaning: as you are now, so once was I. As I
am now, so shall you be.

Abhani did the only thing left to her. She fired. Legio Solaria
were the Emperor's Hunters, swift, subtle and deadly in war.
They weakened enemies, deceived them and then used the
might of their engines' weapons to deliver a killing blow. 'The
blow that can't be resisted only needs to be delivered once,'

her grandmother, and the founding Grand Master of the Legio, had said. There was nowhere left to run. No cunning switch of movement and feint to play. There were tears on her face as *Bestia Est* roared at the Warlord with the full force of the last inch of its being. Abhani saw the cruel jest of life's circle at that moment.

The deluge of laser blasts and mega-bolter shells struck *Carnifector Noctis* in its head. It had no shield. The metal tore and ran. Cracks from its kill-wounds split wide; ash and embers and blood poured out, showering to the ground. It twisted, shaking like a human caught by a gout of water. Its cannon fired. Explosions lit in the battle that surrounded them.

A beam of light, smaller and narrower but star bright, sliced into its right leg. It slid backwards, staggering. Abhani saw the auspex outline of one of the Vyronii Knights jinking around *Carnifector Noctis'* legs, slicing up into its bulk with a beam of white light. The dead Warlord trembled, half falling. Molten metal was pouring from it, but whatever thing of the warp had been poured into it after it had been dragged from the grave would not let go. Its gun arm swept around. Explosions fountained lake mud and black water into the air. It was still moving forwards, too, dragging its legs even as they came apart and its torso became slag. *Bestia Est* kept firing as it walked backwards. The mega-bolter failed, barrels yellow with heat, auto loaders jamming.

Abhani swore.

'Capacitors at four per cent!' called her moderati.

'Reactor output at critical.'

'Hold on it!' shouted Abhani.

Carnifector Noctis raised the ruin of its right leg to step. Its foot came down. Half-molten pistons burst. Struts sheared and suddenly the dead Warlord was an avalanche of cracked metal and flame.

'Get clear!' roared Abhani across the vox. *Bestia Est* danced backwards. At the edge of sight Abhani saw the Vyronii Knight pacing away as the bulk of the Warlord hit the mud and water. Steam billowed up, followed by a wash of coiling red flame as whatever had driven its frame shrieked away into the sky.

Bestia Est halted, its weapon arms limp for a second. Heat coiled from the cherry-red barrels of its mega-bolter. Its head dipped. Inside its cockpit, Abhani Lus Mohana closed her eyes. She could feel her own rage boiling across the manifold and being reflected back by her engine as its exhausted reactor rebuilt power. She opened her eyes. *Bestia Est* straightened.

'Get us moving,' she called. 'Shields up, power to the guns, and mark targets.'

The sky was bright with fire, she realised. All down the shore of the lake explosions flared. Strobing light bleached banks of smoke white. The water itself was burning, as oil poured onto its surface and ignited. As she watched she saw a Titan, a Nightgaunt she thought, stagger through a bank of billowing plasma fire, the metal of its back and limbs stripping away into the inferno.

'Find the others,' she commanded. 'Bring us back into formation and get us something to kill.'

At the edge of her sensorium she saw the lone Armiger Knight come around in a circle locking into wide formation with *Bestia Est* and its kin as they loped back into sensor range. She keyed transmit.

'Knight of Vyronii,' she called, and then stopped. The formality of what she was going to say failed as it came to her tongue. 'My thanks,' she said.

'My honour,' came the reply.

<Merge shields! All maniples, merge shields!> Tetracauron shouted the command across noosphere and vox. *Reginae*

Furorem stepped back; *Ignis Vespula* and *Sun Fury* stepped into
the space off each of its shoulders.

A blast wave struck *Reginae Furorem* from the left side. Tetracauron was not even aware of the source. The explosion burst,
spreading in an eye-blink across the curve of its shields before
vanishing with a thunderclap.

<Calculations complete,> came the voice of Xeta-Beta-1.
<Synchronisation achieved and propagated.>

<Begin,> he willed.

<As you will it,> replied Xeta-Beta-1. <Bring us together.
Make us one.>

Merging the void shields of multiple Titans was not a simple
undertaking. A single error and the result would at best be
the failure of the shield envelope, and at worst something
more catastrophic and spectacular. The soul and spirit of each
machine had to be brought to the point where they were functioning to the same rhythm, where the vibration of shield
projector and electro output were matched. The engines of
a legion used sacred code choruses passed from engine to
engine, the patterns and solutions to the hyper-complex equations soothing and agitating the system of each until they
were vibrating to the same tune of input-output. To achieve
this took exceptional skill and training. To do it in battlefield conditions took nerve and precision beyond what most
Titan crews could achieve. To merge fields between the Titans
in multiple maniples while surrounded by detonations and
hostile engines took something more again: it took the ability
to touch the divine truth of all machines. It took a miracle.

Amongst the fire, the shields of the three Titans glimmered,
a shower of cold silver lost in the glare of a burning world.
Lightning ran through mid-air as void enclosures met, clashed,
pressed, and flowed together.

The spirits of the other engines bled over the meshed bridge of data. Tetracauron could feel the weight of the two Reavers' presence and the call of their crew. Blurred ghost-images flickered through his sight. The roar of three reactors locked to the same heartbeat was an anvil-struck rhythm in his chest.

<Step,> he sent, and the three Titans stepped forward as one.

A shape was lurching towards them, towering, lopsided, its gun belching cracked globes of plasma. The spheres of light struck the air before *Reginae Furorem* and its kin. The first layer of void shields collapsed, but the shared generators of the trio were already regenerating them as they fell. Across the data-links to the rest of his command he could sense the rest of the other Titans doing the same: merging shields, matching weapon fire and reactor output. Going forwards. Into the fire. Killing.

<All weapons lock to target,> he sent, <cycle reactors and ammunition. Continual fire... Order the secutarii reserve in, now. Full engagement.>

Enemies drawn in green. Machines rising into sight. Gun barrels turning. The ground shaking. The power of a god all around him. Iron and light and this moment of oneness. He was not Tetracauron. He was not *Reginae Furorem*. He was the will of fire, and the fury and the light. Soaring... Becoming... Burning.

<Compliance,> came the chorus from the god-machines, and deepening night vanished into bright tatters.

The secutarii came apart. Charred flesh and torn armour blew into the air like fine ash caught in a gust of wind. Tetracauron saw it happen through the eyes of the machine. A stream of las-fire sawed through them, punching through armour layers and vulcanised rubber. Shapes stalked from the smoke pall, small and swift, like giant insects cast in oil-slick metal. Each would have been three times the height of a mortal had they straightened up, but they ran hunched over, gun

mounts blitzing light from their backs. In *Reginae Furorem*'s
sight they were a spilling swarm tide.

<Hunter automata, left flank,> he pulsed.

<Executing,> came the response from *Sun Fury*. The other
princeps' sending was a sharp burst of light. An instant later the
other Titan pivoted, the barrels of its gun arm spinning. Muzzle
flash breathed from the barrels. Shells exploded amongst the
automata swarm. Metal tore into shards. The ground heaved
under the impact. *Sun Fury* panned the spinning barrels across
the ground, chewing through the enemy even as they bounded
forwards. There was a frenzy protocol driving the automata,
Tetracauron could tell, something all-consuming and corrupting from a code data set that had been placed beyond reach.
Before now, before the war made all that was unthinkable real.

Sun Fury's cannons fired a last spit of fire then spun on for
a second.

<Ammunition exhausted,> sent *Sun Fury*.

The secutarii were reforming, shields locking together in
ranked lines, three hundred metres from *Reginae Furorem* and
its kin. Bodies lay in front of the shield line, a tideline of torn
silver and mashed red.

They were advancing down the line of the lake, the rest of
the battle group with them. The enemy were pushing light,
fast ground units in from the south. The noosphere was buzzing with scrap code and connection breaks. Cohesion was a
matter of sight and instinct as much as communication now.
That was the Ignatum way, though: in war as one, of one will
and drive. The fast ground units could only mean one thing –
another major force was closing. They were facing greater than
their numbers already, and now the enemy had brought still
greater strength to the field. Their tactic was simple: pin Ignatum in place while bleeding their ammunition and numbers,
drive them into a pocket and then hit that pocket with another

force. Victory. A victory that should not have been possible without greater losses than the enemy could bear. The numbers that Tetracauron had engaged on the edge of the lake were not enough to hold his battle group. Not if they had been Titans alone. They were not though. They were something else – the loyal dead of hundreds of battles animated by unclean spirits and sent to walk against the living. It was an insult, an abomination, and it had worked. They were still here, hours into engagement, bracketed between water and fire.

Two maniples of the battle group had waded into the lake, churning the water to foam as they strode up to their waists. If they had been able to create an engagement angle from the north, they could have encircled and burned the enemy. As it was, the lake was deeper than the scant survey data had said, but shelved off into a subsurface abyss. The engines could not cross and so had to wade through the water parallel with the shore to engage the enemy flank. Mist roiled across the rippling lake as the heat from weapon discharge flashed water to steam. Munitions detonated under the surface. Geysers of water fountained up. Pressure waves ripped through the water to slam into the shins of red-and-yellow Titans.

On the shore, fire and smoke hid the ground. The wall guns had stopped firing, unable to pick clear targets or communicate with the battle group to mark fire points. The long-range comms had collapsed under a blizzard of static and data corruption that had blown up as the battle deepened. Even the intra-Titan communications were sporadic. Ghosts and screams shrieked across the noosphere. The engagement was now a bloody, burning brawl, but it could only have one outcome. The risen Titans of the enemy were falling, the metal of their frames melted to slag and torn to atoms and dust, the unclean spirits within sent howling into the pyre.

<Auspex contact, multiple engines and ground units one

hundred and thirty-five degrees south,> sent Divisia. <Estimate eight thousand metres and closing.>

<Incoming munition–> began Cartho.

An explosion bleached the sight of the land. A howl flared across the incandescence. The sheet of light resolved to a billowing fist of flame and plasma punching up into the sky a kilometre away. Tetracauron felt *Reginae Furorem* shake with sympathetic rage. A blink of shock and fury transmitted in iron and electro current. He knew what that was – full reactor breach, a pair of Ignatum Titans dying in a single bright instant. The blast wave blew into them a moment later. Void shields flared. The incandescence spun with crystallising data.

<That was *Vulcanis Furio* and *Pyre Jackal*,> breathed Cartho, his sending flattened with shock.

<Kill shot source,> he snapped.

<Long-range, multiple sources,> replied Divisia. <Coordinated laser and missile burst. They have our range.>

<Then we have theirs,> Tetracauron snarled. <Coordinate and fire when ready.>

Fire breathing from his lips, blistering his tongue.

Reginae Furorem, *Sun Fury* and *Ignis Vespula* were coming about, moving forwards. Behind them, four other maniples manoeuvred to follow. The battle with the risen Titans was still rolling across the shore and surface of the lake.

The incandescence was near totality now. The voices of crew merged into that of the machine. He felt the target runes lock, cold ice reaching into the blaze. Weapons swivelled. His kin moved with him, two giants made smaller only by the size of their Warlord. The weapons left to them were volcano cannons, plasma destructors and turbo-lasers. Their racks of missiles and rockets were empty, the ammunition of cannons drained. They could only fire on what they could see, but they could see. Eight thousand metres away the first true engines of Legio Mortis advanced.

These were not the damaged, risen abominations that had come first. Clad in crimson and black and edged in gold they walked forwards. Unhurried. Skulls rattled on cables slung beneath their pale heads. Tattered banners and chains hung from them. Even as Tetracauron perceived them, he felt the drone of scrap code break over him. Troops and battle machines moved in the shadow of the Mortis vanguard, glistening, a carpet of gloss red and corroded chrome. Warhounds bounded forwards. Clutches of Knights in the colours of old bone and iron paced at their side. Behind them, Reavers walked. In the incandescence their guns and eyes were blots of darkness. Notes of corrupt code spun from the target runes as they locked on to the distant engines.

Part of him, the part that was a human mind and a human will, noted that the engines were coming at quarter speed, lighter engines running and walking in lines, staggered so that they could fire up to seven lines deep. It was the Configuration of Annihilation, the way that Mortis had walked to war against enemies marked not just for defeat but for complete destruction. As though they sensed Tetracauron's gaze, the lead Mortis Titans sounded their war-horns. Sound boomed and ululated across the smoke-covered ground.

<Fire,> impulsed Tetracauron.

Beams of las leaped between the god-machines. Blue, white and red light gridded eight kilometres of air. The cacophony of battle rose in pitch, roiling up to the sky. The beams from Ignatum blew out the shields on a Warhound. It paced aside as its void bubbles burst in sheets of light. Its feet crushed a line of spider-limbed tanks. Explosions blossomed in its tread. Tetracauron felt the cold of the target lock, and the answering roar from within. A line of blue-bright energy cut the world. The volcano cannon burst hit the Warhound as it was half turning in its stride. The beam burned through its cannon arm. The rounds waiting in the hopper and chamber became vapour and light an instant before the beam passed through the Warhound's carapace and into the compartment within.

The Warhound had not been blessed with the greater ascendancy and changes made to its kin. For it, the father of the scythe had given only a taste of its breath. Enough to fuse its servitors and enginseer to its bones, and fill its internal spaces with congealed blood and jellied bone that gurgled across the vox. They died in a blink of fire as the volcano beam lanced into the core of the engine and blew it apart with the plasma from its own, corrupt core.

<Engine kill.> Tetracauron was not sure whose voice it was or if it was his own. It did not matter. He was walking with the shore and lake behind him, his kin at his side, as the enemy emerged from the distance, more and more of them. He felt the presence of *Sun Fury* beside him, heard its voice speak to him as they walked in lockstep and drew breath to fire again.

<We are–> began the voice.

There was a ripple in the air, a scratch dragged across the night, a shriek like a dagger point pulled down a sheet of glass.

Sun Fury's head blew apart. The Reaver's leg kept moving for an instant. Then it fell, collapsing, its void shields misfiring. The synchronised envelope of shields burst. Tetracauron felt the snap of feedback as a spike of white pain inside his skull. *Sun Fury* hit the ground. Fires rolled through its torso.

<What–> began Divisia.

<Warp missiles,> roared Cartho in reply as another shriek ripped through sound and code.

Warp missiles… Ancient, precious, abominable for their intent and use. Fired from an engine, the missiles burrowed through the fabric of space and passed through the realm beyond before tearing back into being and exploding. As they bypassed natural laws, shields were no proof against them, armour was no proof against them. They were like the needle dagger thrust under the plate and mail of kings by assassins in ages past.

A bright explosion enveloped *Ignis Vespula*'s back and tore its dorsal missile racks and half of its carapace off. The Reaver bellowed a stream of damage and code invective. Beams of plasma reached across the distance and burst on its failing shields. *Reginae Furorem* and Tetracauron roared as one, striding forward, and into the line of fire.

Sharp pain as voids burst.

<Target lock.>

<Firing.>

Light pouring into the distance, the scream of reactor and weapon the death call for the dead lying at its side and its wounded kin.

<Target shields failed.>

<Engine strike.>

<Engine strike.>

The shrieks as the devil weapons struck engines across the battle group, exploded, crippled, scarred metal falling in torn shreds… Burning… The world burning…

Calculations spun into his mind from the cold cognition of Xeta and the minds of Divisia and Cartho: mounting enemy numbers, weapon and reactor condition, engines lost and damaged, the cold ratios of cause and effect in war. They would die here. The rational turning of the numbers spoke to that. He thought of the emissary Gerontius-Chi-Lambda, and the tech-priest's words:

'I wish the data were not as it is, but above all I am a servant of the machine's truth – annihilation is coming.'

No, said a voice that he knew was his own. *There is only one way, and that way is forward. We are strength enough. We are victory!*

Reginae Furorem moved to his will. Enemy strikes lit the distance.

<All units, cohere and maintain fire – we are victory!>

All the world burning, the success calculations dropping away into the blaze of connection with his engine and the moment, bright beyond measure. The shadows of the enemy multiplying on the horizon, and him going towards them, closing the distance, firing, and the engines of his kin firing, the ground heaving with detonations and the air burning. The shots from the enemy were multiplying, forming a streaked sheet above the ground. The numbers and ratios and odds falling into black motes at the edge of the blaze in his sight. The voices of the incandescence a chorus. Was he moving in war or dreaming through war?

<Target lock…>

<Weapon discharging…>

<Target lock…>

<Shields down…>

<Weapons charge cycling…>

<Reactor output rising…>

<Carapace impact… >

<Damage…>

<Weapon discharging…>

He was bleeding, molten blood rolling from his shoulder… The cloak of his shields a glimmering set of tatters. So many… there were so many in his sight. He blinked and found that he was seeing with his own eyes, the battle a glare beyond the viewports. The cockpit smelled of charring wire. His left arm was wet, sympathetic wounds pulsing blood down his chest from his shoulder. He could not feel anything; he was floating, his mind and thoughts carried elsewhere, aware of the impacts on his metal skin and the Titans of his command pushing forward into the oncoming fire. He did not feel fear or disconnection, for he was connected: he was one with the machine at war. This was just a moment, a last gift from the machine that he had given his spirit to.

Explosions lit the distance. Rolling down the first line of advancing engines, ripping tanks and automata into the air, swallowing the shapes of Mortis. Missiles stretched from behind them, beams and pulses of plasma, torrents of shells lobbed to fall like deadly seeds scattered from an unkind hand.

Tetracauron slammed back into the brightness of the incandescence.

Fresh motes of data spun across his sight. Impacts across the enemy advance, spreading across the land in a wall of roiling fire and light. From over a hundred kilometres behind them the guns of the wall were firing, curtaining the kill-zone, slicing it across with a stroke over a hundred kilometres wide.

At his back, Tetracauron heard the scratching of a voice forming over the vox-connection.

<Ignatum.> Even through the storm of distortion, Tetracauron could feel the weight of the word and recognised it, the focus, the raw will to victory, the ages of knowledge bound into it and the machine it spoke for. <We walk at your side, my kin,> said Princeps Maximus Cydon. From towards the Mercury Wall, the first of the Ignatum main force Titans marched into the battle sphere. Over a hundred engines of war, bonded Knights and cohorts of ground troops moving with them, and at their centre two machines greater than all the rest. Towering, hung with city-killing weaponry, their backs hunched under fortifications that they carried with steps that summoned thunder from the earth. They had names, ancient names that had been spoken with fear and awe in places of victory and devastation.

Imperious Prima, Warmonger, and with it *Magnificum Incendius*, Imperator, both of the Emperor class of Titans, greatest of the avatars of the Machine-God's majesty and wrath, leading the remainder of Ignatum to war. Tetracauron felt the fire of

Reginae Furorem rise. The world was sound and thunder and the light of flame.

Command Bunker, Shard Bastion, Mercury Wall

'Tactical read-outs are incomplete,' Kurral called to Nasuba. 'But it's a macro-engine advance coming straight at the Ignatum battle group.'

'Get a link to them,' she called.

'Negative general, vox-link cannot be made.'

'Do they even know what's coming?' asked Sulkova.

'They are still fighting, it's a full-level engagement – visual estimate they are maintaining total weapon discharge,' said Kurral. 'By all that is true, they are advancing.'

'They are Ignatum,' said Sulkova softly. 'It is what they do.'

'General!' The call came from the door. She turned to see a figure in the uniform of a Cordozian Arqueber. Sweat was pouring down his face, his eyes were wide. 'Runner from the Ignatum principal strategium.'

'Runner? The internal vox- and data-conduits are reading as functional.'

'All communication systems below the seven hundred height mark are down…' He shucked another breath. 'Just… static… and…' He paused, his wide eyes rolling around the bunker space. Nasuba wondered how long the boy had been running. He looked exhausted, and worse, he looked on the edge of turning and running again. It was a look of more than exhaustion; it was the look of someone who had already reached the end but was somehow still moving. 'Can… can you hear it?' he said, voice low, puzzled, eyelids blinking rapidly.

'Deliver your message,' said Nasuba. A sheet of light snapped through the viewslit, blinding even at this distance, curdling to a false sunset red.

'It's out there...' the runner mumbled. His eyes were on the viewslit. 'It's just there...'

'Trooper!' snapped Sulkova, and the boy's eyes darted up to her, blinking faster. He was breathing harder, Nasuba noticed.

'I have this...' He held out a plastek-wrapped furl of parchment. Sulkova took it, snapped the seals, eyes moving over the code wrapper, fingers checking the truth marks on the print.

'Checked and first authentication,' she said. 'Ignatum are walking.'

'How many?'

'Mass deployment, twenty maniples at full stride.'

'This is all going to be over by then. Lock all guns, all levels – saturate across the line and by depth.'

'General, the resonant vibrations will shake the wall apart,' said Kurral. 'We must calibrate the regulation.'

'If we lose this they will be at distance zero before dawn, and the damned guns will be useless.'

'General, vox to Master Efried and Bhab are broken. Scrap code is wild in the–'

'Get me Commander Oceano.'

'*General...*'

'Commander, I'm ordering my section of the wall guns to full fire, all levels, graded saturation. Bracket the engagement zone, hammer the rest.'

'*That cannot be maintained for long, Nasuba.*'

'I know.'

'*I concur. Our wall section will begin fi–*' The vox cut out, then shrieked and kept on shrieking.

The messenger runner moved then. The young Cordozian must have run a kilometre upstairs and clambered up the access shafts that honeycombed the Mercury Wall. It was no small distance, no small effort even for a fit human in the prime of health. For someone who had most likely only slept

in shreds and in the clutch of unquiet dreams, it was an effort
that would have left them empty. But somehow the boy had
enough strength left to run forwards. His eyes were wide, his
teeth bared. For an instant Nasuba thought that she was about
to die, that all of her years of war would end here in an attack
by a wild-eyed youth who looked as though he could barely
stand. Her hand closed on her pistol before the troopers in
the door began to move, but the runner was already on her…
and then past her. He leapt, diving at the viewslit.

It was narrow.

Too narrow for a human skull.

Too narrow for a body.

There was a crunch, a gasp, a wet writhing and snapping.
A sobbed word.

Nasuba lunged for the trooper's foot. Another sob as her
fingers touched his boot and began to close. Another crunch.
And he was gone. And then there was just a wet, jelly-red
smear across the edges of the viewslit and the wail of static
coming over the vox, a noise that in the moment sounded to
Nasuba like a voice, like a final word uttered as the speaker
began to fall without end.

'Paradise,' she thought she heard.

A second later someone yanked the cables out of the vox-
speaker, and for a heartbeat everything was still; then the wall
and world began to shake as the guns began to fire.

Enemy distance to wall: 106 kilometres.

FOURTEEN

Stygian angel
Falling
Breathing

Marmax South

There was a dead man on the wire who would not lie down. In the remains of the blockhouse, Katsuhiro could hear the wires flexing, and the feet scrabbling in the dirt. He tried not to listen, bent his head and began the silent words that he spoke to himself. The words were his own, a simple string of pleas and reminders stitched together from the thoughts that gave him comfort.

Protect me as I stand in service of You…

He dug through the fog of his exhausted mind, saw the light in his memory unfold from the woman called Keeler. Saw, for an instant, the day become bright…

Protect those that I cannot…

Out on the line, the razor wires thrashed, snapping in the still air. He tried to pull his thoughts back to the light, back to the words.

Please give me strength…

'When's it going to stop?' Steena's voice snapped out. Katsu-hiro opened his eyes. The words and the golden memory faded into the grey-and-ochre murk of the present. It was dawn again, though the divide between day and night had blurred so that now it meant little. Three others sat in the blockhouse. Steena and two others that Katsuhiro did not recognise. He might have seen them before, but he was not sure and he didn't want to know.

Marmax South had changed since he had come onto the line. There was barely anything of it left now. The lower walls were torn and existed only in sections. There were not enough repair crews to patch them up any more, not enough of the wall to be patched up either. The lines were an archipelago of broken walls and shattered bunkers. Piles of rubble lay in the place of the gun towers. Katsuhiro did not know where the original emplacements had been. They had pulled back and then moved to occupy the ruins that remained. Mine launch-ers had scattered mines and spools of razor wire into the new no-man's-land. The enemy had changed too. The colours and madness of the attack on his first morning were gone. In a way, in moments when the cracks of weakness grew wider, he wished they would return. Somehow the horror would have been a solution. Katsuhiro knew he was not alone in thinking that.

Another gurgling cry rose from outside the bunker. Wire pinged and jingled.

'Shut up!' shouted Steena. She was shivering. She tried to sleep a lot, but there was little peace for rest, and when dreams came the waking was somehow worse than the exhaustion. Steena had been weeping as she dreamed for the last four days. 'Shut up! Shut up!' She was really shouting now, hitting her hands against the floor. Drawing blood. The other two troop-ers were looking at her. One of them had moved his finger to the trigger of his gun.

'I'll deal with it,' Katsuhiro said, and pulled himself to his feet. He put a hand on Steena's shoulder. 'I'll deal with it, all right.' He looked at the other troopers, caught their bloodshot gaze and nodded, hoping that the gesture looked stronger than it felt. They did not respond, but he noticed their fingers come off the triggers.

He turned and went to the main firing slit. A ragged hole opened the shell of the blockhouse's eastern face to the waste-land beyond; the firing slit sat beside the breach. He went to the slit, raised his gun and rested it on the metal lip. It had been quiet, but it was safer to use the slit rather than fire from the breach. You never knew when ill-luck or a watching enemy would choose that moment to blow you apart. He had seen it happen. Several times.

The butt of the rifle went into his shoulder. He took a breath, tried to see the golden light. A small glimmer in the distance, just enough. He put his eye to the gunsight and looked. Clouds of yellow vapour drifted and curled to white and grey. The ground slid into the hazed distance. Craters and the soft, folded lumps of corpses and parts of corpses formed crests and dips, like the frozen waves and troughs of a sea. He tried not to look too far into the distance. You never knew what you would see there, standing in the half-seen band where the sky and ground merged.

The dead man was just fifty paces out. An explosion had taken off his right arm and scooped away the left half of his torso. The neck was broken. Bits of the skull had peeled back from the soft meat inside. He had probably been caught in a mortar blast, as likely from the lines as the enemy. He had died further out, then dragged himself until he had been tangled by the wire. He had nearly made it to the lines. Katsuhiro had not been able to shake that idea since the corpses had started to rise and walk, that whatever drove them was not hunger or rage, or the fighting instincts that had driven them in life. That it was something simpler, something smaller, the first and last instinct of all living beings – the drive to reach home.

He looked at the dead man through the gunsight. The razor wire was wrapped around his neck and hands. Every time the corpse moved, the barbs cut deeper. Maggots were moving in the eye sockets. Katsuhiro saw the dead man open his mouth as though to try to speak. He fired. The las-bolt hit the skull and blew it apart. He put another one through the upper torso. Then waited, watching the steam rise from the corpse. It did not move.

'Be at peace,' whispered Katsuhiro. 'May He guide you to rest.'

'Waste of ammo,' said one of the other troopers. Katsuhiro did not answer. The trooper was right. Charge packs, bullets, grenades, mines, food, water… all of it was dwindling. The last resupply had been… he was not sure how long ago. Everyone took what they could from the dead but even so, the number of shots he had left to fire was counting down. He would rather waste the shots than let Steena keep listening to the sound of the dead man on the wire. He went back and squatted down next to her. She had tilted her head back, eyes closing, helmet resting against the rockcrete. He nudged her. Her faced twisted.

'You do that again, script, and I'll–'

'Can't sleep,' he said, looking at her. 'Not out here. Remember? Forward position, right? Have to keep our eyes open.'

She closed her mouth, shook her head, but she did not rest it back again. Katsuhiro went back to watching the waste-land through the blast hole in the bunker. Out of the edge of his eyes. It was safer that way; never look straight at the way trouble came. That was a lesson that had become a rule in the last… however long it had been. Don't look straight, don't look at things you saw, not directly.

A shadow moved across the breach and he flinched his gun up, ready. Baeron moved across the view, blotting it out for a second as he pivoted his head to look into the blockhouse. The Blood Angel was a ruin of half-shattered armour. His left pauldron was gone, leaving the mag-plates and connectors dangling. The right forearm was flayed of ceramite down to the flesh. Gouges marked every plate. The red lacquer now only clung to recesses and small patches. A crack ran down the left cheek of his helm, just next to the eyepiece, dark and jagged, like the signature of lightning. He buzzed and clattered as he turned away from them and moved on.

Katsuhiro whispered a murmur of thanks that such warriors still stood, still endured. There were fewer of them though – like everything, they dwindled.

'Rise! Weapons ready!' Baeron's voice boomed out. Katsuhiro came to his feet before his mind had really heard the words. Steena did not move until Katsuhiro pulled her up. The other two were moving slowly, too, like men wading through mud. Katsuhiro had his gun up and steady on the firing slit. 'Rise!'

It was coming again. He could feel it and taste it as he tugged the mask of his breath hood down. The thing was nearly useless, the carbon plug filthy, the hood frayed and the edges of the eyepieces bleeding rust across his sight. It would not save him from a plague wind, or gas attack. It was as good as useless, but it gave a little glimmer of hope that it might save him. Little hope. But sometimes a little was all there was. His eyes fixed on Baeron. The Blood Angel stood five paces in front of the line of broken fortifications, gaze fixed on the lost horizon, bolter held loose in his hands. In the distance down the line, just in sight, another angel in shattered red stood. Katsuhiro could see the shadows of soldiers moving up to firing points behind the remains of parapets and in trenches. There was no sound. No one spoke. Everyone was just trying to look for what was coming. Look and not look.

'Two hundred metres, front,' called Baeron, voice booming.

Hold. Just hold this time. Fire and don't go back. Don't let them close. Don't let them reach us... Please don't let them reach us.

He saw them. Out of the corner of his sight he saw them. They came silently, no cries or shouts, faces masked in rotting cloth, weapons that might have been tools held in bare hands. Slowly, walking forward, first just a loose line and then a close press of them. Larger shapes moved behind them. Katsuhiro felt his eyes twitch to look.

Great hulks lumbering through the mist, shaking and shivering, skin stretched too tight over bags of fluid, stretched past breaking.

Katsuhiro snatched his eyes down, breathing hard, the taste of offal and acid in his mouth. His eyes were streaming. The glimpse of the rolling shapes smeared his retina yellow and red.

'Protect me as I stand in Your service...' he gasped. One of the other troopers was vomiting, green bile and blood spattering the rockcrete.

'Fire!' called Baeron. His bolter roared. A portion of the oncoming tide vanished in a stream of explosive rounds. Bodies exploded. Bone shrapnel tore figures to either side. Limbs blew off, legs stumbled. Katsuhiro pointed his gun and began firing. He was not aiming but he didn't need to – just to point into the distance, brace and squeeze the trigger. Down the line others were firing, too, a disordered squall of las-bolts and rounds whipping across the closing gap with the enemy, punching into it, tearing it, burning it. Somewhere behind the blockhouse, mortars opened up. Shells whistled through the air, hitting deep behind the first ranks and punching clouds of shrapnel and torn flesh into the air. Heavy guns followed them. The sound was a gathering thunder roar. Katsuhiro felt his gun dry-fire, and ripped the charge-mag out, slamming another in, dropping the empty to the floor. No one was conserving ammunition, there was no point – lose here, lose now, and there wouldn't be another battle for them to fire all the shots they saved. Baeron was going forwards, walking towards the closing enemy, firing and firing, steady, like a king walking towards the flowing tide. Down the line the other angels were doing the same. Not going back, going forwards, a few red figures walking towards a horde, firing and firing.

Throne and truth but it was a sight… Not backwards but forwards, broken-armoured, but unbowed.

'Protect me as I stand in service of You…'

Katsuhiro could hear them calling, voices rising in a booming dirge that broke over the gunfire. It was a song of sorts, beautiful as it was terrifying, like the call of a great beast and the voices of old, old souls calling out to all they had lost. The angels had begun to do this in the last days when the surge attacks came. He had asked Baeron the night before what the song was. The angel had looked at him for a long moment, the eyepieces in his cracked helm an emerald glow in the dark.

'It is the Death Lament of Baal,' he had said, at last. 'The song of passing from the world.'

'You are singing of your deaths because you know we will die here?'

'To die is our purpose.'

Something in the oncoming enemy fired back. Yellow-orange energy exploded across the ground next to Baeron. The rubble flashed to slag. Dust fizzed to smoke. Hard rounds began to spit from the horde, first a few, then more. The air was buzzing. Impacts pinged off the wall below the firing slit. Splinters of rockcrete flew up. The left eyepiece shattered in Katsuhiro's breath mask. He flinched back.

'Shit!' shouted Steena. A shard had hit her left hand as she steadied her gun, and torn through the leather of her gauntlets and into her flesh. He could see blood pumping. White bone. 'Shit!'

'Keep firing!' he shouted at her. 'Keep firing!' One of the other troopers firing through the breach staggered back, blood pumping from a hole punched into his throat. He fell, gurgling, legs scrabbling and kicking. Blood pumped out.

Katsuhiro was still firing. He saw smoke rising from the enemy, twisting and rising, more and more fog. The figures were falling. The wail and thump of mortars was beating like a drum. The looming shapes waddling forwards behind the horde were closer. Throne and truth, they were closer! He wanted to look, wanted so badly to look to see what was coming. He could smell spoiled milk and salt, taste acid and copper. The fog was moving, flexing, distances breaking at the edge of his eyes. The smoke rose and rose from the enemy. Except it wasn't smoke. It was a swarm of insects. Black bodies the size of bullets buzzed and circled on grey wings. He could hear them as they rose and turned in the air. He could hear his own breathing coming in gasps. The tide was almost at Baeron now. The Blood Angel fired straight forward, drilling into the bodies of the enemy. They were still coming, ranks falling as they met the hail of gunfire from the line. They still came, forming a bank of chewed flesh that the living scrambled over to die. Limbs and torn bags of meat tumbled. Black bodies rose from the red slick, rising into the air, scattering blood. The air reeked of iron and burst organs. They were at the line, filling the outer ditch with offal and shredded meat.

Baeron was reloading, snapping a magazine into his bolter, going forwards, striving into the tide, drilling into it with gunfire as it curved and crested above him. His armour was red again, red and glistening.

Katsuhiro realised he was staring. His finger was working the trigger but his gun was not firing. He scrambled for a charge pack.

'What is happening?' Steena was gasping. She had frozen, hands slack on her gun.

'Keep firing!' he shouted. His hand could not find the charge pack that should have been there. He looked down, trying to see the pack in his ammo pouch.

'No...' He heard the moan from the other trooper in the bunker loud and shrill.

His hand found the charge pack, last one.

'No...'

Katsuhiro snapped the pack into the port. The other trooper in the bunker dropped to his knees. Steena gasped as though punched in the gut. Katsuhiro looked up. Eyes fully open, he looked through the opening into the wasteland beyond.

Bodies tumbling over and over, blood and burst skin falling like sea foam at the crest of a wave. Shapes in the distance, so close... The buzz of insects loud enough to swallow the boom of guns. Black flies like polished jewels. Blood a mist on the air. The sky above flashing, pulsing with filthy yellow light. Baeron amongst it, red, so red, standing, but not going forward now. Fighting not to go back.

And above it, unfolding in the air, at the edge of seeing, a shape growing larger, sucking in light like a hole cut into his sight. A hooded shape, wings spread behind it to blot out the flash of light, the shadow of a scythe in its hands. He thought of the scraps of dead myths and stories that still persisted even in this age that should have been one of bright truth without the superstitions and fears of old humanity. He thought of angels, not noble, not born of light, but which passed as shadows.

In his mind he heard the voices of all that he had seen fall,

all the people he had loved and wished were not gone calling to him out of memory, gurgling last words out of fluid-filled lungs, speaking words that they did not realise were last farewells. The sounds stitched together, pulsing through him like the vibration of a great bell. Not a sentence spoken, but a meaning that Katsuhiro felt to his core.

As we are, so shall you be…

He felt his breath rattle as it drew between his teeth. His sight was greying, his eyes clouding. The tide of figures was still flowing forwards, but the fire cutting into it was slackening. The world before him was slowing, stretching, moving with the agonised slowness of the time before something feared becomes something which cannot be escaped. Beside him, Steena slumped to the floor. The other trooper in the blockhouse dropped his gun and began to run. Katsuhiro felt himself want to follow, to run and run until this was not real, until it became a dream that he could wake from…

Just lay down, said a sweet voice in the back of his head. It was soft, gentle, the voice of the peace of sleep and the kindness of dreams, of fresh water, sunshine and laughter. *Just lay down and come to paradise*. All he needed to do was stop and close his eyes, and the living world would go. He would not need to live it any more. He could walk in sleep, and leave the world to its nightmare.

'No!' he gasped, breathing hard. 'No! He protects me as I serve Him. He protects me as I serve Him!' He was bellowing, gun up and firing, as the shadow of the angel of despair passed across the light and people fled back from the oncoming tide.

Magnifican

'On the world I was born, you would not get a name until you had ridden alone for three days and nights, and returned.'

Shiban felt Cole look at him.

'I don't think that applies to this one,' Cole said, and nodded at the infant. He sounded tired. Shiban had tried to keep the man talking. Talking kept the blood moving, kept the feet moving and the mind from thinking too much. There was something out there, back the way they had come. Shiban knew it. They had kept moving at night and passed half of the day in the shell of a tower. Its walls were marble, its floors glass tiles – both now shattered. Jewelled fragments of crimson, dulled under ash and dust.

There had been water, too, still drinkable, caught in a pressure-sealed tank that must have fed the flower vines that now hung like burnt hair down the tower's sides. Nothing to eat though. Shiban had shut down the gnawing feeling in his gut.

He could go for weeks without food, but the damage to his body and the demands of walking were burning his reserves like a furnace. He had thought of eating the various carcasses and deposits of rotting biowaste that they had come across. He had decided not to. He had noticed that even the corpses of the recent dead were gathering films of iridescent slime. Blooms of bright fungus clustered in the sockets of the skull of a dead trooper he had seen. The smell of putrefaction was different, too – sweet and sickly, like flowers and burning sugar.

Cole was getting thinner and weaker. The child persisted though. Somehow it persisted.

'He should have a name,' Cole said.

Shiban did not answer. His senses were fixed ahead. They had been getting closer to the Palace Anterior, and the rumble of gunfire had grown louder with each step and hour. He took a form of comfort from it – if there were sounds of battle, it meant that all was not lost.

'You don't think so?' asked Cole in reply to Shiban's silence.

'I think that his name matters less than the fact that he lives.'

'Where are you going, Shiban?' The man's question stopped him, turned him. Cole was standing, head slightly cocked, looking at Shiban with beyond-tired eyes.

'We are going to what safety remains.'

Cole frowned, smiled, swayed.

'That's not what I meant. Where are you going?'

Shiban paused. The answer that came to his lips formed and then faded. *To fight until my last*, had been the first words to come. They were not his though, not any more. No backward step… he would take no backward step, not into the past, not into the warrior who had fallen from the sky and lived.

'I am going home,' he said at last. 'I am going back to the home that has carried and made me. I am going home to die amongst my brothers.'

'To die?'

Shiban shook himself, and let the pain of the movement wash the thoughts from his mind.

'We all die,' he said, and took a step.

Cole did not follow for a second, and then Shiban heard the infant mewl, and Cole whisper a hush before following.

The ground they had been crossing began to slope down. They were in a bowl of rubble and dust. Multiple munition impacts had dug the depression through the buildings that had been there and left them as ragged stacks of rockcrete, plasteel and stone. Water had gathered in the bottom in a bright green pool. Pink blooms of fungus floated on the surface. The air tasted of open guts. Shiban skirted the pool. He was tired. He had not thought that could ever be a possibility but there it was. He needed to take another step, needed to keep going.

Something breathed across the back of his neck.

He paused.

Cole was talking about the infant's name again, chattering as he breathed hard.

'If we reach the lines, he will need a name,' said Cole. 'Paper-work is eternal.'

'Cole,' said Shiban. The feeling was growing, a breath of ice just behind him that stayed out of sight even as he turned.

'They will have to put a name on some form or docket.' Cole was looking into the fog above the crater lip, swaying, blinking as though trying to focus.

'Cole, be quiet and get down.'

'What?'

A cold gust of air. Bubbles formed and ran across the green mirror of the pool.

'Get down!' Shiban roared, grabbing Cole and spinning him to the ground.

A sound like a knife scoring glass shrieked through the air.

A shape came out of the fog above the crater in a single bound. Shiban had an impression of skin and ribs, of fangs in a wide mouth.

Shiban whirled. The shape passed over him, landed and turned.

Its body was long and famine-thin, like an apex hunter left to starve. Shiban could see bone and grey, necrotised flesh through tears in its skin. Six legs bit the ground. A seventh hung from higher on its flank, wasted and slack. Matted fur covered its head. A trio of milk-white eyes sat to the left of a snout that split into a grin of splintered teeth and raw meat. A collar of corroded bronze ringed its neck. It howled, the air rasping from a tumour-clogged throat. Shiban spun the metal pole into both hands. The beast sprang. Shiban stepped back and struck. The metal pole hit the side of the beast's head. It distorted, soft bone mushing, blood sludge and broken teeth scattering. It landed half on him, claws scrambling on his chest. He let go of the pole with one hand and slammed it into the thing's neck. His flesh was screaming. The beast's hind claws scrabbled at his chest. Its wound of a mouth was wide. He closed his fist around its throat and felt vertebrae shatter. The thing's head burst. The bottom half of its jaw snapped on threads of muscle. Its legs were still raking sparks from his ceramite. His world was pain now. Edge to edge. Lightning pinning him to the ground. He shoved the thing away from him, and spun the metal pole up as it leapt again. Torn muscles in his shoulders screamed as they bunched. The pole struck the beast in mid leap. It hit the ground, tried to rise on broken legs. Shiban stamped down on it. Its body exploded.

A cry turned him around. Cole was scrambling away from the pool edge, clutching the infant, trying to draw his pistol.

The pool was foaming. Black cracks were forming in the air.

Figures were rising from the liquid. Sodden hair trailed from lolling heads. Water-bloated limbs hung from wasted torsos. Flies rose from the bursting bubbles. Fever heat was pouring into Shiban's flesh. He went forward, the pole rising in his right hand. The first figure staggered from the pool. Shiban threw the pole. It hit the spasming figure like a javelin, punched it back and skewered it to the ground. It writhed. Flesh shredded from its fingers as it pulled itself up the pole. Shiban charged, ripped the pole free. The body flew up. He spun the pole in a wide arc. It hit the next corpse coming from the pool and broke it in two. The blow whistled on into the first body as it fell from the sky. It burst in shreds of flesh and shards of bone.

Shiban could hear true breath sawing through his teeth, could hear the thunder of agony within, and somewhere back in memory or dream the voice of Jubal Khan, Lord of Summer Lightning, as he taught the hurricane guan-dao form. *'Laugh as you strike them down. Smile at the least. When you fight like this, the chances are you are outnumbered. Fate picks such moments for us to die. Best to treat that as it deserves.'*

He met the next figure with the tip of the pole to its chest and rammed it through the bone and flesh, then turned, slamming staff and body into two more. They came apart. And he was beyond them – pushing down to the shoreline, sweeping, crushing. His teeth were bared, locked together against the roar of pain trying to break out from within him.

Not laughing, Jubal, he thought. Not laughing yet.

A las-bolt burned past him. His head snapped around. Cole had his pistol out. He shook, eyes wide.

'Move!' roared Shiban, turning back to the pool as a figure grabbed his arm. Steam burst into the air as acid burned through white lacquer. He slammed his head into the ruin of its skull. Its grip broke and he kicked it back down into the liquid as he moved towards Cole. The man was almost at the lip of the crater. He saw shapes moving in the fog beyond, bounding forwards. Gurgling growls arose. There were still figures coming from the pool. He was at the crest of the crater.

His stride faltered.

'No backward step!' he roared.

There was a taste of copper on his tongue again, and a band of neon stars danced at the edge of his sight. He felt himself stop, sway, caught himself. The metal pole dug into the ground.

'No backward step…' he hissed to himself.

'Are you alright?' asked Cole, voice sharp with fear.

Shiban nodded, but did not reply. He blinked. Fog blurred his eyes. The ground was moving. He shifted his hand on the metal pole for balance and stared at the red handprint on the shaft. Blood was oozing from the cracked joints of his gauntlets. The sweat on his head was cold.

'Shiban?'

The pain was not there. It had gone. Terrifyingly it had gone. There was just numbness radiating out from his heart.

'Shiban!'

Figures running closer…

The sound of hard rounds in the air…

Fizz-snap… Fizz-snap…

'Falling from the saddle before you reach the horizon,' said Yesugei's voice, clearer than the sound of gunfire and shouts, and his blood roaring in his ears.

'No…' he tried to say. 'No backward…'

The world was turning over. The sky rolled down to fill his eyes.

Yellow and grey.

'Shiban!'

'…step.'

And then it was all grey, and he could not tell if he was still falling.

Terran orbit

Thousands of ships crowded the orbits of Terra. The troop ships and bulk haulers had departed, their guts now emptied, their work done. Only the warships remained. But there were still enough to clad the orb of Terra with iron. They clustered in packs stacked from high to low orbit or in loose gatherings of Legion or loyalty. Above the Palace itself, set like a dagger, was the *Vengeful Spirit*. Beneath and around it the ships of the Sons of Horus and the most exalted craft of Kelbor-Hal's New Mechanicum. The other Legions' ships held close to the greatest of their kind, like schools of proudly coloured fish above a reef. Thousands more lay in the gulfs around and beyond Luna, ships of the less favoured or those placed to watch the approaches for signs of raiding forces. There had been few since the Warmaster's hand had encircled the Throne-world, but picket ships watched and waited for any who might try to open a second front in the void.

Almost none of the watchful ships saw the *Imperator Somnium* until it was well within their sensor and gun ranges. It was vast, a palace shaped in gold and set free in the stars. A thing of such size should not have been able to burn so deep into the spheres of Terra unseen. But it had. It had been born above that world. The last ores of its continents and the metal of its conquered cities laid down as its bones and woven into its skin. Within its hull, technologies that existed nowhere else had shrouded its approach, scattering its mass and engine returns into the background radiation of space. Now, though, it could not hide. Now it needed to be what it was.

It had already accelerated to the edge of its engines' tolerance, and it did not slow or change course. Had the Emperor's flagship appeared two nights before, perhaps it would have died sooner. Then it would have met greater order and greater strength in the Warmaster's fleets, but the *Iron Blood* had broken from orbital dock with the Lion's Gate space port and quit the orbits of Terra with all but a handful of IV Legion ships. Some of the traitor host had tried to prevent them after hails and calls for information had gone unanswered, but Perturabo had taken clarity in battle with him, and when it became clear that they were quitting the battle sphere, it was too late to prevent or punish. In their wake they left fractures in the control of the void. Not enough that even a ship like the *Imperator Somnium* could have hope of anything but destruction, but enough that it cut deep as it burned towards Terra.

Battle groups scrambled to meet it, but half were still trying to chase and disrupt the Iron Warriors ships. Some broke their pursuit and turned back; others carried on after the IV Legion's vessels. Panic sparked in the picket craft. Auspex screens lit with readings. Threat calculations multiplied in the minds of the Mechanicum ships. Guns began to fire. Torpedoes slid into the night and lit. Blossoms of fire flashed across the *Imperator*

Somnium's void shields. On it came, the light of the impacts gleaming across the gold of its hull.

The Warmaster's ships recognised it; shocked demands for primary confirmation flicked back and forth between command officers and bridge crew. The Emperor's ship… It could not be… It could not mean that the Emperor was fleeing… What could it mean?

Three minutes after the *Imperator Somnium* appeared, word reached the Warmaster. His eyes did not move from the view of Terra's surface held in the circle of the viewport. After a long heartbeat of time he spoke.

'It is nothing. My father will not leave. He remains. He endures yet.' He paused, blinked, and in the blink there was a stutter of explosions beneath the clouds covering the Palace. 'Kill it,' he said, and then nothing more.

The long-range gunfire became a boiling storm of detonations. The void shields of the *Imperator Somnium* began to stutter under the weight of fire. In the near-silent engine decks, the shield generators began to creak. Mechanisms that had known the touch of the Master of Mankind Himself began to protest, began to fail.

Corswain watched the blaze of fire on his helm display. The *Wrath's Descent* and the other Dark Angels ships were holding just inside the *Imperator Somnium*'s wake, the great ship's bulk and shields hiding their presence and protecting their hulls.

'Corswain of the First Legion.' The voice of the Custodian filled the inside of Corswain's helm. He could recognise the tones of one of the Emperor's guardians who had met with him and Su-Kassen. Ihohet was the name he had given, though he had never removed his helm to show his face.

'I hear,' said Corswain.

'The *Imperator Somnium*'s shields shall fail, but it shall endure long enough. Do you stand ready?'

'We are ready,' said Corswain. 'Are you and your cadre ready to launch at the moment?'

'My fellow Custodians will go. I shall remain.' The finality in the words reminded Corswain of the edge of a blade.

'May honour go with you, Ihohet,' said Corswain. The Custodian did not reply, and the vox-link cut.

Corswain did not move for a second. The light of explosions and fire flashed in his eyes. The beast looked back at him from the memory of the last dream, its death blood on the snow. Locked into the mag-harness inside the belly of a Stormbird hung in a launch cradle, the plunge down towards Terra felt like nothing.

As he watched, a stuttered line of explosions cut across the *Imperator Somnium*'s prow shields. They blinked, bursting, tattered layers flickering as they tried to relight. A stream of plasma sliced through the gap and scored across the keel. Gilded feathers a hundred metres long flashed to liquid and scattered into the dark, burning tears from a falling eagle.

The traitor ships were moving coherently now. Squadrons of line-class warships were forming into clusters, manoeuvring so that their guns could maintain fire as they tracked the burning eagle of the *Imperator Somnium* on its descent. There was no panic now, no confusion. A will had steadied them and they moved like a pack of dogs ready to kill their prey, arranging themselves so that they could deliver optimal fire, certain that they would. They had noticed that the golden ship was not firing, and even if that was a ruse, they knew they had the teeth and numbers to prevail. Whatever gesture the death of this symbol would serve did not matter; it was irrelevant as its end was inevitable.

Corswain blinked the command vox active.

'All units,' he said, 'stand by.'

A battle group spread across its path began to fire. Forty

torpedoes loosed from tubes. The batteries of half a dozen cruisers fired. The beaked prow of the *Imperator Somnium* began to distort. Globules of white-hot metal the size of tanks spun behind it. Shells burst from its fins. Burning gas streamed past it. And on it came, faster and faster, engines brightening. Inside its hull, the automata tending to its systems bent to their tasks as the hull shook and shook with impact. It was within the outermost edge of the orbital well, and it was not dead.

Now the killers were moving fast, the leisure and confidence gone as they burned to keep their guns on the plunging ship. The greater vessels of that swarm above Terra began to move. A quatro of World Eaters heavy cruisers accelerated at it, prow to prow. The *Imperator Somnium* fired then. It did not have the human crew or manpower to run an exchange of fire, but it had claws and teeth, claws that had pulled down star-kingdoms and teeth that had ended empires. Nova shells loosed from clusters of barrels set along its keel. Each shell was the size of a Battle Titan, loaded with time-delayed fusion reactors, volkite storm accelerators and rad-fusion warheads. Accelerated by mag-coils to the edge of light speed, each shell was a squadron killer. A ship of the line could only mount one such weapon and fire it with ponderous irregularity. The *Imperator Somnium* fired ten shells within the span of a human heartbeat.

The World Eaters cruisers vanished. Shoals of frigates became fire, became dust. The great Emperor's Children barge *Serpentis* burned and then detonated. Transports still rising from Terra became flashes in the spreading blast storm.

The *Imperator Somnium* loosed torpedoes. There were no crews to sight its guns, but the torpedoes could find their own targets. Dozens of warheads cut through the dark, curving towards the scent of reactors and engines. Some were so close that the ships did not have time to evade. New explosions lit the dark. Blisters of fire blew outwards from hulls.

The recoil from the nova cannon had sliced speed from the *Imperator Somnium*, but its engines pushed it on, plunged it down and down through the orbital spheres.

In his gunship, Corswain felt the first explosion shudder through the hull as Terra filled his sight.

'The moment is now,' came the voice of Ihohet across the vox.

'You honour us, Custodian,' said Corswain and then switched to his command channel. 'All units, by my word: strike.'

The *Wrath's Descent* fired its engines and kicked free of the *Imperator Somnium*'s gravity shadow. Void shields sheathed its hull. Its sisters followed, scattering from the great ship. They did not pause to fire guns but cut down, reactors pouring power into their flight. Blinded by the unfolding detonations, the traitor ships did not see them at first. Some hesitated, thinking them debris falling from the dying giant. Then they realised.

The *Wrath's Descent* was already at the edge of near-orbit. Fire reached for it. Its void shields shimmered. Gas and flame spilled after it. It would not take long for them to fail, and then the lance beams and shells would punch through and burn the assault pods clinging to its hull. Not long, but they had long enough.

Corswain watched the distances to surface drop at the edge of his sight. Void shield status was an amber glow at the corner of his eye. Just a little further.

The *Imperator Somnium* was burning, fire and light dragging behind it. Down on the surface of Terra, away from the storms shrouding the Imperial Palace, fires sliced across the belly of the sky.

A squall of macro shells struck the *Wrath's Descent*. It shook. Hull plates buckled. Gas blew into the void. In his gunship, Corswain felt the impacts an instant before his helm flashed.

'Loose,' he said, his voice calm.

The cradle holding the gunship slammed forwards. The engines lit and it shot into the vacuum. Another followed it and another. Drop pods punched from launch tubes. Assault craft detached from the hull and fired thrusters. They scattered and fell, pushing down into Terra's upper atmosphere. Interceptors launched and raced the falling craft down. Behind them the *Wrath's Descent* was turning with the last command sent to its thrusters. More fire hit it. Above it, its sister ships were turning too, craft scattering from their flanks and bellies. Shells impacted across their hulls. Lances sliced into batteries of silent guns. There were no command crew on board now, just the servitors and low serfs following their last protocols and orders.

Force slammed through Corswain. The gunship was juddering. Fire streaked the thickening air behind its wings as it dived.

The *Imperator Somnium* was a smear of fire now, hurtling down in the wake of the Dark Angels ships. Enemy craft wheeled around them firing without cease. In Corswain's helm he could see the falling ship and the ships of his Legion begin to tumble as shells punched their hulls. The swarm of drop and assault craft were all inside the outer atmosphere, racing down before the burning eagle met the warships that had carried them this far and would carry them no further. Inside the quiet of his soul, in the place where the beast died and lived in his dreams, Corswain felt sorrow like a shiver of wind through a forest. Such a price to be paid. He thought of Vassago's words and wondered what would be left after this war, and who would be left to see it.

The *Imperator Somnium*, chariot of the Master of Mankind, bearer of illumination to the galaxy, hit the *Wrath's Descent* as the battle-barge rolled over. For a moment, time missed a stitch.

White light filled the universe. Complete and total, the skies wiped clean of darkness and of stars. Then the whiteness became golden fire, became the red of vaporising metal. The blast wave screamed out, swallowing the abandoned Dark Angels ships that had carried Corswain's assault force. It struck the traitor craft that had closed to use their shorter-range guns. It slammed into the great warships that had been moving to circle it. These were the venerable queens of war that had led the Great Crusade and then the war against the Emperor – and had endured countless battles without scar or mark. Chunks of half-melted hull stabbed through the prow armour of the *Conqueror* and lit fires in its decks. Slime and corrosion burned from the hull of the *Terminus Est,* and the things living in its bones shrieked at the touch of fire. In the throne room of the *Vengeful Spirit* the blast flashed in the depths of Horus' eye.

A few of the Dark Angels assault craft that had not made enough distance were caught by the fire wave. Corswain saw them blink out of being in his tactical display.

'*Astronomican drop zones locked,*' said Tragan's voice, crackling with vox distortion.

The gunship was shaking. Red heat swallowed the black of its hull. Beside it, spread in a swarm of over five hundred, craft fell from the burning heavens to the earth below.

Marmax South

'He protects me as I serve Him!' Katsuhiro heard himself shout the words. His throat was raw. His hood and helmet had gone. Blood caked his face. The buzzing of insects filled his ears. He turned and fired at the shapes cresting the slope of corpses. Steena stopped and swayed. 'Say it!' he shouted.

She looked at him blankly. Her breath hood had gone too. Boils dotted the skin at the edge of her lips. There was something in the air, something corrosive that made Katsu-hiro want to hack up his lungs. 'Say it with me!'

'He...' she managed to say.

A dead thing came out of the mist. It was quick, bound-ing over the rubble on long arms, trailing coils of guts after it. He could see a set of jaws running down the front of its head between pus-yellow eyes. Katsuhiro fired. A shot from the burst hit the dead thing's side and spun it back. It hissed. Liquid pulsed out of it. It twitched and then pushed itself up. He shot it again. The shots burned through its skull and blasted chunks of burning meat into the air.

The gun went silent. He scrambled for another charge cell, found the last one at the bottom of the satchel. It was sticky with the blood of the dead trooper he had taken it from. He snapped it home, still pointing the gun at the dead thing on the floor.

He had no idea where they were, other than they were closer to the walls. Arcs of rockcrete and fingers of reinforcing bars rose above them. They had gone backwards. The yellow murk of the sky above flashed with a sudden brilliant light. His eyes went up and he stared as the blazing light stuttered and flashed, and dimmed. For a second, just a second there was something that might have been quiet. He could hear the ringing in his ears and feel the pulse in his head. The world had shrunk to small numbers and small spaces.

'He protects,' he said to himself.

A figure ran out of the murk. Katsuhiro raised his gun. The figure fell. A black cloud enveloped him. Katsuhiro had a second to see the bodies of the insects swarming over the figure, burrowing between folds of clothing, pouring into an open mouth, chewing into eyes. Katsuhiro felt the prayer falter on his lips. Another figure came from the murk, and another and another. Insects wheeled around them. Gunfire chased them. People fell. None were firing back. The tide came into sight then, rolling forwards, human figures and things larger by far. The air was shimmering with heat. Bodies hit the dirt and became slime. Maggots writhed and split and rose on clusters of wings. Katsuhiro felt his vacant stomach try to empty. He was frozen, and the tide was closing, rolling across the hundred paces he had just crossed, eating the crowd of troopers that ran in front of it. There were no angels here. No bulwarks who could stand. There was just this, a wash of humanity running before death.

Gunfire spat from beside him, punched into a section of the tide.

'He protects,' called Steena, firing, face set. The tide edge was fifty paces away. Thirty paces. A fly hit him on the shoulder. Another on his head. All he could smell and taste was sour milk, ashes and raw meat. The sky was still flashing above, red lightning arcing across it like veins in a bloodshot eye.

And in that flash, the murk and fog was clear. He could see. He could see the folds of rubble that had been the lines and walls and redoubts that had been Marmax South. Over them came a sea of bodies.

Katsuhiro raised his gun.

'Back,' he shouted. 'We have to get back.'

And then he was running. Acid tears falling down his cheeks, his prayers and hopes catching in his throat.

Hatay-Antakya Hive, East Phoenicium Wastes

Rain fell in the tunnels as they climbed. Graft was still carrying Krank. The old soldier was starting to get back the use of his limbs, but they were still twitching, his arms hanging limp down to the fingers, legs like lengths of rope. Krank had not said anything about how he had come to the orchard dome or what had happened, and Oll had not asked. The hollow look in Krank's eyes was enough.

They had got into one of the fluid conduit pipes that moved sludge and grey water around the hive's propagation levels. The pipe was empty now. A tunnel of black-brown water ran down the centre. Droplets fell from the rivet joins. It smelled, in part of rotten vegetable matter and damp, but there was a scent of the flowers, too, cloying and insistent. Bright green stems crawled over the inner walls of the pipe. Large, vivid leaves spread across the moisture-beaded metal. There were thorns on the stems and leaves, pale and hooked, like fish teeth. White and indigo bell-shaped flowers hung in thick clusters from the vines. Oll thought that he saw them shrink as their stablight beams touched them.

'How do they grow?' Oll turned at the sound of Krank's voice. The old soldier was staring towards a spill of blossoms, bright in the glow from the lamp on Graft's shoulder. 'There's no light in here – how do they grow so green and bright?'

Ahead, Katt stopped. She had been leading them, the pendulum swinging in her hand like a dowsing guide, moving to its tug and sway. Oll had not known that it could be used that way.

'Trouble?' he asked.

Katt frowned and panned her stablight up the slope of the pipe. Flowers and leaves rippled back from the light. The brown water frothed past their feet.

'I think we are close to something. The pendulum answers, but I'm not sure what to.'

'Rane? Zybes?'

She shook her head.

'No, maybe, but there's something else... *someone* else. It feels like someone looking for us. It's getting confused.'

Shuffle-tap... shuffle-tap... following him down the corridors of the Labyrinth...

He coughed, swayed. Shook his head to clear it. There was too much ahead to look back now.

Don't look back... don't look back into the underworld...

'Okay, let's go,' he said, and began to trudge up the pipe again. The slosh of flowing water almost washed away the sense he had that he could hear steps behind them.

They did not have to go far. The pipe curled around and up like a corkscrew and emerged into the base of a wide chamber. Shafts of light fell from grates in the roof above. The green vines flowed up out of the tunnel into the chamber. The beams of the stablights showed a great tangle of the foliage and flowers in the dark. The floor was soft and damp and squelched underfoot. Oll paused as the beam of his light reached into the distance.

'Do you see that?' he asked.

'What?' asked Krank from further back.

'The flowers,' said Oll, holding the beam steady on a wash of blooms. 'Their petals, they are opening and closing.' As he spoke, the vines shivered and puffed pollen into the air. Oll coughed, and pulled the fabric of his kerchief over his mouth and nose. It was hellish hot. Oll felt smothered as though he wanted to lie down and...

He caught himself.

'Katt,' he called back over his shoulder. The sugar-sweet scent of the flowers was thick in his mouth. 'Katt, is Zybes here?'

'Oll...' It was Katt, she was swaying, the pendulum in her hand spinning in place. 'Oll, there is noise in here... Why is it so noisy?' Her voice was slurred, her eyelids blinking closed, head nodding lower on her chest.

He caught her as she began to fold to the floor.

'Katt?' he said. 'Katt!'

But she did not answer.

'Oll,' came Krank's voice, urgent, sudden. 'Oll, there! Over there!' Krank was struggling to get out of Graft's grasp, waving his stablight over the heaps of tangled vines. Oll followed the direction of the beam. The flowers shrank in the brightness. 'There!'

Oll looked, and saw.

Carefully, very carefully, he moved forwards, nudged aside the stems and leaves with the barrel of his gun. The flowers furled to white-and-purple spikes. He saw it then, down amongst the close tangle of stems and thorns.

He panned the torch beam lower. There it was, the shape of a human, so tightly bound in thorn stems that it reminded him of one of the midsummer sculptures woven from green corn. He held the beam on it for a long moment. There was a hand. A hand projecting from a tight, green mass.

He suddenly was aware of the space around him and behind him, the dark and the thorn vines filling the pipes they had climbed and the chamber all around him. In the light he saw the plant-wrapped shapes flex, a tiny, repeated rhythm, like a slow pulse, like a sleeping breath.

'Katt…' began Oll.

A patch of knotted thorns unravelled, uncoiling, thorns withdrawing from meat with a sucking sigh. John Grammaticus' face looked out at Oll. Blood poured from punctures in his skin. His eyes opened.

'Oll!' gasped John. 'Oll, get away. Run…'

Oll heard gasps and cries from behind him, started to turn. The flowers on the vines opened. Pollen spat into the air. He could smell burning sugar, spoiled milk, citrus and shit. His feet were tangled, wrapped with stems and leaves that now squeezed. Thorns punched into his flesh. He could hear Graft's confused machine buzzing, the sound of panic in something that should not be able to panic. The flowers and vines coiled tense. Venom was flowing into him, flowing through him in a warm, numbing wave. He just wanted to stop, to sleep, to lie down and rest… Around him, a shivering ripple ran through the vines. Flowers opened and spewed pollen into the air. Everything was clouded, and moving away…

Too slow, he thought, as softness and darkness rose to catch Oll.

Falling again, said a voice in his head as his thoughts unravelled. *Always falling…*

FIFTEEN

To the promise of a better world
Seal Sinister
Inferno

The Imperial Palace

It began on the western walls, on a section between Eastern Hemispheric and Bastion Ledge. The section was a kink of poured rockcrete and raw metal slabs layered on top of a natural fist of granite that pushed from the plateau like a tooth. Its allotted name was Gun Cluster 251, but the troopers called it the Stump. Guns dotted its upper tiers. There were mag-cel mortars, cyclo-trebuchets and cannons that swallowed shells meant for warships. Each one was a regiment killer, an engine killer. Until given new purpose, none of them had fired since the last battles of Unity. They were old, drifting towards rust and decay until hauled from the stores and trophy dungeons where they had been kept, and placed on the wall. Tech-priests from Zagreus Kane's new Adeptus Mechanicus had reconsecrated their functions and woken their spirits. Ammunition forged before Unity had come from the Graveyards

of Blades in the far north to feed them. As the night deepened on the western wall, each gun had been firing for five
hours. Light fountained up and out from the battery barrels.
Explosions lit out beyond the wall. Crawling and slithering
machines slid forwards metre by metre, braced under domes
of energy, which spat lightning as they took the impacts. The
sound was continual, a rolling, irregular drumbeat that shivered from air to bone.

On the lowest of the gun tiers, Julius Cam-rey closed his eyes
for a second and swayed. His ears were bleeding. He had been
on the wall since the siege had started. At first he had thought
it lucky, a place far from the lower lines, high up, covered by
layers of void shields that sat within the aegis shield – as safe
a place as you could find in war. Then the enemy had come,
and the guns had started firing. At first the sound had made
him weep with the shock and force of it. Then his hearing
had gone. That did not matter; he was a ranging officer and
you did not need to be able to hear to look at the fall-pattern
of shells. His ears bled continually. Deafness did not help.
The sound of the guns just found its way in through his flesh
and bones. Every discharge slammed through him. The times,
the dwindling times when he was off the wall and slept, he
woke again and again as his pummelled muscles and bones
lit with pain. He was young as the year turned but now he
hobbled and limped, and shook and shivered to the breath
of the guns. It felt like they were pulling him apart, that the
guns were monsters raised up from the stories of Old Night
and he was their prey, toyed with before he became their food.

The darkness behind Julius' eyelids flickered to red as the
flash of the guns shone through the skin. His veins stood out,
like lines of crimson lightning.

Flash...

He would have to open his eyes soon.

Flash…

He would open his eyes and look at the bursts of fire and key range corrections, and then go back and sleep and weep…

Flash…

Would it ever end? Was this life now? Was there nothing else but an eternity of war, and the slow breaking of the world?

Another flash as though in answer to his thoughts. But… but the light was not red now, but yellow and bright, the glow of a bright sun. It did not fade. The light brightened and brightened until he wanted to turn and look away. He could not look away. He could not blink. He could not scream as it burned…

Then, just as quick as the flash of the guns, he could see. Not the view of the land beyond the wall, or the splash of plasma and explosives, but something else, something so clear that for a moment he could not believe it.

A wide platform of grey rock extended out beneath his feet towards a blue sky. A trio of sickle moons hung in the blue depths. Vine-hung trees swayed beneath the platform, heavy with flower heads. He could smell the pollen and scent. It must be blossom season. The flowers would turn to fruit soon. The insects were busy in the branches, moving with deft purpose as they flitted between petals. Iralkeaos… this was Iralkeaos and the platform of the orchard house. Home, real home. Yes… he must have slept deeply and tumbled into a nightmare that had lasted until well past dawn.

Yes… a nightmare. A nightmare…

But it was past and he was home. He was twenty summers young and the dream where he had been trapped in a war on a faraway world was nothing… nothing… a fancy gestated by too much rich food and last season's nectar-wine. Yes… that was it. He looked out on the land beyond the edge of the platform, a sea of swaying green leaves and orange blossoms. He would go down amongst the trees in a moment, walk to the edge of the platform and hop down and walk amongst those trees. There was time for a long walk before the sun reached its height; then he would come back and there would be food waiting, and perhaps his sisters and father would come back from… wherever they were.

'Julius…' The voice came from behind him. He did not look around. He did not need to. The voice was his betrothed, and she would be standing there, alive and well. The lung rot that he dreamed had taken her, and his going to the army of the new Imperium to escape the image of her with grey skin shrunken over her bones… just a nightmare. She was there, behind him.

He felt her hand slide into his. For an instant he hesitated, but then he remembered that, of course, it was right that her fingers felt like a curve of chitin. It was as it should be. This was all he wanted. Here and now.

'Come, my sweet,' said her voice. It was rich and purring. Perfect. 'Come, let's walk through the trees, you and I.'

He nodded, smiled, but still he did not turn to look at her. Part of him, a very distant part of him, knew that he should not look, that something would break if he did.

'How long can we walk for?' he asked.

'Forever, my sweet,' replied her voice. 'Come, show me the way.'

He nodded and began to walk. Around him the wind stirred the scent of the trees into the air and the sun was bright on his face.

Julius Cam-rey stepped off the edge of the gun platform. He fell and did not open his eyes. A second after his last step, another person walked from the platform ten metres from him. Then another and another, down the tiered platforms and across the walls. Some walked, some ran, some leapt with the light of paradise in their eyes. A few tried to stop them, to grab them. Officers and comrades shouted, lunged and tried to pull them back. They did not succeed. Bodies fell from the western walls like corn swept from a table. They tumbled, struck, burst apart.

The fire of the guns began to stutter. Munitions hoisted from magazines stopped. Orders and commands for response broke. In a plasma relay junction beneath the gun cluster, a senior prefect set the conduits to overload. The rest of the overseers were already dead. She wept and smiled as she keyed the last control. Fire geysered up the heat shafts and blew into the darkening sky. In the instant before the overseer became vapour she saw the light of a distant place, and knew that now she would never have to live outside of that dream's embrace.

High above the Palace's shields, the fires of the dead *Imperator Somnium* curdled from blinding bright to black. The colours of stars became smeared ochre and shattered red. The light of the sun that touched Terra curdled into shadow. Crimson aurorae unfolded across the heavens, swallowing the light of the sun as though it were a cosmic lamp now shining through a blood-slicked glass.

On down the walls the exodus spread like a scent carried on the wind. It touched those inside the wall and without. Like water flowing into a fractured rock, the siren call of paradise had found every fissure and crack. It had found those who resonated to its melody. Now its sound and call was a cacophony. People woke with the song in their eyes, and their hands already red.

Those who were not in its grip felt it. In his chamber, alone for a rare moment between the comings and goings of war, Malcador felt his shoulders dip and the weariness within him make him close his eyes and think of a time when the future had been alive.

In the depths of shelters people cried out in their sleep.

Some woke and wept as the golden promise that they could not remember vanished out of reach.

On his own, a tank commander lit a last lho-stick and let the falling ember ignite the promethium pooling at his feet.

Looking at the documents scattered and stacked on his desk, Kyril Sindermann found himself noticing the title of a small fabric-bound volume that must have been on one of the few shelves in the Symposium. *Ignace Karkasy*, read the lettering on the spine: *To Dream of Empire*. He felt himself thinking of old times, times that seemed simpler, times that now seemed like a precious and delicate thing. He found he was weeping and could not stop.

Over and along the walls it spread, like the fire of an idea and the breath of a god.

On Sanctus and Europa some of the men and women who had stood for months simply lay down, while above them the shields flared and their comrades shouted and the fire from the enemy lit the sky.

In the caverns of the Adeptus Mechanicus, Gerontius-Chi-Lambda locked the door to the augmentorium. The data of the cause-effect projections that he had been running hung in his data-buffer, glowing, as clear a sacred truth as he had ever seen. Inevitable. A certainty with no margin for error. Slowly, he climbed into the primary-process cradle. He incanted and the saws began to spin to life. Laser cutters lit. He began to shut down his cognition in sections, but a part of him was still aware and awake as the machines disassembled his metal and flesh.

And on the hundred kilometres of the Mercury Wall, hundreds of people simply began to walk towards the horizon. They were soldiers and tech-adepts and labourers, officers and menials, veterans and scripts alike. They walked and they did not see the blaze of the inferno and the burning god-engines.

All they saw and all they heard was a promise that they could escape despair. A promise that they just needed to reach. They still saw it as they fell and they fell silent to the last.

Grand Borealis Strategium, Bhab Bastion,
Sanctum Imperialis Palatine

The door to the chamber closed. Seals and locks activated with a rattle and purr of field generators and fine cogwork. Rogal Dorn did not move for a moment, but looked at the door. The shadows in his face darkened. He blinked once, but did not move. In this moment, almost alone, he was a statue caught between poses.

'*You are troubled,*' said the voice from the vox-transmitter set on the table at the room's centre. Even through the rasp and crackle of distortion, the voice was a melody.

'Circumstances allow for no other response,' said Dorn.

'*Yet you see victory,*' said Sanguinius. '*You know we will prevail.*'

'Victory is not fate. It is an act of will.'

'*Perhaps, my brother. But perhaps it is both.*'

'Both?' breathed Dorn, and turned. He pulled one of the stone chairs from the table and sat. The metal and ceramite of his armour clinked against the marble and granite. He ran his hand across his jaw, and then rested his chin on the knuckles of his fist. His eyes fixed on the flecks of crystal and mineral in the polished stone of the tabletop. He did not speak. The vox spat and crackled.

'*I must go soon, brother,*' said Sanguinius. '*They have sent a horde against the downed Argus Plate on the Europa Outworks.*'

'Everywhere the tide comes in,' said Dorn.

'*As it always has and always will,*' says Sanguinius. '*You are the wall against which it breaks, brother.*'

'Am I equal to it?'

'A question that you have never asked before, and not the question you want to ask now.'

'There is someone here for the Praetorian, Lord Archamus.'

Archamus looked up from the data scrolling across the slate in his hand. The senior command aide was standing at attention two paces from him. Calith, the man was called. New, a fresh face to replace Hayleigh. The man looked uncomfortable.

'The Praetorian is unavailable at present. If it is of critical importance, they can see me.'

He looked back at the data feed. Half of the strategic status feeds from the walls were grey – lost or incomplete data. It was like losing one's sight piece by piece.

His mind went to the Praetorian, who he had left in the council chamber. The other members of the war council had already left an hour before. Most had attended as ghosts of distorted hololight, or as voices that crackled from failing vox-links. Archamus had remained with the Praetorian after all but the link to Lord Sanguinius had been disconnected. It alone was almost clear. They had talked of the details of the situation and then, at a signal of subtle dismissal, Archamus had left his lord alone to talk to his brother. Shadows had gathered in Dorn's face as he sat beside the table and the chamber doors closed. Archamus wished he had not glanced back and seen them.

'Lord...' the aide began, voice trailing. Archamus heard the man swallow.

'Yes?'

'I... I do not think that this personage will... I believe they have to see the Praetorian.'

Archamus raised his eyes, and shut down the data flow. He saw now the moisture on the man's skin, the vibration in his frame. He was terrified. No... this was not just terror. This was a mortal flight response. The old primal drive to flee from the dark and the gaze of the predator. The human wanted to run, but not from Archamus.

'Who is it?' Archamus asked.

The man did not answer but stepped back, his hand rising to indicate the figure who stood at the far end of the antechamber.

Archamus looked up. He saw...

He saw a man in black.

Dark eyes looked back at him from a web of tattoos that sprawled across neck and cheek and scalp. Centaurs, beasts and stars reared and snarled and turned, all in coal black. The man held his arms behind his back. The grey-black uniform held no mark, apart from the lion's head pins on the high collar. Archamus felt the instinct to look away grip him. His head began to turn, his eyes to blink. He held his gaze on the man, who offered the smallest of nods.

The aide shifted beside Archamus.

'Lord, I did not know what to–'

'You may go, Senior Calith,' said Archamus, his eyes still on the man.

'Yes... I... Thank you.' The aide hurried away. Still Archamus did not move.

'I do not know you,' he said at last.

'I am Aurum, First Prefect of the Fourth House.'

'The Praetorian is engaged.'

'He will see me,' said Aurum. 'He must.'

Archamus still did not move.

'Why are you here? The Titans of the Ordo Sinister do not bow to the Praetorian's command.'

'Just so,' Aurum said, and held up a hand. A cone of golden light projected from a ring on his finger. Within the light a symbol of a lion and an eagle circled each other, one roaring, the other shrieking as it took to wing. It was a symbol rarely used, but Archamus knew it and knew what it meant. And it meant one thing.

The cone of light vanished.

'I will see him,' said Aurum.

Archamus gave a single, slow nod and turned to the chamber door.

Rogal Dorn was silent for a long moment in the quiet of the chamber. Perhaps behind his eyes battles fought and unfought turned in an orbit around his thoughts. Perhaps for a moment he felt the tide of eternity lapping against the fortress he had made himself.

'Why does our father not speak to me?' he said at last.

'We have this battle to fight, and He a greater battle still,' said Sanguinius. Over the crackle of the vox, the sound of a distant detonation rolled like thunder. *'You know this. You know He trusts you above all others, Rogal.'*

'The darkness is at the walls, and there is no sign of aid on the horizon, no word from the Lion and Roboute. Yet our father is silent.'

'The forces of despair press close in the aetheric realm, my brother. You know this, you have listened to Malcador. The ocean flows and breaks over and through us. We are now stones that break the tide or are broken by it. We are part of it. It is us. Trust yourself, brother. Just as our father has. He knows you and knows what we face, and placed you on the walls to face it. Does that act not speak enough?'

Dorn was silent, and then raised his head, looking towards where the vox crackled into the half-dark.

'I cannot see it. I cannot feel its substance. And if these questions come from the warp, then they themselves are an attack, an attack that I can feel but cannot see the sword edge that cuts. That is a battle that I do not know if...'

'Say it,' said Sanguinius. *'The truth is a weapon and a shield.'*

'It is a battle I will fight to the last. I do not know if it is a battle I can win.' The lines of his face seemed like carved marble. 'All the sacrifices that have been made, every deed done in the name of survival, and now the lightning falls. What will be left after a war like this? What can be left?'

Another crackle over the vox, and the sound of air passing that said that Sanguinius was rising through it, the snap of gunfire in the battle that he fought as he talked with his brother.

'What could our father say that would undo that?' said Sanguinius, and Dorn's head rose as he heard the note in his brother's voice. *'There are sacrifices yet to make. The end is coming, brother. This, like all things, shall end, and even in loss much shall endure.'*

'I believe that,' said Dorn. 'From His lips it would be a certainty. That is what I fear I may have lost to this battle, brother – certainty.'

The vox crackled again, as though Sanguinius was gathering a reply.

The locks on the door to the outer chamber released. Override warnings chimed.

Leaves of metal withdrew into the stone frame. Dorn looked up as Archamus entered. The Praetorian sat at the council table, hands clasped beneath his chin. The shadows were thick in the lines of his face. The vox-horn on the table crackled and popped static into the air.

'What has happened, brother?' said Sanguinius' voice.

Under Dorn's gaze, Archamus did not need a question to speak.

'My lord, a prefect of the Ordo Sinister has come. He bears the sigil of the Emperor's will.'

For a second, Archamus thought he saw a flash in the darkness of his lord's eyes.

'Let him draw near,' said Rogal Dorn.

Prefect Aurum did not salute or bow. To be a mortal and stand in the presence of a primarch was an experience that could crush or exalt. No matter what, it was never an experience that passed without impact. Even those who served close to Rogal Dorn and his kin had to acclimatise, to learn to let will override the reaction that their bodies and minds had to such beings. Except Aurum. He stood still, face impassive. Archamus could hear the man's heart rhythm – it had not even risen one beat.

He was a pariah, an ultra-blank. So were all the officers of the Ordo Sinister, last of the Emperor's talons. Thought slid off them. Eyes and minds turned away, unwilling to look at something that looked and moved like a human, but was not. They were empty, holes in reality that had the shape of living beings.

Rogal Dorn looked into Aurum's eyes.

'My father,' he said. 'He sent you.'

Aurum nodded.

'He spoke to you?' A blink of lids over Aurum's pale eyes.

'I am commanded,' he said, and lifted his left hand. On the palm lay a circular seal of stone the black of obsidian but darker, its depths an utter abyss beneath the smooth surface. At first Archamus could see nothing on its surface. Then he saw the lines and curves of the lion's head, its mane flowing and fangs snarling. 'This I give to you, Lord Praetorian,' said Aurum.

Rogal Dorn was staring at the seal.

'Why?' asked Dorn.

'Because He willed and commanded it.'

'Now?'

'Now,' said Aurum with a nod, and he placed the seal on the table.

'The might of reserves committed, the enemy fracturing

and held back from the walls, my brothers coming, the balance rests with us.' Dorn's hand reached across the stone of the table, and then stopped. He was looking at the seal as though trying to look beyond it through a blackened window into a place outside the walls of his world. 'Yet He sends you here now.'

He looked up at Aurum. The prefect's eyes met the Praetorian's. The electoos of beasts and warriors on his face shifted like constellations moving over the night sky.

'Now is the hour. It is written.'

Dorn's hand pulled back slightly, recoiling from the seal and what it meant.

'What does this mean?' asked Archamus.

Dorn was silent, then looked up at his Master of Huscarls. The face was set, the control still there, but there was something in the depths of the eyes now – a crack, and beyond, not the fires of anger or rage, but an emptiness, the blackness of a void that you could fall into and never hit the bottom.

'It means that matters are not as I have seen them. It means that my father has spoken. It means that we are closer to disaster than I had hoped. There is no weapon that cannot and should not be used now, and no hope that a victory will mean anything.' Rogal Dorn glanced at the vox-console as though his brother were there, seated across the table. 'I have my answer.'

'Brother...'

'It is the only way we can survive. A last sacrifice. After all, is that not what we were made for?'

Dorn reached out, his fingers spreading to clasp the seal. Archamus felt the instinct within him rise to reach out, to dash the seal from the table. He felt it beyond a level of thought. From here nothing would be the same. The seal and what it meant was an answer to a question that Archamus had not heard spoken.

'Lord…'

'It is as it must be, Archamus,' said Dorn. 'My father has willed it, and so I must do as must be done.'

His hand closed on the seal, and lifted it.

'The seal of the Ordo Sinister is yours, and with it we are yours, too,' said Aurum, and then he knelt. 'The Titans of our ordo walk at your will.'

Rogal Dorn looked at Archamus.

'Give the word to Zagreus Kane and the wall commanders. Open the weapon reserves. All of them.' He looked back at the kneeling Ordo Sinister prefect.

'Rise,' he said, 'and by my will, walk.'

Karalia's Grave, Mercury-Exultant kill-zone

The beam came from the heavens and exploded through a tangle of girders. The rusted metal exploded outwards in glowing gas and a spray of liquid metal. It hit the stuttering shields of a Warhound Titan, blew through them and staggered it sideways. The engine quivered. Damaged limb joints screamed. Half a kilometre away, a macro shell hit the rise of a hill and detonated. The fireball lifted into the sky, spreading and swelling.

<Engine locks!> came Divisia's sending. <Twenty degrees right flank. Multiple returns. Multiple active weapons. Closing!>

<Drawing charge to weapons,> sent Cartho. <If we pull much more, we are not going to have enough to keep moving.>

<Fourth Maniple, respond,> Tetracauron called across the wide connection. Distortion and disintegrating sensations roared back at him. The incandescence was a riot of orange and near-yellow-white. Status mandalas whirred. Target and range data spun in their own geometries. And the fires in the land beyond were black. Great washes of charcoal, their hearts utter

night where the heat was greatest. The outlines of the rest of his battle force were statues of orange and red, ringed by halos of command data. Interface corruption rolled through the incandescence, boiling in spirals of half-formed numerals. Tetracauron could taste the scrap code, ash and bile on his tongue. It was boiling through the world, flowing out and breathing through the Ignatum engines. *Reginae Furorem* could feel it. The Warlord shivered as it took a step back. Shattering stars of code burst in the middle of Tetracauron's sight. He heard himself gasp.

They were in the tangle of Karalia's Grave, the knot of girders and half-demolished stumps of metal that had been the roots of the nascent Karalia Hive. Dorn's levelling had not been able to remove the macro structures around which the rest of the hive had begun to accrete, so they had been left, twisted and mangled in a fold in the ground of the kill-zone. It was a bad place to be for any battle – surrounded by high ground, dead centre to the direct-fire weapons mounted on the Mercury Wall. It was a place to die.

The battlefront had spread out from Lake Voss' shore. There were hundreds of enemy Titans in the field.

Hundreds.

The Legio Ignatum had walked to meet them and then spread from the first point of combat into a line that was stretching across fifty kilometres. Engagement had been continual: reactors working close to overload, engines cycling and covering each other while each drew fresh fire into its heart. The fire from the walls had held the balance. They had advanced, pushing at full-force strength into the enemy advance. Then the wall gun fire had slackened and the sky had turned bright with fire and the flash of detonations: an orbital explosion, massive, multiple ship deaths. Debris had begun to fall, streaking the sky. The advance had stopped, become a brawl spread across dozens of kilometres, Ignatum engines and Mortis carving the air with lines of fire. They could not contact the wall, and when they tried the only reply was a gurgle of static, like a last breath. Tetracauron's battle group, the first of the Legio into the inferno, had been ordered back to the wall. Forty Titans from the fifty-five that had walked beyond the wall. All of them had scars, many of them were damaged; none had any kinetic munitions left. So they were going back to Mercury to refuel, rearm, and then re-engage.

They were ten kilometres back from the main line of engagement when the orbital fire had begun. Beams of energy had reached down through the clouds. Bombardment shells fell, burrowed into the ground and blew earth and fire into the air. Subsurface shock waves opened cracks beneath the feet of Titans. At full strength, their void shields could weather an orbital bombardment. With those shields merged, and weapon and reactor outputs synchronised they could do that and win a battle group-level engine battle. Moving fast as they had been, fire flowing to their strides, they were not ready.

They had been caught in the perfect place to die. Pinned. Caged.

Another beam struck down onto empty ground and fused it into a glowing puddle of glass.

<Engine returns to front lost,> sent Divisia. <No returns. Where in all the machine's truth have they gone?>

<All units, maximum alert.>

<Engine lock!> shouted Divisia. <Eighty-five degrees right flank!> Tetracauron could feel her question – how had it got there, on their flank?

The other maniples and engines in the battle group saw it, too – warning and sighting signals fizzing into the incandescence. Tetracauron turned *Reginae Furorem*'s gaze towards the new direction of threat. A shadow in the red-and-orange world, an image made of charcoal scattered over crimson.

<I cannot lock on to it.> Cartho.

<How is it there? How did it get through the Legio lines?> Divisia.

<Focus,> he willed, and felt his own calm slam through the link.

Tetracauron's sight blinked and the enemy engine was close now, much closer, as though a section had been sliced out of the ribbon of time and space. Divisia was right; the engine should not have been there. The main Legio engagement was a full three kilometres forwards, lighting the bellies of clouds with weapon light.

<Weapons charged.>

Heat whipped up his spine. His right fist was burning. He could taste lightning.

<Power to shield recharge dropping.>

Colossi drawn in the colours of the pyre turning with him, his kin, his siblings in fire and iron.

<All units, wheel and power weapons.>

Scrap code blurred the incandescence, boiling like wind-blown ash. The shadow was there, coming closer, staying still, a spot cut in truth that should not be looked at. The voices of the Titan crews were blurring and merging as power filled the war engines and their spirits blazed.

<Weapons ready to fire, gross area saturation.>

<What is it?>

<Weapons failing to lock.>

<Switch to visual targeting.>

He could hear and feel a rhythm now, a pulse in the buzz and scratch of the storm of scrap code.

<I…> The voice was Clementia's, coming from half a kilometre away, chopped and distorted. <How many targets can you see?>

The image in the incandescence was flowing, layers of data

skipping and vanishing, distance and scale stuttering. There was one smudge of darkness, with legs and limbs and hunched back… two, then three, then one again.

<All units…>

Another skip-blink and then it was there. Closer than it should have been. Much closer than it should have been. A war-horn boomed out, rolling and echoing, then another and another. The enemy engine was there, on the hill above the broken spars of Karalia's Grave, taller than the Battle and Scout Titans that looked up at it. Its skin was blackened, crusted with soot. Growths of bone and desiccated flesh jutted from its back. Clouds of white insects breathed from vents in its torso. It had been an Emperor-class Titan, greatest of its kind, city killer, destroyer of armies. Now it was something else. Something greater and something that had fallen. Despair and the hunger of the grave filled the hearts of those that looked on it. Substance unravelled into decay at its passing. Behind and with it were seven engines that had been Battle Titans, each now a shell for powers that bubbled and rasped in the warp. Each was a horror of distorted metal. Fluid dripped from cracked metal. Things with eyes and soft, half-formed hands writhed in blisters that bulged from rusting metal. One dragged the head of a dead engine on a chain, digging a gouge through the ground as it strode forwards. Another seemed to limp, its head a mass of dry bone where before it had been metal. A litany of numerals rasped from it, audible over the din, as though whispered next to the listener's ear. The dust of the ground burned as they stepped behind their unholy king.

In the incandescence, Tetracauron saw the Emperor Titan and knew what it was and its name.

Dies Irae, the day of judgement, the reaper enthroned in iron.

Mortis had breached the main battle line. He knew it without having to try to connect with Cydon or the rest of the Legio. They were not held. They were advancing.

For a moment, the incandescence was still. Tetracauron could feel his flesh sweating. He could hear the buzz of broken data links and taste the acid burn of terror, the old reaction of human flesh to facing death. He was not human though. He was the interface between the world of fear and flesh, and a god of metal and fury.

<All units,> he willed, <fire.>

Enemy distance to wall: 91 kilometres.

PART THREE

I SHALL EITHER FIND A WAY
OR MAKE ONE

THE WARP

∞

It is noon in the desert. It has been noon here for all time. It is fixed at that point, at the idea of the heat beating down and the light giving no room for shadows. The eyes of the man beneath the tree have closed to slits. Above Him, the dry branches of the tree rattle. His shape here is not truth. It is just a reflection of His nature at that moment: pain and suffering and the relentless hammer of vast forces crushing in on Him. His skin is a parchment pulled thin across a skull. Cracks have opened on his brow and cheeks. Dried blisters cling to His lips. He has not moved for a long time. Longer than a lifetime. The scoop in the ground, where water rose from the tree's roots, is dry. This is a realm of thirst now. There is no water here any more, just His will pushing against the idea of this desert, holding it back from Him and the only tree that gives any shade.

The rattle of the first snake rises into the air. The man's eyes open a fraction wider. The serpent sits on the cracked earth. Its head is raised, its black eyes unblinking. As the man looks at it, a tongue flicks out to taste the air. Its scales are blue, the colour of an ocean under the sun. It flicks its tail and again the dry rattle rises. The man meets its gaze. From behind the serpent the head of another rises. The scales of this one are the green of summer forests, and the light draws a gleam of copper from a bone crest. It hisses. The fangs inside its pink mouth are black, needle splinters of night. Another hiss and the man has to open His eyes and turn to see the third and fourth shapes gliding over the ground behind Him. There will be two more, He knows, lying still, out of sight, coiled in the dust like a promise that is in truth a threat.

'Almost time,' says Horus. He is there, sat on the ground just outside the tree's web of shade. He wears a robe of black, the edges threaded with gold. A circlet sits on his head. It might be brass, but under the noon glare its points look like flame. A red eye with slit pupil looks out from its setting on his brow. Horus gives a sad smile. 'Almost time,' he says again as he scoops up a handful of dust and lets it fall from his fingers. The serpents coil close to him, sliding around him. He reaches out and runs a finger down the head of one. For a moment the finger is not a human digit but a talon, long and sharp. The snake squirms under the touch and hisses. 'Why did you do it?' says Horus. 'Why did you lie? Why did you try to stand in the way of the inevitable? The powers of this realm cannot be defied or stopped, but they can be mastered. Their ascent is inevitable but so is our domination of them. They serve if you have the will to shackle them. You do not lack for will, father, so why did you not make them your slaves? Is there weakness in you that held you back from doing what I have done? Did you fear it? Did the Master of Mankind fear becoming Master of All?'

The man beneath the tree opens His mouth. Skin splits on His lips.

'You have lied to him,' He says, and the voice holds no crack or note of the wasting that marks His face. His eyes are on the serpents, and they rear up at his words, mouths open, fangs showing, eyes black pearls in the glare. 'When he sees what you have made him, there will be nothing left of him for you. Nothing. You create only hollow things. You make a desolation of hope, and a wasteland of the future.'

'Hope...' says Horus. He rolls the last of the dust between his fingers. 'There is no hope for you, father, and there never was. This was inevitable. *I* was inevitable.'

Horus smiles, and nods. He flicks the last of the dust.

The man beneath the tree coughs, the sound a rattle in a dry throat.

'He shall undo you,' says the man to the serpents. 'I made him. I know him, his strengths and his flaws. To you he is only a slave, but he is still my son.'

Horus' face hardens, and suddenly there are shadows pooling on the ground as he rises to his feet. The sky bruises above him. The serpents lash towards the man beneath the tree.

'You are a lie!' Horus' voice is the dry growl of thunder, and he is stepping forward, breaking the ground with his tread. A hurricane wind blasts past. The idea of Horus' shape is a dust-edged blur. His eyes are burning coals.

The man beneath the tree stands. Behind Him the tree bursts into flame. Smoke pours into the sky. Branches blacken in the blaze. The man towers before the flames, a shadow cut into their light. Fire rains from the burning branches. The serpents recoil, seared and hissing, black eyes scorched to blind white.

Horus halts but does not step back.

'You are nothing!' Embers fall from his mouth.

'This shall end,' says the Emperor in the voice of the fire. 'As all things must.' Then for the first time, His gaze, which holds only night, lowers to look at Horus. 'And I wait for you.'

SIXTEEN

The tower
Hollow Mountain
Thunderbolt

Before time was counted – Hatay-Antakya Hive,
East Phoenicium Wastes

'We are ready, master.' The man was sweating, droplets running from under his red leather cap down his forehead to gather in his beard.

Oll – except he wasn't Oll yet, and wouldn't accept that name for a long time – looked at the officer, and then down the slope to where the engines sat on the dust of the plain. Twenty of them, the ropes and timbers tense, the crews waiting beside the piles of boulders that had been dragged from the river shore. There were no trees large enough here to make the frames so they had floated them down the rivers from the northern forests. Only a quarter of the trunks had been sound enough to be used. The rest had gone to make screens for the wall assault troops to advance behind. If he turned, he would see the nearest camp of those troops, the sea of tents ringed by palisades, smoke from cooking fires rising into the sky to streak the blue heavens. Thousands of warriors, and not just farm-ers pulled from their land – true warriors, drilled and trained and bound to the greater cause. Banners hung in the still heat above the camps, images of beasts and fire and memories of the conquered land where these legions had come from. A host to remake the world.

Oll looked back to the officer, who still had his head bowed.

'Begin,' he said.

The officer straightened, brought his fist to his chest and snapped out an order. Flags rose in the hands of heralds. Behind them the war-horns and trumpets blared. The air shook in Oll's ears. At the bottom of the slope the arm of the first engine released with a thump. The boulder arced through the air as it loosed from the sling. Oll watched it tumble over and over, tracing down to the outer defences. His eyes pulled up to look at the tower beyond the wall. It thrust into the sky like an accusation. Tiers of rock and brick the colour of a sun-baked riverbed. His gaze caught the arches, and windows, and the wooden scaffolds circling the highest point like a crown.

The lofted boulder struck the first parapet. Stone, wood and mud brick burst into the air. Even through the heat haze he could see the men running along the wall tops. He imag-ined the blood, the broken bodies, the shouts and screams.

'A little long,' came the voice from just behind him. He did not turn as he answered, even though he had not heard his friend join him on the slope.

'They are adjusting,' said Oll.

The next engine released as he finished speaking, then the next and the next.

Thump-thump-thump. Stones cast up into the sky, tum-bling dots.

Oll watched the first stone hit the wall.

'We should send another envoy,' he said.

'We are past the point where that would make a difference,' said the man.

Oll frowned. 'Do we ever really pass that point?'

'This has to happen.'

Oll said nothing.

'You do not agree?' asked the man.

'I'm here, aren't I?' said Oll. He was watching the crews pull the beam arm of the first engine down. A sweating pair were hauling a boulder to where the sling was lowering to the ground.

'It can't be allowed to stand,' said his friend. 'If it does, then the words and powers that it holds will spread from here across the face of the world.'

Oll was silent again.

Clouds were collecting above the tower top, white folding into black and grey. Lightning flickered in the building mass. The crew of the engines faltered as the sound of thunder rolled across the plateau. Hail began to fall. The heralds and officers were shouting, horns sounding through the legion camps. Men ran for their weapons. Falling ice rang on armour. Half the sky was black, boiling, flashing. The spirals of wind rose from the ground, spinning ice and dust into the air. The siege engines began to rock in place.

'You see, my friend,' said the voice from behind him, carrying above the roar of the storm. 'This has to be ended.' Oll turned. His friend stood amidst the running troops and the hail. The circlet of silver leaves around his head gleamed. His eyes were dark, steady, a reflected flash of the storm caught in their depths. He looked sorry, Oll thought, the bearer of bad news to a soul who did not deserve that unkindness.

Oll opened his mouth to say his friend's name.

And the world stopped.

The hail hung in the air. The flash of lightning shone in a

frozen sheet. The running troops and the spinning columns of air were still.

'This was it, then?' said John Grammaticus. 'This was when you two were young.'

'We were never young,' said Oll.

Oll turned and looked at the storm above the tower, the frozen whirl of white and coal grey.

'I'm dreaming,' he said. 'Right?'

'You and me both,' John replied, and smiled, but Oll could read exhaustion in his eyes. John was wearing a faded desert cloak over a bodyglove. Scuffs and stains mottled the leather and rubber of the suit. Oll could see the edges of the ceramic armour plates poking out through micro tears.

'Seems very real, for a dream,' said Oll.

John shrugged. 'It's not your conventional type of dream.'

Oll kept looking.

John shook his head and flicked a hand. 'Stop it. It's really me, alright? You want proof? Then we are going to have to be a bit old-fashioned, my friend – but sure. Ask me something only I would know.'

Oll kept looking at him.

'What do you want?' asked John. 'When we first met? The colour of the smoke over Sennchar? Or all the stuff we never spoke about from that time I tried to have you killed on Oos-Lua? No one else walked away from that, so the chances of someone being able to fool you would be minimal.' John opened his hands and shrugged in the way that he had for centuries. 'Not much else I've got, old friend, other than stories. No talisman or sign. Sorry.'

'Okay,' said Oll after a long pause.

'What convinced you?'

'Only you could talk that much without someone actually asking you a question,' said Oll. He frowned, bent down, and picked up a handful of the dirt that was about to become mud as the rain fell. He rubbed his fingers through it. The grit felt as real as the cold stone of the Labyrinth. He let it fall. It dropped a finger span from his hand and froze.

'Sorcery, right?' asked Oll.

John nodded.

'Secrets and infinite dreams. That's what we are caught in. Somewhere out there you and I, and whomever you brought with you, are lying all wrapped in thorns, dreaming of our deepest secrets.'

John looked up at the half-constructed tower, and the lightning playing above it.

'I've been down into the deep past, Oll, seen all the bits of the past that I have tried my best to forget – Nurth, the whole shitshow with the Cabal, and before… This place pulls you down into the dark and then throws all of the things you try to hide back at you.'

'This is a trap then,' said Oll. 'This place, your message.'

John laughed.

'A trap alright, but not just for us, Oll. We just fell into it. This is a trap for humanity. All those people you saw coming here, they chose to come, and wanted it enough that they left everything to follow the call of the dream. It's like your sirens, Oll – those that hear cannot help but get up and follow.'

'I saw,' said Oll. 'The hive is feeding on them.'

John bit his lip and nodded.

'All the things you ever wanted but feared, all the terror, all the things you can dream given back to you, infinite and beckoning. Fulgrim's Children planted the seeds, I think, hothoused it in the blood and warp fallout from what's going on in the Himalazia.' John paused and shivered. 'This is Fulgrim's garden of earthly delights, his vision for the future. They have a name for it…'

'Paradise,' said Oll.

John nodded.

'I am sorry, Oll,' he said. 'I came to the Hatay Hive because the augurs said that this is where you would arrive.' He gave a bitter chuckle. 'And you did, just not before I did.'

'I came here because of you,' said Oll. 'I heard you.'

John laughed again.

'A self-causing loop – you came here because you followed me here. I came here because this is where the signs said you arrived.'

Oll was quiet for a moment, looking up at the glare of the unmoving sun and the frozen flash of lightning.

'We went off course,' said Oll. He frowned and looked at John. 'You said you read the signs and they said that I would arrive here. So if you thought I overshot, you must have got to the original rendezvous. You must have seen Her...'

John nodded.

'You saw Her?'

'Yes. Not pleased to see me, but yes – I saw Erda.'

Oll looked away down the slope at the running troops in their hauberks and skirts of scale. Wild eyes looking at the lightning-filled sky, mouths open to shout.

'I miss Her,' he heard himself say. It was not what he had intended, but then he was not sure what he had meant to say. He frowned, shook his head. 'She's not coming with us, is She?'

John's shrug and smile was half a grimace.

'She sent help, a warrior, and She set me on my way – couldn't have done that without Her. You know Her better than me, Oll, but something tells me She's as much with us as history lets Her be.'

'She's still angry,' said Oll.

'Yeah, I reckon so. Angry at Him, at what He's done – angry

that She helped Him make the twenty things that brought the whole show crashing down. And most of all, angry that if He fails then that's it.'

Oll shook his head, his gaze on the tower.

'No,' he said. 'That's not why She is angry.' He knew without looking that John was frowning. 'She is still angry about the same thing I am.'

John came to stand beside him. Oll felt the wind on his face. Above him the storm was turning. The frozen arcs of lightning blinked. A drop of rain hit the skin of his cheek. 'She is angry about what happened here.'

'And what was that, Oll?'

Oll shook his head in answer. His armour was gone. The fatigues he had worn when they had made the last cut to Earth hung from him. His limbs were a little heavier, a little older – a lot older – than they had been back then, back before the tower fell. Rain pattered on the fabric. He had a feeling that if he had turned to look behind him he would have seen himself all in armour, standing next to a man that he had called a friend.

'I get it, Oll,' said John from beside him. 'You have history, and more than most. Even if you don't want to tell me about it.' The rain was heavy now; men were running again. Thunder vibrated through the air. 'Anyway, I don't think you will have a choice.' Rain was streaming down John's face and his cloak was sodden. 'That's what these dreams are, Oll. They are not just a trap – they are taking secrets from us here, whether we like it or not. That's what the thorns are feeding on. That is what they drink. All the secrets we keep.'

Oll shivered. Above them a bolt of lightning began to fall from the clouds like a spear reaching down through the air, faster than a blink but slower than a falling feather.

'What secret do you prefer I didn't see, Oll?' asked John,

and there was sadness in his voice. 'Because that's where we are going.'

The Hollow Mountain

They called it the Hollow Mountain. Before the will of the Emperor had remade Terra, it had borne other names, all now lost. Tunnels and caves had wormed through its heart since before humanity had struck an edge to flint. Its summit had caught clouds and spun storms in times when the seas had covered the land that men would bleed and die to conquer in the aeons that followed. The mountain had always been an unquiet place. The ghosts of the dead sung on the ice winds that spun over its flanks. The shamans that first went into its caves would dream and die, and live and dream and die over and over again in a single night. Crystal threaded the walls and floors of those caves. Sometimes these threads would seem black. Sometimes they would glow violet, or burn fire-orange.

Civilisations and species would rise and fall and rise again, and the mountain would endure, gathering whispers and legends and names: Daemon Barb, Eater of Souls, Gate of Sky and Earth. Images were daubed in the outer caves, and bones gathered in the dark. Once in an age, a mystic would come down from the summit with fire in their eyes. Wild wars and revelations sprang up in their wake. All the while, the mountain slept and spoke only in whispers.

Then the Emperor had come and broken open its heart. Drilling machines turned caves into tunnels and burrowed into caverns that light had never touched. The layout of some of these passages followed the needs of construction, opening the mountain for the excavators and labour armies that would follow. Others had no obvious purpose: shafts plunging down or up into the mass of the mountain, volumes of space excavated to precise geometric design and then sealed so that they hung in the rock, voids of darkness in cold stone.

Workers vanished, most by night, but others would take a wrong turn into a well-lit tunnel and never be seen again. Once the tunnels and caverns were complete, masters of aetheric resonance assembled machines that made the crystals in the walls sing. The first psykers arrived a little later. There were a thousand of them, enough to kindle a flame. They burned with the last song of their souls, and the Hollow Mountain echoed that song. In the void between the stars and beyond thought, a light lit in the darkness...

The first drop pod hit the mountain's summit. Snow and ice flashed to steam. Assault ramps slammed down. Warriors in black armour emerged. Another pod struck, then another and another. Plumes of white vapour punched into the thin air. Fire criss-crossed the blue dome of sky above. Gunships and drop pods trailed red and orange behind them as they plummeted down. Interceptors spiralled after them. Fuselages burst into fragments. The shadows of warships crossed the sun like serrated storm clouds.

Corswain's gunship skimmed low. The assault ramps were already open. Alarms and warning lights flashed through the cabin. Oil and flame spilled from the craft's wing. A fresh spit of cannon fire sliced through the air beneath it. A chrome interceptor went past above, engines shrieking.

'Get us as close as you can,' he shouted into the vox. His mag-harness snapped free and he was at the assault ramp. A wall of ice and black rock blurred past. Heavy las-fire burst through the open door, and punched through three Dark Angels as they climbed out of their harnesses. The gunship skidded across the sky. Corswain could see the world spinning around and around through the open door.

'*Deploy on signal,*' came the pilot's voice over the vox, flat and calm. The gunship slewed around, tipping over on its burning wing. Corswain's boots mag-locked to the deck. His armour growled as it fought gravity and G-force. He was looking straight down through the open door. The flank of the mountain plunged away from his sight. As he watched, an aircraft tumbled past, clipped a crag of grey rock and became a fireball. The ready rune flicked to amber in his helm. Corswain braced. The gunship snapped level, and then up. A cliff edge blurred past beneath it. Sensor spines snapped on its belly. The rune in Corswain's helm blinked green. He jumped.

The mountain came up to meet him. He landed in a tuck. Stone and ice exploded out. He rose, sword in hand. A stream of heavy rounds hit the warrior that landed beside him, but Corswain was already bounding up the frozen slope. He could see the gun-box above him, set into a crag of rocks. Auto-cannon barrels jutted from a half-sphere of plasteel. He leapt. The gun barrels swung down. Laser rangefinders touched his armour. He caught the rockcrete edge under the gun mount and sliced up with his sword. Lightning-wrapped steel sliced through the gun as it fired. Corswain caught the momentum of his cut and swung up. The dead guns swung side to side like the head of a blind man. He rammed the sword down. The point went through the gun fitting with an explosion of metal fragments. He sawed it sideways. He could hear the spluttering buzz of the servitor wired into the gun controls. Then his blade cut through the ammo feed. The explosion blew the gun out of its mount, and sent it tumbling down the mountainside. Above him, the domed cap of the mountain rose up and up.

Corswain looked down at the slope of snow and scree beneath him. There were warriors in black climbing, firing. Las-bolts and auto-rounds sheeted from the mountain peaks to meet them. Drop pods and assault craft lay scattered on the ice crust. Some burned. Smoke breathed into the air. The enemy had full control of both the mountain and its defences. If his assault force stayed on the outside too long they would be slaughtered.

A shape blotted out the light. Corswain's gaze snapped up. A figure stood on the top of the gun-box. Its armour was bronze, polished, weeping jewels on chains. A coxcomb of green hair rose above a helm dotted with dozens of circular speaker grilles. There were no eyes. The gun in its hands writhed with chrome pipes. Corswain heard a sound like a swarm of insects and the shrieks of dying crows. He exploded upwards. The gun in the traitor's hands spoke. A sonic wave hit the rockcrete next to Corswain and blew it to dust. He landed but the traitor in bronze was fast and was just beyond blade reach as Corswain's sword sliced out. The traitor laughed and the sound shattered the crystal of Corswain's eye-lenses. He staggered. The traitor levelled its gun again. Corswain raised his sword.

The traitor jerked up into the air. It hung for a second, pinned to the sky. Then its armour plates buckled. Its helm crumpled. Blood and pulped meat gushed out of cracks. Corswain could smell storm charge and smoke. The warrior in bronze gave a last shriek, then its form was crushed into a bloody ball of armour fragments. Blood sprayed out, melting ice and snow to a pink slurry. Corswain looked around at where Vassago stood on a rise of stone beside the gun-box. Coils of ghost light drained back into his armour.

Corswain bowed his head in thanks, but the Librarian moved stiffly, as he began to climb.

'This place…' he called. 'There is something within it. Something that interferes with my abilities.'

More Dark Angels were moving past them up the mountain face. Most of the force was down on the ground, now, or would never be landing at all. They climbed and leapt, moving up and up, over jagged faces, punching grip holes in ice, toes finding purchase on blade-thin ledges.

'Resistance is lighter than anticipated,' said Vassago, bounding up the ice and scree again.

'I would not consider that comfort,' said Corswain.

Streaks of energy flicked through the air as gun-boxes fired at the Dark Angels climbing up the slopes. Aircraft shrieked overhead. Clusters of blue unit markers blinked at the corner of Corswain's sight. He pulled himself over a lip of rock and looked up.

The door in the mountainside sat beneath an overhang just above him, sealed and unyielding. The door was a circular plug of metal set into the stone of the mountain: twenty metres across, riveted, frost dusting its wind-pitted surface. There was no sign of a lock or hatch. There were supposed to be seven of these door seals dotted down the mountainsides, but to what end Corswain could neither deduce, nor gather. Most inaccessible to anything but the kind of aerial approach the Dark Angels had just completed. But no matter their intended purpose, they offered a way in. He had chosen five of the seals and sent a Chapter-strength force to each of them. This was the highest door, set closest to the main structures within the mountain, the closest to heaven.

Around him, the fire from the gun turrets slackened.

'Breach it,' he said as his warriors joined him.

The seal blew in moments later. Glowing liquid metal sprayed into the darkness inside. The first Dark Angels were through the breach before the metal had cooled from white to yellow. Corswain was amongst them, sword drawn and lit.

Silence and darkness greeted them. No gunfire or shouts or guns braced behind readied positions. He slowed his charge. Amber threat and targeting runes flicked across his sight, searching and finding nothing. A circular tunnel angled down from the seal they had breached. The walls were smooth, almost mirrors. The glow of the breach and the radiance of Corswain's sword glimmered in broken reflections. A thread of air flicked at the edge of his robes and he heard a low moan in the distance.

'Lord?' It was Tragan, his voice so clear and loud over the vox that Corswain almost flinched. His brother was two kilometres away but he sounded as though he was right next to Corswain. *Fourth and Third have breached into the lower mountain. All vox signals are holding true. Resistance encountered, but less than anticipated.*

Corswain was silent. The breath of air tugged the edge of his robes again.

'This shaft should lead directly to the main choral chamber,' said Vassago. Threads of green-blue light arced over the head of his mace. He shivered, the movement amplified through his armour. 'There is a… a voice. Whatever has darkened the light of the beacon knows we are here. They… *it* is waiting.'

Corswain looked down the shaft. The angle was such that it would not be an advance from here; it would be a drop, and a race down into the dark without the choice of stopping or slowing.

'At this point, Brother Vassago,' he said, 'I do not think that we have any choice. All units, descend,' he said, and dropped himself down the shaft.

*Before time was counted – Hatay-Antakya Hive,
East Phoenicium Wastes*

The soldiers who reached the chamber at the heart of the tower died before they could cross the threshold. Armour tore. Bodies blasted back and up into the air, and then burst apart in turn. Armour plates crushed in on flesh and mashed bone.

Legs sank into marble that was now liquid. Pieces of shattered armour extended into smears of blinding light. Time froze. Flesh slid into red ribbons, organs and muscle peeling away and unravelling into nothing. The air was red and screaming.

At the centre of the chamber beyond the door twenty figures stood still, hands locked together, mouths open, lips and tongues charring as they spoke, runnels of blood crusting their cheeks. Frost covered the obsidian beneath their feet. Spears of flame crawled over the silver pillars behind each of them. Words covered every inch of the floor, walls and domed ceiling. Above and beyond it, the tower rose to the sky, reaching up to touch heaven. The circle of twenty spoke and sung, but they were using no tongue of men. Un-words and nil-sound came from their throats, biting chunks out of the shouts and screams of the soldiers trying to get into the chamber.

+Enough.+ The word somehow carried through the babble of un-words pouring from the twenty.

There was a figure at the door. Blood streaked his armour and face. His crown gleamed like a circle of flame. The circle of twenty trembled. The man in the crown grimaced, and then stepped into the chamber. The air around him thickened. He pushed on, his footsteps forcing their way down towards the stone floor of the room. The shriek of un-sound rose beyond hearing. The man in the crown forced himself forwards, face set. Fire haloed him. The metal of his armour was red with heat. Shadows and rainbow light burst and spun in the chamber. The frost on the walls thickened. Dust and snow billowed from nowhere on gusts of wind.

The man in the crown surged forwards. He was burning, the flesh of his face charring. But still he pushed forwards. Light exploded out from him, blinked to blackness and then back to blinding white. Cracks split the stone floor. Frost flashed to steam. A pressure wave ripped into the nearest of the circle of

figures and tossed them up into the air. And now the man in
the crown was coming forwards, not with one step but with
strides, sword drawn, flame gathering on its edge as it rose.
Behind him, soldiers were coming through the doorway. And
the circle of speakers and singers were twisting, panicking, the
howls coming from their throats now the simple sounds of
human rage and fear.

Stillness.

Complete stillness. Faces frozen. Embers and ashes suspended
in mid-air.

John Grammaticus walked into the middle of the tableau.
Oll stood in the place where he had been when he had lived
the dream in reality, two steps behind the man with the crown
and the burning sword. Oll shifted, and heard the fish scales
of his pearl-white armour chime as he moved. He watched
John circle the man in the crown.

'You and the big Him,' said John. 'Did He call Himself
an Emperor back then?' Oll shook his head. 'Wore a crown
though,' said John, nodding at the image of the man.

'To service a higher ideal demands that those who can act
sacrifice themselves to authority,' said Oll.

'Those are His words, right? That's what He said about why
He took power. He had that ambition even then. Was there
anyone then who could go up against Him?'

Oll shrugged. 'There were some but He was the first.'

'You mean the first psyker.'

'The first witch, the first wizard, sorcerer, shaman, druid…
the first. There were others who were different, but none like
Him. Not in the beginning.'

'What changed?'

'He did. He was… weaker than He is now, much weaker,
but always stronger than anyone else. People change, people
stay the same. He was always driven. Always.'

'But different?'

'He had… limits. Or maybe I just wished He did.'

'I knew you two knew each other, but this is not just an acquaintance between two fellow travellers I'm seeing here, Oll. You fought along with Him, *for* Him, right?'

Oll did not nod, did not shake his head.

'I have always been a soldier, John.'

'So you brought the tower down?'

Oll nodded, tried to close his eyes for a moment, but nothing happened. His eyes simply remained open.

'Yes,' said Oll. 'We brought it down.'

'Too dangerous to stand, right? A place of sorcerers, right?'

Oll looked down. There were ashes frozen in the middle of drifting across the symbol-etched floor.

'The people of the tower thought of themselves as something else. They were scholars of a sort, thinkers, fools…' He found a humourless laugh on his lips and shook his head. 'I think they thought they could unify humanity, elevate it, make it something… higher…' He could feel John looking at him, but he did not look back. His eyes found the frozen face of a man in the circle of figures at the chamber's centre. A drop of blood hung, half-formed from the man's open lips. 'They built their tower, and up and up it went, and out there, their word spread across the lands. Cultures, people, language, art, they changed it all.'

'So He decided to stop them and you decided to help Him? Must say I'm still surprised, Oll. I knew you two had history, but I never thought you drank the water of ideals, or whatever.'

'The people of the tower had something very dangerous, John, something that no one should have. There wasn't a universe to balance it out back then. That's the kind of thing that you can't let happen. Not if you are one of the only people with the perspective to see it.'

Oll shook his head. He wanted very much not to be here.

'Whatever happened to not wanting to be involved?'

'That was later. After this… because of this.'

John Grammaticus frowned.

'What was it they had, Oll? Psyker stuff, sure, witch and warp stuff, but that's not all, is it?'

John looked at the cracked floor for a moment, then flinched back, shaking. Oll watched, and waited.

'That's…' gasped John. 'All the carvings… it's Enuncia. It's shitting Enuncia.'

'It wasn't called that back then,' said Oll. 'Things didn't really have the names they picked up later. Enochian, Glossolalia, Enuncia, Babel… In some ways that was the problem – names, concepts, power, illumination – it all started here. In the fallout. Like everything else.'

'The primordial language of creation…' breathed John. He was not looking at Oll now, not really listening, his eyes moving across the figures and chamber as though seeing it for the first time. 'The first symbol system to span the gap between reality and infinity, and they just had it carved on the walls like kids' graffiti on a hab.'

'A near-complete lexicon,' said Oll.

John whistled.

'I've seen a few symbols before, never wanted to understand it – the definition of knowledge that should not be known, right? Had to be careful when I ran into it before, in case I just started having it screaming in my head.' He grinned briefly. 'One of the few downsides of the whole psychic ability to understand all language and communication. This though, I'm not getting anything. Must be because it's a dream rather than the real thing – just how you remember it, an impression, not the real thing.'

Oll did not reply, but bent down, to where a crystal bowl

lay on the floor. It had shattered as it hit the tiles. Pieces hung in the air above the impact point. He saw the image of a bull-headed man, neck thrown back as another man opened its throat with a knife.

'How did they get hold of so much of it?' John asked, bending down to look at the pillars, and then at the robed figures. 'Enuncia is a shattered language now, but I'm guessing it was still pretty rare back then.'

Oll shrugged. 'I'm not sure, but they had it alright, and they were using it.'

'To do what?'

'The same as everyone with power – to change things. They wanted to elevate humanity, or at least that was what they said. Ideas, art, knowledge, power, all of it. Spread it, channel it, master it, and it would make humanity something bright and shining. They wanted to unlock potential.'

'Sounds dangerous,' said John.

'It was.'

'Sounds not a million miles from what our big man in the crown over there has tried.'

'Yes,' said Oll. 'And no. They did not concentrate all their power and ideals in one figure. The idea was that over time the knowledge and understanding would spread out, that we would all be illuminated.'

'Lovely ideal. I'm guessing the reality was less lovely.'

'Cities turned to ash and salt. Predator ideas. Words that once you heard them would sink into the brain and kill you if you started to think the wrong things.'

'But all in the service of a higher ideal,' said John.

'It always is.'

'Didn't do them much good, by the look of things.' John nodded at the circle of figures in robes.

'Some of their students survived,' said Oll, 'but not many.'

'Really? I would have thought He would have been more thorough.'

'They persisted and still do, seeds and ideas scattered from this tower and this moment. Ideas of a common origin and derivation.'

John gave Oll a hard look.

'Common origin and derivation?' said John carefully. 'As in words with the same root, as in things that are connected to each other? As in cognate?'

Oll nodded.

'Everything starts somewhere.'

The air shimmered, the motes of ash shifted, and the tableau was suddenly moving, blurring with unravelling seconds.

Flames poured from the robed figures' lips as the un-words in their mouths slipped beyond their control. Their bodies collapsed into ash. The man in the crown came forwards, still burning, eyes dark holes. His skin was blistered, but no expression of pain touched His expression. The ash spiralled into the air.

'It's over,' Oll heard himself say, his mouth moving in an echo of the words spoken a long time ago. 'Do whatever you need to do to grind this stuff into dust and it's done.'

The man in the crown turned and looked at Oll, who looked back just as he had all those ages ago. He could feel the armour on his limbs, as heavy as it had been back then. He could feel the sweat and blood on his face. Ashes and sparks stirred through the air. Flames billowed beyond the doors as the tower burned.

'Not yet,' the man replied, and moved towards one of the twenty carved pillars, reaching out with blackened and blistered fingers.

'What are you doing?' said Oll, the words on his lips just as they had been then, when the chamber and the tower had been not just a dream.

'The future…' said the man with the crown. 'When we found each other that is what we talked about. "Live past the span of man and you can see the patterns of what is to come." That was what you said. You were right, but also not. You cannot see the future, my friend. But I… I can see it. I can see the future's shadow.'

Oll felt himself stare at the man, his friend. In his mind he felt the memory of his denial and disbelief falling through him.

'We agreed.'

'We agreed to put the argument aside. I am still right, my friend. Humanity's future cannot be left to chance. You might not agree, but your denial does not alter the truth.'

'This place must become dust and its secrets with it.'

'There are things that cannot be imagined coming,' said the man. A mote of fire glowed in his eyes now. 'The sorcerers and gods and horrors of today are nothing. The tide will rise, and with it the powers that will destroy everything. The world of humanity is small, but one day it will not be, and we won't be able to topple a single tower and save mankind. We will need to be able to do more.'

'Maybe, perhaps… You can't be certain, you *know* you can't be certain. What of causality? Interfere and what happens? Maybe we *cause* what you see in the future by trying to stop it.'

'It must not come to pass. I will not allow it to.'

'We are not gods!' Oll heard himself shout. 'We can't tilt the world on its edge or carry it on our backs. Try to and we will only make it worse. What about leaving things to figure themselves out? What about letting people choose?'

'Let them choose, and they will kill the future.'

'That is not our judgement to make.'

'Is it not?' asked the man in the crown, looking around. The fire had gone from His eyes.

Oll felt himself move next to the pillars. His eyes moved over the symbols. He flinched but held himself steady.

'And this? What has guiding the future got to do with this?'

'Tools,' said the man. 'Weapons, knowledge. We cannot throw aside any of it. You are right – we cannot see the clear path to salvation, but we *will* be able to. This is a step. There shall be other steps and other paths, and we shall take them in turn as we must. This though, is the first real step. Come, my friend. We are fighting a war the end of which no one else shall see. We cannot turn from the weapons that we have, nor those that providence provides.'

'A glass to see further, a word to open hearts, a sword to kill unborn gods...'

The man in the crown nodded, and gestured to the symbol-covered pillars and walls.

'Take this knowledge and the fate changes. Leave it and it unravels. It is a simple choice.'

'There are no simple choices,' said Oll.

'But there *are*,' said the man. 'It's just the consequences that are complicated.'

The dream froze again.

'My stars, Oll,' whistled John. 'You two *did* fall out, didn't you? I mean I always thought... I suppose I thought that you were a bit more distant, a bit less close, and that it was more that you decided to leave each other to whatever you were doing, but...'

'Secrets and things we would rather forget,' said Oll, his voice low. He wondered how far this dream was going to drill. He thought he knew: all the way down into the Labyrinth... 'That's what you said these dreams are showing, so there you go.'

'Hell's teeth, though,' said John, shaking his head and pacing towards the man with the crown, and looking at Him closely. Oll watched John raise a hand as though he was going to touch the man's face. 'You two really went at it, big things, big ideas. You were right, too, weren't you, Oll? I mean, as much as He is the play we are backing in this circus – He is the problem, not now but back then. He tried to control it all and caused what He feared most. This is it, His main problem right here at the start – gazing at the horizon but not seeing the drop at His feet.'

'Maybe,' said Oll.

'Maybe? He was wrong – you knew it then, and you said it, and time came along and proved you right.'

'Right is not what I would call it.'

'Why? Because you walked away? Because things don't come down to one side and another. Oll, when will you get off the fence and just commit? All in.'

Oll shot John a hard look. 'I'm here, aren't I?'

John raised his hands, placating.

'All in – that's the problem, John,' said Oll, and he could hear the anger in his voice. 'The same problem as you and your damned Cabal, and Him, and all the rest. You all want people to be *all in*. No one thinks that they don't have the right to pick an answer. That there might not be an answer!' He realised he had moved towards John. That he had a knife in his hand, fingers clenched around it. He relaxed, stepped back. 'Sorry,' he said.

'It's alright,' John replied, and then looked back to the frozen image of the man in the crown. 'This is really how it all started, though, isn't it? Him, His plan, what He would go on to do – it's all here. At war with anyone who would not get into line, that would not toe the line, like these poor bastards.' John nodded to the crumbling forms of the burning figures in robes. 'You must have seen it before this point, though, Oll. So I still don't see how He got you to fight in His war?'

Oll shook his head. 'I'm not sure about that.'

John frowned. 'About what?'

'About whose war it was.'

'We are standing in your memory, and it seems pretty clear from here.'

And now it was coming, rolling up out of the dark like the voices of the dead calling from the underworld…

'I just want an ordinary life…'

Summer in a meadow in a land drowned by time.

'My dear friend, you'll have as many of those as you want…'

The wind and spray and the bow of a ship splitting the waves…

'Don't look back…'

Down in the dark with the shades behind them…

'Give us the winter and you can have the summer…'

Poor Persephone looking at him with sorrow, her tears gathering as pearls in her eyes…

'You will need to take a thread…'

Down in the Labyrinth, lost in the dark…

'You always made better choices, Oll…'

An old hand turning a card on which a bolt of lightning fell to break a tower…

It was all going to happen again, just as he remembered.

'You've lived a long time, John, but not long enough,' said Oll. 'After a while you forget, and then you forget what you have forgotten. You remember some things and they seem clear, but then you wonder if you are remembering what happened or the story that you told yourself.'

'But He, that man right there, the whatever of then and the Emperor in the now – He found you, got you onside for a while, then you left and He went on to do what He did. That's what happened. That's why you two have history…'

John stopped, and Oll could almost hear the pieces dropping into place. Oll looked at John, and gave a tired sigh.

'I was always a soldier, John. Remember. Always a soldier, never a leader… But then… back then I was something else, and I had a different name.'

John was looking at him. Oll could see the realisation in his eyes.

'You… This war, the whole thing… the warriors that brought this place down… They were not His–'

'Ours,' said Oll. 'They were ours. He was the king and I was…'

'Oh… Shit.'

Oll nodded.

'Warmaster – that is what I was called.'

John Grammaticus stared at him. Oll gave a sad smile.

'Stories, memories… Live long enough, John, and you see the past coming around wearing a different face.'

John opened his mouth to reply. Then he stopped and swayed. The frozen shadows and flames shifted. The frozen embers drifted in the air for an instant. Oll saw John's eyes touch the words covering the stones, then he was doubled over, convulsing as though vomiting, but all that came from his mouth were dry moans.

Oll did not move. He had feared it would come to this. It all had the feeling of something familiar and inevitable.

'I can hear it,' gasped John Grammaticus. 'The Enuncia… Oh, stars-and-time… I can hear Enuncia in my head!'

Oll nodded, and turned to look at the man in the crown, the man who had been a king and was now an Emperor. Something was unlocking inside him. Something he had buried down a long way, locked in old stone and built over with other memories and other deeds.

'This is supposed to be a dream…' gasped John. 'I shouldn't be able to hear it.'

'You are a logokinetic, John,' said Oll, softly. 'You can

understand and gloss any language that someone near you is thinking or speaking.'

'No one is thinking in Enuncia here, though, no one real. It's a dream.'

'I am here, John. Here in the dream and back then, and I'm about to make a choice. You are hearing the memory of my thoughts. You are understanding what is about to happen.'

'Oll… Oll, what did you do?' John was shaking now, body blurring like a smeared drawing of chalk. 'Oll!'

'You are a good man, John. Better than you think you are. Better than me.'

And the dream began to move again. The heat from the flames washed over him. The ash and cinders were thick in the air.

Oll felt his gaze move to the man in the crown, the man who had been his friend and who had trusted him.

'I am sorry,' said Oll to the man in the crown. 'I made the wrong choice.'

The knife was in his hand, just as it had been then. He felt himself step forward. Felt the un-words he read from the floor and pillars form in his mouth. Saw the crowned man turn.

Oll rammed the knife forward and up: up under the scales of the crowned man's armour, up into the flesh beneath, up into the heart that beat within. The black eyes of the crowned man were wide and open, staring into Oll's.

Then Oll spoke.

'_'

High above the burning tower, which had reached from earth to clutch at heaven, the thunderbolt fell.

The Hollow Mountain

The walls of the shaft blurred past. Trails of sparks rose from where armoured fingers and boots dug into the stone. Echoes filled Corswain's ears as hundreds of warriors slid downwards in his wake. Down and down, rushing into the dark.

Heartbeats sliced seconds.

The shrieks of their descent struck the walls, reflected, wrapped around him. The flash of sparks reflected from the circle of the walls, gold streaking black, and the hole they plunged down like the pupil in the eye of a beast. From a place at the back of his skull, the smell of snow and blood breathed into him and the beast looked up as he struck down with his sword.

The black circle beneath Corswain vanished. The darkness was an opening. Colour and light blazed into his eyes, and he was hurtling almost straight down, unable to slow, unable to stop. He hit the edge of the tunnel and then he was not sliding but falling.

Light blazed into his eyes. Sound shrieked through his bones and earpieces.

His helmet display overloaded. Blood vessels in his eyes burst. Bile and acid filled his mouth. He was falling blind. Colours and jagged patterns spun across his retinas. The shrieks vibrated through him, rattling through armour and bone. He could feel sinew and bone splitting. He could not think, could not feel, could only sense and listen. There were voices in the deluge of sound, babbling, calling to each other, calling to him, singing, humming and crying in dozens of tongues.

He hit something. Armour cracked across his shoulder. He spun through the air. Another impact, and this time the pain reached through the storm of sensations. He rolled, tumbling, halted, nerves and thoughts flooding.

In his mind's eye he looked up. A beast was rising above him, sword held point down. It snarled.

He gasped. Pushed himself up, gripped his helm and wrenched it off. The world swam in front of him. He staggered as distances stretched and then snapped tight. He sensed the falling blow as it arced towards his head. He jerked aside. The weapon hit the ground with an explosion of light and lightning. Corswain came up. His sword was in his hand – gripped even as he had fallen. The enemy warrior was a mountain of chromed metal. Amethysts plugged its eye sockets. It had been a Legion warrior once, that was written in the lines of its Terminator armour, still visible beneath the growths of polished metal and jewels. Its neck bulged in its collar ring, inflating as it swept up a mace with a head of silver. Even over the din surrounding him, Corswain heard the traitor inhale to shout. Cartilage clicked in its mouth. Sacs of skin inflated. Corswain rammed his blade forwards. Its power field was inactive, but the sharpened steel punched through the warrior's throat and into the meat of its neck. It shook, vibrating for the instant it hung on the sword, gurgling with a moan of deflating lungs and air sacs. Then it moved, mace still rising. Blood gushed down Corswain's sword. He activated the blade's power field. Lightning exploded out. Flesh and blood blew to smoke. Corswain wrenched the sword back and turned it into a cut that sliced off the hands gripping the mace at the wrist. Warrior and weapon fell. Blood and yellow fluid poured out. Corswain stepped back, turning his gaze.

The deep choral chamber of the Hollow Mountain shimmered around him. The chamber was a sphere cut into the heart of the mountain, three hundred and forty-three metres in diameter. Lining the internal surface were the choral tiers. From there the psykers would sing the song of their souls and merge that song into a single beacon flame. Circular platforms hung on pillars from the roof, each one dangling from the one above like the leaves of an inverted plant. The disc of each platform held a subtle convexity or concavity.

A heat haze shimmered over Corswain's sight as he tried to take the view in. The fall from the shaft opening had tumbled him down and into one of the circular platforms. He must

have hit the edge of a platform above, and spun sideways.
Amethyst, serpentine and clouded quartz threaded through the
stone of the platforms. Flecks of gold gleamed in the light. And
what light there was… Colours and patterns flashed through
the air, sliding together, merging and ripping apart. Sound
boomed and sawed through the chamber.

There were Dark Angels falling from the open shafts above,
striking the platforms, rising, forming into units, moving and
firing. Some triggered jump packs as they fell. Cones of flame
caught them and boosted them up onto the tiers on the inner
walls. He saw three units of Destroyers plunge down, weaving
between shimmering blasts, firing pistols, grenades shedding
from harnesses. There were enemies scattered across the platforms, warriors, giants in armour that rioted in colour. The
colours clashed and blurred. Light reflected from polished
plates and shattered into blinding mirages. They were fast,
too, Astartes fast, but the nobility of their breed was gone.
Only discord and obscenity remained.

As he watched he felt something shift at the edge of his
senses. Above and around him, reality cracked. Soft, pulpy
flesh oozed into being, clotting into muscle and fat and skin.
Horns formed and hardened. He felt screams in the back of his
head. The ground shifted beneath him. He leapt back as a claw
punched through the floor where he had stood. Figures pulled
themselves out through the wounds in reality, lithe muscle and
chitin forming as they moved. Black-pearl eyes looked back at
him. Glass-needle smiles opened. He felt his skin tighten. The
figures leapt. He stepped back, sword rising, and…

…fell upwards.

The creatures sprang after him. The stone of the platform
flowed up into the air, growing into a spiral of razor crystals.
The figures bounded up the steps after him, laughing, spinning, smiling at the mockery they made of the laws of reality.

He hit the platform above, spun into a roll and came up. The chamber that had been below loomed above him. The first creature leapt from the crystal stair towards him. Corswain's sword swung. The creature's claw extended as it reached for him. His blade went through its arm and on into its torso. It blew apart, black ichor crystallising in the power field's flash. Another came through the remains of the first, then another and another, and he was cutting and cutting, the world defined now by the reach of his blade. Claws bit through his armour. He was bleeding. He could feel warmth spreading through him, slowing him, pulling him down, a promise of rest without end. He stepped back and the floor folded like paper, twisting as he moved over it, spiralling and opening into different shapes every time it was not in his sight. Sensations poured into him with each instant: needles in his skin; the taste of ashes and sugar; the smell of forests and flowers and rot; blasts of colour in his eyes; laughter and voices, louder than the roll of thunder; whispers that stabbed into his mind. He could not see the rest of the battle now – it was a blur beyond the reach of his senses. Time creaked and stretched. Was he remembering the blur of cuts and parries, or was he living them? Where were his brothers? How long had he been here? He was a single, shrinking point. He was not even real, just the dream of a knight in the mind of a boy who died to the claws of a beast, long ago and far away… There had been snow on the ground and the sound of wind in the trees.

A beam of cold blue light struck the figure in front of him. Its substance blasted to ash. The light leapt to the next figure and the next. Iridescent flesh became dust. Glass-blade smiles vanished. Vassago advanced on Corswain, a rope of lightning uncoiling from his raised hand. With him were warriors in black hoods and robes and chequered pauldrons, swords drawn, bolters firing. They were climbing up a spiral stair that had grown from nothing. Vassago held the cord of lightning until the last creature was ash. He jumped and landed next to Corswain.

'My thanks,' said Corswain.

'This place,' said Vassago. 'It is…' The Librarian staggered, almost fell. 'It's shouting, calling out. Can't you hear it?'

'What?' he called.

'He asked if you could hear my song,' said a voice that came from all around.

And then, as though it needed the words to be spoken to make it real, Corswain heard the cacophony. Distances expanded and contracted in time with the rhythm. Colours flared and burst into shards in his eyes.

Then the world became perfectly clear, as though a window had been wiped clean. The heat-haze blur and the riot of broken colour was gone. All was silent. All was slow. The taste of gun smoke and lightning in his mouth was clean and perfectly balanced. He looked up and for the first time since he had entered the choral chamber, he saw it clear and true.

The psykers of the grand choir filled the choral tiers on the chamber walls. All of them. Pinned in place, the stone and metal of their chairs grown through and over them, limbs and skin stretched so that the only features that remained were their mouths. Corswain's eye found the face of a psyker on a tier level with him. Swirling light surrounded the man's head. Chrome tendrils squirmed over and through his torso, threading his ribs. A mouth of metal fangs surrounded his neck like a collar. He was looking straight at Corswain. The psyker's mouth moved silently, lips fluttering. Along the tiers above and below, hundreds of mouths took up the murmur until it was a hiss of words.

'Do you not hear my song, Corswain, Lion's son?' said the Chorus. It was talking just to him, even though a part of

him knew that it would be whispering to all his brothers, speaking their names like a parent to a child. *'Listen and be at peace,'* it said.

Hatay-Antakya Hive, East Phoenicium Wastes

The tower exploded in Oll's memory. He tasted lightning: salt and metal on his tongue. Over and again: lightning stabbing down, blocks of stone and mud brick blowing outwards, wood and plaster blasted to ash and cinders. Darkness and night... and the idea of two figures falling from the ruin, survivors, victims, the Emperor and the Warmaster... always falling, from then to now, forever.

'Get up! Move now! Come on, you old bastard!' A voice. A voice that was not the dream or in his mind, but real and near. He heard hissing and a whoosh and a soft thump. Fire blazed behind his eyelids. There was pain across his body, digging into him, biting, chewing. He gasped. Tried to move. Cords were twisting around him. He felt the thorns in his flesh. Something grabbed him, pulled him. The thorns bit. He could smell smoke and flame. The thorns held him for an instant and then released. He half fell. Eyes blurred as they opened.

'Come on, Oll! Come on!' Zybes was there, standing beside him, pulling him up by the arm. There was fire in the chamber, yellow and oily. Clumps of thorns were burning, twisting as they became ash. Sap sizzled to smoke. Zybes had an arm hooked under Oll's arm, his lasgun in the other hand. A plastek canister of promethium hung on a strap at his side, sloshing as he twisted to fire. Las-bolts burned into a clump of thorns.

Katt was there, red from head to foot. Thorn punctures covered her, seeping blood. She tossed promethium in an arc around her, brought her pistol up and fired. The fuel ignited. Flame breathed out. They were in a burnt circle in the middle

of the chamber. The thorns flowed back like a tide gathering
to crash back down on a shoreline.

Oll forced his limbs to move, found that his gun was still
hanging from his arm by its strap, grabbed the canister off
Zybes' shoulder and sloshed the fuel in a wide arc. He fired
as the fluid was still falling.

'How did you find us?' he called to Zybes.

'She called me,' said Zybes, now pulling out a wide-bladed
knife and hacking into a burning wall of thorns. Katt was
beside him.

'Left,' she called, pointing as she ignited another wash of
fuel. Zybes hacked into the thorns on his left. A machine
hand glinted, under the cut vines. 'Her mind voice found me,
reached out, guided me.'

'I thought you were gone your own way,' said Oll. He was
beside Zybes, ripping the torn vines back from Graft. The
servitor gurgled, tracks spinning but not gripping, machine
limbs thrashing.

'I was gone,' said Zybes. 'But what else have I got other than
you, other than all of us?'

Oll paused for an instant, looked at Zybes as the one-time
pay-by-day grunted and heaved Graft back onto its tracks.

'Thank you,' said Oll.

Zybes looked at him, nodded.

'Trooper Persson…' Graft's voice buzzed, slurred. 'I… I did
not know where I was, Trooper Persson.' Its limbs twitched, its
head moved from side to side. 'I do not… I do not know…'

'Over there!' shouted Katt. 'Two metres in.'

Zybes was already hacking forwards, firing into knots of
vines, peeling them back from the shape of Krank. The old
trooper did not move as the thorns came free.

'Graft,' said Oll.

'I…' buzzed the servitor. 'I am… I saw… a…'

'Graft, he needs help.'

Graft rocked for a second, then moved forwards, and lifted the unconscious Krank up.

'Let's move!' shouted Zybes.

'Not yet!' called Oll.

'You're kidding!'

'John,' said Oll, and he snapped his eyes around to look at Katt. 'John Grammaticus, he's here.' He called out, shouting, 'John! John!'

Somewhere under his senses he heard a reply. 'There,' he shouted, pointing into the mass of thorns. Fingers protruded from the vines. Zybes was already there, cutting and hacking. Oll was next to him, battering and yanking the vines. John gasped as his face emerged. Zybes gripped him, under the chin and by an arm.

'Shoot,' called Zybes. Oll fired into the thorns around John. They burned, coiling back. Zybes pulled. The vines tightened. Oll fired again, and Zybes yanked him free. Oll fired another burst as Zybes tried to steady John. The psyker swayed, shivering, bleeding from puncture wounds. He looked thin, drained, the skin of his face slack, like the surface of a deflated balloon. He doubled over and vomited.

'Shit...' he gasped. 'Reality tastes bad.'

'You said you had someone with you,' said Oll, catching John's arm and tugging him up. The movement was rough. He could feel anger in him. The dream had touched things in his very old soul that he did not want to waken, things he had hoped not to have to look at yet. Part of him blamed John Grammaticus for that; the rest of him blamed himself. 'Who came with you? Where are they?'

'Nice to see you in the flesh, too, Oll,' coughed John, spluttering, hand shaking as he wiped vomit from his chin.

'Here,' said Katt, already hacking and shooting into the thorns.

John suddenly jerked up alert, his eyes on Katt. Oll could read the trained tension-relaxation of muscles, the predator readiness. Katt's head snapped around. Her gaze locked with John's. Oll felt a jolt in his muscles like the discharge of electric current.

'Where did you find her?' asked John, his voice suddenly low and controlled.

'Along the way,' said Oll.

'She's…'

'She saved us all.'

'Out of fuel!' shouted Zybes. 'Whoever is still in there, you had better get them out fast.'

John hesitated for a second and then nodded.

'Here!' He moved up beside Katt as she hacked at vines. Oll moved with them, clubbing the butt of his gun into barbed knots. Milk-white venom was pooling on the floor. Something grey amongst the coils. Hard, smooth edges, cracked and pitted, a shape emerging as the vines tore from it, ripping from where they had sunk their fangs into the soft rubber between plates. Oll almost stopped as he recognised what it was.

Armour.

Dull grey without colour, just the scratches of time.

A helmed head, beaked, like a broken memory of a crow.

Huge.

A giant.

A Space Marine.

Oll stepped back as the grey warrior ripped free, and stood. Its head turned towards him, gaze like an aimed gun barrel.

Zybes cried out. Oll saw him think about shooting. Oll brought his hand up to stop what would be the man's last act if he wasn't still.

'You are Ollanius the Pious,' said the Space Marine.

'She sent you with John?' he asked.

'She sent me to *you*,' it said. 'I am called Leetu.'

A sound like nails pulling over rusted metal split the air. Oll whirled. The wall of thorns was rolling inwards, bending around the fire that was still eating it, contracting like muscle fibres, thorns gripping the floor, roiling towards them in a wave.

Leetu moved.

Oll saw the movement as a blur.

There was a sound like the ripping of steel and the roar of thunder. Explosions burst amongst the thorns, phosphor bright. Leetu had a gun in his hands. It was long-barrelled, ribbed, and wound with pipes and wires that gleamed with the work of technology that Oll had not seen since wars that were now long past. Fire spat from its muzzle, stuttering as the Space Marine held the trigger down. Blinding white light strobed from the shell impacts. Leetu reached the end of the clip, and reloaded in the time that it took Oll to draw breath. The gun exhaled again.

'We must get out,' said John. 'Down to the lower levels and out as fast as we can.'

'No,' said Oll.

'Oll,' began John. 'What–'

'Rane is still in the hive somewhere. We are going to get him.'

'Oll, come on! He's just one person. There is more at stake here.'

Oll checked the mag on his gun. Still green. He looked at Zybes and Graft and the unconscious Krank. 'We go on together, all of us. No one left behind.'

In the Labyrinth at the back of his memory he saw Theseus close his eyes, and heard abandoned Ariadne shriek from the shoreline vanishing behind the stern of a ship with black sails.

'You were always good at choices…'

'Okay?' he said, and looked around. Zybes nodded. He thought Katt gave a smile.

'I was sent to help find you,' said Leetu. 'I have succeeded. Best I keep you in sight, so that I do not have to find you again.'

'I follow…' burbled Graft. 'I follow you, Trooper Persson.'

He nodded a brief thanks, not certain what to say or if there was anything that could be said.

'Katt, can you find him?'

'Up,' she said. 'That's all I can feel. We have to go higher.'

John Grammaticus snorted.

'You are actually kidding, right?'

Oll shrugged and began to move towards the shaft opening. He thought of the tower, all that time ago, of the knife in his belt now and the lightning falling from the sky. Small choices. Big choices. After enough time they were the same thing.

After a moment, John Grammaticus followed.

The Hollow Mountain

Corswain saw the daemon. How he had not before was not fathomable. There at the heart of the chamber, in the void between all the platforms and apparatus, burned a sun. It was golden, rayed, its light the light of a new day on gently rolling waves. He looked at it and felt the heaviness of his thoughts fall away. The burdens of will and command, of certain death and hopeless struggle, vanishing. He had never realised he was carrying so much, that he had borne the weight of existence on his shoulders. It was gone now. He was free. He was the master of his universe. From here, only what he desired and willed would exist.

'You deserve more,' said the Chorus. *'You deserve everything.'*

The orb of the sun split into three and then again into six, each a yellow yolk of light orbiting its kin. Then each of the orbs stretched, took on the shape of limbs and hands and features. Six figures stood in a circle in the air, rotating around each other. Each was a perfect image of humanity; mouths opened and closed over the glowing surface of their skin, wings of light unfurled from their backs. Corswain felt as though he was looking at six images, but also one – a figure with layers of limbs and wings placed over each other.

'*I am the voice within you,*' said the golden image, and all around the walls the voice of the psykers echoed it with perfect harmony. It was getting closer, though Corswain did not see it move, spinning, arms and fingers and wings moving in time with the thrum of echoes. All he wanted to do was submit to the endless fall of sleep. There were dreams waiting for him just behind the flicker of closing eyelids. '*I am the promise of the dream, and the Song of Endless Rapture. I am the Chorus of the Denied. I have waited for you, my beautiful son. I am so glad you came. There shall be no more waking. No more strife. No more beasts in the forests of your memory. Only peace.*'

'You are a creature of the warp,' he said. There was no effort to the words, and the mouths of the Chorus smiled as though charmed.

'*I am a prince of truths so great that fools call them lies. This is my nest, my place on this mortal Earth while it is seeded. From here I call and the dreams of the living ring to my song. The Children called me here, made this my temple, my light-house from which to shine into the night of lost souls. So many follow the call now… but will you join us, my beautiful son? Will you listen? Will you hear? Will you follow?*'

He did not hear or think of the words, but *felt* them. They slid into his mind: the words needles, the promises hooks. Then there was warmth and peace, and he knew that all he needed to do was believe the words and to let his life become the dream…

Dream…

Dream…

Dream…

The beast was dead on the snow, still at last, not baring its fangs as he faced it, not looking at him as it bled out, and he raised his sword to give it mercy. He could set aside his sword. He could leave the past and the beast he bore in his mind and on his back. A knight of swords no longer… a warrior who fought only for what he believed, that did not see the shadows, that did not have to live and wonder why the beast would not let go of him.

He looked over his shoulder as he reached the treeline. The beast lay where it had fallen. Its blood was red on the snow. Except it was no beast and never had been. A man lay in its place, hair matted with clotting blood, torso and neck split by pistol shot and blade edge, eyes closed. His brother. His true brother, who had come out of the woods with murder on his breath. Slain in the snow and left behind, a beast slain by a knight. He felt his head drop. All he had to do was keep on walking and this would be no more. Keep moving into the light, following the song…

He looked up and turned towards the trees and the blazing light that was now shining through them. He paused, looked back. The beast was on its feet, looking at him, blood and entrails draining onto the snow. It bared its teeth and Corswain turned back, sword rising.

The choral chamber snapped back into being.

The sixfold daemon of sunlight was right in front of him, reaching for him. His Legion brothers were unmoving, transfixed. Creatures with razor claws and gloss-black orbs for eyes bent over them, talon tips poised, needle smiles wide. Warriors in twisted armour stood further back, tube-barrelled guns held low, watching. The choir of psykers shivered. Pale knots of fire wound through the air. The air was a reek of blossom scent and spoiled meat. The daemon hands recoiled from him an instant before he surged to his feet. The heads of the creatures crawling over the platform twitched up. The traitors began to hoist their guns.

Corswain came up and cut faster than any of them. His sword struck the first of the six bodies of the Chorus daemon, and cut through to the two beside it. Time stuttered. The remaining figures were bleeding, darkness pouring out of them as their brightness curdled to shadow. Corswain spun his sword to strike again, as across the chamber the Angels of the First Legion came to their feet with a roar of gunfire.

Sound vanished. Silence swallowed the choral chamber as the last sixfold daemon screamed. Corswain swept his sword up. The platform was alight with bolt-round detonations. Everything seemed slowed, time stretching to allow every detail of what was happening to shine. Bodies of iridescent flesh blew open without sound. Blood, jewel-bright, gushed into slow-falling arcs. Fragments of shrapnel tumbled through smoke, winking, reflecting the flash of the explosions. Dark Angels were moving down and across the platforms, black armour gleaming like oil in firelight. He saw things with half-chitin skin materialise and vaporise. Warriors in multi-coloured armour came from side tunnels. The blast waves of their guns formed silver shivers in the air. Corswain saw one of his brothers hit by a blast and come apart, blood, armour and pulped organs forming concentric rings in the air.

He felt himself drawn to stop, to look, to watch and fill his eyes with the pattern and colour of blood spray and fire blasts.

He wrenched his gaze back to the crumbling forms of the sixfold daemon in front of him. They were shadows now, smudges of heat haze around him. Blade-like embers spiralled through the air. One struck Corswain's shoulder and burrowed through the ceramite. He swung his sword, and the blade went through what little substance remained of the daemon. A neon-white blast wave ripped out, passing through mass and matter. Corswain felt it spill over him and through him, silence, filled with images: the perfect feathered pink of a rad explosion over a city, a drop of blood hanging from a polished smile of steel, the spiced scent of flesh turning to sugar in a flame's heat. Then it was past. The lesser daemons blew into silver mist as the wave struck them. Warriors in neon-bright armour staggered, quivering. Bolts tore into them, ripping armour plates in rolling drumbeats of detonations. The wave of psychic energy struck the psykers in their choral tiers. Skulls crumpled. Teeth blew out of mouths. Ribs exploded. All in silence, like an image projected from a pict-feed without sound. Blood coloured the air in a wet, red spray. The wave rebounded. The remains of the psykers flashed to pink-and-red ice. The wave picked up slivers of bone and shards of armour as it ripped back towards the core of the chamber. Dark Angels fell as debris sliced through joints and punched into ceramite. At the centre of the chamber, Corswain saw the wave contracting in on where he stood and knew he could not escape it. In the slow second before it struck him, he raised his sword, an old salute to duty and a life given to see it done.

The wave reached for him, glittering with razor fragments and witch-ice. He kept his eyes open.

A sphere of blue fire surrounded him. The wave of fragments hit the flame. Sound roared back into being with a thunderclap. Light blanked out sight. Corswain felt his pupils contract to pinpricks.

The sound of gunfire and shouting broke over him. A hand gripped his shoulder; he spun to see Vassago, haloed by blue fire, mace in hand.

'It seems I must give my thanks again,' said Corswain.

'What else is the meaning of brotherhood?' replied Vassago.

SEVENTEEN

Vortex
Our own monsters
Invigilata

The Cradle Basin, Mercury-Exultant kill-zone

<Fire!>

White heat speared into the shadow engine. Sparks burst from it. Tetracauron felt his skin blister.

<Reactor at overload threshold!>

He could feel it. His heart was beating fast, sweat pouring from his skin. He was breathing hard in sympathetic fever. His thoughts and emotions were swirling and blurring.

<Fire!> he willed again. *Reginae Furorem*'s volcano cannon bored a line of white heat into the shadow of the enemy engine.

<Strike fail!>

He felt Divisia's frustration flare, felt Cartho's steadying presence switch reactor flow to the motive drives. He was losing the balance of the incarnation. Exhaustion. Beyond exhaustion, and the will of the engine and the Legio to turn and walk into the fire, into the guns of the enemy. He could still feel the flame presences of his battle force engines and maniples, all below strength, all running at the edge of reactor tolerance, munitions gone, damaged, battered, filled with rage. He felt it too. The enemy had breached their lines so now they had to fight a different war.

Water channels braided the basin they had crossed from Karalia's Grave. *Dies Irae* and its court were six kilometres distant, advancing, unhurried, firing as they came. Knights and tanks and insectoid war machines swarmed about their feet.

<Tetracauron.> The signal voice cut into his sensations. Distortion laced the connection, fizzing with data corruption and system error, but the voice of Princeps Maximus Cydon was like a breath of pure air into the heart of a dying forge. <We are ready. Clear the zone.>

A pause, the briefest interruption of the flow of data between him and the princeps maximus. He thought of the old man, enthroned in the skull of *Imperious Prima*. Old in war, hardened by time. Tetracauron wanted to voice an objection to what was about to be done, but knew that it would be wasted, and worse, that it would be wrong. The enemy had breached the lines. They were closing through the kill-zone. Fire from the wall guns had become erratic. Across a hundred-kilometre front, enemy engines and forces were pressing forwards. The hole could not be sealed by engines standing only to die. It needed other strength to be brought to bear.

<Yes, my princeps,> replied Tetracauron, and switched to battle group-wide transmission with a thought. <All engines, move to grid lambda-one-two by gimel-thirty-four-five, maximum stride. Acknowledge and action.>

<I have partial target data integration from the Ninth and Tenth maniples.>

<Divisia, confirm and integrate our target systems.>

<Yes, my princeps.> There was a pause, a shudder through

the incandescence, a cold and hollow knot of realisation. He could feel the edge of his youngest moderatus' thoughts like a shadow of his own. That they had come this far, one unthinkable act piled on top of another.

<Time to firing, twenty-one seconds,> sent Cartho.

<*Helios* and *Furnace Child* are not clear of the fire zone.>

He saw then, the two engines. Arthusa's *Helios* keeping pace with a Reaver, its left legs twisted, armour plates warped by damage. It was limping, void shields stuttering. Arthusa was pacing the Reaver, sheltering it with her engine's own shields, firing back at the advancing Mortis engines fording the water channel. As he watched, *Helios'* volcano cannon fired. The discharge cooked the river surface to steam as it passed over. Light splashed across an enemy engine. Sprays of luminescence arced into the air. If it had done anything to slow its advance, Tetracauron could see no sign of it.

<Time to firing, thirteen seconds.>

Tetracauron threw his voice into the incandescence.

<Arthusa, move. For the turning of the cog, move faster!>

At the back of his awareness he could feel the presence of *Imperious Prima* and its maniple. The Warmonger and its court of four Warlords had gone still, their weapon systems synchronising. Their threat and fury was a growing blue ache at the back of Tetracauron's skull.

<Advance,> he willed. <Get next to them and merge shields.>

He felt Divisia's curse as *Reginae Furorem* strode down the slope towards the two engines.

<What are you doing?> came Arthusa's sending.

<What I can,> he replied.

<Fire launch.>

<Merge now!> He felt the void shields syncopate and then slide into those of *Helios* and around the wounded Reaver.

The first missile landed. Fired from thirty kilometres away, it hit the ground in front of the Mortis Titan and exploded in the riverbed. Fire and steam billowed up. Then another landed and another, the payloads of three Warlord Titans saturating the world with fire.

Tetracauron had a fraction of a second to see *Dies Irae* and its court vanish behind a wall of detonations, before the secondary munitions exploded. *Helios'* and *Reginae Furorem's* merged void shields tore away in a drum roll of collapsing energy.

<Move!>

Reginae Furorem strode up the slope, wall-wards, dust and flame boiling around it. The two other Titans were with it. A kilometre towards the wall, the remainder of his battle force were retreating in staggered order, half looking back at the others striding towards the wall. Southwards he could see the glimmers of three maniples and half a dozen Knight lances moving to fill the line as they withdrew. To the west the towering presence of *Imperious Prima* stood, its lethal intent a building flame. Tetracauron felt the burning flow from reactor to drives, the burning hunger of weapons, the rage of *Reginae Furorem* that they were not turning to face the fire and the enemy within it.

<Terminus launch wave in ten seconds.> Divisia's emotion was held just beneath the surface. They were fourteen strides from the top of the slope and edge of the fire-zone.

Behind them a scorched figure broke from the wall of fire and smoke. The warp creature had remade its skin, swelling its eye-ports to multifaceted blisters. Pale fluid drooled from a proboscis that dangled beneath its jaw. The weapon of its right arm coiled with ghost-light. Rust flaked from its barrel. Colour drained from the air as it drew breath to fire.

Four strides to the edge of the fire-zone.

Imperious Prima's cold intent was now a blue supernova.

The Mortis engine fired. A beam of shrieking light struck the Reaver limping beside *Helios* and *Reginae Furorem*. It took another stride. The light of the beam was crawling over it. Another stride. Rust fell from it, and then chunks of armour that broke into dust. Its back was bending, its stance breaking under its own weight as joints and pistons corroded in an eye-blink. Tetracauron felt his mind freeze. The Reaver's death cry flowed across him, a hissing, desperate wail of guttering power and crumbling metal. Its torso broke open. For an instant, its reactor core was visible, the fire within shrinking and guttering faster than its failing containment. It fell, bones and spirit breaking. The Mortis engine took another step. Behind it the shadows of its kin loomed.

<Terminus launch,> sent Divisia.

Thirty kilometres back towards the wall, *Imperious Prima* and its maniple fired.

The purpose of First Maniple, the primary of the Maniple of Maniples, was not to walk into the heart of the inferno – that purpose was for the Second and Fifth maniples. *Imperious Prima* was a Warmonger, an Emperor-class Titan armed with weapons to end civilisations: Deathstrike missiles, vengeance cannons, multiple rocket and missile clusters. The four Warlords that walked at its side each bore a fist, both a symbol and a means to defend the First Titan of the Legio. On their backs and other arms they bore weapons that aped those of *Imperious Prima*: Apocalypse launchers, quake cannons. Armies became ash when they spoke. To this battle they had brought more than fire, though.

To the Titan legions born of Mars, the vortex missile was both sacred and profane – a wonder of technology and the lost mysteries of ancient techno-arcana, and a bitter blade that once drawn in war brought only sorrow and loss. During the old wars, the use of such weapons had been a mark of irrevocable intent – a sign that conflict had passed the point where it could be healed by diplomacy, or even the peace that followed victory. To use one such weapon signalled an intent not to destroy but to annihilate, and to expect the same in turn if it failed. Amongst the Legio Ignatum they were called the Bitter Gift. Only the other legions of the Triad Ferrum Morgulis held as many in their armouries, and even they used them sparingly.

Seven vortex missiles loosed from *Imperious Prima* and its maniple in a single, synchronised launch. The missiles flew free, accelerating past the limits of sound, trailing thunder.

In the incandescence, Tetracauron felt the data-echo of the launch as a cold shiver on his skin. The Mortis engine before them arched up, a creature sensing the flight of an arrow.

The first missile struck and detonated forty metres behind the Mortis engine. It did not have a precise target. Even with Tetracauron's targeting data the spirit of the missiles had been launched half blind. That did not matter. The mechanism in the warhead ripped a hole in the sheet of reality.

Darkness beyond darkness.

Existence screamed.

Matter vanished into the growing sphere of unreality. Light curdled to neon smears as it vanished into the vortex.

To Tetracauron, the incandescence showed him the vortex as a white space of data failure.

The Mortis engine twisted as the vortex grasped it. The warp entity within the Titan roared as its essence was pulled from the metal shell it had possessed. Ephemeral shapes of insect wings, feelers and endless eyes bubbled into being and vanished into the darkness. The machine twisted as physical laws went into wild contradiction. Armour and mechanisms compressed, liquefied and twisted between states. The shell of its torso ruptured. Blue-hot plasma exploded out and then stopped, held in paradox, and began to tumble into brilliant shards like leaves of sun-fire caught in a tornado. Then it was gone and the vortex grew and spun into the air. Black lightning arced across it. The next three vortex missiles hit deeper in the fire zone. Then the next one and the next, each tearing existence apart with a sound that Tetracauron felt inside the metal flesh of his Titan. Commands failed, the incandescence shivered.

<Walk!> he willed, and the force of his mind drew fire from its stuttering heart. *Reginae Furorem* took a step and another, and then it was striding from the basin. He could see the wall, could see the maniples manoeuvring to meet whatever came from the rolling storm of violated existence. The fires of other engagements glittered in sight and awareness, destruction shrunk in the face of the vortex bombardment.

The vortices were moving across the basin. Two collided, slid together, swelled, and rose into the air like a black mockery of a sun. The fire and dust of the first bombardment spun upwards into it, whirling a burning cloak before vanishing into its heart. The shapes of Knights, of tanks, of spider-limbed war machines flew into the wounds. Tetracauron saw the silhouette of a Warlord Titan rise and tumble into the void, its shape coming apart as it hung for an instant on the edge of unmaking. He could not look away. He felt the eyes of his crew and the spirit of his Titan transfix, drawn to watch this atrocity committed in a war that was defined by atrocity.

<Focus, and walk.>

He took another step, turning the Titan and the focus of Divisia and Cartho by will.

Then he saw the shadow step into sight between the vortices. *Dies Irae* dragged the debris and smoke with it as it strode on.

Scrap code bellowed from it. Tetracauron felt it strike his sensors and roll into his thoughts, burbling like laughter. The vortices moved around it, close but not pulling it into their embrace. It sounded its war-horns. The sound slid into the warp and boomed beyond sound. In the incandescence, the princeps and crews of Ignatum Titans across the two hundred kilometres of the kill-zone heard it. On the ground, the princeps and tank commanders felt it boom into their vox-sets. In the warp, the daemons of despair and loss heard and followed its call.

The vortices shimmered, the edges billowing ragged as the flow of matter into the warp stopped and the warp breathed through the breaches. Amorphous shapes slid into being, congealing into false substance – creatures that dragged themselves across the ground on broken limbs as thick as battle cannons, swarms of fat-bodied insects spiralling on asymmetric wings, grubs that slithered and oozed through the air as though it were water, lumbering figures writhing with tentacles. The vortices shrank as the creatures drained from the warp into reality. Four of *Dies Irae*'s surviving court were at its side now. Beneath and around them, the air and ground writhed. Munitions were already exploding amongst them, blowing chunks of false flesh to slime. *Dies Irae* gave another booming cry and took another step towards the Palace.

Shard Bastion, Mercury Wall

General Nasuba and her command entourage came out onto the viewing platform and paused to look up. The ragged edge of the aegis shield flickered above them. Lightning arced along it, and rain poured from the field interface edge in a grey curtain. A gust of wind blew past her face, warm even up here, heavy with the smell of energy discharge. There was blood on the viewing platform, dancing in dilute pools under the falling rain. Command troopers spread out. Tech-priests made for the vox and data signal nodes that rose from the platform like bare, iron trees. There were bodies on the platform, scattered and crumpled, different uniforms, limbs slack, empty eyes pointing at the sky. A trooper in bloody greens and blues rose from where he was crouched over a mashed corpse and charged at Nasuba. She aimed and fired her serpenta without pausing in stride. The trooper was blasted to ash.

'Time?' she called.

'Three minutes twenty-one seconds,' replied Sulkova.

'Secure the platform for landing.'

'We have a link to Indomitor,' called a vox-officer from beside an aerial-pylon. 'It's intermittent.'

'Better than nothing,' said Nasuba. 'Start building a picture of the section, piece by piece, unit by unit. Use ink and parchment if you have to.'

'Our units have control of the wall top south to Section Forty-Five and north to Indomitor,' said Kurral. He was limping, leaning hard on a comms trooper. Blood was coming through the bandages around his right leg. He looked very pale.

To the left and right of the platform the rockcrete blisters of two turbo-laser emplacements rose, the barrels of the guns levelled at the land beyond the wall but silent. Beyond them, down the top edge of the wall, other gun emplacements rose like teeth: macro plasma and lasweapons of a dozen different configurations and purposes. From the top tiers and edge of the bastion and wall they could draw their lines of fire to a horizon line a hundred and twenty kilometres away. They could also fire without shaking the wall apart. The heavy kinetic guns were mounted lower down the wall, cushioned and fired to precise patterns to stop them setting up lethal resonance waves. The weapons on the wall top did not recoil and so could fire as long as the power and plasma flowed from the bastion's reactors.

At that moment, though, neither power nor vibration from mass bombardment were a problem. The problem was that the crew units were not functioning and the direct command chain was down. The guns of the Mercury Wall had fallen silent as their crew fled. A few, those crewed almost solely by servitors and the tech-priests, kept firing. Troops fled their posts. Some simply sat behind firing steps or in corridors or arming chambers and wept. Nasuba had spent hours gathering near-stable forces in the bastion and sending them along the wall to take control of weapon and control installations. Some on foot, some in vehicles along the wall tops. Take control... It felt like she was invading her own zone of command. That was exactly what she was doing. Some of those manning the wall had not fallen to panic – some had begun to try to kill anything that came near them. They had lost several of her command staff to learn that lesson in the last few hours.

'How long until we have the top batteries functional?'

'I... Forty minutes for the bastion guns, the rest...'

'Kurral...' she said, stepping closer.

'I'm alright, general... I'll get a better answer on the wall guns.'

She nodded and straightened.

'Time?' she called again.

'One minute twenty seconds,' called Sulkova.

'Do we have vox-link or visual?'

'Negative.'

'Ready status?' she called.

'Command fidelity estimated at forty-five per cent.'

Command... Nasuba had seen commands come apart before, had seen battle zones fragment into anarchy. But she had never seen it happen as quickly and as thoroughly as it had on Mercury. Comms-failure, suicide, desertion, insanity. Command was just not a word you could wrap around the situation. She could not reach half of the units on the wall, and those that she could reach were in a state a long way from viable. Violence and disorder was spreading through the wall. There were enclaves of order, but central direction and control was partial at best, and out there in the kill-zone the largest battle Nasuba had ever seen was lighting the land with fire and shrouding it with smoke. She had made contact with Princeps Maximus Cydon once since the Legio Ignatum had walked out in full strength. The vox-link had lasted for moments and then failed, but it had been enough for her to confirm an on-the-ground assessment of the situation with what she could see: bad. Very bad indeed. The Legio were fighting un-covered by full fire from the wall's guns. Worse, the lack of local near-orbital fire had let the enemy's ships come in close enough to begin tactical ground bombardment. Nasuba had seen pillars of energy punch down from the sky just eighty kilometres from the wall.

Eighty kilometres... The enemy were advancing across the full width of the kill-zone, and had pushed through Ignatum on a line that cut from Lake Voss through Karalia's Grave and into the tangle of run-off rivers called the Cradle. Pushed right through two full battle groups. How in the light of Illumination you did that, Nasuba did not know, but Mortis had done it. You didn't need engagement data to know – you could see it in the rolling cauldron of fire spilling towards the wall like a living storm.

Something dark blinked out in the distance on the edge of the firestorm. Nasuba felt herself wince, tasted metal on her teeth. Then another and another, black detonations amongst the fire.

'Tears of the sun...' breathed Sulkova, straightening and coming to stand by Nasuba. 'Those are vortex detonations. The enemy–'

'That was us. Ignatum are throwing everything they have.'

Nasuba blinked, turned away. The pinprick detonations hovered in her sight as black spots.

'Inbound,' came a call a moment before a sonic boom rolled across the wall top. Three Stormbird gunships in the yellow gold of the Imperial Fists came in across the wall top, low enough that Nasuba felt the pressure wave try to slam her to the ground. Lightning Crow strike fighters in black and gold turned in the air above, hugging the edge of the aegis shield interface. The gunships banked hard, assault ramps already open. The lead craft slammed to a hard hover and descended onto the platform. Thruster jets sent pools of bloody rain-water rippling away. Its two kin followed it down. Warriors in amber yellow dropped from the open hatches before they touched the ground, spreading out across the top of the bastion. Rogal Dorn did not wait for the gunship's ramp to touch the rockcrete but dropped from its open mouth and stood as it lifted off again. The roar of engines filled Nasuba's ears as she knelt as the Praetorian strode towards her.

She knew him as well as any human might – forty years of campaigns and conquest could attest to that – and the hardness in his eyes as he advanced sent a wave of cold through her.

'Rise,' he said when he was within three paces. She stood.

'My lord,' she said.

'My apologies, Lord Praetorian,' called Sulkova. Nasuba looked at her adjutant. 'General, we have a vox report of Titan engines moving into the wall base sally chambers using critical command overrides.'

'Which Legio?' asked Nasuba.

'Unknown, but the vox- and data links are at full clarity. They are reporting… They say that the Titans are screaming inside people's thoughts.'

Nasuba looked around at the Praetorian.

'*What* have you brought with you, my lord?'

'All the weapons I can wield,' said Rogal Dorn.

Sortie Cavern 78, Mercury Wall

'Princeps…' began one of the tech-priests as Abhani Lus Mohana pulled herself from the hatch into *Bestia Est*'s engine space. A wall of hot air met her with the smell of oil, metal and burnt plastek. The cavern was filled with movement. Tech-priests calling to each other in binary. Servitors hauling plasma feeds and ammunition hoppers. Sparks showered from welders and thermal cutters as tech-adepts tended to the Knights and Titans. They had barely arrived, and the first of the outer doors was still closing, but the activity was already frantic. The hunter force needed to be out in the kill-zone again, and fast. Abhani had seen the glow of the firestorms as Ignatum engaged along the line. They were fighting, cog of truth but they were fighting, but the enemy were advancing, pushing closer to the wall, relentless, seeming to grow stronger as they fell. She and her sisters needed to be hunting again; every engine and machine needed to be engaged.

'Auspex returns are failing to lock and vox-link is not connecting,' she snapped at the tech-priest before he could continue. 'Clear the error.'

'Signal and scanning errors are acute across all engines and systems, princeps,' said the priest in a modulated whine. Abhani was already swinging down the crew scaffold, taking in the activity around the other Solaria engines and Vyronii Knights. 'Data corruption and ailment of spirit…'

'Just make it so that we can see what to shoot,' she said, not looking at the priest. There was something wrong in the cavern, a frantic, ragged edge to the attendance of the machines. As she looked, a heavy servitor hauling a stack of piston rings slewed into the path of a loading rig stacked with macro bolter shells. Crates and machine parts tumbled across the cavern floor. Shouts rose. She blinked, feeling fatigue crush onto her. She turned at the sound of a louder shout and the bark of a high-calibre pistol shot.

A man in the livery of a scion of House Vyronii was standing above the remains of a menial servitor, pistol drawn. The servitor was still trying to rise; it had the Knight scion's helmet in its brass hands. Blood and oil were sputtering from its body and mechanisms. The man half turned and she recognised Caradoc. Behind him the pilots of the two Vyronii Armiger machines were climbing out of their cockpits. She began to stride towards them. Caradoc spat at the half-dead servitor and fired again. The bullet ripped the top of its skull off. Caradoc had picked up his helm and was holstering his pistol and halfway through turning towards the Armiger pilots, when Abhani's kick cannoned into his side. His suit was heavy, layered with ballistic padding and chain mail, but she ploughed her armoured shin into his torso, folded him in two and sent him staggering. He came up fast, face red, fist rising.

Abhani did not move.

'Do it and I will have you shot where you stand. Then I will have your corpse wrapped in the banner of your steed and sent back to your house as a mark of dishonour.' The red of his face was ripening, his teeth bared. 'Go on,' she said to him, with a hunter's smile. He breathed hard, eyes glistening with rage.

'Honoured princeps,' he said, biting down the vibration of anger in his voice. 'You have no–'

'In the engagement, you failed to maintain cohesion. You ride with us to aid our hunt, but where were you when the prey turned? I would think that incompetence might have guided you out of harm's way, but I do not think you are unschooled in war. I think you are a coward.' Caradoc closed his mouth. His eyes were glittering pearls of pure hate. Abhani held her smile. 'Fail again, and I will gun you down.'

'You would not–'

'You do not see even the edge of what I have done or would do.' Abhani looked to Acastia, who had hung back, watching. Was that a glimmer of satisfaction in the Armiger pilot's eye? 'Acastia, you did your house great honour and my legion high service. Solaria honours and thanks you.'

Caradoc's face had paled around the mouth now. He looked like he might explode.

'Get your machines ready,' she said coldly. 'We go to battle again.'

Caradoc looked like he might have been going to say something, but then stopped. His eyes had fixed on something behind Abhani, something towards the inner doors of the cavern. He blinked, shivered and suddenly the rage was gone from his face. His lip trembled. He was blinking rapidly.

Abhani turned.

Her skin was clammy suddenly.

The door at the far end of the sally chamber was opening. Figures in black came through. Gloss-black visors hid their faces. Each of them wore graphite black and deep green without sign of rank or unit. The long staves in their hands tapped the ground, marking each step. The tech-priests and Legio personnel pulled back from them as they advanced, and behind them the doors opened wider and wider.

'What?' said Acastia, her voice fading to a whisper. Caradoc was already backing away, skin grey, eyes wide, shaking.

And then Abhani saw it. A Warlord Titan stepped into the cavern. Dull black-grey edged by worn bronze. Its face blank. Towering. Walking. Tiny worms of light shook from it as it moved. Frost spread across the walls and across the floor. Bile rose in her throat. She felt herself want to scream, but held it behind her teeth. She tried to keep her eyes on it but it was blurring in her sight, as though her mind were trying to unprocess what it was seeing. She wanted to run, to lock herself into the throne of *Bestia Est* to loose its weapons and pour fire into this thing that looked like a Titan but could not be. That was not. That was a thing with the shape of something great and noble and holy. Abomination. That was the only word that came close to it. Some in the cavern were crying out, shrinking back.

She had heard whispers of the Titans Sinister. Rumours and stories passed through the Legio Solaria. They told of witch Titans, of engines that nightmares clung to, that were a fusion of the powers of the empyrean, and the Machine-God's greatest weapons of war. Few believed they were true, but Abhani had once been there when one of her sisters had asked the oldest of the Legio's enginseers if there were such a thing as 'Psi-Titans'. The enginseer had become very still, and then given a single shake of his head.

'Such things are not talked of,' was his only reply. For decades Abhani had forgotten the moment, but now, as she looked up at the engine above her, she remembered and understood.

'Blood of ancestors…' whispered Acastia, and the words made Abhani turn her head.

Another Titan followed the first, a Reaver, and behind it another Warlord and another behind that. The ground was shaking now. The witch-ice was thick on the walls. Breath was falling as frost. The smell of ozone filled Abhani's nose. She could feel her fingers shaking.

The first door to the outer wall was already open, and the four Titans walked towards it, dragging silence with them. The black-visored figures walked at their feet as though to keep back any who might try to cross the Titans' path. None did.

When the last engine had passed and the external door was

sealed, the silence lingered. Abhani shook her head and made to turn towards her crews.

'What was that?' she heard the Armiger rider ask.

'That...' she began, and then swallowed in a dry throat. 'Our own monsters. Those are our own monsters walking to war.'

Adeptus Mechanicus enclave, Sanctum Imperialis Palatine

Vethorel walked into the Titan halls. She was not prone to emotion. Despite her appearance, which was calculated to minimise the discomfort for those outside the priesthood, the mind inside her perfect skull was a thing of calibrated logic and process. Her decisions followed the sacred laws of the sixteenfold methods and pathways of deduction, inference and completeness. Everything else fell into the zones of intangibility and error potential, pollution to the manifestation of knowledge. But at her root she was human and at that moment she saw no weakness in letting the rage within her have its due.

'You shall heed my words,' she spoke, and the noospheric overrides carried her voice over every vox-link, speaker grille and loudhailer in the engine-caverns. Noospheric incantations poured from the priests of her entourage. There were eight of them, each a tooth in the cog that turned around Fabricator General Zagreus Kane. The code lines flowing from them were amongst the highest mysteries salvaged from Mars – machine-spirit imperatives, data-override-djinn and command-entreaties. They spread through the folds of data connection, partially waking systems, stirring the spirits of sleeping machines. They did not have the power to take control but they carried one thing that echoed in time with Vethorel's words: authority and anger.

She marched along the central apse. Heads and sensor

clusters rose to see the source of the voice as it rolled and echoed louder than the sound of machines and turning cogs. The octigal of magi around her struck their staves and pole-axes on the floor as she halted in front of *Luxor Invictoria*. The Warlord Titan stood in its niche. The enginseers of Legio Solaria stood on gantries about it, ready to anoint the engine of the Great Mother to walk. In the other vaults the engines of the legions that had refused to walk to war stirred as their subsystems heard Vethorel's machine voice. The voices of their priests were whispers of code, trying to placate the waking spirits of their engines.

Vethorel turned a full circle. A crowd was gathering. Eyes were gazing at holo-projections of her.

'You have waited,' she said. 'You have watched. You have refused to perform the function given to your design.' The anger in her voice rolled through the air, shaking dust from the arches of stone. 'You have judged that you are above the call of war, that your knowledge is greater than the Fabricator General, than the Praetorian, than the Omnissiah Himself. You think that to stand apart from sacrifice is to serve a higher purpose. Yet that ideal is just the corruption of pride and the failed progression of fear.'

She paused and the quiet held.

'Engines fell in the war, in the Titan Death, and so you fear to lose what remains. You fear that you are the last, and that if you fight then the Legios will be no more. You are fools!' The last words were thunder. Spirals of code gushed into the noosphere, each a hammer blow of formulae and axiomatic authority. 'This…' Vethorel said, and raised her hand as though casting an object into the air. A vortex of green and blue and red hololight spun into being above her. Pixels sparkled in the cone of light. The sound of explosions, of void shields bursting and metal tearing apart filled the cavern. The whirl of distortion resolved into the image of a Warlord Titan. It was burning. Half its head was gone and thick fluid fell from its shattered skull and wounds. Blisters of rust pocked its skin. An old wound could be seen in its carapace, a through-and-through wound that said the engine should be dead. It was a ruin, but on the armour plates the heraldry it had worn when alive could still be seen. The image flickered and merged into the image of another Titan, a Reaver, its spine half broken so that it listed as it walked. Its carapace gleamed where insects swarmed over the soft flesh that had filled its wounds. The projection held long enough for the tatters of the banner dragged behind it to show clear, and then it was replaced in turn.

The silence flowed out. Data spools wound to single-value code streams, cogwork spun to the end of momentum. Eyes watched and saw.

'There it is,' said Vethorel, and there was no anger now, just an all-too-human weariness. 'There is the war you refuse to fight. The dead, your dead, *our* dead violated with the warp and sent against us.' She tilted her head back to look at the cascade of imagery. It was flowing in real time to each Legio remnant in the caverns, stamped and ciphered for authenticity. 'Solaria, Amaranth, Atarus, Defensor, Gryphonicus, the dead of this war sent back to us.'

She bowed her head.

'Yet of you, only a few walk. In the face of this you do nothing.'

The growl was silent, carried in data transmission and noospheric broadcast. First one, then another, and then the entire cavern was roaring with silent, machine rage.

'Rage is no answer.' Esha Ani Mohana Vi, Great Mother of the Imperial Hunters, spoke with the voice of her engine as *Luxor Invictoria* took a step forwards. From the niches to either side of it, the last few engines of Legio Solaria followed their queen. 'There can be only one answer to this shame – fire and death. I shall walk and my sisters shall walk, and I shall fight at the side of any that hunt with me.'

A moment and then the roar of voices and of machines; the sound rose and rose.

'No,' said Vethorel. The word sounded like a gunshot over a baying crowd. The head of *Luxor Invictoria* turned to look at her. There had been no time to align and coordinate with Esha Ani Mohana. She was alone here. No carefully positioned and prepared political moves, just her voice and the fact that what she would say was true. She felt *Luxor Invictoria*'s eye-ports fix on her. It was like being under the lens focus of a star. Data-pressure built in her skull as the spirits of her augmetics recoiled from the god-engine's gaze. She held her eyes steady. 'That time has passed. A rabble of leaderless engines walking for honour and vengeance. That shall fail, and you all shall fall to join the dead you wish to avenge.'

Coolant vented from one of the Solaria Titan's plasma destructors as power flushed into firing coils. Death held on a thread.

Luxor Invictoria did not move.

'The dead shall be avenged,' said Vethorel. 'But this is a battle of legions, not engines. Walk as a rabble and you do no more than spend the spirits of your engines for pride. You must walk with unity, with command and the purpose of being not many but one.'

The silence came again, but now it was of a different texture – a question, a balance.

'We are many,' said the augmented and noospheric voice of an Amaranth princeps. 'We are not a Legio.'

'But you are, and if you walk from here you shall be. Guards of the Omnissiah's last fastness and truth, avengers of the dead.

'The Adeptus Titanicus wills it and it shall be. I bear the authority and seal of both to forge here and now a Legio from the splinters of broken legions, so that they may walk not just to vengeance but to victory.'

<This is a dangerous ploy, even for you, emissary,> came the sending of Esha Ani Mohana, ciphered and transmitted to Vethorel alone. <These princeps and engines will not shed their honour and traditions lightly.>

<They will if you do,> replied Vethorel. <They will if you lead them, Great Mother.>

<I cannot.>

<Only you can,> replied Vethorel, and turned from *Luxor Invictoria* to look across the crowded faces, both real and data-ghosts.

'It is the will of the machine,' she said. 'Who shall serve that will?'

There was a pause and then *Luxor Invictoria* took another step, so that it stood above Vethorel and her circle of magi.

'*Luxor Invictoria* answers,' said Esha Ani Mohana with the voice of the god-machine.

Then the other engines of her sisterhood stepped forward. Then the engines of Amaranth that were ready to walk, and then the princeps of Atarus and Defensor, the scattered few of broken legions, and the noosphere was ringing with assent and battle cries written in the code of war and iron.

Vethorel looked around, still for a moment. The human part of her that had come to this place in anger and felt fear in the face of what was happening, felt something that she had only experienced in the presence of the highest and most humbling mysteries of cog and craft.

She bowed her head. Then she reached out and took the ritual stave from one of the magi that had come with her. Electro-circuits in her hands lit and meshed with its spirit.

Ciphers of authority unwound through it. A wave of instruction and command formed in the datasphere, waiting, ready to roll out through machine and history. She brought the tip of the stave down on the floor and spoke her command.

'In this place, in this time, by the authority of the Omnissiah and the will of His Fabricator General I consecrate the Legio Invigilata, and call all its engines to walk to war.'

Mercury-Exultant kill-zone

The guns of the Mercury Wall began to fire again. Half of those on the summit parapet turned their gaze to the heavens. Spears of light burned up through the cloud and smoke layer to sting the warships manoeuvring to close orbit. Some struck and tore the shields from heavy bombardment barques. Some vessels pulled back, some altered position. None fled. The burning of the *Imperator Somnium* had drawn them away from their objective, but they had been willed to their task by the Warmaster and they could not disobey or fail. A sustained stream of plasma caught the *Torment Born* in the hull as its void shield envelope opened a second before its gun fired. The plasma bored through its hull plates into its guts, and burned through chains of macro shells waiting to be dropped into gun breeches. Fire detonated through the hull in a rippling line of explosions. The ship slewed, its engines dying as the force of the blast rocked it free from its orbit. It began to fall, its half-kilometre-long carcass pulling fire with it as it dropped. The other ships began to fire. Shells and lance beams raced the *Torment Born* down into the skies above the Palace. They struck as the fire from the Mercury Wall guns reached out into the kill-zone.

Near the wreckage tangle of *Nerek* in the south of the zone, an armoured company vanished as quake shells burrowed into the ground and then detonated. Soil and rock fountained into the air as a sinkhole opened beneath the tanks and dragged them down in a cascade of debris. On the mid elevation above the water-filled void of Silver Tarn, plasma streamed from the sky, rolling across advancing cohorts of skitarii, fusing ground, armour and flesh into glass. In the cratered land between Karalia's Grave and Lake Voss, a force of Imperial Army tanks and Knights of House Tyranus were bracketed by automata, pinned in place and then scoured from being by orbital blasts from the Dark Mechanicum ship *Omicron-Aleph* that fell from the sky like emerald coils of lightning. Dust and radiation was all that remained after nine minutes and nine seconds of precisely timed fire.

In the sally chambers across the Mercury Wall, units returned from the kill-zone swallowed ammunition and drank fuel. Tank crews sat on the rockcrete floor, and stared into the distance as the sparks of welding torches filled the air. Knights and war machines shed damaged armour. Blood and soot sluiced from hulls. There was little order; commands from the bastion and regional control nodes were few and laced with signal and information corruption. The last clear order, though, gave a clear purpose – hold the enemy in the kill-zone. That was enough to keep the momentum of war turning.

Linked into the primary data and vox-feeds, Commander Oceano swam in the polluted tide of battle. Four decades had passed since a rad-strike on Kizar had taken his ability to fight without the machine that now wrapped him in amnion and metal. He was blind without the Dreadnought chassis that carried him, reliant on its systems for life and sight. Linked to the failing tactical data and communications across the Mercury Wall, he felt for the first time that blindness close in on him. Curdir Bastion and half the wall was his responsibility, delegated to him by Sanguinius at the will of the Praetorian.

An honour and a burden, and one that now felt like it had turned to sand in his grasp. Mutiny, unit failure, deaths, and worse. It was as though something had reached through the stones of the wall, through the flesh of those who stood on it, and torn them apart from within. The only surety that held were his own brothers, the few hundred that he had scattered across the defences to bolster discipline and aid morale. Now those Blood Angels were the points of light in the dark, sure and true, unwavering. Orders flowed from them to the mortal units; bit by bit commands flowed out from him in words spoken from one person to another. Nasuba had got the guns of Shard Bastion and the northern sections firing again, now Oceano added the voice of his command to that.

From Curdir the light of devastation began to pour down into the fire and smoke-shrouded land. Oceano watched it through a static-filled feed from the wall sensors and deep in his old warrior soul wondered at the power they still had, and hoped that it would be enough.

Enemy distance to wall: 57 kilometres.

EIGHTEEN

Paradise found
Path of lightning
No backward step

Magnifican

Shiban's eyes opened. The sky was above. Storm clouds filled it. Lightning whipped across their bellies as they sped across his sight, now white, now fire red. The clouds vanished. Stars spun in blurred arcs. Not Terran stars. Chogorian stars, the guides to the Path of Heaven. The ground was passing beneath him, the wind rushing. He could feel the steed between his legs, the jolt of its hooves on the ground.

'Lo, I ride with you, my brother,' said Torghun's voice. Shiban saw him now at the edge of his sight, just off his left shoulder. Torghun sat high and straight-backed, cloaked in the fur of his northern Terran birth land. He smiled at Shiban.

'I too, my brother,' said Yesugei, and there he was too, riding at his other shoulder, black hair spilling behind.

'We are here to bear you to the horizon.' Jubal Khan, smiling, rode in front of him and to his right.

'You have come far,' said a voice deeper than the rest, and

there was the bearded face of Camba Diaz, strong, stone-like, riding on his other side. 'There is only a little further to go.'

The riders turned their faces towards the point where the distance met the sky. The stars and sun and day and night wheeled above. The horses gathered pace. He could smell the dust kicked up by their hooves, their sweat, the thread of cold air that rose to meet them as they rode.

'What waits for me?' he heard himself say. 'At the ride's end, what waits for me, brothers?'

'Rest,' said Yesugei.

'Peace,' said Jubal.

'Eternity,' said Camba Diaz.

'And that is it?' asked Shiban. 'What of the battle? What of the world I leave behind?'

'The concern of those who still ride and walk on the earth,' said Torghun.

'Not yours,' said Jubal.

'Not ours,' said Yesugei.

'From beyond, it has already happened. The battle is done. The end set,' said Torghun.

'And how did it end?' asked Shiban.

Silence from them all. Just the wind.

He thought of Cole, just a man trying to get back to some-where safer than the wasteland he found himself in. He thought of the child, too young to know it had been born into an apoc-alypse. He thought of all those dead at the Eternity Wall, and all those still living and standing in the path of the forces of anni-hilation coming for them.

'Look,' said Torghun, jerking his head up. 'They come to bring you home.'

Birds turned in a gyre above them. Vultures and hawks and eagles, wings catching the wind and thermals of the plateau.

The sun, only moments risen, sank below the curve of the world before them. The thunder of the horses' hooves was the roar and beat of blood in his veins.

He knew that somewhere very close and too far to reach, he was falling to the ground, and that the man Cole was scrambling to reach him, and bullets were passing overhead and that things of rotting flesh were pulling themselves closer. He knew that somewhere, beyond a different horizon, his Legion brothers still lived and waited, and that there was more pain and the laughter of total sorrow.

'No,' he said. 'I am not finished. This does not end here.'

'For you it does,' said Yesugei. 'Your part is played. You go onwards, as we all must.'

'No backward step,' said Torghun.

No backward step... only forwards... onwards, through pain, through darkness and desolation.

No backward step...

Camba Diaz with his shield and sword standing on a bridge against a howling tide.

No backward step.

Torghun torn apart, falling, a son of Terra and a White Scar to the last.

No backward step!

Blinks of night and blinding light and red.

Shiban gripped the reins of his mount, and wheeled it about. The sky behind him was a tatter of torn night.

'No backward step...' said the voice of Torghun behind him.

'No backward step,' echoed Shiban and spurred the mount on. Behind him he heard a snap of laughter from the throat of Jubal, and then Yesugei, his voice fading into the wind and the call of the birds above.

'Ride well, brother. Ride for us all.'

* * *

Hatay-Antakya Hive, East Phoenicium Wastes

'She didn't tell me,' said John after a few hours of climbing up through the hive. 'Erda, I mean. She didn't tell me about you and Him. Not a word... Hints that you were all closer than I had thought, but not a raised eyebrow about... what happened.' Oll did not reply. 'Guess there were no real reasons to tell me you tried to kill Him, other than it being pretty central to the whole reason we are here.'

'I never lied, John,' Oll said softly.

'And I never thought to ask, so I guess that makes me ten times the fool and half the genius I thought I was. Getting you *involved* again – hell's vomit, but I think you might have been right to just stay away.'

'Having second thoughts?' asked Oll.

'Too late for that, isn't it? Unless I want to try and ditch or kill you, or give you to the other side, the only way seems like forward... whichever pissing way that actually is.'

John rubbed his eyes, blinked.

'Headache?' asked Oll. John nodded.

'Like a pneumatic hammer.'

'Never touched Enuncia before,' he said.

John shook his head.

'I can feel it,' he said, 'like it's alive in here.' He tapped his head.

Oll lapsed back into silence. They were still climbing, scrambling up through the vegetation-filled pipes and tubes of the hive. The stems of the plants were thick and flexed as they touched them. When they had to cut their way through a tangle, the sap that leaked from the cut stems was like thick, dark wine.

'You know what this place is?' asked Zybes, as they pulled themselves through a chamber where the sap drained from slit vines into large glass bottles. The fluid was forming big, gelatinous droplets as it oozed down the glass. The air had a thick scent, like solvent, spice and sugar. The fluid in the bottles rippled as they passed, sloshing up against the crystal as though trying to reach them. 'It's a farm.'

Oll did not reply. He had been thinking the same thing since Ugent Sye and the orchards.

'The song of paradise brings people and then this place gives them the endless dream they want,' said John. 'And the Emperor's Children take what they want in turn.'

'Fruit from the orchard,' muttered Zybes. 'Wine from the vine.'

They found the proof of their fears in a chamber that had been a bubble of stained glass on the outside of the hive. A warrior in purple and acid-green armour sat on a throne of human vertebrae. Its monstrous weapons lay in the hands of shivering, wasted slaves, their eyes, mouths and ears stapled shut. The Space Marine, for a Space Marine it was, did not move as they entered the chamber. They approached slowly, Zybes and Leetu moving to check the ways out, while Oll looked at the thing in the throne of bone. Glass tubes curled from spherical jars, and ran into sockets in its helm. Sap liquid bubbled and foamed down the tubes. Air hissed from fleshy valves in the Space Marine's chest, burbling and purring.

'It is bathing in dreams and secrets,' said John without looking around. 'The fluid is saturated with them, psychoactive. Refined from the desperate and devoted. Harvested and refined like honey.' He shivered. 'I can feel it. Your man Zybes is right, that's what this garden of paradise is – it's a farm for dreams.'

Oll kept his gun aimed at the enthroned warrior.

'We should be careful,' said Leetu. 'The Emperor's Children know we are here. Cause too much damage and they will find us before we find the man you have lost.'

Oll considered Leetu's words for a moment.

'We leave it,' he said at last. 'Let's go.' They did, reluctantly, looking back at the chair of bone and the figure on it. The pendulum in Katt's hands kept moving, guiding them as they climbed.

Oll tried not to look at what they passed as they moved up through the dreaming hive: tableaux of pastoral bliss that wound through chambers, silent and pulsing; the great machine pits that turned over and over, breaking matter and mixing it into the soil; pits where limbs and shreds of fabric surfaced in the dark loam. Plants grew everywhere, blooming, pressing and squirming against crystal domes as though trying to strangle the sunlight before it could reach inside. It was quiet, the sound of the honey-hive, a low pulse disturbed by moans that shivered from the distance and then faded, remaining only as a haze in the mind. They did not encounter more of the Emperor's Children, though their signs marked the ground, and occasionally they found a human body so totally deconstructed that it could only have been done by an Astartes.

'Paradise found,' said John without humour as they pressed on.

Oll did not answer.

Magnifican

White dot on black.

Pain.

No, an echo of pain, a promise of what was coming. Shiban knew it.

The dot became a line across black. He could hear breath, the beat of hearts.

The line was growing thicker, growing closer.

The bubble of blood and the gasp of air all around.

Forwards, just forwards, into the pain, into the promise of the white horizon.

Sounds buzzing. Shouting. Thunder.

The whiteness was right in front of him. He could taste acid and iron.

White. Blinding. Edge to edge. Pain as a lightning bolt.

He gasped air.

He pushed up.

The pain was him, every inch of him, within and without. Cole was half crouched on the ground, the infant gripped with one arm, firing his pistol with the other.

'Shiban!' he was calling. 'Shiban!'

A round buzzed through the air and the man was tumbling back. Blood splashed bright on the shoulder of his uniform as he fell, twisting to shield the infant.

There were figures on the lip of the crater, humans in filth-drenched uniforms and gas hoods, spitting hard rounds from rust-covered guns. There were dead things rising from the pool at the bottom of the crater. Bloated bodies, dragging themselves up the shoreline. Gleaming clouds of insects flowed and wheeled through the air. A vomit, gut-acid reek threaded every breath. Shiban found the metal pole on the ground under his fingers. A staggering, drowned thing was almost on them. He came to his feet, hands gripping and lifting the pole into a blow that hit the thing in its central mass. It was not a clean blow, not efficient, nor timed and weighted for optimal effect. No poem of war was written by it. But it was enough.

The drowned thing came apart. Soft bones and bloated flesh were crushed, and burst apart. Shiban heard the roar explode from his lips. He went forwards, fast, the pain almost blinding. He rammed the pole through another drowned corpse and whirled. The impaled thing writhed as Shiban swung it into two others that had just dragged themselves onto the shore.

They burst apart, and Shiban was wrenching the weapon free and turning. Rounds sparked from his left shoulder. A stutter of lightning through his flesh and nerves. Cole was on the ground, trying to rise, blood running from his fingers. Shiban reached the man's side in a bound, and pulled him up. Hard rounds exploded across the spot they had been occupying. Shiban's head snapped up; he saw the shooter, ten strides up the slope, saw the man's finger begin to squeeze the trigger for another burst. He cast the metal pole like a spear, one-handed. He surged up the slope even as it released from his grasp. The pole hit the man in the left eye. It punched through the eyepiece of the gas hood and into the skull behind, and the man was falling. Shiban was on the man before he hit the ground. The pole ripped free from the skull and hit the next figure coming over the lip of the crater.

He could hear the thunder roar of pain within. Lightning flashed inside his skull, but he was moving, going forwards, only forwards, killing without pause, flowing like a thunderbolt reaching for the ground. One strike and another, impacts shuddering through him. One figure and then another and another, all falling. Blood and brain matter. Rounds rang as they struck him, and he pivoted to shield Cole and the infant. Flies hit him like spots of black rain, flogging his joints, smearing his sight, but he did not slow, and only went forwards. He had a second to see the tide of figures surging from the fogbound distance. He did not stop. To stop was to end, to go back to the ride across the plateau with his duty undone. Forwards, only forwards, killing and killing, the agony and taste of blood the sign that he was still in the world of the living.

He spun the pole and the impact sent a human to the ground, with a pulped bag of bone for a head. He spun to the next target... and found that there was none.

Quiet, sudden stillness, broken only by the curl of fog on a sluggish breath of air. The swirl of insects had gone. The dead lay unmoving on the ground. Blood and gut fluid trickled slowly over rubble.

He took another pace, unwilling to let go of the momentum that had kept the pain from overwhelming him.

A shadow moved in the ochre haze, a bloated smudge swelling in the murk.

Shiban turned towards it, breathing hard.

Cole moaned and staggered against him. Half of the man's torso was black with blood.

Shiban felt the pain inside him dim, felt the numbness rise. He took a pace towards the shadow, and let the agony relight. A snarl came to his lips.

'What...' began Cole.

The mustard fog ripped aside and the warrior came at them. It was huge, a mountain of shaking fat and rotting armour plate. Bulges of soft matter, corroded tubes and chain mail drowned the shape of the Astartes warrior they had grown on. Mucus-thick breaths heaved from the vents on its back. Chains rattled against its armour as it ran. The corpses of dogs and humans and other things that had lost their features dragged behind it. It had a huge billhook, its blade pitted and clotted with blood and rust, and it swung as it charged. Shiban met the blow, deflected it past him and struck once high, once low. Pieces of flesh burst from each strike. The rotting warrior grunted. Shiban turned and rammed the pole tip-first into the join between helm and body. It drove deep. Black fluid gushed out. The vast warrior shook for a moment. Then it reached up, gripped the pole and pulled it free. Lumps of fat ran out of the wound on a bubbling slick of blood. It stood for a second, looking at Shiban with an eye slit of cracked glass. Then it swung its billhook up. It wasn't slow, Shiban realised

in that moment, not slow at all. The blow sang a ragged song
as it arced down at Shiban's head.

Hatay-Antakya Hive, East Phoenicium Wastes

The pendulum stopped spinning in a dome high on the outside of the hive.

Katt looked at Oll. 'Rane's here,' she said, 'somewhere.'

Oll nodded and looked at the place she had led them.

It had been a garden dome, one of those that the high-born
of the hive used to demonstrate their power to make an oasis
in a world reduced to dry seas and pollution by war and waste
and time. Water had cascaded from a great copper sphere that
hung from the dome's apex, down into a hundred-metre-wide
bowl with a six-metre-wide hole at its centre. Hidden jet
systems had spun the water in the bowl so that it whirled in
a slow vortex before draining through the central hole into a
lake that filled the bottom half of a crystal and plasteel bubble
beneath. Bathers had swum the spinning waters, fighting the
current and laughing until they were caught by the final spin
and yanked down to fall, whooping with shock and excite-
ment, into the lake below. From there, sluice gates could be
opened to channels that looped out and down the sides of the
hive, arcing past other domes and suspended pools and lakes.

The plants that had filled the dome were examples of the
rare species saved from Terra's past, propagated and preserved
over hundreds of years by the forebears of the Hatay-Antakya
Hydro Clans. Tall trees with silver bark had swayed in artificial winds of purified air. Flowers had grown from meadow
ground and sent their pollen and seed into the air. Birds and
insects had buzzed and flitted between nests and blooms. In
the half-light balanced between night and dawn, it had been
possible to stand on one of the low banks of grass, breathe the

smell of dew and sap and earth, and think that one could smell the plants reaching towards the growing sunlight.

That was as things had been.

Fulgrim's Children had made the garden anew. The water still turned in the pool, but things grew within it now – things with huge, thick-petalled flowers and red roots that dangled into the currents like a vascular system without a body. The trees had withered to bare branches, or had grown and grown to press against the crystal of the dome above. Their leaves had taken on the colour of copper and mother of pearl. Reptilian creatures pecked at the trunks with metallic beaks; dark red sap oozed from the wounds and slid down the trunks to silver pails and tangles of gulping glass tubes. Every now and then the trees would shiver, even though there was no breeze to stir their branches. Shadows and sunlight dappled the ground, so deep in most places that it felt like you could only see the surface of the false forests. Pollen drifted in thick clouds beneath the dome – mauve and yellow and dust grey. Fountains sat in the open spaces between the trees, thick jets of purple liquid gushing from the mouths of stone and ivory figures that twisted around cornucopias of barbed fruit. Other sculptures peeked from amidst the undergrowth, their stone sinews caught in song, or dance, or scream.

Oll blinked at the view. Beside him, Leetu stood still, the warrior's head turning in place as he scanned the dome. John stood a small distance away to the other side. He had Krank's lasgun, and had thumbed the safety off.

'Anything?' Oll said to him. John shook his head without looking at Oll.

'This whole place is a lie,' he said. 'There could be Horus himself out there and I wouldn't be able to tell you right now.'

'This is a place of dire threat,' said Leetu.

'Quite,' John said, then jerked his head to where Katt stood a little further back. 'What do you see, Katt?'

She did not answer for a moment. The pendulum was spinning on its thread, almost jerking free of her fingers. Beads of blood were forming inside her nostrils.

She shook her head.

'Rane is here,' she said. 'Somewhere near. That's all I can tell.'

'It's a trap, though, right?' asked John. Katt shrugged.

'Almost certainly.'

'Great,' sighed John. 'So what do we do, start poking about in the bushes?'

'No,' said Oll, looking around at the others. 'You, Katt and I do that, the rest wait.'

'In case we need rescuing again?' asked John.

'Given how things have gone, it seems reasonable,' Oll replied.

'Fair point,' said John. 'Alright, let's go. I've got point, so if my head explodes or something rips me in half you'll know that there is something out there.'

John slid forwards through the edge of the foliage. Oll watched him for a second, reminding himself that John Grammaticus was, on top of everything else, one of the best covert warfare operatives he had ever seen. It was not a showy thing, but somehow through the way he moved he became part of the ground he walked upon. Katt followed, not as smoothly but quietly, gun in one hand, pendant in the other. Oll glanced at where Zybes was, and Graft bent over Krank. Then he looked at Leetu.

'Keep them safe,' he said, 'and get them out if this goes wrong.'

Leetu gave a small nod.

'As you wish.'

Oll turned and followed Katt and John. Soon the others were out of sight and there was just the sound of dripping sap and the rustle of leaves as the trees quivered. Oll looked back after twenty paces and could not see the others. The next time he paused, he could not be certain how many steps he had taken. The light under the trees was dappled gold, the shadows maroon. Mulch squelched softly underfoot. Sap and pink fluid foamed around the soles of his boots. He felt his eyelids becoming heavy, then blinked them wide again. Ahead of him Katt moved through the gloom, and somewhere beyond her the shadow that was John. Oll glanced around. He thought he could feel eyes watching him, out there, just on the edge of his own sight, staring through the leaves. He thought of tigers in jungles now long burned. He thought of a boat chugging its way up a wide, still river to a place he had not wanted to go. He thought of the sirens, the Laestrygonians and the lotus-eaters. He knew this place. He had been here before. Not exactly, but he knew the shape and taste of it. He thought of all the heroes and fools and friends that he had seen go into the mouth of the monsters. Now here he was – old choices and old mistakes come around to be made again.

+Oll.+ It was John, speaking with a low whisper of telepathy. Oll dropped to one knee, gun up, eyes alert. +I think we have found your lost sheep.+ A pause. +You better come and have a look.+

He saw Rane as soon as he reached John and Katt. They were on the edge of the cover of a copse of trees next to a vivid green sward of grass. Statues dotted the space, and a marble-paved path curved through them. The statues looked like human figures in the classic heroic form. It was only when you looked a little longer that you saw the differences the sculptors had introduced. Oll tried not to look for long. Fountain sprays rose and fell in pink arcs, splashing into wide bowls. Rane was there, still in his boots and kit, rifle gone, but his pistol holstered at his waist. His hands were loose at his sides, and he was gazing up at a cluster of white marble statues dancing on a wide plinth.

Oll sat still for a moment and let his senses and thoughts

settle. Nothing unexpected moved or made a sound. There was a tension there, though, a taut threat.

'Yep,' said John, softly from beside him. 'All wrong, that oh-so-old set of soldier instincts are just screaming to get the hell out and see if there is a way to call in a fire-strike.' He sighed. 'Without that option, I guess you are going to go out to the kid.'

Oll looked at John and then Katt.

'Watch my back,' he said and then slipped out of cover.

He kept his head down until he was within five paces of Rane, then dropped into the cover of a statue plinth. This close the marble looked almost fluid beneath the surface, alive with phosphorescent things with pale feelers, stings and pincers. He waited but the only movement came from the shivering trees.

'Rane,' he said, raising his voice but keeping it level. The boy did not turn. Oll caught himself – no, not a boy. Rane had not been a boy even when he had been a newly signed-up soldier on Calth. He had just been young, and full of not very much life and a lot of naivety. But Oll could not see him as anything else other than a kid in the wrong place and time. Rane had changed in the years since Calth, they all had – except, maybe Oll himself – but Rane had always been furthest back, always closest to the kid who just wanted to find the young wife he had never had a chance to say goodbye to. A part of Rane still thought that she was out there, that there would somehow be a way back to what he had lost. 'Bale Rane,' said Oll again, a little louder and with a little of the soldier's authority in his voice.

'I made it, Oll,' said Rane, but he did not turn around. 'Never thought that I would, but I did.'

'Rane,' said Oll carefully. There was something in the boy's voice that raised the hairs on his skin. 'Rane, look at me, please.'

Oll stood up and took a step towards Rane. He thought

he saw something move at the edge of his eye, glanced aside before he could stop himself. A statue of a man stretching his arms up to support a wide bowl stood right next to him. The man's face was screaming, an image of agony caught in marble. For a moment Oll thought he had seen the man's mouth move.

'Thank you, Oll,' said Rane. 'You brought me here. I would never have made it if it had not been for you. Thank you.'

He could see half of the lad's face now. There were tears on Rane's cheeks, running from his eyes, which were looking up at the statue in front of him. Oll did not follow the boy's gaze.

'Who would have thought that we would both end up here? I fell and slept and woke up and I heard her, Oll. I heard her calling for me, just like back on Calth. She has been waiting for me all this time.'

'You need to come with me, Bale,' said Oll, gently. 'We need to go.' He reached out a hand and touched Rane's arm. The boy lashed out without looking around. The blow was fast and strong, and Oll only flinched fast enough to avoid it hitting him full in the chest. Rane's hand caught him on the shoulder and sent him staggering back.

'You two have never met,' said Rane, his voice still filled with joy, as though what had just happened was nothing. He was still staring up. 'I forgot that. Neve, my love, Oll did not mean anything by it. I have talked about you so often that I just forgot that he doesn't know you, my love. It's my fault. Let me introduce you, yes?'

Oll was picking himself up, gun coming up with him as Rane, without looking away, stepped aside from the statue in front of him.

'Oll, this is my darling wife.'

Oll looked up.

* * *

Magnifican

Shiban jerked aside, but not fast enough. The billhook hit his left shoulder between collar-ring and pauldron. A spur of the blade found a join in the armour and punched through. Shiban felt his left arm become numb. He tried to break the hook free, but the bloated warrior yanked the billhook down. The blade bit into plate and bone, and Shiban staggered, fighting for balance. The thing was strong, monstrously strong. A fresh cascade of blood and slime poured from the hole in its throat. A laugh, a chuckle of indulgence made with fluid-clogged lungs. Shiban tried to bring the pole up in his right hand. The warrior yanked the billhook and Shiban jerked forwards before the blow could begin to unfurl. He stumbled to one knee. The numbness was spreading, drowning sensation and the pain that meant he was still moving. The warrior gripped the haft of the billhook, crushing Shiban further to the ground. The pole fell from his fingers, and rolled across the dust. Shiban rammed his right hand up, gripped the haft of the billhook, and pushed up, trying to force the barb out of his flesh. The enemy warrior tilted its head, and then jerked the weapon. Shiban felt the barb bite deeper.

A las-blast hit the warrior in the middle of its helm. Rotten ceramite blew out. Its eye visor shattered. Behind him, he heard Cole moan. The warrior's head rose to look at this fresh distraction. Shiban could see an eye socket beyond the blown visor. A finger-sized piece of crystal was embedded in the flesh just beneath a fogged, yellow eyeball. Another las-blast, this one wide, then another that burned a furrow in an exposed roll of fat. The warrior shifted. Shiban felt the pressure in the billhook give fractionally. He rammed his weight forward with all the strength of his muscle and armour. The hook sliced through flesh and out through the back of Shiban's armour.

He came to his feet. The bloated warrior recoiled, fast, but not fast enough. Shiban slammed his right hand down onto the billhook's shaft just below the blade. The shaft broke. He caught the blade, spun it in his grasp, then rammed it into the hole he had made in the thing's neck, and sawed up through softened bone and half-rotten flesh, up through skull and brain, up through the crown of its helm.

Fluid gushed out, black and crimson and yellow. The warrior juddered, croaking. For a second it stood, a mountain of already dead flesh refusing to fall. Shiban stepped back. His own blood was flowing down his armour. Then the warrior toppled, slumping, flesh and armour folding with a grinding squelch. It hit the ground and lay steaming and oozing. Shiban dropped the billhook blade. White stars burst in his eyes. He felt himself sway. Blood was still flowing from the wound in his shoulder. He looked at his left arm, willed the hand to form a fist. The fingers twitched, though he felt nothing.

A small cry turned his head. Cole was on his back, pistol in one hand, the infant clutched close in the other. Shiban lurched over to the man. The blood from the wound in Cole's shoulder was still flowing, slowly. The infant was crying, tiny balled fists gripping the air. Cole's eyes were half-closed, the eyelids sagging. Shiban could hear the shallowing breath in the man's chest. He had seen a lot of the fading moments of life; it was part of the craft that was his existence, a by-product of lethality. He reached down, into the man's wound. His gauntleted fingers clamped shut. The man gave a gasp, and his eyes fluttered open.

Shiban looked down at him. There must have been little in his appearance to inspire comfort: streaked with blood and filth, a remade monster of war before and a wreck of armour and blood now. But Cole's breath stilled as he looked up. A smile began to form.

'You…' he began. 'You are still here.'

Shiban nodded once.

'The child…' said Cole. 'Take the child.'

The blood had stopped flowing from the wound, but he could tell that the man's life was falling from him – too much of it had already drained onto the ground.

'No,' Shiban said, and saw a shadow form in the man's eyes for a second. Then he stood, lifting the man and the infant.

Shiban closed his eyes for a moment. No voices came from the wind to speak to him, no call of birds guiding him home. He opened his eyes. The wasteland lay before him, and somewhere in the distance the lines and the Palace waited. He was not sure how far now. His sense of place and distance had been left behind. He knew which way was forward, though.

'No backward step.'

NINETEEN

Burned horizon
Orientalis-Echion
You are Solaria now

Mercury-Exultant kill-zone

Fire burned the dawn light from the horizon. Detonations bubbled in a wall of smoke that reached from the ground to the bruised cloud layer above. Light strobed and smouldered. The air trembled. Hot winds coiled smoke and flame and debris into fire-devils that spiralled through the murk, howling, eating the dead that lay on the ground, scattering ash and flakes of scorched bone.

The battle line was a crescent drawn from the north, where the Palace wall kinked west at Indomitor Bastion, to the south where it swung away from the guns of the Exultant Wall. The centre of the curve pressed in towards the Mercury Wall, pushing in from the blind zone one hundred and twenty kilometres out and reaching through the rivers of run-off towards Shard Bastion. The engines of Mortis walked across the entire arc of the line. Hundreds of Titans, with the greatest strength layered in maniples in the central engagement zone.

On the flanks the concentration of engines was lower, but here the abomination machines of the New Mechanicum swarmed across the ground, bodies of shimmering chrome or coal black, belching warp-polluted plasma that shrieked as it burned the air. It was not an assault; it was an ocean's storm tide.

Against it the defenders of the wall poured the strength they had hoarded over the months of the siege. Their purpose was simple: to keep the enemy Titans from the walls. In the shadow of the Exultant Wall, five regiments of heavy armour rolled across the undulating plateau. Stormhammers, Executioners and assault carriers pulverised the already broken ground to dust as they drove to meet the enemy advance. They spread out, unfolding into lines and diamonds like the cavalry of old, stretching across five kilometres. In their turrets they saw the towering figures emerge as shadows from the clouds.

The first machines to fire were those of Shadowsword squadron Antonine. Their volcano cannons were Titan killers. Lines of white heat reached through the air in an eye-blink and struck the void envelope of the Reaver Titan *Soul Sickle*. Layers of shield blew out in a radiant halo. Inside the Shadowswords, the commanders were already shouting for their secondary weapons to fire, as capacitors began to build charge for another shot. Lines of shells and the blasts of lesser weapons were already blazing from the squadrons to either side of them. The Titan's last shield vanished in a scattered wash of explosions. The Shadowswords of Antonine Squadron were at a near halt as their guns drained power from their drives. *Soul Sickle* turned its head towards them. The metal of its skull was enamelled white, its eyes crimson glows. It fired its own greeting in the instant the first volcano cannon beam struck it. The beam sliced through *Soul Sickle*'s thigh plate in a spray of molten metal. Twin lances of heat struck the Shadowsword and bored into its core. Plasma coils burst and rolled their fire into a blast wave that boiled through the hulls of its kin. Spheres of sun-fire were ripping across the line of advancing armour. *Soul Sickle* gave a bellow and strode on, limping, bleeding but already firing as more of its Legio marched into sight and the machines rode to meet them.

In the north, twenty Knights of the vagabond House Canis spurred across the plateau. With them three Warlords of the Legio Gryphonicus walked. The rest of their engines fought far to the south where traitor forces flooded against the weakened zones of Saturnine and Europa. These three had taken damage weeks before and returned at the call of Wall Master Efried. They bore quake cannons and ground-boring missiles in their launch racks. They met the northern edge of the Mortis forces a hundred kilometres off the wall. Six Warhound Titans, their black and red and gold armour shedding scabs of rust from their pocked and pitted skins. With them came swift tanks and speeders carrying slave-wrought Mechanicum troops. The three Gryphonicus engines rocked to a halt, banners rippling, stabilising pistons venting gas. The Warhounds loped towards them, growling scrap code. The Gryphonicus Warlords fired. Missiles loosed, arced and bored into the ground before exploding. The earth tore apart. Fissures opened. Soil and dust rolled like an ocean in a storm. A Warhound's foot fell to the ground and vanished into a fissure. Its void shield burst as its chin slammed into the earth. The subsurface blast wave hit a lance of House Hermetika Knights and tore them apart. Its packmates danced over the heaving terrain. The stricken Warhound's reactor failed as it vanished into the maw of the ground. A blister of light and burning earth rose as the engines of Horus and the Emperor tore at each other.

Across the Mercury-Exultant kill-zone the pattern repeated, magnified, and multiplied across hundreds of kilometres. In the centre of the kill-zone, the Legio Mortis met the force of Ignatum head-on. At the fore of the march of Mortis were the engines that had been opened to the daemons of the warp – god-engines given as libation to the powers that allowed knowledge, life and perfection beyond the old limits of artifice and cog. Reality boiled around them. Armour tore like skin and knitted like flesh. Blood and pus wept from the air at their passing. Static filled targeting systems as they tried to look at the daemon Titans. With them the remaining corpse-Titans walked, staggering, screaming their death calls over and again. True daemons slid from the gaps between light and shadow – hollow things of dead flesh and rattling bone, bags of pus and rotten fat that waded across the ground. Ignatum Titans were dragged down, gouts of acid enveloping them, metal softening and sagging as they struggled. Swarms of warp-born larvae writhed from the ground and the clouds of smoke, bursting and unfolding into things with wings that bloated as they rose. Washes of flame sliced through them, reducing them to ash.

At the centre of the kill-zone, the advance of Mortis pressed towards the wall. The battle line bulged inwards for forty kilometres. Forced backwards, the engines of Ignatum folded maniples and the largest of their engines in to meet and slow the surge. The Maniple of Maniples, three Emperor-class engines and their attendants, formed the fulcrums around which battle groups moved. Seen from within the incandescence of Princeps Maximus Cydon, the engines of his Legio moved in unfolding arcs and geometries, each balanced against another, none isolated, all parts of a whole. That was the majesty of Ignatum: even when engines and princeps moved by their own will or fury they followed the will of the whole, the fire of the Legio's soul. Not through control, not through mere orders, but because they were echoes of a single greater spirit – the fiery hearts of hundreds of engines that had walked and burned their enemies, and did not forget and did not forgive.

They held. In the south the towering *Magnificum Incendius* advanced as it engaged. Its plasma annihilator wailed as it drew charge. Lightning played across charge coils as wide as battle tanks. A plasma shell fell from the sky and struck its shield envelope, blowing out eight layers of energy. Blue and white fire cascaded to the ground as the Titan strode on. Secutarii in blue and red and chrome spilled from the bastions in its legs, dropping from assault ramps at the second the machine's foot touched the ground. Ten Warhounds of its guard ran as its heralds, firing streams of vulcan shells and bouts of liquid flame. The fortress mounted on its shoulders shed explosive shells and beams of las energy into the lesser engines and troops that followed the Mortis Titans. Then its great guns spoke. The barrels of its cannon turned. Shells the size of tanks chugged from its muzzle. Fire surrounded it and poured from it as it walked, vanishing into the maelstrom, swelling the blaze.

In the north, the Imperator *Exemplis* strode at maximum speed. The ground shook and shook at its tread. Five maniples came with it, spread in a battle mandala. They drove into the traitor forces pushing up towards the Indomitor Bastion. These were the swift machines and forces of the assault: long-shanked Knights and the nimble murder-automata bred by the New Mechanicum on Mars. They burned. The Ignatum engines fired plasma munitions deep behind the enemy advance, cutting a wall of fire across the following enemy forces, and then engaging the trapped engines at point-blank range.

High in the skull of *Imperious Prima*, Princeps Maximus Cydon saw the kill-zone through the light of the incandescence. His engine, the wondrous link to his Machine-God, smouldered with rage and exultation. Its spirit was old and vast. Others of its kind crushed the minds of those that guided them, but his engine was a Warmonger of the Emperor class of Titans, and its purpose was to break cities and watch civilisations die. The currents of its spirit were like the tides of magma beneath an old volcano, slow and relentless. All things bowed to its might in the end, all enemies, all who stood against it. The old enemy, the Death's Heads would come no further.

The world was fire now. It fell from orbit and the walls, and burned the air as the god-engines threw their anger at each other. The air clotted with smoke and blast clouds, shivering as shock waves ripped through it. In the far heart of the Inner Palace, hundreds of kilometres beneath the earth, the prisoners of Blackstone felt the battles roar as a tremble hovering on the edge of hearing. The storm of flame and shredding reality did not fade but grew, reaching up and curling over, a billowing curtain stretching across the kill-zone, a burning mockery of the wall that stood across its path.

In Cydon's mind he held it as an image painted in crimson and night. This would be the end, the moment his Legio's soul was laid bare; faced with the impossible, where there was no way to victory, they would make one.

Shard Bastion, Mercury Wall

'Battery frequency is falling,' said Rogal Dorn. Nasuba looked up. From up here, on the top platform of Shard Bastion, you could look each way and down the wall and see the light of the turbo-lasers and plasma bombards opening up. Even in the far distance, you could see the flash from behind the curtains of rain and smoke. Flash and thunder, on and on, like the sound of the world cracking under the blows of false gods.

They had got the wall guns firing again – forty-five per cent active to seventy-five per cent effectiveness. Not good. A long way from good, in fact, but better than it had been. There was a measure of control on Mercury. The presence of the Praetorian and the four hundred Imperial Fists he had dropped along the wall had helped. They had comms down to the Titan legion caverns and sally-vaults, too, intermittent but functional. Unit cohesion and loss could not even be measured. There were dead everywhere, and clusters of wild violence inside the wall mass. They were holding, though. That was what the presence and command of a primarch did.

Nasuba watched and listened for twenty-two seconds before she picked out the distortion in the rhythm of the guns, like a stutter in the pulse of a heart struggling to beat.

'It's surging,' said a warrior in the yellow of an Imperial Fist but with blue pauldrons and a caul-like hood framing his helm. He had been identified to her as Chief Librarian Massak. Nasuba was old enough in making war for the Imperium to know what a Librarian was – a psyker of the Legions, a wielder of aetheric energy as a tool of war.

'What?' she asked, looking directly at the Librarian. He returned her gaze. Sparks were flicking from his hooded helm into the air.

'The warp, general,' said Massak. 'The tides of the immaterium wax. That is why the guns stutter. The crews are wavering. The machines are breaking. The tide of the Great Ocean is finding the fractures in our will and strength.'

Nasuba frowned, looked back along the wall at the flash of the guns – forty-five per cent active... enough to hold an army from the wall, but they were not just facing an army.

A white-blue flare of plasma burst from one of the nearest batteries. She blinked, the glare clinging to her retinas.

'We must be ready to shut the batteries down,' said Dorn.

He looked at her, the pupils of his eyes the levelling of gun barrels.

'My lord?' she said.

'The plasma reservoirs and generators – teams should be sent to secure them and shut them down.'

Kurral looked up sharply. The presence of a primarch was often enough to silence mortals before they could even think of speaking, but Nasuba saw no sign of fear in her aide.

'Lord Dorn, the top guns are our primary functioning weapons – if we shut the plasma feeds down…'

'Then they cannot be used against us,' said Dorn. His voice was steady, but somehow managed to sound clear across the platform over the thunder roll of gun discharge. 'Consider this – how do the enemy intend to breach the walls?' Dorn looked around at them, his face set but calm. Control radiated from him. 'This wall is within range of the largest ordnance mounted on their engines, and they can hardly miss. But they have not fired directly against the wall. Why?'

'Because they would do nothing,' said Kurral, and Nasuba saw realisation spreading in the lines of the officer's face.

Dorn gave a single nod.

'Hundreds of metres of rockcrete, plasteel and armour. They could concentrate fire and blow out the void shields on a small section, and then… how far would they get trying to create a breach?'

'Some damage,' said Kurral. 'Perhaps penetration through four layers, three hundred metres depth, but no wall integrity threat.'

'And while they are applying that firepower to the wall, their engines sacrifice themselves and battle-sphere dominance for nothing,' said Nasuba.

'Unless they can reach the wall in the dead zone beneath our guns,' said Dorn. 'If there is nothing to threaten them then they can bore their way through the wall base. Not enough for a full escalade, not enough to even be called a threat, but if that breach goes deep enough to hit a primary plasma conduit or generator, then…'

'They bring the wall down,' said Nasuba, flatly.

There was a moment of quiet even with the noise of the guns.

'Secure the generators,' said Dorn. 'Make preparation to shut them down on your command.'

'But the guns are keeping them from the walls, my lord,' said Kurral.

'They are not the only thing,' Dorn said, and he turned to look out into the fire-killed night.

The Cradle Basin, Mercury-Exultant kill-zone

<Full stride,> willed Tetracauron, and he felt *Reginae Furorem* speed forwards an instant after the thought became transmission. The ground before it glittered with a skin of gleaming metal shells, and crowds of soft rotting flesh. Targeting mandalas spun. Black silhouettes strode towards them. Weapon fire streaked the orange of the world. To his left, Arthusa's engine-presence was a column of flame. Their maniples had fused into one, and walked into the kill-zone at the head of an arrowhead of Battle Titans. The Warhounds ran at their flanks. They were fuelled, rearmed, but the data halos of most spun with damage. There had been no time for anything but primary repairs. They were a Legio walking with the blood of their last fight still on their skin. They had returned from their hours in the wall with new weapons in their hands – vortex and warp missiles, and rad-impellers – weapons taken from the Legio's deep magazines in numbers that Tetracauron had never seen.

The tide of ground units rolled towards them. Gunfire spat at them. Void shields chimed with swallowed fire. *Reginae Furorem* and its kin waded into the tide, stamping down, mashing troops, sending vehicles tumbling. They were thrusting into the centre of the Mortis advance, while the maniples of the two Imperator Titans held the far flanks twenty kilometres distant to either side. At their back, Cydon and the maniple of Arthusa had locked in place, their fire arcing above to strike deep in the enemy advance.

<Point defence weapons firing.> Divisia, her focus and fatigue fused.

Tetracauron felt the tingle of the lascannon and bolter shots shed from his shoulders. A spider-limbed walker scuttled towards *Reginae Furorem*. The cannon on its back pulsed with red threat markers. Tetracauron sent a surge of will and spite into the incandescence, and the engine lashed its next stride into the machine. The fire was rising, flowing into him, obliterating the pain and exhaustion building in his flesh. He was the focus and wrath of his god now.

<Reactor at optimal.>

<Enemy engines sighted.>

<Weapons lit.>

<Target lock.>

<Fire.>

Light reaching across the distance, burning the air across kilometres, and beside him Arthusa and his engine kin firing to a single converging beat.

<Engine strike.>

He could feel the weight of the vortex missiles on his back, the black hunger at the heart of the spirit of each warhead.

<Here they come,> said Divisia, and an instant later he saw them too. Two blurred and jagged shapes, striding to close, static target mandalas overlaying them. They were from the court of *Dies Irae*, no longer incarnations of the divine, but vessels for blasphemy. The fallen Imperator had vanished from the battle sphere, melting from being as Ignatum punished

its lesser vassals. But the two that remained in Tetracauron's sight were still formidable.

The Ignatum Titans began to fire on the pair. Explosions boiled across them, vanishing into clouds of insects and whirls of filthy yellow light.

<Close and engage,> he willed across the noospheric links, and saw the pairs of Warhounds sprint forwards, vulcan bolters breathing shells at the daemon engines. They would close to point-blank range while the rest of the battle group saturated the targets. Then the Hounds would take the kill with melta cannons and maximal plasma blasts. Lesser fire traced the Warhounds, but the two daemon engines did not respond.

<Something's wrong.> Cartho, his sending sharp. Tetracauron followed the direction of the moderatus' intent. The read-outs for the Warhounds were fizzing, data degrading.

<Reactor output dropping fast!> came the sending from the first Warhound princeps, and then the others were echoing it, and the Warhounds were slowing, stumbling like humans feeling the beat of their heart fade.

The daemon Titans walked on unconcerned, dust-filled winds blowing around them. Tetracauron thought for a second that he heard a low, rasping chuckle in the wash of static.

The fires of the Warhound guttered before Tetracauron's sight. Weapon target runes fizzed as they tried to lock.

<Lone engine approaching from rear!> Cartho, urgent. Tetracauron turned his gaze. For a moment he could see nothing. Then the lone Titan formed, coalescing from partial signal returns and gaps in auspex feeds, like a shadow cast by someone he could not quite see. A Warlord Titan, walking alone into the battle sphere, a single blue rune marking its fealty to the Emperor. Tetracauron felt his mouth go dry and the world of the incandescence seem to fade.

'Princeps senioris,' came a voice that sounded clear and cold in the vox. 'I am Prefect Cadamia of the engine *Orientalis-Echion*. I am entering your immediate combat zone. Prepare to launch a single vortex payload on transmitted coordinates and then give supporting fire.'

The Titan's image blinked through basic visual data feeds: black bleeding to dark green, edges of bronze gold without mark or heraldry. He was old enough in the service of the oldest of Legios to have heard the whispers of the lost Titans given to Terra, of the engines that walked with hollow spirits. Some thought those stories just the old fears of the flesh bleeding into the rationality of data, but Tetracauron had never dismissed the possibility of there being a shadow of truth behind the whispers. Now he saw that he had been wrong; the truth was beyond the fear of stories.

'This is Princeps Senioris Tetracauron of the Legio Ignatum, I have battle-sphere command. You will state your tactical intentions and integrate with my command.'

'Negative,' came the reply. 'My command renders your authority null, and your compliance mandated. Your first act will be to launch a vortex warhead on the transmitted target coordinates.' The voice was cold and grey in the swirl of the incandescence. A blurt of data and command code clearance unfolded from the transmission. The authority was undoubted.

<Those coordinates fall short of the enemy engines,> came Divisia's sending. <We would be firing into nothing.>

'Princeps senioris, compliance is necessary,' said Cadamia.

Tetracauron held the contradiction of thoughts and emotion still in his mind for a moment, felt the breathing fire of his engine and the pulse of his own blood.

<Do it,> he willed.

The engine responded. Fuel flushed into the missile ignition. Cloud spread across his shoulders as the vortex warhead armed.

Orientalis-Echion walked past them towards the daemon engines. The air around it shivered.

<Missile armed,> sent Cartho.

<Launch.>

The vortex missile struck. A black, hungering hole opened between the Mortis engines and the Psi-Titan. The breach yawned wide, a bullet hole shot in reality. Warp energy and collapsing matter whirled at its edge, flaring through every colour of the spectrum as they balanced on the edge of oblivion. Tetracauron saw it through his engine's eyes, the incandescence turning the absence into a circle of blinding white. There was blood on his teeth. *Reginae Furorem*'s head twisted, the god-machine trying to turn its sensor gaze away from the violation. The air around the wound rippled. The pair of Mortis engines shivered. Scrap code burbled across the noosphere and vox, a chuckle of dying stars and radiation death. They heaved forwards, turning to pass the vortex, weapons inhaling to fire. *Orientalis-Echion* kept moving, striding directly forwards. Shells rattled from its shields as the daemon Titans blazed at it. The Psi-Titan's shields flared and burst as it strode into the fusillade. Beams of pale light stabbed through the curtains of explosions. Armour vaporised. Metal scattered from cuts. Still the Psi-Titan walked, its gun silent, its skin bleeding. The vortex was spinning towards it. It was going to die before it had even drawn blood.

<Synchronise and lock fire to those engines,> Tetracauron roared across the link to his maniple. <Now.>

He felt *Reginae Furorem* already turning, its targeting a narrowing circle of fire-etched symbols in his sight. *Orientalis-Echion*'s carapace was glowing with wounds, trailing burning oil and sparks, the vortex directly in front of it.

'Princeps-Senioris Tetracauron,' came the cool voice of Cadamia over the vox-link. 'Maintain your previous target tasking.'

'You will be–'

'We will be what we are,' said Cadamia, and the link cut. In the battle sphere, the Psi-Titan had reached the threshold of the vortex.

<Ever-turning cog of truth...> Cartho's shock breathed across the incandescence. <It's walking into it.>

Orientalis-Echion stepped into the black abyss of the vortex.

The ragged edge of the hole flared for an instant. Ghost lightning arced through the air. Reality howled. And then the vortex drained into the Psi-Titan, spinning, half-daemonic energies clawing at the air. Then it was gone. *Orientalis-Echion* took another step. Its wounded skin glowed. Eldritch power poured into breaches and damage. Armour plates flickered back into being. Tetracauron could hear a high-pitched shriek rising in his thoughts as he watched the Psi-Titan remake reality. It flickered, time and space blinking, and now it was closer to the two daemon Titans – much closer, and they were turning, war-horns droning, the entities bound within their shells sensing the anathema of the foe they faced.

<Hit them now!> willed Tetracauron, and his maniple answered. Beams of plasma and las bathed the Mortis engines. Ghost shields coiled. Fire clotted to black slime. Void shields shattered.

The weapon on *Orientalis-Echion*'s left arm fired. White to black, straight and true, like a razor line pulled through light and sound. It touched the first Mortis engine and unmade it. It took a step, the substance of its shell unwinding into grey ash. The daemon in its core blazed out, folding light into shadows of claws, insect wings, horned heads and spindle fingers. The beam of unreality cored into it, shredding it, drinking its false substance with a hungering howl. The second daemon Titan gurgled static. Flies shook from it as the cannons on its back and fists fired. Light exploded across *Orientalis-Echion*.

Its shields were still charging, but the shots exploded half a metre from the Psi-Titan's skin. It turned to face the second Mortis engine, slow, unhurried. Its cannon sucked the light from the explosions. The daemon Titan's head split along a crack. Iron teeth spread wide in a wet maw. *Orientalis-Echion* fired. The beam hit the daemon Titan on the left shoulder. For an instant the substance of its armour held, and then it began to dissolve into dust and smoke. The daemon engine slumped to its left, tried to take a step, fell gurgling, its substance unravelling, and *Orientalis-Echion* was walking towards it, carving the beam of darkness through it even as the entity within tried to hold on, tried to fight. A sudden black star opened where the daemon Titan had fallen.

Orientalis-Echion strode on, the air howling with ghost light around it.

<What…> Divisia's question breathed across the incandescence. <What just happened?>

Tetracauron looked towards where the Psi-Titan walked alone.

<The Emperor's Talon's have opened the way. Forwards!> replied Tetracauron. *Reginae Furorem*'s war-horns sounded as it strode, weapons firing, its surviving kin following in its wake.

Remnant Dunes, Mercury-Exultant kill-zone

Elatus came around the dune crest at full stride, and fired. The thermal lance hit its first target, blew it to slag and sliced into the one behind it. Machines in oil-slick black and iron poured down the opposite dune face. *Elatus*' stubber pivoted and sent a burst of hard rounds into a cluster of kill-servitors bounding up the right flank. Inside the Armiger's cockpit, Acastia was breathing hard. Target and tactical data blurred across her screens.

The enemy ground units were coming in a tide, flowing across the northern kill-zone where the remains of the ground-down hab-districts had formed dunes of metallic dust and powdered rockcrete, blown and sculpted into a still sea by the winds that curled and rebounded from the Palace wall. It was dry, baked by the heat and untouched by the storms that poured water from the edge of the Palace shield canopy. The hunters of Solaria and Vyronii had strode into this dust sea and run straight into the enemy.

Acastia reined in *Elatus'* stride and wheeled. The enemy were already filling the gap she had blasted in their ranks. Amber runes spun on the weapons console. The stubber was almost dry. Bolts of las-fire and rad-heavy rounds lashed at *Elatus*, and she swung her steed's ion shield around. It flared bright. The enemy would be all around her soon, but she needed only a few seconds more.

'Onwards...' she hissed to herself.

A clutch of cyborgs with scythe limbs scuttled towards her. Gun-pods arched above their backs.

Thaumas came over the dune crest to her left. It fired. Heavy rounds punched into the cyborgs. They spun back, metal and half-rotting flesh bursting into blood and sparks. Pluton's Armiger bounded down the dune face, landed and locked its legs. The recoil shook the light Knight as it pivoted, guns chugging out a stream of rounds. The tide of the enemy curled to face the new threat.

'Ammunition depleting...' came Pluton's voice in Acastia's ear as she kicked *Elatus* forwards and gunned her chainfist to life. A thing like a scorpion cast in black iron leapt at her. She met it with the teeth of her blade and chewed it to fragments. Something in its unholy heart detonated with a blast of green lightning. *Elatus* flinched back.

The neural tether to Caradoc burned in Acastia's skull. She

felt her hands curb her mount back as Caradoc's Knight came into sight. *Meliae* was at full stride, the pistons of its shank driving it forward in a blur. Acastia felt her half-brother's rage spill into glee as his Knight's bolt cannon fired. A tongue of muzzle flame breathed from the spinning barrels. Enemy machines vanished in a burning crescent of impacts and explosions. *Meliae* drove its charge home, ploughing in, stamping, crushing, sweeping its blade arm around in a reaping arc. Acastia could feel the rage and joy of slaughter flowing across the neural tether from Caradoc. She brought *Elatus* onto *Meliae*'s left flank. Pluton was moving slower, *Thaumas*' stride jerking awkwardly.

Caradoc was driving forwards, pulling more and more of the enemy machines to him. An enemy Knight stepped into sight on the horizon – first one, then a second, and then three more, their filthy shells the colour of dried bone. Banners of skin dangled from their weapon arms. Runes cast in dark iron spidered across what remained of their heraldry.

'My liege,' Acastia said into the vox. She was watching the blurred image of the auspex. 'We need to turn. Solaria needs us to pull the enemy south.'

Caradoc answered with a lash of neural command. She and *Elatus* went forwards into the oncoming press of enemy, towards the enemy Knights, towards the glory that Caradoc felt the universe owed him and had never given him.

'My liege,' she said, forcing the word out. 'Please, we need to pull back–'

But it was too late.

The plan had been simple, a hunter's logic applied to war: hit the enemy hard and draw larger prey before pulling back as the true killers did their work. Once Caradoc and the Vyronii Knights had engaged, they had had a few moments to pull back, because the first of the Solaria Titans would have begun a run that would land it in the middle of the enemy like a spear thrust into the side of a charging beast. That was the plan and the will of Princeps Abhani Lus Mohana. It required courage and daring, and risk, but more, it required control.

The Solaria Warhound crested the dune to their left at a run and leaped. Acastia felt her breath catch with awe at the sight. Nothing that size should move with such feral grace. Pistons bunched. The call of its war-horns sounded.

The enemy Knights turned. Caradoc, halfway to them, faltered in his charge. Acastia felt the leash on her mind and limbs slacken, and strafed *Elatus* to the side.

The Solaria Warhound had seen them – had seen them even as it leaped from the crest of the dune; had seen them and known they were out of place and directly in the impact path of its leap. The Warhound twisted, trying to pull itself around. Caradoc's Knight was frozen. Acastia kicked maximum power into *Elatus*. The Armiger hit *Meliae* at only half stride. The impact spun the larger Knight back and to the side. Hammer force whipped through *Elatus*. Acastia felt her head and sight fill with spinning light.

The Warhound landed. Twisted, its left leg came down at an angle. The full weight of the god-machine hammered down into piston joints. Metal sheared. Void shields stuttered. Gas and liquid burst from broken cylinders. It fought to stand. The automata crushed beneath it exploded. The tide of enemy crashed into it, driven by momentum and suicidal kill protocols. The Titan fired, mega-bolters cutting a wild arc around it. The enemy Knights came forwards. Shells and beams of energy exploded across the Warhound's back as it struggled to stand.

Acastia shook the pain and blinding light from her sight. She latched *Elatus*' targeter on to one of the enemy Knights and triggered the thermal lance. The beam of blinding heat exploded against an active ion shield. The enemy Knight shifted its gaze, gun aligning on *Elatus*.

The second Solaria Titan arrived then. It came from behind Acastia. It was *Bestia Est*. Its strides sent dust pouring down the dune faces. Vulcan rounds and blinding light slashed across the enemy Knights. One fell, ion shield blown out, torso cored. The others fired back, but *Bestia Est* had already switched direction with the speed of a gust of wind.

Then a third Solaria Warhound hit. Like *Bestia Est*, it came at full stride, guns firing, slicing into the enemy as they poured into its kill arc. *Bestia Est* changed direction still firing, pivoting around the enemy. Another enemy Knight blew apart, another fell.

Acastia was hacking around her again, stubber and thermal lance firing, all thought of conserving ammunition gone. The ground was shaking, her mouth filled with iron.

Seen from above, the battle would have seemed a spiral: Caradoc and his Armigers and a Solaria Warhound at the centre, surrounded by a mass of enemy machines and infantry; *Bestia Est* and its sister Warhound on the outside, turning in wide arcs as they herded and slaughtered their prey. It was over in under two minutes.

Acastia watched *Bestia Est* slow its stride and fire a last blast from its guns into a pair of still-moving automata. Then *Bestia Est* turned its guns and gaze on where *Meliae* and the Vyronii Knights paced amongst the slaughter. The last flashes of a reforming void shield lit its hound features. It took a ground-shaking pace towards Caradoc's Knight.

Caradoc must have transmitted something over a direct vox-stream to Abhani, but the princeps' reply snarled over the unit-wide vox.

'I will gun you down, and live with whatever protest Vyronii wishes to make for sending a fool and a coward to war.'

No reply came, but Acastia could feel Caradoc's rage and shame across the neural tether, a migraine glow behind her eyes. The moment lengthened.

Bestia Est's guns cycled down and the Warhound turned and began to lope across the dunes.

'We need to move before the enemy advance pins us,' growled Abhani. 'Follow.'

Acastia felt the anger smoulder from Caradoc, then the goad as he spurred his Knight after the Warhounds.

The Achilus Line, Mercury-Exultant kill-zone

Along the centre of the Mercury Wall the sally doors opened. Spaced ten kilometres apart, they had opened to let the engines of Ignatum through, and now again to let a newborn Legion walk. They came in maniples formed by necessity. Where they could, the Collegia had merged the engines and crews of a common heritage, but for most, the formations they now belonged to were driven by blunt pragmatism. Warhounds that were once of the Nova Guard paced ahead of a Reaver formerly bound to Legio Amaranth and a Warlord once of Solaria. All still bore the colours of the Legios that they had once belonged to; there had been no time to grant them the colours of the newly born Legio Invigilata, but all bore its mark, either painted on a heraldic shield or simply etched into their armoured skin: a red eye haloed in silver casting lightning beneath its gaze. Wrathful, unblinking, holy in the sight of the machine and its god.

They walked, horns blaring as the light of battle touched their sensors. Static and scrap code washed over their systems, buzzing out of the distance like a cloud of insects. In her amniotic tank, Esha Ani Mohana heard the vox and data commands of her princeps call and respond as they spread along the wall line. They were distorted, speaking in a base Imperial battle cant rather than the dialect and code-ciphers of the dozen individual legions they had come from. Before them lay the Achilus Line – the cordon of blockhouses that lay fifteen kilometres out from the foot of the wall. Beyond that the kill-zone burned and flashed with the light of the battle. Esha Ani Mohana noticed the tactical data links update, mapping the known real-time picture of the battle sphere to the spirit of *Luxor Invictoria*. The links to Princeps Maximus Cydon showed active but not clear – nothing in the battle sphere was untouched by entropic failures. Out here everything was dying, either fast or by the slow seconds of falling sand and decaying metal. Nothing would walk away from this whole. She was sure.

Far off she saw a cluster of communication markers flicker deep in the battle lines. Swift moving, following a hunter's path. For a second she hesitated. She had not had the time nor the means to contact her daughter after Vethorel's proclamation and the strange birth of the Legio Invigilata. Command queries pinged in her awareness. She held her silence and then opened up a long-range vox-link. Around her, *Luxor Invictoria* strode towards the engagement lines. The link fizzed.

'*Honoured Grand Master.*' Abhani's voice echoed in the connection, flexing from distant to close. Esha Ani did not answer for a long moment. She suddenly felt the silence of her amnion tank, disturbed only by the jolt of her engine's strides moving it forwards.

'Hello, my daughter,' she said at last.

Remnant Dunes, Mercury-Exultant kill-zone

Abhani heard the machine simulacrum of her mother's voice and blinked. She swallowed in a dry throat. There was something in the words that reached through the cold modulation of her mother's false speech. Beyond *Bestia Est*'s eye-ports, the land passed stride by stride.

'What is your will?' she said at last.

'*Only to speak with you,*' came the reply.

'The legion walks?'

'*I walk,*' came the reply, then the catch in the sound. Then her mother told her. Just a few words, no elaboration, just a direct transfer of information that sank into her cold as quiet steel. She felt *Bestia Est* respond to her. Data cleared, became distant. The fire of her reactor became a cold chill. She thought of the sisters and their engines dead on Beta-Garmon. She thought of the Titans and crews still out there amongst the stars, perhaps still alive, perhaps still hunting. She thought of the machines that walked with her mother now, machines that walked under a new name, Imperial Hunters no more. All the honour and heritage and loss from her grandmother, carried by Imperial Hunters through conquest and civil war to her. She thought of her mother, and thought she heard a catch in the machine-made voice as she spoke again.

'*You are Solaria now, Abhani Lus,*' said her mother. '*You are all of us.*'

'Legio first,' she said and felt how those words, spoken so often but never truly understood until now, would follow her.

'*Hunt well, my daughter,*' said her mother. Static filled the link, speaking into the silence. Then the link faded, and *Bestia Est* ran on into the cauldron of war, while before the wall *Luxor Invictoria* marched forwards with its new kin towards the engines of the Death's Heads and the falling lightning and tatters of reality.

'Princeps.' The voice of a moderatus broke the silence that had settled in her. She blinked, her thoughts pulling from the distance to the world in front of her. 'I am getting multiple returns ahead, maximum range.'

Abhani felt the catch in the moderatus' voice as she felt *Bestia Est*'s void shields spark and cycle, a hound's hackles bristling. She looked out, but there was just the swirl of smoke and the flash of explosions. The auspex sounded a return, the pitch rising. The fog parted for a second, and there in the distance she saw what walked to face the defenders.

Mercury-Exultant kill-zone

First the dead had walked, hundreds of Titans taken from the engine graves of the galaxy. Then the great maniples of Mortis had come, and with them the god-machines that were now hosts to daemons of despair and decay and death. Hundreds of engines marked with the livery of the Death's Heads, pressing against the Legio Ignatum and the other forces scrambled beyond the wall. The kill-zone was a cauldron of fire in which the flames of sorcery and warp light bubbled. But the enemy had not reached the walls, and the last steps under the sight of the walls' guns were blocked by the red and yellow and black Titans of the Fire Wasps, the abomination engines of the Ordo Sinister, and the motley-coloured Legio Invigilata. Enough to hold. Enough to kill the reapers of Mortis, even if the cost was total.

But the strength of the Death's Heads and the will of Horus had prepared for this last act of defiance. Behind the main advance walked engines made to do one thing – break other Titans and tear down fortresses. Only the Emperor-class machines were greater in size and destructive power, but these engines had a special purpose and the tools to complete it. Void shield generators blistered on their backs, enough to protect a warship. Fed by chains of reactors, they could cycle and restore their shield integrity without drawing power from their weapons. And what weapons they bore. Layers of batteries and clusters of engine-killing ordnance, guns that could scour armies from their feet. They had not marched to battle in the Great Crusade, the secrets of their making and their might held back by the Mechanicum, perhaps through fear, perhaps as a threat, the jealous hoarding tolerated by the Imperium. The name of their class and pattern had only been spoken in machine code, a scarred cipher that held the kernel of their purpose and divinity. Now as they walked to war, they bore a name in the tongues of those unblessed by knowledge of the machine. Warmaster Titans, they were called, in honour of the one that had brought this new age into being.

They walked together, a single block, each engine no more than a hundred metres from another, their reactors burning to a single count, their void shields merged into a single shroud that glittered with shrapnel impacts. Trios of Knights and packs of Warhounds circled them like lesser fish around a school of behemoths. On they walked, unhurried, their tread the slow countdown of inevitability.

Enemy distance to wall: 24 kilometres.

TWENTY

Oath
All that we had hoped to never lose
Pious to a different creed

The Blackstone, Sanctum Imperialis Palatine

'Ready?' Mauer asked as she stepped through the cell door. Keeler looked at Sindermann.

The two held each other's gaze, and then Keeler nodded.

'We go from here as a three,' said Mauer. 'Once we are out of the fortress, we are going to be transferring to a ground-car convoy. That will take us to the checkpoint at Ganymede Zone Intersection.'

'That is where you believe the incident will occur?' said Sindermann.

Mauer shook her head.

'If they want to stop her, they will hit us there. If that happens, you know the contingency – we vanish you both out at the point it occurs. We could get beyond the checkpoint as a group, but the variables go up and not in a good way – too many angles, too many people.' Mauer took a breath, looked at them both: Sindermann, his old face open, eyes sharp; Keeler looking at the

leaves of parchment in Sindermann's hands. 'Contingency route
is you both get out of the vehicle, move to the third building
on the left. There is a door that's normally sealed. Knock four
times and it will open. Ahlborn will be there. From there do
exactly what he says, when he says it.'

'Is there another way of responding to Conroi-Captain
Ahlborn?' said Sindermann lightly, but his expression was
grave. 'You have reason to believe an attempt is likely.'

Mauer shrugged.

'If forces inside or outside the Imperial hierarchy are going
to make an attempt to kill or capture Mamzel Keeler then a
time and place close to her release is likely.'

'Fewer places to look, and bottlenecks we have to pass
through – I appreciate the thoroughness, boetharch, but the
details from the first briefings are still quite fresh. I am presuming that none of us will know where Conroi-Captain
Ahlborn will take us in this eventuality?'

'From this point, information must be segmented,' said Mauer.

Mauer noticed the old man was rolling an autoquill through
the fingers of his right hand. She had spent enough time with
Sindermann now to know that he was not prone to fidgeting.

'Nervous?' she asked. He glanced at her, a small ghost of a
smile in the wrinkles of his face.

'Of course,' he said. 'The stakes are rather high, don't you think?'

She felt her mouth twitch.

'Fair point,' she replied, and looked at Keeler. The woman
looked back at Mauer, face calm, gaze settled. Mauer almost
flinched. It was like looking into the heart of a cyclone, still
and calm, but edged by a storm. For a second, she wondered
what it was that they were setting in motion.

'All shall be as it must, boetharch,' said Keeler; then she
looked at Sindermann and held out her hand. 'The pen, Kyril.
It is time for me to tell my lie.'

Sindermann held up the autoquill and the docket of parchments, a heavy wax seal of the Order of Interrogation hanging from each leaf.

The quill scratched in the quiet.

'There,' said Keeler. 'It is done.'

Sindermann looked like he was about to say something, and then closed his mouth and bowed his head. Keeler put out a hand and touched the old man's face. He looked up. Mauer saw the passing of a sad smile on Keeler's face. Then she rose and turned to Mauer. 'Let's go.'

Hatay-Antakya Hive, East Phoenicium Wastes

A face of marble smiled down at Oll with needle teeth. Orb eyes held his. He saw nothing else but had the impression of clawed fingers and curves and scales.

I have waited, Ollanius.

He heard its voice, and it was the same voice that he had heard call across the waves of the Aegean and had dragged the crews of ships down to the midnight beneath the waves. He knew that he never wanted to move again, never wanted to leave, and that he would not need to. He would become stone like all the rest, living in perfection. Was that not everything he had always wanted – to not play a part, just to be still, and belong and be?

The statues were spinning and howling, and there were figures coming from the shadows beneath the trees, the riot of colours on their armour making their shapes swim and flicker. Space Marines, daubed in orange and mauve, in crimson and lime, in copper and emerald. Shrunken, amber-encased heads swung on silver chains. Bulbous weapons hooted as they armed. The air reeked of faeces and roses.

A trap, it was a trap, of course – he had known that; but he wondered how far back they had stepped into it. Back in the tunnel when they had arrived and he had heard John's call for help? Before? On Calth when Rane had lost his wife and heard the siren song for the first time? And now here they were, all the way down in the Labyrinth with the beast and without a thread to follow out. Time was not what people thought it was, Oll knew that better than most. The false gods of the warp saw it true. What had been and what would be were eternally present to them. There was no paradox in them setting up Rane in his path years before so that he would be a lure now.

The statue above Oll – that was not Rane's wife and never had been – bent down to him, luminous marble limbs flowing, smile wide.

A burst of las-fire hit it in the top of its skull and blew the crown of its head off. It arched back. Stone fragments and black-crimson ichor flicked through the air. Rane shrieked. Oll shivered. Another burst of las-fire, but this time the statue tumbled aside.

'Neve!' screamed Rane. He whirled and his pistol was in his hand, aiming back at where John and Katt had come from the treeline. Oll came up and slammed into the boy. Rane's gun went off. The las-blast hit the statue of a man bearing a bowl of red liquid. The point of the statue's chin blew off in a spray of blood, and the stone man screamed. Oll felt rather than heard it. He and Rane were on the ground scrambling. The boy still had the pistol. Oll's rifle was tangling with its strap as he tried to wrap his arms and legs around the boy, to hold and pin.

The bleeding statue of the man with the bowl screamed again, twisting, feet ripping from its plinth in a spray of blood and bone. Its arms tore free of the bowl on its shoulders. Red liquid showered out.

A cacophony of screams rose from the statues. Oll felt something burst inside his nose. He could smell copper and taste iron. John and Katt both staggered as though drunk, gun barrels dropping. More statues ripped from their places. Some left parts of limbs and bloody pockets of flesh inside broken stone shells.

'Neve!' shouted Rane. 'He killed Neve!'

But John had not killed the thing that Rane thought was his lost love. Not killed it even by half. It pirouetted into sight. It was still bloody, but it had shed its skin of false stone now. Iridescent hair spilled around its head as though floating in water. It was taller, much taller, its limbs grown into curved talons, pearl-white scales gleaming over flexing muscle. It was laughing, but the sound coming from its mouth was colour and shape, a great spill of vibrating red and neon-green sound. It was moving fast, but somehow also slowly, growing as it moved, lengthening, the shadows of its whirling arms forming new arms, its head lengthening into a snout, folds of skin unfolding into spills of silk. Oll saw it and felt a jolt of pure terror spark through him. He wanted to run or to wait, but also wanted it to reach him. He wanted to let it speak to him and only him. He wanted to stab a knife into his ear so that he could not hear and think any more, so that he did not have to be in a universe where a thing like this existed.

It was the promise of all that had been lost and could not be given back, and it smiled at him and reached down with a hand that grew black-glass talons.

Ollanius, it said. *Ollanius... Pious Ollanius, brief Warmaster, first of those without death. Ollanius, you are home... No need to run. No need to sail further...*

A spear of las-fire reached for the daemon and exploded into insects with burning wings before it could touch its skin. Katt was firing at it, John trying to pull her back. The thing did not even look at them, but trembled and a shockwave rippled out. Katt and John tumbled back, like leaves caught in a gale.

The daemon's image was blinding as it reached for Oll.

'_'

Blood sprayed from John's lips as he spoke the un-word. It stole colour and sound from the air. The glittering daemon staggered and fell, becoming for an eye-blink something grey, wasted and ugly.

'No...' Oll tried to say, rolling over, ears bleeding. 'No, John! Don't!' The words crumbled to a hiss as they came from his mouth. He could see John Grammaticus on his knees, blood pouring down his face. Wounds had opened on his cheeks. The veins under his skin were black, bulging. Blood and broken teeth fell from his mouth. Katt was half on her feet, her hands clamped to her ears, vomiting uncontrollably. The un-word that John had spoken, that he had learnt from Oll's memory of the tower, hung above his head in a synaesthetic halo of colour, jagged yellow, neon purple.

The daemon began to stand again. Ash fell from it. Muscles writhed under loose, grey skin. Its face was a ruin of cracked features and black, rotting teeth. It bellowed, and the sound vibrated through the air in a black cone. Marble slabs shattered. It jerked forwards, cloven feet spreading flames. Bale Rane came to his feet, screaming a cascade of red agony. His eyes were wide. Tears boiled on his cheeks. Oll wondered in that second if Rane saw the daemon true, or if its lie of hope still clung to his sight. The daemon's talon was a brief blur, a stutter in time, so fast that it seemed the passing of a shadow.

Rane stood for a moment. Then his torso hinged open. Blood gushed out. Rane collapsed, the halves of the bisected body folding to the ground. Oll cried out as the boy's head hit the ground, mouth and eyes still open.

A pulse of shriek-sound ripped through the air, its blast forming ripples of cyan and magenta. The writhing statues blew

into fragments of stone, flesh and bone. Waves of ultra-sonic
pressure shuddered through Oll's bones. The colour-daubed
Space Marines were advancing, chromed weapons levelled.

The daemon coiled. Conjured muscles tightened under vein-
threaded skin. It hunched to spring forward. A beam of crimson
energy hit it in the flank. False flesh blew to ash. It roared in
anger and complete silence. Oll was halfway to his feet as the
second beam hit. The daemon's substance sucked back into it
as the beam bored through it. Oll turned to see a figure in grey
armour blur as it ran through the garden of shattered statues.
Leetu fired another pulse from his serpenta pistol, clamped
it to his thigh and pulled a rib-barrelled gun from his back.
A tongue of flame breathed from the muzzle. Rounds hit the
daemon and burst into white starbursts. John was standing,
trembling. The daemon leapt towards Oll, white fire falling
from it like raindrops reflecting the noon sun.

'–!' shouted John Grammaticus.

The phrase of Enuncia broke the light. Spectrums inverted.
Blood glittered green. Shadows blazed bright. The sky above
blinked to a black void.

Oll saw the daemon unravel. Flesh spooled into ropes of
ash that fell upwards. Its shape dissolved into a chalk-smear
blur. He could taste salt and smell bitter ozone. He thought
he saw its mouth open to scream. Then it was simply not
there. Motes of ash and stone, and globules of blood hung in
the air. Oll was shivering. Sweat poured from his skin, blood
from his ears and the corners of his eyes. He could feel the
un-word John had spoken still echoing beyond hearing, an
angel summoned and sent to end existence, the sound of a
tower falling under the fall of lightning.

The thunderclap came. A blinding light bleaching his sight.
Sound returned with a roar.

And he was pushing himself up, his hand finding his rifle.

'Two things make a soldier,' he had said to Rane once, years ago, as the boy had followed him through the labyrinth of time and misadventure to Terra. *'First is the ability to do something damned stupid without knowing why, and second is letting go of your life before you let go of your weapon.'*

Rane lay on the ground. The blood that was pouring from him had begun to bubble and burn in the sorcery-rich air. Oll lifted the boy's head, calling for who knows what help from anyone that could hear.

A shadow fell over him. Grey, massive, holding a gun that breathed fire into the Emperor's Children that were still coming from the undergrowth.

'You must leave him, sir,' bellowed Leetu, pausing to reload in the time it took to draw breath. A shivering scream of sound hit the grey Space Marine. Layers of ceramite blew into dust. Leetu flinched, then fired back. A warrior in silver-and-amethyst armour fell, its head a ball of white flame. 'Now.'

Oll saw Zybes then. The pay-by-day had crossed the distance well behind Leetu but was firing as he ran, ducking down amongst the stone plinths and pulped trees to fire a stream of shots into the distance. With him was Graft, clanking forwards, supporting a grey-faced Krank. The veteran had his pistol out and was firing, covering Zybes as the other ran to Leetu and Oll.

Zybes dropped beside Oll, aimed his gun into the distance and fired.

Graft clanked into cover a moment later.

'Move, Oll,' Zybes shouted, and jerked a hand towards the centre of the dome and the whirling pool at its heart. 'That way – it's the only way the bastards aren't coming from. Get the others and move!'

Zybes, resentful Zybes, not clever and gifted like Katt, not a kid like Rane. A man who never wanted to be a soldier, who had never signed up to fight, dragged along by Oll and the others. Now shouting, now here like all the rest, ready to die just because Oll had made a bad choice. Like all the rest, like all the crews and units he had been part of – all too damn loyal to someone they did not really know.

He stood and turned, began to run to John. The psyker was on the ground. A circle of broken slabs surrounded him. The skin of his face was blistered and blackened. Lips almost burned away. His eyes were open, though. Wide open. He gasped, and tried to move. His hands were twisted as though the bones inside the flesh had shattered. Katt was trying to pull him up. Blood covered her face and hands. Oll grabbed John under the other arm.

'You shouldn't have done that,' growled Oll. 'You shouldn't have spoken the Enuncia.'

John Grammaticus grinned through his mask of blood.

'You might have a point,' he hissed. 'Next time you can do it.'

A scythe of sound sheared across the dome at head height. Stone and wood blasted to pulp and dust. Oll looked at Katt and nodded. They began a stooped run, John Grammaticus hanging between them, gasping up blood-froth. Behind them Zybes, Graft and Krank were following. Oll could hear the roaring blast of Leetu's rifle.

They reached the end of the row of statues. Oll could see the way through the shredded trees, could see the light glimmering off the water in the whirlpool at the dome's centre. He caught a glint of colour out of the corner of his eye, and twisted. Space Marines in multicoloured armour were closing on them. A legionary in bloated chrome armour lumbered to a halt. Sound shivered around it, the air popping with impossible colours. Pipes arched over its back. Its mouth was a tunnel into its head. Twin weapons hung from its limbs, power feeds shivering as they inhaled to fire.

Oll opened his mouth to shout, and began to pull Katt and John down.

Down and down… past the river that cut the living from the dead.

I have coin for you, ferryman…

Will you take it from me?

A woman in red tatters stepped across the path in front of them. She was tall, very tall. A red veil hid her eyes, and finger bones hung from the hooks in her lips and chin. Her mouth was smiling.

A towering figure moved in front of her. It moved fast, far too fast for something that size. Billowing fabric surrounded it like multicoloured smoke. Silvered armour plates glinted beneath the snout of a helm. A Space Marine, or something written on that scale. It raised its bolter. Oll's eyes met the black circle of the barrel.

'Down,' it growled, an instant before it fired.

Sanctum Imperialis Palatine

The vehicles already had their engines running as Mauer reached the courtyard. Troopers in the red armour and silver visors of the Command Prefectus stood ready beside each vehicle, guns ready, eyes alert. Mauer had her pistol in her hand. The vox-bead in her ear clicked and buzzed with code phrases. Sindermann and Keeler were shimmer blurs to her left and right. Both wore false-hoods that broke their image into things without clear depth, size or colour. They moved to the left groundcar. All the buildings were empty, and she had sent people she trusted to check all of them.

People she trusted…

'Trust no one, might be a wiser maxim…'

Her eyes went to the empty sockets of the windows. Above, the skin of the aegis shield flashed against the sky.

She could hear her heartbeat in her ears.

The groundcars chuckled exhaust fumes into the air. Their roof-mounted cannons twitched. Rain fell, exploding silver across the water pooling on the flagstones.

Now, here; this was the time. If someone had betrayed them then they would hit them now.

The red troopers moved as they crossed the ground. Folding in. She reached their groundcar. Its doors were open. Solsha looked at her from the driver's cradle, visor up. He nodded.

'In,' she hissed at Sindermann and Keeler.

They moved to the doors. Raindrops smeared where they hit the falsehoods.

The outriders gunned the engines of their machines.

She turned to look up at the buildings. Ghosts danced down her spine.

Another flash in the sky above.

She swung into the seat beside Solsha. The door slammed closed.

'Go,' she said. The engine gunned and then it leapt forwards. Acceleration shoved Mauer back into her seat. The vehicle in front of them was already out of the courtyard. The outriders blurred past. They hit the street and the groundcar accelerated. The facades of buildings blinked past. There was nothing else on the street.

'Status,' she said.

'Auspex zero,' said Solsha, his voice iron calm. Lights blinked across the groundcar controls. 'Time to intersection, four minutes.'

Mauer mag-clamped her pistol to the dashboard, and pulled up a lascarbine from the footwell. The rain was exploding and rolling down the armourglass.

'Contacts,' buzzed her vox-bead. 'Coming in from the west. I count three.'

'Visual?' said Mauer.

'Negative,' said Solsha, 'but they read as military.'

'Everything in here is military,' said Mauer. She glanced out of the narrow slit in her door. Lightning blinked high above.

Mauer nodded, eyes on the drenched gloom beyond the windows.

'They will intersect with us just after we reach the checkpoint.'

'Trouble?' asked Sindermann from the rear compartment.

'Just be ready to move when we reach the checkpoint,' she replied.

The street was narrowing. The outriders moved closer. Water rose in arcs from their rear wheels. A cliff of buildings rose ahead of them. The road arced to the left around a forty-metre statue of one of the Emperor's dead generals.

A light blinked on the dashboard.

'Someone is out there,' said Solsha, his voice level. He switched to vox. 'We are coming up on the checkpoint. One vehicle ahead of us is moving through now. All units, stand by.'

'Ready?' she said to the blurred shapes of Sindermann and Keeler. 'One way or another you follow the plan, right?'

'Understood and ready,' said Sindermann.

They took the corner, water spraying up, engines growling. Mauer could see the checkpoint ahead – five hundred metres – gun towers, troopers in rain-slicked greatcoats. The street was only just wide enough for two vehicles to pass. The lightning-lit sky was a narrow slit above. A cargo hauler was just ahead of them, going fast but braking. Militia stencils covered its sides.

'*Contacts rear*,' came a voice over the vox. Three vehicles turned onto the street behind them. Block shapes in drabs and greens. '*They are coming in fast.*'

'Stand by,' said Mauer.

Ahead, the cargo-hauler skidded as it braked. One of its

load doors flapped. The cargo segments on its back shifted. It braked again.

'Shit!' called Solsha.

The cargo-hauler slewed across the road. There were figures running beside the gun towers of the checkpoint. The hauler's wheels and tracks locked and then shrieked to full spin. It hit the gun tower and checkpoint gate. Rockcrete exploded out.

Shouts, running feet, gun barrels pointing.

The escort car behind them reversed. The outriders had kicked wide.

The guards at the checkpoint were shouting. The rain was a curtain of silver fragments.

Mauer had the butt of the carbine at her shoulder.

'Out,' said Mauer, releasing the door and pushing it open. 'Now.'

'Three contacts to rear still closing at speed,' said Solsha.

'This is it,' she said. 'All units, engage on contact.'

Mauer dropped to the street. Keeler and Sindermann were behind her. The roar of engines was loud over the rain. Figures were getting out of the drive unit of the cargo-hauler. A guard near the wrecked gate was shouting, gun half rising. Mauer saw the autogun in one of the hauler driver's hands. The guard did not see it, and was still shouting as the burst of rounds hit him in the face and chest.

Mauer fired. The round hit the hauler driver in the shoulder as he turned, and punched him back.

The cannons on the rear convoy vehicle opened up. Then there was a roar of metal slamming into metal as something hit the tail vehicle.

Running feet, shouts. Gunfire streaked through the rain.

'Go!' she shouted.

Three figures came out of the rain, guns up. She saw dark helmets, breath masks, infra-goggles. She fired. The burst hit the lead figure. The cannon on the groundcar roared. The figures scattered.

Solsha rammed the machine into reverse. It kicked back, slewed around. Down the road, a cannon opened up. Heavy rounds slammed into the groundcar's frame. Then the lead vehicle went up with a dull rolling boom. The blast wave picked Mauer up and slammed her down. Her ears were ringing. Blood in her mouth. Colours spiralling in her eyes.

All gone to hell, all gone to hell as fast as she had feared. She did not know where Keeler and Sindermann were, but she had anticipated that this might happen, planned for it. All Keeler and Sindermann needed to do was follow that plan.

Something shrieked in the air overhead. Mauer pushed herself up. Burning promethium floated across the dancing puddles. A gunship came in low, block-framed, thrusters spinning raindrops into mist. Rotor cannons spun. Rounds drilled into the groundcar behind her. She ducked an instant before its fuel and ammunition exploded. The gunship slid sideways, panning fire across the road. Las bolts and rounds spat up at it.

'We're boxed in!' shouted Solsha from the groundcar, as he released his harness and dropped through the open door. The gunship was coming around, the gaze of its cannon swinging towards them. There was fire coming from the gun towers on the checkpoint gate, from the crashed hauler, from Mauer's troops as they returned fire.

'Where did the gunship come from?' shouted Solsha from beside her.

The buzz-roar of its cannon paused, like a fire-breathing beast drawing breath.

'Move,' Mauer shouted, and pushed away. A tongue of fire reached down from the gunship. Rounds hit the groundcar. Armourglass and metal distorted. Mauer was running for the crashed hauler and the checkpoint gate.

For a second, in the blink of cannon fire, she wondered just how everything had got this bad.

'All units, break and evade,' she shouted into the vox.

Their groundcar distorted, crumpling like paper in a balled fist.

A figure came out of the rain beside the hauler. Mauer had the impression of worker's overalls, grey, striped with yellow and black, and the barrel of an autogun. She fired. Two bursts hit the figure in the gut and chest. He slammed back, stumbled, rolled, then tried to rise. She saw the body armour under the torn overalls a second before a burst of las-fire hit the man in the head. The top of his skull blasted to fragments.

'Thanks,' she called to Solsha, as they ducked behind the mass of the hauler's front wheel.

She looked up, suddenly aware of the breath sawing between her teeth. A gunship. Whoever had moved against them had mobilised a gunship inside the Sanctum Imperialis. That spoke to a power, and a recklessness, beyond what she had anticipated. That was going to be a problem. Keeler was likely loose and free, though, that was what mattered. Now all she needed to do was try to live past the present.

'…Boetharch…' The voice fizzed from the vox-bead in her ear. Overhead, the gunship was coming around. Mauer suddenly felt cold. It was Ahlborn's voice.

'Ahlborn,' she replied, shouting over the din. 'What has happened? Where is Keeler?'

'She's–' His voice cut out.

She saw Sindermann then, staggering forwards in the rain, the falsehood half shredded from him, blood on the visible sliver of his face. Mauer began to run. She reached the old man a second before a stream of las-fire blazed across the street. They tumbled to the ground. Solsha sent a stream of fire into the dark. Mauer pulled Sindermann up and dragged him into a staggering run.

'Where is she?' she shouted. 'What happened?'

'Someone…' gasped Sindermann; there was fresh blood flowing down his face. 'Someone was waiting… Waiting for us. Almost got us… Euphrati… got… she got away.'

'Where?'

'I don't… I didn't see which way she ran.'

'Who was waiting for you?'

'Oh, shit!' said Solsha. Mauer's head snapped up as another aircraft came in above the building tops. She had an instant to take in the lines of a Storm Eagle, before missiles loosed from its back. The gunship above them had enough time to jerk in mid-air before it became a fireball. The Storm Eagle's assault ramp was open. Mauer saw a giant in armour braced on its edge. The aircraft banked and then slammed still with a shriek of thrusters. The figure jumped. Mauer's instincts screamed at her to run, to get as far away as she could. Even if she had listened, there was no time.

The armoured giant hit the remains of the groundcar and crushed its roof with its landing. Eyes glowed red in a blank-faced helm. Mauer met its gaze for an instant. The sound of the rain and gunfire seemed to dim. Everything was held in that red gaze – a lifetime of war, and the promise of the only gift its kind could give. A blast of las-fire splashed across the Space Marine's shoulder. It did not flinch, but stood and began to kill.

Marmax South

Katsuhiro watched the angel die. Baeron was trying to stand. Blood smeared the ruin of his armour, brighter than the filth and soot-darkened ceramite. A ragged hole had punched through the left side of his chest and gouged through armour, flesh, bone. The wound… It wasn't a wound. Something like that didn't fit the word. It had been there before the last wave.

Now… now there was worse. Katsuhiro watched the angel try to move. He did not know what to do. Baeron had half fallen through the remains of the firing wall, knife gripped in his remaining hand. He kept on trying to rise. Parts of his armour kept twitching as though trying to amplify a misfiring movement. The attack had drained back, the gunfire slackening to leave a quiet for the angel's gurgling breaths to fill.

Katsuhiro did not know what to do. The sight of it, the sight of Baeron, red now only from his own blood, held him still.

'Lord,' he said.

'Be quiet,' hissed Steena from beside him. She had her head in her hands. The others… he didn't know who or where the other troopers behind the firing wall were, living bodies, caked in mud and blood and dust. Their uniforms and marks of distinction had disappeared: officer, high-born, script or veteran professional, all of it was gone. There was just the fact that they were here, in this small piece of the world, hemmed in by grey smoke and yellow fog, watching one of the Emperor's demigod warriors breathe his last. 'Just let him end,' said Steena, and Katsuhiro was not sure if it was a plea to him or the universe.

Baeron shivered again. Fresh red dribbled from cracks. Katsuhiro had not seen him after the last attack, after they had pulled back and found a still-functioning bit of wall to shelter behind. They had pulled back twice more since. Once at the command of an officer who had vanished soon after, and once because the enemy had just kept coming. He had no idea what the chain of command was right now, but others had gathered to him and Steena, most likely because they were not running and that meant that people presumed they had authority or a plan. He supposed he did – have a plan that was, a very simple one: hold until he couldn't any more. That was all there was to do. The universe, even this nightmare within a nightmare, had become very simple to him – trust in the Emperor and hold, or run and feel the last thing that was his break inside his soul. He was going to die, one way or another, and it would be soon, he knew.

The dead were everywhere. Some fell, overcome by fever, mouths and throats filled with pustules, gurgling last breaths as they shivered and clutched the waiting ground. Bullets found others, or the fumes that drifted across the ground and then rolled back like a ghost sea. Not everyone died though. People walked from bunkers that had crushed dozens of others. Diseases swept through groups in hours, but left half alone for no reason that Katsuhiro could grasp. At least no reason he wanted to grasp. There was a thought that had been growing in him since he had seen the shape of the black angel against the sky – the idea that there had to be some left alive so that there were souls to suffer. That somehow the fear and desperation mattered more than slaughter. It was an idea that he had tried to drown with the words of prayer and the golden memory of the saint. It sometimes worked, but it had begun to fail when the dying angel had walked from the fog and fallen at his feet.

'Lord Baeron,' he said again, edging closer so that he was within touching distance of the Blood Angel. 'You are… you are wounded…' He heard the words fail as they came from his mouth. What was he trying to do? What was there *to* do at this moment? He turned his head to look at Steena.

'I…' The word growled through the air. 'I cannot…' Katsuhiro turned back, looked down at the mangled lump that was the angel's head. Skull and flesh and helm blurred. Red bubbles popped. Jelly-soft lumps quivered. 'I cannot… see.'

'Lord, I am… my name is Katsu–'

'I know… I recog… Your… voice. You are under my… comm…'

Katsuhiro heard the breath gurgle out with the last word. He thought of the moments he had seen the Blood Angel in the last days or weeks, always a fleeting glimpse. He was not sure he had ever heard his own name spoken in Baeron's presence.

'I am under your command, lord.'

The angel took a great breath that shook his frame. Red frothed from the helm and from holes in the armour. A stump rose. There were just a finger and a thumb at the end. Katsuhiro did not know what will or strength drove it, but the remains of the hand suddenly had him by the front of his uniform, pulling him closer.

'You...' gasped Baeron. 'You did... not flee.' Katsuhiro shook his head, opened his mouth, but the angel forced more words out. 'You will... you will hold... this section.'

Katsuhiro blinked, swallowed. He did not know what he had been thinking to hear from the mouth of such a warrior in his last moments.

Not this... came the answer.

Baeron's back arched as he took another breath and raised his voice, so that it was heard again, loud and strong enough to jerk up the heads of the other troops behind the firing lip. 'Follow... this one,' he said. Katsuhiro found his head was shaking. 'I am... giving... an order,' called Baeron, still loud.

Katsuhiro went still. He was suddenly cold, the weight of what was happening and what would happen next waiting for him after these few moments of life had passed. He found he was thinking of how long ago it had been, and how far he had come, since he had stepped onto this section of the Marmax South line. It felt as though that tiered wall and that time was a long way away, but it was not. It was not because here was Baeron beside him, and that meant that this must be the same section, that the rubble and firing lines and scrap trenches were the parapets and bastions he had stood on in the past. He had moved very little. It was the world that had moved. He looked up at the clutch of filth-stained soldiers close to them. He wondered how many of them had been there on the morning he and Steena had climbed the steps, and he had looked out and paused at the light of the dawn in the distance. Some, perhaps. They all looked like nothing and no one he could recognise. He guessed that neither did he.

'Yes, lord,' he found himself saying to Baeron. 'I will die for...'

He found the word he had wanted to say falter, but something in the remains of the angel moved and Katsuhiro realised it was Baeron shaking his head.

'We all die... for one another... in... the... end...'

Then there was a last, great shiver and the mutilated hand gripping Katsuhiro released its grip.

He did not move. He could not move. Only look at the stillness that had been a thing of wonder and terror and strength. He wondered what he should do for a long moment, and then stood, pulling his rifle up and checking his pouches for ammunition. He thought of the man with the gun who had got off a macro train in another life. He looked at his hand; it was shaking. That would have to stop. He couldn't shake, couldn't do anything that would let those around him find a reason to do anything but stand and fight.

To us He gave His angels... The words ran in his head.

'Steena, and you.' He pointed to another of the troopers near her. 'What's your name?'

'Jacobus Solex,' said the trooper, clutching his lasgun tight. 'Albia, First Sappers...'

'Make a sweep down the line and check for ammunition, Jacobus. You and you,' another jab of his finger at two other crouched figures, 'run the line south and link up with any unit in the next section. Find out if they have command infrastructure. If they do, update that this section holds.'

They moved without hesitation. Just like that. He almost

smiled. He was moving now, standing, turning to look at the distance where the next wave would come from.

'He protects!' he shouted, and turned to look at the other troopers.

'He protects,' called one, not loud but with enough strength to carry. Then another echoed the call, and then another, and it was loud now, voices calling out in released fear and rage and defiance.

'He protects!'

'He protects!'

'He protects!'

Katsuhiro nodded and looked at the dead angel whose grave would be the wasteland that he had bled his last on.

'As we protect Him,' he said to himself.

Hatay-Antakya Hive, East Phoenicium Wastes

'So, do you wish to leave paradise?' Oll looked around. The woman in rags and tatters was next to them. Oll's gun came up. The woman shook her head. There was ice in the air, forming in a haze. Oll felt the pressure in his skull. The woman was still smiling. +That is not in your interest, Ollanius,+ said a voice in his head.

Katt made a sound like a hiss of steam. Oll felt heat blaze on his skin. The shadows on Katt's face had swallowed her eyes. Her mouth was open in a snarl. The woman in red tatters turned her head towards Katt. Inside his skull, Oll felt two pressure waves meet like a hammer striking an anvil. Blood and soot coloured the air. Katt was shaking, teeth bared. The veiled woman's smile had vanished.

'Unexpected,' she said. Then she turned to Oll. 'All of us need to leave and leave now. The path of opportunity is narrow, Ollanius, walk it now or be lost.'

'No…' gasped John Grammaticus, trying to straighten. 'No, she is…' He shuddered in Oll's grip.

'I am an ally,' said the woman. 'I am not one of the Children's slaves, not Horus' puppet. I serve truth, and in that we have common purpose.' In the back of Oll's mind he heard Ariadne's voice and Medea's and Niumue's.

'This thread will lead you out…'

'I will tell you how to pass through the flames and send the sleepless dragon to the land of dreams…'

'You were always better at choices, Oll…'

'This is a moment of alignment, not fracture,' said the woman. 'I am here as an ally.'

'Who are you?' Oll asked.

The bones hanging from the woman's lips clinked. The air was shimmering around her as though rippling with heat.

'Surely the real question is, what do I want?' she said. 'And the answer to that is that I want to see mankind live. I want to see it ascend. I want to see it outlive what is coming.'

'Oll, she is a liar,' gasped John from beside him. 'Kill her now. The Primordial Annihilator has her. She is a reborn, a new one of us. The Cabal tried to… Damien went after her, but…'

The woman raised her hands and lifted the red veil from her face. The eyes beneath were silver-white with blindness.

+I have walked the path of gods, Ollanius,+ she said, and her voice sounded clear in Oll's head. Everything else was distant, a thin slice of time that would not be noticed as having passed. There was a smell, too, a bleed of scent into his senses – ashes and incense, the smell of burned civilisations and sacrifice. +I have crossed into the underworld and come back. I have seen the face of the universe's shadow. I know its truth and its lies. Nothing is one thing, nothing wholly evil nor good, nothing is kind that is not also cruel. You know that truth, too. You know the Emperor, just as I know Horus.

You know that the Emperor is powerful and bathed in insight and will lead humanity to destruction. I know Horus and the ashen war he brings. I know that even in victory, Horus will lead us not to triumph and power but to slavery and Chaos. I have seen it, and I have done what I can to see that it does not come to pass. There is another way, a way that lies neither in Horus' tyranny nor the Emperor's delusion. I am an echo of you, Ollanius – though I am pious to a different creed. I have died and am born to live again. You have never died, but lived to see all that you know become past. You see power as a sin. I see it as the only way to salvation.+

He almost smiled. Almost wept. In the back of his mind, all the line of Hecate's daughters screamed at him from their places of abandonment. Wronged, ignored, dangerous, brilliant.

+You smile at that?+

'No,' he said, and knew that only she would hear, and that in the stopped-clock moment nothing had moved. 'You just remind me of someone… of people I once knew.'

+The truth,+ she said, +is that the realm of the gods cannot be destroyed. The warp is and was and will be forever. We can either be its slaves or its rulers. This is the moment where we decide which it shall be.+

'And you are here because it's not going to come out that way, and you think that there is something I can do to… what? Tip the balance?'

She stepped forward then, raising a thin-fingered hand as though to touch Oll's face, but stopped. Oll felt a spider dance of sensation on his skin.

+I think you are a fulcrum – a small one, but on such things does the future balance. You want to take the next step on your path, and I want that, too. You and those with you carry the scales of fate.+ The woman nodded to herself and lowered her hand. +And I have come too far to see the future fail now.+

'I know the feeling,' he replied.

+There is no reason to do anything other than unite our purposes.+

'There is always a reason not to do anything,' said Oll. 'Most of the time it's a pretty good reason, too.'

+Not now, Ollanius, not with what is at stake. And besides, I have something you need, just as you are something I need.+

'And that is?'

+A way of reaching Horus.+

Oll paused, holding her blind gaze.

'You still have not told me your name.'

+You may call me Actae,+ she said.

'That is not your real name,' he replied.

Her smile shifted, and for a second it was something almost human, almost amused.

+I will tell you mine, if you tell me yours, Ollanius.+

Time and sound roared back into full flow.

From behind Oll, he heard the boom of gunfire and explosives.

Leetu was standing ten paces away, his armour chewed by explosions and impacts. A grey-black pall hid the view of the dome now. The trees were ablaze, howling as the sap inside them cooked. The gun in Leetu's hand was rock-steady, levelled at the woman called Actae. Zybes and the others were paces behind him.

'Shoot!' coughed John Grammaticus. 'Shoot her! Now!'

'Master Ollanius?' said Leetu.

Oll did not have time to reply.

Actae's towering companion strode from a spreading pall of black smoke, as though sliding into being on a breath of wind. The silken wrappings had torn and burned from it so that the armour beneath was visible: silver and pearlescent darkness, the hint of scales in the pattern on the lacquer.

'Shit!' shouted John, forcing the sound out. 'Shit no! No!'

'Greetings, John Grammaticus,' said the warrior, its voice a growl from a helm speaker grille. 'It has been a long time.'

Oll looked from the warrior to Actae.

'Do we have an understanding?' she asked.

'Oll,' gasped John. 'Oll, this is not… they are not…'

Oll was looking at Actae.

Choices, prices, consequences, just like there always were…

'Okay,' he said at last. 'We have an accord.' Then he looked up at the warrior who had come with Actae. 'And you?' he asked. 'Who and what are you?'

'I am Alpharius,' replied the warrior.

TWENTY-ONE

Mercury burns
My honour
Engine kill

'Direct wall fire!' shouted someone from across the parapet. The Titan fired. The missile loosed from its back in a streak of rocket flame. Then a blink, a ripple blur, and then suddenly nothing. Nasuba had an instant to inhale a breath.

The laser battery exploded. Fire blossomed out from inside the parapet. Rockcrete showered out in a blister of flame and superheated gas. A twenty-metre-wide gun dome blew upwards, tumbling on a geyser of debris, bodies falling from its shell. It struck the edge of the parapet and spun down the face of the wall, pulling chunks of masonry to crash into the lower tier of guns three hundred metres down.

'Warp missile!' Another shout, fighting against the din.

Warp missiles... rarest of technologies. Launched in the real world but flying through the warp, they bypassed shields and armour before blinking back into being and detonating. They were unreliable, prone to misfires, failure and inaccuracy, but the Death's Heads had waited until they were practically within touching distance of their targets. Nasuba realised that they must have been plotting and gathering targeting data since the wall batteries fired for the first time. As the guns had failed, Mortis had watched, and marked those positions that had come back online. They had calculated and refined the esoteric data needed to guide the warp missiles as true as possible. Now they were merely executing what they had planned since the advance began.

Cold realisation spread through Nasuba – they had fought and scrambled to get the guns firing as soon as possible and by doing that they had pinpointed which were still working, and which the enemy needed to target in this last phase.

'Shut the guns down!' shouted Nasuba. Down the wall, a plasma array went up like a ragged sun.

'Now!' Esha Ani Mohana's voice echoed through the static and the assault maniples crashed forwards. Armed with chain-fists, power claws and melta cannons, they also carried another lethal cargo. Assault groups of Imperial Fists rode in barb-tipped assault pods slung from the Titans' arms.

Luxor Invictoria fired its full weapon complement. The fire was phased, mass-detonation weapons and shield-killers first, then the raw fury of energy blasts sent a second later. The Titan braced. Pistons released and tensed as the engine absorbed the recoil. Coolant and steam vented. The Reavers in her maniple added their fire, and the screen of Titans and Knights vanished from mundane sight.

'Target shields down!'

'Target shields down!' The calls came across the data-link and vox, as the Invigilata engines fired.

'Engine strike!'

'Engine strike!'

The assault maniples crashed through the fire line, stride at maximum, reactors pouring power to shields and motive drives. One of the enemy came out of the cloud of debris. Its shields had gone, but it dragged a sphere of spiked plasteel by a chain, and it swung it with piston-driven force. The wrecking ball cannoned through the void shields of an Invigilata Reaver, and slammed into the engine's right arm. The Reaver staggered. The Mortis engine ripped back the spiked sphere. Pieces of armour tore away on its barbs. The Reaver tried to pivot, but the ball swung and crushed the metal of its skull. The Reaver juddered and began to fall as the Mortis engine turned, war-horns droning.

The rest of the assault group had not stopped or paused. They crashed into the first of the warp missile-armed engines. The first to strike was a Reaver once of the Warp Runners. Shields cycling to maximum, it opened its assault pod. Armoured doors ripped open. Warriors in yellow armour lit their jump packs and leapt into the air. The closest Mortis engine was a Warlord, its armour edged in rotting bronze, its red-ember eyes weeping skull-shaped kill marks. The Imperial Fists landed on the engine's back. Boots mag-locked to the engine's skin. It twisted, a great beast feeling the insects landing on its hide. The Imperial Fists knew their business; they had avoided the access hatch and the anti-personnel weapons mounted beneath the Titan's carapace. On its upper surface the risks were the venting of heat and energy from the engine's shoulder guns, that and standing on the back of an enemy Titan in the middle of a battle. The Space Marines did not linger. Their charges set, they triggered their jump packs. Two seconds later, fire ripped across the Mortis engine's back as its void shield projectors became slag.

'Switch fire, now,' said Esha Ani Mohana. *Luxor Invictoria*'s weapons blazed into the unprotected Titan before it could react. Laser fire bored into its chest through its head, and a great fist of heat punched into the sky.

'Engine kill,' said Esha Ani Mohana, coldly, already tracking the Imperial Fists as they landed on the back of another engine. More were loose in the air, lifting from assault pods like lethal wasps. She saw a burst of cannon fire catch one squad, and swat three warriors from the air in bursts of blood and chewed armour. The shields of another Mortis engine vanished, and Esha Ani Mohana was already firing.

'All engines, full speed, close order,' Abhani said, and felt *Bestia Est* already moving to respond. 'Target the screen of Knights and light engines – let's see if we can put a crack in their shields.'

Before her the block of Warmaster Titans grew, their shadows looming in the smoke. She could see its escorts now too, packs of Scout Titans, Knights and battle tanks riding and spreading in the shadow of the great engines. The unified void envelope covering them shimmered as it kissed the smoke-drowned air. She keyed the vox transmission and sent the latest auspex data shooting back to the wall and the engines fighting in its shadow. No confirmation data returned, no link, just the answering rumble of distant fire and explosions. The primary battleground flashed and roiled with light.

The air itself looked like it was burning, thought Abhani.

They could have run back to the main forces before the wall, could have… But they would not. She was Solaria now… The words of her mother rang in her ears. *Legion first* was their motto, and the nature of that legion was not to burn in glory; it was to hunt, to draw blood and create victory by weakening the enemy in mind, body and will until they could be brought down. No matter the quarry or the chances of survival – Solaria would hunt.

'First targets, entering into weapon range,' said her moderatus. They were coming over water-carved ground, *Bestia Est* bounding up scree drifts. The Knights of Vyronii were on her right, her kindred Warhounds trailing on her left.

'Hit, and then left flank fast,' said Abhani into the unit vox. *Bestia Est* vibrated with the speed of its quickening pace. Beyond the viewports, she could see the shape of a tracked war machine. It had not seen her yet. The auspex started to ping in her ear. She felt the shiver as the spirits of *Bestia Est*'s guns aligned with its targeters.

'Target lock,' said her moderatus.

'Kill,' she said.

The blast cored the war machine like a fruit. Fuel and ammunition exploded. Tracks and armour plates spun into the air. Abhani was already feeling the tug of the next target, and then the roar within as the guns spoke again and again.

The Warmasters were close enough now for Abhani to see the reaper emblems and jagged symbols on their banners. Some of the Mortis Titans began to turn in reaction. She felt the sting of low-grade void impacts.

'A little more…' she breathed to herself.

'I think they have noticed us,' came the dry voice of her moderatus. Above and beyond them, one of the Warmaster Titans rotated. She saw lightning flicker down the barrels of its guns.

'Turn left flank!' she called into the vox. *Bestia Est* jinked sideways. The Warmaster fired. The blast sliced through a block of its own escorts. Armour flashed to vapour, the ground beneath to glass. The blast wave clipped *Bestia Est*'s shields. It kept moving as the escort column began to fire at them.

'Vyronii,' she called over the vox to the Knights. 'Now!'

A burble of static answered her. Something in the column of enemy vehicles fired, something with an engine kill-grade weapon. *Bestia Est*'s shield vanished in a thunderclap.

'Diverting power to shields!' said the moderatus.

Abhani's eyes flicked to the auspex, expecting to see the fading death markers of the Vyronii Knights. But they were still there, still blinking green, their pace slowing.

'Vyronii, what are you doing?' shouted Abhani into the vox.

Acastia clenched her teeth as the neural feedback lashed through her. She saw the electro blast hit Abhani's Warhound. The machine that had fired upon it looked like a Knight, but of no pattern she had ever seen – six-legged and centaurine, its long head dragging a mace of chains, its right limb a lance of glowing discs. It reared, fuming coolant and lightning. Acastia had a shot, a near-clean shot, into the thing's flank, but she could not shoot, could not move, could do nothing but feel *Elatus* strain to be free. The neural tether to Caradoc was burning. Raw emotion blazed across it, translating into fire that sliced down her spine. Her fists were balling, muscles spasming.

Terror. The kind of terror that humans had carried since before they had been human. The terror of a soul looking into the eyes of death. Overwhelming, drowning all other thoughts and instincts. Perhaps it was something from the aether that flowed in the Mortis engines' wake, searching for cracks in the souls of those that would oppose them. Perhaps it was the promise of death in the red gaze of the god-engines as they looked down at the mortal world beneath. Perhaps it was that Caradoc had never had the courage to see that he was a scion of House Vyronii in name only; that his hunger for glory was just the cloak he wore to cover the fear that he was nothing, and all he had desired was ash already blowing from the pyre.

'Caradoc!' Acastia forced the word across the vox.

She felt the neural tether tighten, felt her hands slow *Elatus* to a standstill. Caradoc's own Knight was stationary, head twitching.

'Vyronii!' Princeps Abhani's voice was a shout of rage on the vox.

'Caradoc, you coward!' hissed Acastia through the pain flooding her skull.

'My liege…' She heard Pluton's voice then. Thin with the effort of speaking. 'Our, our duty…'

The enemy had noticed they were immobile. Guns turned towards the Vyronii Knights.

Acastia tried to move her hand, pushing against the force holding her. The pain spiked. Colours exploded behind her eyes. The neural control bit deeper.

This was not how Knights of Vyronii should die, she thought. To ride to war for a just cause was honourable. To die in a lost cause was true glory. Death was the nature of the warrior, perhaps the nature of all things, and from it all wonder and grace sprang like a rose threading a corpse for food.

But to die like this… bound by weakness and dishonour. Was there anything worse?

A blast of light sliced across Caradoc's Knight, clipped the edge of its ion shield and burned across its midriff.

Acastia felt the echo of Caradoc's shock, and then his Knight was turning away from the enemy.

Caradoc's panic broke across the link to Acastia – blind, pounding in waves as his Knight ran. Her brother was almost senseless, wild and blind with fear. Acastia could feel it, taste it in the bile-sting in her throat. Pluton's Knight, *Thaumas*, was still unmoving, pinned to its place behind its master like a loyal dog.

Acastia saw what was about to happen a second before it did: the positions of the two Knights, the blind fear driving her brother.

'My liege–' crackled Pluton's voice, sharp with alarm.

Caradoc's Knight hit Pluton's Armiger at full stride. The

smaller Knight cannoned back, hit the ground, legs kicking air. What Caradoc was seeing – a threat, or just an obstacle in his way – Acastia did not know, but she felt the spike of will and anger.

'No!' she shouted.

Caradoc's Knight fired. Explosive rounds chewed into *Thaumas* as the Armiger flailed. Armour plates deformed, tore. Oil and steam gushed out, and Caradoc was still firing as shredded red meat sprayed from the Knight's cored shell. The Castigator kept firing.

Acastia felt the hold on her limbs and nerves slip, and then break. She gasped, head spinning, half blind. She reined *Elatus* around and stepped into her brother's path. The head of the Castigator came up. The barrels of its guns were still spinning, its stride lengthening. Acastia latched her targeter on to her brother's head, heard the ping of a lock, saw the flash of a trigger rune. The larger Knight thundered towards her. Her finger paused on the firing stud.

'My liege,' she began. 'My brother…'

Caradoc's Knight was on her, its blade arm rising.

A burst of energy hit the Castigator. It reeled, twisted, white fire splashing across its ion field and burning into its torso.

Bestia Est sent another burst of fire into Caradoc's Knight.

'Now, Knight of Vyronii!' came Princeps Abhani's voice.

Acastia pressed the firing stud. The lance of heat stabbed from *Elatus* up into the unshielded head and shoulders of Caradoc's Knight. The beam burned through armour, cockpit and out of the top of the Knight's back. Acastia held the lance still for a second, breathing hard, feeling the death echo building across the neural link. Then she sliced the beam down through the Castigator's torso and reactor. She had an instant to wrench the helm and neural connection from her skull before her brother's Knight vanished in white flame.

A world of ringing pain. Echoing from birth to present. She could taste oil and smell a memory of the waters of the world that had borne her. Images of faces fell past her eyes, proud and noble and cruel and broken.

'Ride!' Abhani's voice, suddenly loud. Warning lights were blaring inside *Elatus*' cockpit. Enemy weapon-lock warnings. Damage alarms. Neural link failure. She swung *Elatus*' ion shield around in time to meet a spray of high-calibre rounds, and kicked the Knight forwards towards where *Bestia Est* and her kin were curving back out from the column of enemy machines.

What had she done? The image of her brother's Knight coming apart lingered in her eyes.

I can never go back, she thought, and then almost laughed despite herself. Would there be anything to go back to?

'My thanks, princeps of Solaria,' she breathed.

'My honour,' came the reply, then a pause. 'Cog of truth… they are firing.'

Light blinked across Acastia's eyes from *Elatus*' screens. The thunder roll came seconds later, shaking the skin of the Knight. Light and fire streaked from the Warmaster's shoulders. Flashes lit the underside of the clouds. Towards the wall, new fires lit as the phalanx of engines advanced.

<Close with me.> Cydon's will flashed across the incandescence.

<Compliance.> Tetracauron's reply flashed out.

<Compliance.> Arthusa's reply a second later, a blink of light as her engine pivoted and fired a stuttered stream of las energy.

Tetracauron's thoughts were whirling. Circles of target runes bubbled across his sight. There were engines in front of him – black shapes blurring with static. He was barely conscious of *Reginae Furorem*'s fire. Targets and power cycles and engine strikes flowed from and through him, the thought to send a blast merging with the sensation of plasma pouring from the reactor to fill the cannon's hunger. Xeta-Beta-1's link with the engine's reactor was a dance of code as she spun power into shields, motion, sensors and weapons, balancing the hunger of each component. It was frantic, almost overwhelming. He felt his grip on his own thoughts breaking, felt the pulse of wills and systems that were his and not his.

He could feel the promise of the machine, of true incarnation. It was pulling into the distance, he realised, not getting closer. The world of fire and destruction slid away from him as he sank, the light of war like the flash of lightning seen through the surface of an ocean as he descended into its heart. Burning… always burning…

Will I die? he wondered, the thought sudden in his mind, and he was not sure if it was his or Divisia's or Cartho's or the engine itself. A mechanism turning over and over in the blaze of forge fire, a turning wheel that raised you high before plunging you down into ashes, again and again.

He could see the lines of the enemy before them. Ragged but advancing with slow, remorseless tread. He could sense Cydon and his First Maniple closing from behind him. The hands of Ignatum were pulling in as Mortis pressed towards the wall. Before them, walking out beyond the lines, were the Psi-Titans wading into the tide alone. The blockhouses of the Achilus Line, just twenty kilometres from the wall, were firing now, hitting the closing engines with heavy bolter fire, lascannon blasts and cannon shells. There was no stillness any more except here beneath the ocean of fire.

<Mass engine formation incoming.>

Data prorated through him as the signal reached and spread through the noosphere. It had come from Solaria scouts reaving into the flanks of the enemy. He saw the shadow of the approaching engines then, dark ghosts in the snow of auspex distortion.

<We are with you.> Cydon's voice, a furnace growl. <Synchronise void shields and reactor cycles. We are Ignatum, we go only forwards.>

The stuttered burning of dozens of machines pulsing to the same heartbeat.

Around and behind him the Titans of Princeps Maximus Cydon's maniple walked into place, and he felt the volcano heat of *Imperious Prima*'s spirit wash into his own.

<Full engagement,> willed Cydon. <We drive them back.>

Tetracauron stepped forwards, his will no longer just his own but also the will of the machine. *Reginae Furorem*'s foot splashed through the slurry of a run-off river. A blast of energy hit the ground just in front of it and blew the water and mud to steam.

There was a flicker in the distance, and a bloom of ghost light from where the figure of the Psi-Titan *Orientalis-Echion* was holding ground.

<Wall gun fire effectiveness falling.> Cartho.

<The Great Mother's engines are engaging the engines firing on the walls.> Arthusa, her voice meshing into the vox, taut with the war fire of her own engine.

<The damage is done,> came Cydon's voice. <The enemy will begin orbital fire. We are the wall now, my kin.>

<Compensate our shield cycles,> willed Tetracauron.

As if in response, the heavens lit. Beams of light stabbed down from the cloud layer. Shells exploded across the ground and slammed into void shields. Tetracauron felt layers of skin ripped from the shared envelope of energy. The ground heaved. Earth blasted into the air. Power flowed to the shield blisters and they relit. The heat was draining from weapons. *Imperious Prima* and the rest of the battle group were loosing missiles and munitions at the growing shadow of threat returns.

<Threat data received from Solaria scout forces.> He felt the

message unfold an instant before the data pack unfolded. He stared at it for a nanosecond that felt like an eternity.

<They have loosed the Warmasters...> sent Arthusa, echoing the thoughts of all of the battle group.

Tetracauron looked into the distance as the block of shadows in the incandescence shivered into form. Towering engines advancing in line and rank, stretching in a block almost three kilometres across and deep. They began to fire.

Tetracauron felt the impacts. A cluster missile struck the shields directly ahead of him. They burst like soap bubbles in a gale. The orbital fire was stabbing down, a deluge dancing on the upper void envelope.

The ground between them and the enemy was glittering as a surge tide of infantry, machines, and things that lumbered or buzzed or oozed flooded towards them. The noise of static and failed code rose in the incandescence, rolling like the muffled tolling of a bell.

<Forward, cycle power to fire,> came Cydon's will, and the Ignatum battle group roared. Volleys of white light streaked into the oncoming enemy. It struck their void shield envelope in a drum roll of flashes. Power flicked between weapons and shields across the battle group, spinning from one to another in perfect time across dozens of engines. Fire ploughed through the tide of infantry. Warp-born flesh and tainted iron burst into ash. The weapons spoke without cease, the shields holding against the bombardment from in front and above. They were advancing, and in his half-machine soul Tetracauron felt a raw rush of joy. This was their way, and now would be no different. They could not break the shield envelope around the Mortis advance, so they were closing until they were within that envelope and where the fire from the traitors' ships would have to cease.

<The Great Mother's new legion is pulling onto our flanks,>

sent Cydon. <This is the crucible, my kin. This is where we live. This is where we speak.>

Ahead of him Tetracauron saw *Orientalis-Echion* begin to march backwards. Its skin glowed with witch energies. Darkness breathed from it, scything at a pair of rust-crusted engines marching in front of the block of Warmasters.

Tetracauron felt the volleys striking the void shields ebb. The fire from the first rank of Warmasters stuttered. He felt the head of *Reginae Furorem* rise, twitching up, as something within its spirit sensed a shift. A gap opened in the line of advancing Mortis engines.

Dies Irae walked from the lines. Its court of abominations came with it. The towering engine sounded its war-horns. The things of false flesh moving across ground and air raised horned and rotting heads.

Orientalis-Echion paused in its retreat, brought its weapon up.

The front rank of Warmasters fired at it. Its shields vanished. Beams of energy and a torrent of shells slammed into its body. Armour broke, melted, reformed as the Psi-Titan tried to repair and heal even as fresh wounds were burned into it.

'Prefect Cadamia!' called Tetracauron over the vox. 'Pull back and merge with our shie–'

The Psi-Titan exploded. A shrieking sphere of cold light expanded out and collapsed back, folding in to become a singularity of utter blackness. Tetracauron felt blood dripping from his mouth.

Dies Irae sounded its war-horns again and began to stride forwards. The tide of monsters and machines at its feet surged towards the Ignatum war machines. A volley from the Warmaster Titans struck their merged shield envelope. Tetracauron shivered as layer upon layer of fields blew out. They were dancing on the edge of the mysteries of reactor and power flow now, balanced between disaster and invulnerability. Other

Legios would have begun to fail, would have lost engines, would be dying. Ignatum were not another Legio, though, and they would go forwards.

Warhounds paced ahead and fire washed the ground. Things made of fat and chewed bone writhed, became ash, but the rest came on.

<Those things will be in the shield envelope within twenty seconds,> sent Cartho. <Twenty strides to close-engine engagement.>

The deluge from the heavens was still falling, ripping away void shields almost faster than they reformed.

<They will taste ashes.> Cydon's will filled the incandescence.

Tetracauron felt the rush of growing power as commands propagated through the maniples, felt the heat growing in his hands, saw the fire order unfold in his eyes. Arthusa and all the others would be experiencing the same moment, each locked by instinct into a pattern that was the fury of the machine. For an instant the battle formation went silent as dozens of reactors drew breath.

Imperious Prima's main guns fired. A second later, fire ripped from *Reginae Furorem*, and from *Helios* and the rest. The volley passed from one Titan to another so that it drilled into *Dies Irae* and the Mortis engines. Tetracauron saw the enemy vanish in detonations an instant before one of the daemon Titans collapsed, shields ripped from it, limbs torn to ichor-slick tatters. Its death scream poured static across Tetracauron's sight.

<They burn now!> growled Cydon, and the sending became a wave through the incandescence, spreading like a shout that could rise up to the sky and pull the sun from its setting. Part of the Warmaster formation was hidden by the detonations, but they were still coming. Tetracauron was half blind with static. Another pulse of will from the princeps maximus. <We take them at the edge of the blade.>

Tetracauron felt the power flare in his hand as *Reginae Furorem*'s fist ignited with lightning.

Dies Irae came out of the cloud of static and fire. Above them. In front of them. Congealing into sight. Impossible. Abominable.

Tetracauron felt the impulse to shout, but it was too late. Its eyes were holes drawing light into them, extinguishing them, pulling all that it saw down into an abyss where there was only cold, dark and the slow count of atoms decaying.

He saw the fire already gathered in the mouth of the gun.

His hand and the fist of his engine rose.

He saw the flick of lightning on the corroded charge coils as it spoke.

He felt the fire touch him, consume him, for the last time, in a moment that stretched for a brief eternity and then was no more.

Enemy distance to wall: 7 kilometres.

TWENTY-TWO

Cold beacon
A little further
Freedom

Marmax South

On… on… one step and then another. On, on… Shiban could not feel the ground beneath his feet. The world was grey at the edge of his eyes. How long had he been walking? Days and nights and hours all gone now. Just him and the way ahead, the way across the land.

He stopped, shook. The man, Cole, was quiet; he had been quiet for a long time. The child, too.

He wondered if he had lost direction. He wondered if the instincts trained and chained within him were failing. He wondered if he had not already fallen, and was now a soul lost in the un-land, neither of the earth nor of the sky. He wondered what would happen. He wondered if any would remember those that he had known and walked and fought beside. He wondered where the next step would take him.

'You have come so far,' said Yesugei in a voice that might

have been the cry of a hawk on a tongue of wind. 'Will you not go a little further?'

'I thought…' said Shiban. 'I thought you had left me.'

The land was quiet, dulled. Grey. Unending.

'We ride with you until the end, brother,' said Torghun from the edge of his sight.

'To the end…' he said to the air. 'Then it is over.'

'Hah!' Yesugei's laugh was a bark of distant gunfire. 'Not yet, Shiban. Not yet!'

His head came up. He fixed his grip on the limp form of the human, bared his teeth at the distance and took a step.

'On,' he snarled. 'On! No backward step. No. Backward. Step. You hear me, Cole! We will not end here. You hear me. I am Shiban, Son of Lightning, Brother of the Storm – I will take no backward step… No. Backward. Step.'

Only forwards.

Only towards the horizon.

'Target,' called Steena, from down the line. Katsuhiro looked up. The sun was setting. Somewhere beyond the fog and cloud, the day was sliding down the last hours into night. The light was bruising to blue. The heat still suffocating, but dark and soft rather than strangling. He had been half asleep, drifting on the line between dreams and waking. He had not meant to, now he never meant to, but the fatigue had pulled him down into the clammy embrace of the land, which was not rest and was not peace. The quiet had done it. There had been attacks – tides of things coming from the fog, staggering, pressing forwards, cut down till they littered the ground with a fresh layer of food for the flies. But there had not been an assault, not a true one. It did not feel like respite. It felt like an inhalation, like the moment before something yet to come.

'Wait,' called Katsuhiro. There was a shape in the fog, moving with a laboured gait, huge and armoured. Someone fired, and the las-bolt skimmed off a rise of corpses and sent a thick cloud of flies to blur the view. 'Hold fire!' he shouted. The figure was a Space Marine, but even from the blurred silhouette he could tell it was alone. Alone and limping, not striding, not lumbering and rolling in the middle of a tide. Alone, its gait awkward. He thought of Baeron and of the other Blood Angels scattered along Marmax. 'Hold,' he said again, but quieter.

'What is it?' asked Steena, and he could hear terror in her voice. Others were looking at him. They were beyond ready to run or shoot.

'I think...' he said. 'I think it's one of ours.'

Shiban could hear his own breathing now, heavy, gasping, muscles fighting to pull air into failing lungs. He could taste metal.

The fog was drawing close. The land grey.

Human, so human, unravelling...

The weight of the man in his arms and the child still in Cole's bloody grasp. Such a weight. Greater than the weight of guns and swords and command.

One more step. One more.

'Now you see,' said Yesugei. 'We are made to be greater than the humanity we serve. The weight of the blade is nothing to us. To ride and fight and bleed for days is nothing to us. Nothing to us... We are made higher and so we lose that part that a child and an old man and a father looking into his child's eyes knows – that the next step is not a promise. That to live is to fight. We forget that. We forget that life is weakness in the face of eternity. To take the next step only matters if you must fight for it, for the last fraction of ourselves. And taking it you see yourself, true and clear – not a warrior, not a hero, not a story of glory and wonder... Just a lightning

flash, a descent from Heaven to Earth, a step taken, bright
and fleeting and then gone.'

'I understand,' he gasped. 'I understand…'

There was someone there.

People, weapons, a ragged line of chewed rockcrete. Ten
steps, a hundred, ten thousand… too many. Just one more.

'Who are you?' came the voice of the birds in the sky above.

His answer was another step and another, onward towards
the walls, towards no rest but just the moment that would
come.

He was at the lines. There were people, humans, shouts,
calls, eyes and guns turned to him. He stepped over the parapet, Cole and the infant clutched close. He looked around, felt
the instinct to keep moving even as he stopped.

Katsuhiro looked up at the Space Marine. Filth and blood
streaked the warrior's armour but it was whole, white beneath
the grime – a son of the Khan, a warrior of the White Scars.
There was a bundle, half draped over his shoulder, half carried
by his arms. The warrior's head was bare, the colour of the skin
drained to grey, hair hanging in a matted mass from above
features that were set. The pupils were pinpricks of pain fixed
on the distance. The warrior was breathing hard. There were
red flecks on his lips.

'Who are you?' asked Katsuhiro.

The warrior did not answer. Katsuhiro wondered if he was
even aware of him.

Katsuhiro looked at the bundle the warrior carried. Not a
bundle, a man wrapped in a greatcoat. The fabric was stiff
with dry blood. Slowly he put out a hand, his eyes steady on
the warrior's face, but the giant made no move to stop the
gesture. Katsuhiro peeled back a fold of the greatcoat. The
man within hung limp and unmoving. There was a wound

in his chest and the White Scar had his fingers clamped into it. That must have stemmed the bleeding, but a lot of blood had flowed. A life's worth.

'Is this…' said the warrior, swaying for a moment as he spoke. 'Is this the Inner Palace?'

'This is Marmax South,' said Katsuhiro. 'The Ultimate Wall is about a kilometre back there.' He began to point, then stopped. The warrior was looking up, shaking his head as though at a voice only he could hear.

'And this…' said the warrior. 'This line holds?'

The image of Baeron, lying in the remains of his armour, bright with blood – a red echo to the white-armoured warrior who had walked from the wasteland.

'It holds,' said Katsuhiro. The warrior did not move for a second, and then raised his head; for a moment the eyes closed. In the folds of the dead soldier's greatcoat, a child squirmed, and then to Katsuhiro's surprise let out a cry that carried clearer than a shout or a gunshot in the still air. He stared, open-mouthed. 'Where have you come from, lord?'

'I must…' said the warrior, his gaze distant. 'There are more steps to take.' Katsuhiro was not certain who the words were for. 'My brothers still fight and wait for me to join them.'

'Do you…' began Katsuhiro, then hesitated as the warrior lowered his gaze to him. He looked at the dead soldier. 'What was his name?'

'Cole,' said the warrior. 'Cole, second lieutenant, Massian Fifth.'

'Do you wish us to take him?'

'No. He comes with me,' growled the warrior, then looked back at the dead soldier. 'I will bear him a little further.'

'The child?' The warrior looked at the infant. Its face was streaked with the blood of the dead man, but its eyes were open, blinking to focus. Katsuhiro shook his head. 'How did it survive?' he asked.

'Because something must,' said the warrior.

Then the warrior shifted, inhaled and took a step towards where the walls of the Inner Palace waited. Katsuhiro found that he was watching the warrior, eyes and breath held still.

A shout rose from the firing step, one and then another and another, cheers not of joy but of defiance, of exhaustion, of hopelessness that had just witnessed the impossible – a warrior walking from the land of death with life in its hands. The warrior did not look around but kept moving, will and pain screaming in silence from every step.

'Who are you?' called Katsuhiro again, realising that he needed to know.

The warrior paused, half turned his head to look back. A flash in the eyes. A blink, and then a look that met Katsuhiro's gaze and held it for a long moment.

'I am Shiban Khan.'

The Blackstone, Sanctum Imperialis Palatine

Basilio Fo looked up. The cell was silent again. He waited, utterly still, senses open, mind blank. Complete stillness was one of the highest skills a being could possess and one that few valued as highly as they should. Not even the one that now called Himself Emperor, really. Too much in a hurry, too focused, too committed to a single path without showing flexibility for the fact that the universe simply did not care and would burn what you had raised up. Not Basilio Fo though; to him stillness was as close to a sacred property as he could think of. It did not require much either, just for him to stop doing all the things that humans found most difficult to stop doing: filtering the world through half-baked dreams, moving, needing, being anything else other than a cluster of matter that happened to be a person at the point of time that was now.

Shut all that down and just wait for the next second to arrive. Patience, that is what stillness really was, the physical expression of patience, and to Fo there was no higher virtue. Patience was the only true strategy to existence, and one that he had built and rebuilt himself around – mind, body and action. Wait, be still, and observe; it had served him well for thousands of years.

The song did not return. The crystalline stone walls had been singing for days and nights, but for a moment he thought he had detected a new pitch, like a fresh voice entering into the chorus. Fo looked back down at the section of wall he had been working on. A long sliver of the black crystal was almost free of the wall. Another seven lay wrapped in rags and placed in the small sling bag he had made from his bedding. Getting the first piece free had been the biggest challenge – the stuff was near diamond hard, and it had taken several weeks of careful experimentation to get a small piece loose. Once he had done that, he had established that, as he had suspected, the stone could be used to cut more of its kind from the walls. If you were careful. If you were patient.

The project for Amon and the Custodians had been useful – a good way of giving him more time, of allowing him more ways of arranging things. Thank all that was true that they had bitten when he had dangled the possibility of a weapon that could end their current problems. A primarch and Legion killer, a means to end the war and those that waged it – too much for the Custodian not to hold in his hands. He had protested that he needed resources to test it, to perfect it, but of course he did not. Like all his art, he could see it in his mind as real as if the molecules and essential substances hung before his eyes, spinning as they combined and transformed. They had not known that, though; how could they? Neither did they know that he could have written out perfect formulae for the substance's creation in a day. The last set of formulations lay on the screen of the dataslate beside him, discarded for now. He had a feeling that the currency of that secret was soon going to be devalued, and besides its promise had already bought him time, and that was all that counted.

The splinter of wall came free. He held it in his hand for a moment. It was heavy this time, heavy and cold, like a shard of black ice. That was one of the many properties about it that was strange: sometimes it was cold or so hot that it was difficult to hold. Sometimes it danced with inner light. The piece in his fingers was currently dark, so dark that it seemed a slice of night. Remarkable. He had seen many things in his life, things greater and more terrible than the sanity or dreams of most humans could encompass, so much that little moved him to horror or rapture. This material, though… it was extraordinary. A hyper-solid, utterly real, and also resonating in the aetheric sub-phase of the universe. A reality polarised substance. What could such a substance do? The possibilities lit a spark in the depths of his mind.

If they had known, would they have put him in a prison of it? He doubted it, but that was another thing that most people did not understand – the power of chance.

He heard the door click shut behind him, and froze. The guard was not supposed to be coming yet, and he doubted that the limping fool would have been able to enter so quietly. That put the list of people who were standing behind him down to a few. The boetharch, maybe? Amon? Likely. A faceless killer sent by an unseen hand? Just as possible. Carefully he placed the shard of crystal in a rag and wrapped it up.

'I take it that I made a mistake somewhere along the way,' he said aloud. 'Some small error in my behaviour perhaps. Or is this simply the inevitable end come a little earlier?'

He let out a breath. His mind riffled through his contingencies. As ever, the crucial factor was time, a little more time.

'You do realise that if I end here,' he said, carefully, still not turning around, 'the work I have been doing shall not be finished.' He extended a finger towards the dataslate. 'It is nearly complete, an end to the war, a new start, a terminus to the folly that has come before.'

'I am not interested in your monster killer,' said Andromeda-17. Fo turned, unable to keep a twitch of surprise from his face. The Selenar gene-witch stood with her back to the sealed door, a laspistol in her hand. He gave a small smile.

'I should have known,' he said, folding the rags over the crystal shard. 'Your gene-hate is strong. Too strong to let me live. I am one of the few creatures in existence who understands that you have very little choice over what you are doing. So much of what the herd of sentient species think is their will is spliced into them from before they were born. The curse of the past visited on the living. People think they control themselves, but they don't. The strings are pulled by instincts and drives bred into creatures that could barely ooze across a rock.' He finished wrapping the crystal and put it carefully into the small sack. 'In your case the imperative to kill me is just a more deliberate expression of the same things that drive others to eat or breed. It is purer even, a deliberate act by your forebears so that you would have no choice if you ever encountered the gene-daemon but to kill me.'

He smiled. The smallest splinter of stone was still in his hand, curled in fingers and palm. Just two steps closer…

Andromeda-17 tilted her head and nodded at the sack on the bed. 'All packed?' she said.

He nodded, and used the gesture to shuffle closer.

'I was intending to be gone shortly,' he said.

'The guard. Warden Vaskale,' said Andromeda, 'you have been working on him for a while, haven't you?'

'Just a little memetic-implantation through linguistic and

voice tonal suggestion. Nothing too impressive. It took a while to build up.'

'To the point where he was going to let you out on command.'

Fo shrugged, and shifted. He was just one step away from being able to strike.

'Essentially, yes.'

'So all the conversations with Keeler and whatever devilry you have been peddling to the Custodians was to give you time to make him yours?'

'More or less.'

'Not the best plan,' said Andromeda-17.

'Oh?' Another subtle shift of weight, just half a step now. 'Do you not think so?'

'No, not really. You see, Warden Vaskale can't be controlled by you…' Fo slid forwards, tensed, the shard ready like a sting in his hand. 'Because he is controlled by me.'

Fo felt the impulse that would have stabbed the shard into Andromeda-17's neck falter. She stepped back, the gun level at him. 'And that little spike of stone can stay where it is.'

He laughed.

'How long? How long has that idiot guard been yours?'

'A while.'

'And I am guessing he is not as much of an idiot as he seems.'

'Far from it.'

Fo let out a slow breath.

'Very clever, very clever indeed. If only your forebears had been so sharp, they might not have suffered so much. What is it that your cult believed they were personifying in your gene-spiral?'

'You want to guess, so guess.'

'Aepate,' he nodded. 'Sister of Dolos, the archetype of guile.' A small smile on his face. 'You knew I was here before you came with the boetharch and Sindermann, didn't you? No need to answer. I know I am right. You knew that I would be here. You knew that Keeler would be in this cell when you arrived. You simulated the gene-murder instinct to cover any suspicion, to put you out of the consideration of dear Amon. You knew that I was going to leave tonight, before this tragic farce of false gods reaches its conclusion.' He smiled again, and saw the flash of his own teeth in the darkness of her eyes. 'I wonder, what else have you watched and set into motion? Your friends, Mauer and Sindermann, and the fascinating Keeler, they won't have got away cleanly, will they? Not as planned at least, maybe some of them in a state of being not alive at all, yes? Set them up, get them out, then change the game. I have a terrible suspicion why you might have done that, but I think I would like to hear it from you.'

'Outside context,' she said. 'I exist to solve problems, big problems, and everyone is looking for simple solutions to the wrong problem. Weapons to end the war. Tactics to win. But that's not the real problem.'

'Survival,' said Fo.

She nodded.

'Survival on the absolute scale – not winning, not keeping things the way they were, not being right, but there just being someone left at all. That is all that I serve. You might say it is bred into me, but I like to think that it is the only choice left to anyone with more than an ounce of wit.'

'Almost altruistic,' he said. 'And in that light, what is a little betrayal and deceit?'

She shook her head. 'The straight-line plans will fail – all plans will fail. The only way a solution emerges is through random chance. I have not stopped anything. I have put factors into play that cannot be predicted. From that, strength and survival might emerge. The more factors there are in play, the more threat, the less clean patterns and plans, the more chance we have… Perhaps Keeler will prove a saint or a martyr or a catalyst for something else. Perhaps none of it will mean anything, and the key to survival is at the other end of the world, unknown by me or you, or even the Emperor. None of that matters, all that matters is changing the path we are on.'

'Evolution rather than design,' said Fo. 'Risky. But a work of art. You have my admiration, daughter of the Selenar.'

'I want nothing of your admiration,' she said.

'And that being the case, the question that is just begging to be asked is why are you here?'

Andromeda gave a snort of mirthless breath.

'To set you free, Basilio Fo,' she said, and opened the cell door behind her. 'To set you free.'

Hatay-Antakya Hive, East Phoenicium Wastes

They fell through water. Down into the whirlpool. Spinning. Turning. Drowning. Oll snatched breath as he tumbled through whirls of foam and spray.

Down… down… always down… Caught by Charybdis to escape Scylla.

That had been the way out, into the vortex pool at the centre of the dome as the Emperor's Children came to find the damage done to their paradise. The plants growing in the pool had reached for Oll and he had dived in. Red roots had tried to circle his limbs. As he had hit the surface he had seen beneath the huge lily pads and flowers that floated in the current. Bodies hung in the water, their fingers and toes extended into knots of root, their skulls open like seed pods from which the flowers and leaves spread up and out. Then the current of the whirlpool had caught him and spun the sight away. The rest had dived in with him, but he could not see them as he plunged down and down.

'*Fear death by water…*' a memory of an old oracle said. Turning a card. He had laughed.

'*Oh, you who turn the wheel…*'

'*Where are we sailing?*'

'*Beyond the edge of the world…*'

'*Keep walking and don't look back…*'

Theseus, a dozen dead monsters at his feet. Giants that just wanted to sleep, just wanted the world to fit, just wanted to be left alone.

'*We have a duty.*'

'*A duty to do what? Interfere?*'

'*To be involved, to be what we are.*'

'*In which case I will go and plant crops.*'

'*You are a soldier, not a farmer, my friend. What do soldiers do but change the world by blood and feat of arms?*'

'*I will not do that.*'

'*The wheel turns. In the end we all return to what we are and to where we began.*'

A hand grabbed him and hoisted him up into the air.

He gasped, choked. He was still drowning.

Something hit him hard on the back, twice, very precisely. His breath stopped, then he gave a great spasm. He gasped again and felt the air fill his lungs. The sound of rushing water filled his ears. He tried to stand.

'Be still, Master Ollanius,' came Leetu's voice. Oll rolled over, feeling his body heave and the colour return to sight. They were on a metal ledge beside a channel of churning water. Blue-white light from chem-illuminators reflected from the water surface and sent glow patterns dancing across the ceiling and walls. Cyan corrosion clotted their rivets and seams. Fronds of pale vegetation hung from the roof, and the noise of the water vibrated through his fingers as he pushed himself up. The others were there, some already standing: Leetu; the warrior who named himself Alpharius; Katt; the woman Actae. Graft was twitching, head shaking as its metal limbs retracted and extended. Krank was on the floor, looking closer to dead than ever. Zybes was beside him. After a moment Krank stirred, shivered and began to try and get up. Zybes hooked his arm under the man's shoulder and helped him. Rane was…

Not there. Oll felt his thoughts lurch, like he had put his foot down on a step only to find it absent.

Leetu was beside the channel, watching the froth and spray. Then, faster than an eye-blink, his arm darted out, and he was pulling a spluttering John Grammaticus onto the walkway. The psyker still looked ill and lay gasping and choking for several moments.

'I suppose we should be grateful that there was a way out,' he said at last. 'But that is not something I will be agreeing to do again.'

'It only gets harder from here,' said Oll, 'remember.'

The warrior called Alpharius loomed next to them, suddenly closer in a way something that large should not have been able to manage. He felt something in the back of his head scream at him to run, the base instinct that sent animals fleeing from the predator.

'I have breached the hatch. From there a passage runs up to the surface outside the hive.'

'How convenient,' muttered John.

The warrior rotated its helmeted head, its gaze steady on the psyker.

'You live,' it said. 'I would reflect on that.'

John shook his head and began pulling himself up, then stopped, limbs trembling. Leetu hoisted John up and set him on his feet.

'Don't tell me you trust… *it*?' said John to Leetu, nodding at Alpharius.

'I neither trust nor doubt, John Grammaticus. That is not the part I was given to play. I follow. I help. I protect.'

'The consolations of a simple life.'

'Okay, let's move,' said Oll, looking around. He still had his gun. It would need stripping down and cleaning before it would fire again, but he hefted it and moved to follow the warrior called Alpharius, both actions as clear a statement as he could give.

They followed. He did not look back to check, but he knew.

The tunnel was low and reeked of stagnant air. No one spoke; there was no room to turn, just to shuffle forwards through the dark. On and on, until there was a clang of shearing metal and a breath of hot wind. Oll felt his way forward until he touched the rungs of a ladder and looked up to see the glow of stars in a circle above. He climbed.

Night had fallen outside, but the air was still warm, the heat yet to bleed out into the cold of the desert night. Ragged holes in the clouds let the gleam of the stars through. Oll's eyes caught the bright lights amongst the familiar constellations – warships turning through the dark heavens. In the distance the spike of Hatay-Antakya Hive rose, glimmering with golden light, dancing in the eye.

Oll turned away from it. For a second it had looked like a tower, frozen beneath the fall of a lightning bolt.

'What is the plan for this unholy convergence of purpose?' asked John Grammaticus as he emerged from the hatch. Oll looked at him and then at the others.

The woman Actae was standing slightly apart with the warrior called Alpharius, her head raised as though in conversation, though both were silent. As Oll watched, she placed her hand on the warrior's chest and nodded before turning to Oll and John.

'Look,' began John, 'if this is a way of the dead husk of the Cabal getting back in the game, then–'

'Those you call the Cabal are dead, and their plan with it,' said Actae.

'Which brings us back to here and now, and what next,' said John, turning to look at Oll, the starlight and the glow of the distant hive catching in his eyes. 'What is your plan, Oll?'

'Same as it was before, get to where we need to be,' he said. He could feel all of the others listening. Even Graft had come close as though wanting to hear. 'We came for you because you are our guide, John, and that still stands.'

'And I thought it was because you cared,' said John, and jerked his head at Actae. 'Recent events show that I am not as informed as I thought – a guide whose map is out of date is not much use.' John gave Oll a long look.

Oll shook his head.

'I am not big picture, John, remember. Not my strong suit.'

'What about *her* big picture?' John flicked a thumb at Actae. 'She is a grade A supernova of a psyker, but then so am I, and I know that you two had a chat in between the seconds up there in the dome. What did she offer, Oll?'

'An alliance to do what is needed.'

'Really, and what version of *what-is-needed* is that?'

Oll shrugged.

'Journeys like this, John, you can't know the end. Trust me.'

'Trust you? You are asking me to come with you on an unknown path, while not knowing the end, and with dubious allies and options, and to do this all on trust… Now isn't that a turnaround.' John bit his lip, half turned away, and shook his head. 'You don't need a guide. It's bloody obvious where we need to be.' He raised his hand and pointed east towards where the Palace waited, far beyond the horizon. 'But that's a hell of a walk, and time has yet to be our friend.'

'There is time still,' said Actae. They turned to look at her. She had shed the bones that had hung from her chin and the talons on her fingers. The veil had gone too, leaving her face and blind eyes bare. She held up a hand, beckoning. Oll hesitated for a second and then followed her over a rise in the ground. The others followed him.

A lighter lay in a shallow bowl between slopes of scree and dust. A scrim-net covered it, blending its blunt form with the wasteland.

'Ready and waiting.' John gave a snort of laughter, lip curling at Actae. 'You two must have been very sure we would come with you.'

'Contingency is a weapon of war, John Grammaticus,' said the warrior called Alpharius.

'So we have a way of getting away,' said Zybes. 'Anyone actually know how to fly it?'

'I can,' said John. 'Got some uses still, I guess.' He trudged over to the lighter, released the side hatch to the cockpit and swung himself up. Console controls lit under his fingers. 'Are you going to get in? I don't want to hang around. It's going to be a hell of a flight, and I don't want to have an attack of changing my mind before we are past the point of no return.'

'I think we passed that a while ago,' said Katt.

John laughed. The lighter's engines lit. A low whine of building power filled the air.

Oll held up a hand and looked around at those that remained of the few he had brought from Calth. Zybes, Katt, Krank and Graft looked back.

'You know what I'm going to say, but I'm going to anyway – you should go. All of you, go south maybe. Fighting might be lighter there, wait it out. I'll come find you later, when this is done.'

They all looked at him, silent, unmoving.

'I go with you, Trooper Persson,' said Graft eventually. The others nodded.

'You know what that means?' he said.

'We know,' said Zybes flatly.

'It's okay,' said Katt.

Oll looked at them all, then nodded.

'Okay,' he said, and turned towards the lighter. 'Okay...' he repeated quietly to himself.

John was pulling the cockpit hatch closed. Zybes and Katt were peeling back the scrim-net. Actae was standing beside the descending rear ramp. The warrior called Alpharius had already vanished inside. Oll moved towards it, slinging his gun. He would clean it in flight, an old soldier habit. He patted the knife in its sheath at his waist. He still had–

Shuffle-tap...

He turned at the sounds of the footsteps on stone. Behind him. Getting closer.

Shuffle-tap...

He looked up, hand on the knife. The light from the distant hive glowed behind the ridge of the bowl.

His eyes moved across the shadows and skyline.

'Time to go,' called Zybes from the lighter's hatch.

Oll blinked, then nodded, turned and ran to the open ramp. The engine noise rose in pitch as the lighter lifted into the air.

Oll did not look back. For a second, he had been sure that something was just behind him, breathing on the back of his neck.

The Hollow Mountain

'Are any of them sane enough to serve?' asked Corswain.

Tragan looked at Vassago. The Calibanite Librarian said nothing. Tragan looked back at Corswain. 'Some perhaps, not enough, and the... equipment.' Tragan nodded up at the choral tiers that lined the inside of the sphere chamber.

Cradles and banks of seats hung from twisted brackets. Drops of gut fluid and still-liquid blood dripped slowly onto the levels below. Most of the dead had been cleared. Those that were not dead had been granted that peace. A few had been so merged with the fabric of the chamber that the only way of ending them was by flamer and grenade. The air reeked of cooked flesh and sulphur. The presence of the Emperor's Children and the warp creatures they had conjured lingered at the edge of every sense – a jagged razor on the nerves and taste on the tongue. They had cleared them from the upper levels and most of the key areas of the mountain's interior. Some had slid down into the dark of the deepest reaches and vanished, but the Hollow Mountain was now the First Legion's. Relighting its beacon was another matter. The mountain was a device of occult wonder that had not just been occupied but violated. According to his Librarians, there were resonances in the fabric of the mountain itself that were going to cause problems. Then there was the issue of the psychic choir itself. They had found psykers in the deep, crowded into chambers – members of the sub choirs and aspirants. Many of them dead, most of them barely coherent.

'The beacon must be relit,' said Corswain.

'Our craft is war, brother,' said Tragan, steadily. 'Not the mysteries of the Great Ocean. This is a damaged creation, and one that cannot be reassembled like a stripped bolter.'

Corswain looked at Vassago.

The Librarian was quiet for a long moment.

'It might be possible,' he said at last. 'It is a realm of knowledge beyond my training, but there are pieces of older lore that might give guidance.'

Tragan, unhelmed, raised an eyebrow.

'Caliban knows much, and teaches more than the circle of common wisdom.'

Corswain paused for a long moment. Part of him wanted to ask the Librarian what he meant. Another part of him, the part that had grown in the forests of Caliban, felt that he could see the shadow of an answer. Not evils, but secrets, things that were known only by a few, hints that lived in the tatters of myth.

'Whatever you can do,' said Corswain.

Vassago nodded. Tragan shifted, mouth opening to speak.

'Brother.' The call came from an entrance onto the balcony. They all turned. Adophel, battered and bloody, came from the opening, and paused to bow his head in salute. 'We have secured the main communication chambers. The machinery is damaged but our smiths believe it can be called to function. We may be able to reach the Palace.'

Corswain blinked.

'Make the connection,' he said, and strode from the balcony, Tragan and Adophel at his side.

Behind them, Vassago watched them go for a long moment and then turned away.

TWENTY-THREE

The test of all we are
One day
Distance to wall

Heads turned as Dorn entered the Shard Bastion command bunker. The wall top was non-viable, so core commands had relocated to inside the bastion. Red lights blinked across consoles. Corrupting data blurred across screens. Fear and exhaustion marked every human face, and did not dim as they watched the Praetorian stride to beside Archamus and a senior vox-officer. The man's left arm and head were still wrapped in bandages. A smell of sweat and static filled the air, like the dead crackle of a broken vox had spread to another sense. The holo-displays blinked and fizzed in the air above the projectors Dorn's command staff had installed. Corruption artefacts and pixel waves washed the displays. Some cut out intermittently or just showed shifting patterns of meaningless data. The walls, ceiling and floor were shaking. Archamus did not need the tactical data or to look out of the viewslits to know that an apocalyptic battle was raging beyond the wall – he could feel it.

'The signal?' said Dorn.

Archamus nodded to the fizzing displays.

'It's confirmed as from the Astronomican fortress. It's coming over one of the hardline backups. It's distorted but coherent, and is using crusade-era Legion cipher codes.' Archamus felt the breath still in a dry throat; only he and the signal officer knew what he was about to say. 'It's the First, the Dark Angels of the Lion.'

A moment of silence formed, echoing through the room like the shadow of a struck gong. Then a gasp of relief quickly stifled, and then a rustle of exhaled breaths, a ripple of heads rising. Archamus could see the relief and joy breaking through the masks of exhaustion. He felt something stir in his chest, though he made no sign of it – they had been waiting for this moment. Not the end, not victory, but the moment that the strategies and sacrifices had been made for – reinforcements were here, the forces of the Lion and Guilliman were coming. The balance of fate had tipped and all they needed to do now was follow the light into the future.

Dorn was utterly still, but Archamus thought he saw a flash in his lord's eyes as he looked at the communication officer.

'Connect us,' he said.

The man bowed and turned, shaking, emotion grounding through him like lightning finally released from a storm.

Static popped from a vox-speaker, growling through the air. Everyone in the chamber looked up, some were standing.

'This is Rogal Dorn,' said the Praetorian. 'To whom of the First Legion do I speak?'

'This is Seneschal Corswain, of the First Legion, sire.'

A cheer then, first one and then another coming from mouths in an uncontrollable rising wall. Archamus saw Dorn let out a breath.

'We have retaken the Astronomican, and hold it,' said Corswain's voice.

The sound of cheers had faded but still lingered. Archamus could hear low weeping. It was the sound of relief, of a final relief that had finally arrived.

A red rune flashed on one of the command consoles at the edge of Archamus' sight. He turned his head, frowned. More red runes, but no one was looking; they were all looking at Dorn, their senses filled with the reality of hope come at last.

'My lord…' began Archamus.

'What strength are you?' Dorn asked Corswain, leaning into the vox-console.

'*We made the assault with ten thousand of our order,*' crackled Corswain's voice. '*The fallen are still being counted.*'

'What of the rest of my brothers and their sons?' asked Dorn. 'When do the rest of your Legion deploy?'

A pause. Vox distortion crackled in the air. The echoes of cheers faded. Archamus could feel something cold form in his chest in that pause.

'*Sire,*' said Corswain's voice. '*We have had no contact with our primarch, nor other forces. We came alone.*'

Alone.

And the word rang in the silence like the blow of an executioner.

'My lord,' said Archamus again, louder, as he moved to the tactical display. Dorn looked around then. 'My lord, Mortis have breached the lines. Cydon is gone.'

Nasuba looked down from the top of Shard Bastion as blast light washed over her. Her helm visor dimmed at the brightness. Sound vibrated through the wall and her bones. Her ears were ringing even inside the noise-baffles fitted to her helm. The breath went still in her throat.

Light linked the sky to the earth in blinding pillars. She could see figures, dozens of towering figures that from this height seemed small. Fire and light surrounded them, drowned them, flowed from them and through them. As she watched, one of them took hits from three sides. Stitched lines of light. A balanced moment where the Titan took another step that would never end, then light.

White and bright. The death of a god in a blink. Another blink. Another blink. The wall itself was beginning to shake.

She turned, started to stride back towards where one of the Praetorian's Huscarls was consulting with Sulkova. They looked around at her, saluting. The aegis shield above was strobing with orbital impacts. Another blink of light from beyond the parapet, closer now. The sound a shiver in her spine.

'Get the teams to the reactors!' she shouted. 'The lines are breached! Drain the plasma off and shut them down, now!'

'Command-and-control data feeds are failing at a rate of nine per cent every five minutes,' called Archamus. Alarms had started to sound, voices raised in barely controlled panic. 'Within the hour we will be data-blind. Fidelity of what field data there is stands at forty-one per cent clarity and falling. What there is says that the whole circuit of the wall is engaged. Unit cohesion amongst mortal units is collapsing in all zones.'

Rogal Dorn did not move for a long moment; when he did, it was a slow turning of his head to look across the chamber. A few eyes went to him, but many heads stayed bowed, as though to look at him was to have to face the truth. Archamus saw Dorn glance down at his hand. The Seal Sinister lay in his fingers, the carved lion's head flickering with reflected hololight.

'Signal Sigismund and our reserves,' he said. 'They come here with full force and full speed.'

'By your will, lord.'

'Open a vox-link, Palace-wide, all viable channels and conduits. Do it now before we lose connection.' Dorn looked up. Archamus saw his lord's hand close tight over the seal sent from the

Emperor, his father. A tech-priest straightened from a block of machinery, gestured to the vox-officer, who bent to his controls and then looked up at the Praetorian.

'The vox-link is open.'

Rogal Dorn gave a nod of acknowledgement. Archamus saw his lord blink for a second and then his gaze harden.

'This is Rogal Dorn.' The Praetorian's voice rolled out, echoing in the static-filled vox and from speakers and comm-sets. 'I speak now to all of you. We have come to it, you and I. All of us. All that has come before has been but the passing of suffering...'

Acastia saw a flash on her screens. *Elatus* slowed. Its head rose as its stride paused. Another flash, larger than the first. Much larger. Then another. White light flashing clear up to the sky. Shadows loomed in the light, giants cast into the clouds and smoke.

'What was that?' breathed Acastia.

'Engine reactor detonations,' said Abhani over the vox. 'Large, very large...'

'Ours or theirs, princeps?'

Abhani did not reply; a second later the Solaria Titans turned into the direction of the light and the wall, and began to accelerate. Acastia kicked *Elatus* into a run and followed. In the distance another light flared. The ground was shaking through the metal bones of her steed. She ran on towards the light of battle.

'The moment ahead is the test of all that we are...'

On the rubble of Marmax South, Section 52, Katsuhiro closed his eyes and took a breath. The shell fire shook the shards from the parapet. The bombardment was shifting, walking back behind the line. He opened his eyes, let out the breath. They were stinging. Steena was looking at him.

'They are coming,' she said.

'Yes,' he nodded.

She did not say anything, just clenched her jaw and gripped her rifle.

He swallowed. His mouth and throat were dry. The ground was shaking.

'You know…' he began. Steena opened her eyes and looked at him. 'One day this will be over. All this will be done. Time will pass and they will rebuild on this spot. Statues and roads and fountains filled with water. Right here where we are now. People will walk and talk, and they will worry about things they think matter. They will laugh at jokes and frown at what they think are insults, and when they pause on this spot it will be because they have dropped something, or wish to rest, or to talk a little longer. Look and listen and you can see them. Not out there,' he jerked his head at the parapet, then tapped his forehead and heart, 'but in here, you can see them. They will stand here one day, and know what happened only as stories that will be kinder than the living of them was.'

She shook her head. He could hear the clash of armour from beyond the parapet. There were flies in the air the size of bullets.

'How can you be certain?' she asked. 'How can you know?'

'I have faith.'

The air was shaking.

'Thank you, script,' she said at last, and smiled at him.

He smiled back, briefly, and then he was standing, gun up, shouting down the line.

'Rise! Weapons ready! Rise!'

* * *

*'What shall be lost, what must be given, is the price of all that
shall be…'*

In the Hollow Mountain, Vassago moved down the passage
alone. It was circular and the plasma-drills that had cut it had
left a ripple in the rock. Like it was something organic. Like it
was the inside of a serpent. His footfalls did not echo on the
bare stone, despite the weight of his tread. The crystal flecks
and seams in the walls gleamed as he passed, light kindling in
them then fading. He could hear the walls sing, too. The song
was low and distant but always there, an echo caught in the
bones of this mountain. He did not see them waiting for him.
There were two standing in the passage, their black armour
showing only when the glow from the walls touched them.

Vassago stopped.

'My brothers,' he said, and reached forwards with his mind
to taste their thoughts and names. His mind recoiled as it slid
off them. A murmur slid into the back of his skull, like the
rustle of leaves and shadows. That should not have happened
even here. Unless… unless… 'I did not know there were any
other of the initiated amongst us,' he said. His hand moved
to where the mace was mag-clamped to his back.

'There are many things you do not know… brother…' said
one of the Dark Angels, stepping forwards.

'You are using the secrets of our order to help relight this
beacon. How does that serve Caliban? We are not here to aid
the dying empire that forsook us, brother. You saved Corswain's
life when you could have let him perish. That was a mistake. The
void left by his death could have been used to our advantage.'

Vassago took a careful half-step backwards. In his mind, his
thoughts were gliding through the doors and coils of knowledge, gathering power.

'I serve only our order,' he said. 'But you have seen what

was here, what beasts have come and made a nest in the War-master's Legion. This is a threat to us.'

'Is it?' The question came from behind him, and he whirled, drawing his mace in the same movement. It lit with blue fire. Warriors in black armour and hooded robes stood in the tunnel. The glow of his mace cast their shadows onto the stone walls. Threads of crystal became orange embers in dark stone.

'How could it be anything else?' he countered, glancing back as he sensed the first warriors shifting closer, encircling him.

'Any power can be made to serve,' said a voice from the circle of warriors. 'And there are things that even you do not see…'

'What happened here will not happen to us. We are not weak, and will not fall to such powers, no matter the gain.'

'Who says you have not already fallen, son of Caliban?'

The cold light of his mace flickered, and the shadows on the wall shifted, and for a moment they were not of men but of things made of feathers and claws and reaching talons.

Vassago felt the cold tighten around his spine. How long ago had he been betrayed? he wondered.

'There is no room for doubt. You have proved that even amongst the initiated, there is weakness still.'

A figure stepped from amongst the others, and lowered his hood. Darkness filled the eye sockets and lines of the face beneath. It was a face that should not have been there, that had been left on Caliban.

'You?' said Vassago in shock.

The face nodded, and then turned away.

'Take him,' it said.

Vassago raised his mace. Blue fire and shadows flickered across the walls. The figures around him surged forwards.

'No matter the price…'

* * *

The engines of Legio Mortis walked through the fires of their burning and dying enemies. The droning count of their scrap code buzzed between them. Above them the face of the Mercury Wall rose. *Dies Irae* walked at the head of its kin, pulling the light of battle to it and shredding it to shadow like a tattered cloak. It reached the base of the wall, and stopped. Debris and fire rained down on it, exploding from the energies that coiled around its frame. Slowly it tilted its head and weapon-laden shoulders back, so that the light of the fire above fell on its face. Its war-horns sounded, booming up the face of the wall of the Palace.

'We shall face what is to come.'

Enemy distance to wall: 0 kilometres.

THE WARP

∞

The horizon has gone. In the land that is just an idea of heat and suffering, the sky and plain of baked dust have merged. The man sits beneath the blackened tree. The flesh has pulled back over the bones of His frame so that He seems a corpse. There is no breath of wind to steal the heat from Him, and the burned tree gives no shade. It has been like this for a long time. It has been like this for an eternity.

Something shifts in the white-hammer heat. The man opens His eyes. He knows what He will see.

A figure in gold armour and a red cloak stands above him. A laurel sits on Horus' head like a crown. The fingers of his right hand are claws. His face is regal, the features set in an expression of calm authority. He looks like the image of a king. He looks like the idea of his father.

He is very close to the man and the burned tree, much closer than any time before. The man beneath the tree stirs, tries to raise a hand.

'Almost, father,' Horus says, and takes a step closer. The man beneath the tree reaches down to the ground, tries to draw a line in the dust. 'No,' Horus says, and bends down so that he is almost within reach of the man. 'There is no need to try. You have a little strength left, enough that this will not be the end, but not enough for ever.'

Horus shakes his head. The man beneath the tree meets his gaze and there is no sign of withering or weakness.

'You have ruined all that you made,' says Horus. 'You did great things, father. Great things… but they are now in ruin and unravel at my will. It is a tragedy, but it is not my doing. It is yours. You burned everything you ever touched, every idea and person heaped on the pyre of your arrogance and ambition.'

Above them the black branches of the tree creak, and in that sound there might be laughter and the chittering of things without tongues but only mouths and teeth. If Horus hears them his face shows no sign.

'Everything that has happened is your doing. All that I have done and must do is but the consequence of your deeds. There is only one thing I do not blame you for…' Horus reaches down with his clawed hand and draws the line in the dust that the man's finger could not make. 'This defiance. This stubborn refusal to bow to inevitability. I wish I could hate you for that too, but I cannot. After all, what else remains to you?' The man beneath the tree is silent. Horus shakes his head. 'It is coming, father. The end of your stolen years and false kingdom. You will see it all become ash before the end. But you will not be alone when death claims you… For *I* am here with you.' And Horus raises his clawed hand and touches the idea of the Emperor's cheek. 'I am right here.'

ABOUT THE AUTHOR

John French is the author of several Horus
Heresy stories including the novels *The Solar
War, Mortis, Praetorian of Dorn, Tallarn* and *Slaves
to Darkness, Sigismund: The Eternal Crusader,* the
novella *The Crimson Fist,* and the audio dramas
Dark Compliance, Templar and *Warmaster.* For
Warhammer 40,000 he has written *Resurrection,
Incarnation* and *Divination* for The Horusian
Wars and three tie-in audio dramas – the Scribe
Award-winning *Agent of the Throne: Blood and Lies,*
as well as *Agent of the Throne: Truth and Dreams* and
Agent of the Throne: Ashes and Oaths. John has also
written the Ahriman series and many short stories.

YOUR
NEXT READ

SIGISMUND: THE ETERNAL CRUSADER
by John French

As the Great Crusade draws to a conclusion, Remembrancer Solomon
Voss seeks to answer one question: why does Sigismund, First Captain
of the Imperial Fists, believe that war will never end? The answer lies
in Sigismund's fraught past of battles, oaths, and bitter duels.

An extract from
Sigismund: The Eternal Crusader
by John French

The storm wind breathed across the Ionus Plateau. Summer heat and dry winds had pulled the dust up into the air so that now a layer of cloud lurked on the horizon, flickering with lightning, bruise-dark smudged with ochre. The plain had once been an ocean, or so the story ran. The waters had long since drained away, leaving dust where there had been a seabed and mesas of stone that had been mountains beneath the waves. The tombs of long-dead kings stared down from those mountains at the drift camps at their feet. They were called camps even by those who had been born in them. They were home to the millions that the great war for and against Unity had pushed from the cities and hives to the north and south. Alleys tangled through walls made from scrap and fabric. Smoke rose from cooking fires, along with the cries of the dying and the songs of the living. On and on it went, rolling beyond sight to meet the edge of the world.

This was the land taken by the lost. Even for the despots who hungered for dominion, it was a shunned place. The monarchs who had bored their palaces and tombs into the mountains had left their mark on the land in the form of stories of enchanter kings and tales of ghost voices laughing from the mouths of deserted palaces. It had been an empty place for millennia, but then new armies had marched across the world: gene-wrought armies in skins of metal. Cities became pyres as warlords new and old tried to make new realms or hold on to what they had. Refugees had come to Ionus, first a few and then tens of thousands. They had made homes and had children, and done what humanity does even as the world is falling into fire – they had survived. Now the wars were supposed to be over. From many warlords there had come one who called Himself 'Emperor', and He had proclaimed the tattered realms He had conquered not many lands but one. One Imperium.

For the people in the drift camps of Ionus, this new Unity had been neither a blight nor a triumph. As with all the other wars in all the other years, the new peace was a distant irrelevance. Life remained as it had been, balanced on sharp edges, unsoftened in its cruelty. The stories of the old kings of the mountains had become the founding myths of murder gangs that ran the alleys at night with sharp knives and crowns of blades. Spring winds sometimes brought poison from the north. Those of autumn, the smell of the dead left on the mountain slopes for the carrion birds. In winter, ice clotted the gathered dew, and in summer Sol breathed furnace heat and summoned thirst to steal the spit from people's mouths. There was no change, nor hope, just the certainty of struggle.

Sigismund could taste the storm on his teeth like he was biting copper. He was breathing hard as he twisted down an alley between two shacks. Behind him the cries rose, ululating up into the storm wind. They were close.

He reached the dead end of the alley and looked behind him in time to see a figure come around the corner at a run: wiry muscle and scarred skin dusted with white ash, a mask and crown of jagged metal, bones and skin hung on cords. The blade in the figure's hand was a hooked smile of pla-steel. It was a Corpse King, one of the gangs that hunted and harvested in this part of the drift.

Sigismund jumped up, grabbed on to the edge of the roof, and hauled himself up. He started running, boards shaking under his strides. Ahead of him, a metal pylon jabbed up from the roof into the darkening sky. The storm was a dark wall, curving up from the land into the heavens. Behind him, the Corpse King vaulted up the side of the alley and landed in a crouch. In the distance, the storm spoke. Thunder growled through the air. Lightning sparked in its depths. It was an angry god of a storm.

Sigismund's eyes caught on a lightning flash, and his stride stuttered. There had been something there in the clouds, glint-ing in the flare of energy. Another flash, and there it was again, and not just one but several, glinting motes in the roiling murk...

'Come down to the kingdom!' shouted his Corpse King. 'The dead want you!' The ganger was closing, almost on him. Sigismund kicked his run into a sprint. A second Corpse King climbed onto the roof. She had knives in her hands and finger bones in her hair.

Sigismund reached the pylon and ducked behind it. For a second, he was out of sight of the gangers. He picked out the metal bar he had left propped against the pylon. The first Corpse King came into view at full sprint. The metal bar hit him in the throat, just under the mask. Sigismund slammed the tip of the metal bar into the youth's chest, and then swung it up into his face. The crude mask mashed into skin and bone, and the ganger was falling, bone fetishes clattering, blood and air gasping from between broken teeth. Sigismund could hear the second Corpse King running across the roof. The one on the floor pushed up, hooked blade in hand. Sigismund slammed the metal bar down once, hard, and brought it up just in time to meet the second murder ganger as she came around the side of the pylon. A blade flashed out towards Sigismund. It was hooked, a polished sliver of scrap, the hilt wound in green-blue plastek and human hair. The cut was fast, but Sigismund was already swinging the metal bar and the Corpse King did not have time to duck back before it crashed into her upper arm. She staggered, crying out, arm dangling. The ganger's other knife sliced out. He darted back. She was up and coming for him, cursing, stabbing and slashing.

Sigismund had heard from one of the other orphans that there was supposed to be an art to fighting, that warriors in the distant wars knew ways of using blades and guns, and hands and feet to kill and survive. He did not know if that was true, but here, in the drift camps, the only art was being the one left alive.

A blade point slashed across his left forearm. A sharp feeling and then a sudden soft lightness in his legs and gut as the shock slammed through him. Nausea followed in a flood. The knives flashed forwards again. Sigismund swung the bar into the masked face. The Corpse King crumpled, blood dribbling from behind the mask.

Sigismund could feel his hands shaking. There were more running feet pounding the roof. Cries rose. He needed to move. There were many of them, at least twenty, maybe more. Too many. They had come hunting again as though roused by the coming storm. Too many to face all at once. He had learnt that since the first time he had fought. In that first fight, he had got the best of it somehow, sent some down bloody into the dust. The rest had run, the cost suddenly higher than they wanted to pay for the skin of a few orphans. Since then the gangs had come for them repeatedly: the Queens of Hades with their manes of cadaver hair; the Blood Spectres in crude armour dipped in red paint; the Breath Stealers, gasping out strings of rattling noise from tongueless mouths. Most were youths little older than Sigismund; with every winter there seemed to be more, and they always came back. He had learnt: you did not face them together, you faced them one at a time.

He ran to the edge of the roof, jumped, hit the dust, crouched, rolled, and came up running again. Blood was dripping down his left arm, the weight of the metal bar dragging at the right. His chest felt like it was going to explode. He ducked down a half-collapsed opening between two shacks. Running footsteps shook the roof panels above and behind him.

'Come back, little one!'

Keep going, he needed to keep going. He reached the end of the alley. The space beyond was a wide oblong open to the sky. A charge reservoir sat in the middle of the oil-stained ground. A web of cables stretched from the machinery up to a soar of electro-kites in the sky above. Sparks were already running down the cords. Sigismund ran towards a narrow gap between the charge reservoir and a shack wall. He reached it just as he heard the first of the Corpse Kings reach the opposite roof edge. He did not look around as they dropped down and ran after him. He slowed, just enough. One of the Corpse Kings was just a few strides behind him, a spiked club held in two hands. There was a niche in the wall, made by the poor join between two sheets of rusted metal.

'You're ours now!' the ganger snarled.

Sigismund ducked into the niche in the shack wall, pivoted, and brought the metal bar around. It hit the Corpse King in the gut and folded him in two. Sigismund's knee met the masked face as it came down. He was not as strong as the ganger, but the falling weight of the Corpse King's head, and the rising knee, were enough to mash the mask into the face with a crack of bone.

Thunder roared in the ochre-and-iron sky. A tongue of lightning struck one of the electro-kites. The flash of light exploded in Sigismund's sight. He staggered. The bar dropped from his hand. He could not see. The world was white dancing with neon ghosts. There were cries close by, the sound of someone barrelling towards him. He jumped back almost too late. A sharp point scored across the meat of his left shoulder. The pain jolted through him.

'The gods of death are coming!' called a voice from close to him. 'They have come to choose! They have come to make us live forever!'

He saw something move behind the blur filling his eyes. He lashed a foot out, felt it connect, heard a grunt. He punched his open right hand in the direction of the sound, felt it hit something that felt like hair and the strap of a harness. He grabbed and yanked. The weight of a human body crashed into him. Arms flailed at him. He yanked again and heard the Corpse King slam into the metal of the charge reservoir next to them. He brought his knee up, felt it hit something soft, and then hit again and again, hearing the Corpse King gasping for air. There were shouts in the narrow space, more blurred images moving in the clearing fog. He landed one more knee, then shoved the body away from him and broke into a run. Lightning split the sky above. Thunder rolled, obliterating the sound of cries and feet behind him. He reached a shack wall, found a door and hauled it open.

The space inside was as empty as when he had scouted this route: lengths of rag folded and stacked in a corner, cooking pots made from cast-off munition casings, lumps of blast glass threaded on strings so that they caught the flashes of lightning from the open door. It was a home. Where the people had gone, he did not know; there were more ways to vanish in the drift than there were to live. He slammed the door closed and dropped the bar he had prepared across it. He turned, half stumbling, looking down at his left arm. Clotted blood and dust covered it down to the fingers. He picked up another metal bar he had left waiting and staggered across the shack as something heavy hit the door he had just shut. There was white fog at the edge of his sight. That one on the roof had caught him well, a deeper cut. He was slowing down. He could not slow down. He just needed to keep moving, keep them focused on him.

He pulled up the length of board he had loosened in the shack wall. All the details he had prepared – the route he had run, when he had turned to fight, the bar to close the door, the backup weapons he had left himself – all of it was so that he could face the murder gangers one at a time, on his terms. The gangs that had come the last few times had given up with only a few of their kind lying bloody on the dust, but not tonight. Perhaps it was the storm, perhaps the Corpse Kings had decided to do whatever it took to run him and the others down. No matter the reason, they were not stopping.

He had ducked out of the shack just as the door he had barred gave way. He started to run. The white fog was spreading from the side of his sight. Above him, the storm clouds boiled with lightning. The ground dropped into a slope. He half ran, half tumbled down it. Behind him, the cries of the Corpse Kings rose and vanished in the drumming of the rain and roll of the thunder. He twisted to look back, saw one on the rooftops, then two, then three, more, more than he had ever seen on a hunt. This was not going to go like it had before.

Bright light surrounded him suddenly, pouring from the sky.

He ducked and looked up. A shape turned in the air above him. He had seen flying machines before. Sometimes they slid across the sky above, trailing white from their wings. Sometimes they flew lower, and you could hear them chewing the air as they moved. Some looked like grey darts, and others like they were made by people who had heard of birds but never seen one. They were always distant, things of another world that did not touch the dust. This one was closer than he had ever seen before. Rain poured from its block-sided body and wings. Cones of blue-white fire breathed from its flanks. The sound of it shook his flesh down to the bone. He could smell the burning-fuel reek of it over the rain. Gun mounts twitched on its wing tips and snout. Its skin was dark in the storm light. The light shining from its belly held on Sigismund for a second and then flashed up to the rooftops, where the Corpse Kings turned their heads up and howled.

Sigismund did not wait: he turned and began to run, feet sliding in the dust as it became mud. Above, the flying machine shifted across the sky, the beam of its light panning across the shack roofs. Sigismund reached an alley and ducked in as he heard the Corpse Kings' cries change in pitch. They were coming and he needed to reach the only family he had ever known before they did.

Four blows of thunder shook the sky as he reached the rock. A thumb of old stone, it jutted up from the sea of roofs. A fissure split its side, barely wide enough for a person to crawl into. There, in the cool dark, there was just enough space for a dozen people to lie or crouch, more if they were small. Faces looked up at Sigismund as he squeezed down the gap. Some were young, others had the years, but hunger or cruelty had kept flesh from their bones.

'Get the light out,' he said.

'What's happening?' asked Yel, rising to her feet, the blade-tipped pole in her hands.

'The Corpse Kings are coming,' he replied. 'A lot of them. We have to move and move now.'

'Slowly now,' said Yel, calmly. Her eyes were steady. Sigismund was suddenly aware that he was shaking. Pain and exhaustion and fear were juddering through him, like power through a charge coil that was about to blow. Yel looked at him, not blinking, waiting, steady. The eyes of the smaller ones in the cave were on them, wide in the light of the flame that rose from a rag lamp. He could feel their tension, the tense instincts that had kept them alive this long in a place that ate the alone and the lost. They were all looking at him and Yel and Coroban, the eldest three, all waiting. He forced his breath to slow and stilled the instincts that were screaming at him to shout and run.

'You're bleeding,' said Coroban, moving up beside them, jerking his head at Sigismund's left arm.

'One of them snagged me,' he said.

'I should have gone with you,' said Coroban.

'You're not fast enough,' said Sigismund.

'Neither were you,' said Coroban. Sigismund almost smiled. Coroban was bigger than him, just as tall, but thicker in limb. He had come out of one of the techno-domains to the south and still had the remains of shackle-plugs in his spine and skull. Whatever had happened to him, he had got out alone, and made it to Ionus. Not fast, but strong. He had broken the skulls of three gangs who decided they wanted the meat off his bones, but he was too slow for the running fight that Sigismund fought. They had agreed on that after they had both nearly died. So, Sigismund led the hunters in a dance and the others held the line, the best chance of survival if he failed. It had worked, too. Until now.

'Is the route north open?' asked Yel.

Sigismund shook his head, blinked. A hammer beat of pain and nausea was rolling inside his skull.

'I don't know. There are flying machines, too. They came with the storm.'

'Flying machines?'

'Hovering low. Tracing the ground with lights, like they are watching. They had guns.'

'The war's come,' said Coroban.

'We go west,' said Yel.

'That's towards the mountains,' said Sigismund. They all knew what he meant. The mountain tombs and ruined palaces were the haunts of the gangs. If they went towards them...

'There will be fewer of them,' said Yel. 'If they are hunting then they won't be watching their own patch. And if the war has come then I'd rather take my chances in the ghost caves than down here.'

Sigismund did not answer.

'You know I am right,' said Yel after a moment.

He looked around, at the eyes fixed on them.

'Where are we going?' asked Siv. The boy was new. They had found him walking on his own on one of the dust paths to the south. He had been clutching a piece of parchment that he refused to let go of, and neither he nor any of the others could read. No tears then, and none now, just a stillness that came from expecting nothing that was here now to be there in the next moment. Sigismund knew the look. It was his own.

'You are going somewhere safer than here,' he said, holding Siv's gaze, before looking back at Yel and Coroban.

'You will have to go now,' he said. 'I don't know how close they are or how long I can distract them.'

He began to move towards the way out.

'Come with us,' said Coroban, and he put his hand on Sigismund's shoulder to stop him. 'They will kill you.'

Sigismund looked around at Coroban and then at Yel and back at the other orphans of the drift, still listening, still watching. He thought of Thera, the eldest of the orphans when he was small. In his memory, he saw her touching her forehead to the piece of metal she called a weapon and going out to face the killers in their ragged crowns. She had stood up and never come back, but he and others had lived.

'I stay,' he said.

Coroban shook his head, but Sigismund was already working his way back up the gap in the rock, pulling the metal bar with him in his good hand.

He found his first Corpse King barely two hundred paces from the bolthole in the rock. The ganger was moving across an open patch of ground that was becoming a swamp, his head turning. He did not see Sigismund until he was just an arm's reach away. The Corpse King flinched back, but the metal bar crashed into his shoulder, and then his legs. He fell. Spray showered up from the boards of the shack roof. Sigismund looked down at him. The ganger was writhing, trying to move with broken bones. Sigismund stood above him, looked up. In the distance he could see the light of one of the flying machines. Then lightning whipped across the belly of the clouds, turning the world blinding silver. The rain was pouring down him. Drops exploded in the sea of mud at his feet.

'I am here!' he shouted as the thunder roar faded. 'If your dead kings want me, then come and get me!' The ganger at his feet screamed – maybe a warning, maybe a cry of pain.

Sigismund saw a masked figure come to the edge of the roof next to the open ground. Another joined it and then another, and then a crowd of them were vaulting and swinging down. They did not come at him but spread out in a ragged crescent, wary.

Sigismund watched them. The blood in his veins was beating a roll of thunder that filled his ears. He could taste metal and bile. He tried to push the sensation down even as he felt it reach through his nerves to shake his fingers on the metal bar in his grip.

The crowd of Corpse Kings watched. The rain poured down them, pulling the white dust from their skin. Masks and crowns glinted in the flash of lightning. Some of them held knives, others switched their grips on hooked blades and spiked clubs.

'The lords of death watch us, little one,' called a taller figure who stepped from the half-circle. Teeth glinted on cords around his neck. A mask of blue plastek and battered metal covered his face. His chest was bare and gaunt, but muscle moved under the taut skin. He held a club capped with a ball of black metal in a crude echo of the statues of the dead monarchs that filled the tombs in the mountains. This was a leader. Sigismund could tell that from the way the others pulled back and waited, listening. 'There are angels watching from the storm. They have come to pick those who will live forever. Your blood and bone will pay my crossing into the land of ghosts.'

Sigismund did not reply but raised the metal bar, fighting to hold it steady as he touched it against his forehead. He closed his eyes for a moment. He thought of Yel, and Coroban, and Siv, and the others running towards whatever safety they could find.

'Look at you,' called the Corpse King. 'You have hurt a lot of us, but we cannot die. We rule death, and you are ours now, little one.' The leader took a slow step forwards, the club resting on his shoulder, a long blade loose at his side. 'We will find your friends, too. We know they have run. We will find them. A few might like to take a crown from us, eh? Live as kings…'